"What do you want?" he rasped.

She slid both her hands up behind his neck, looked up at him with those gorgeous brown eyes and sexy as hell glasses, and stood on tip-toe. "You, Mason. I want you."

Three little words—*I want you*—had the power to break him like nothing else ever had. The dam broke free. There was no holding it back. He grabbed her with all the finesse of that same green youth he'd likened himself to earlier, lifting her against him and slamming his mouth down on top of hers.

The kiss was hot, wild, completely out of control. Someone whimpered. It might have been him. He turned with her in his arms, desperate to get closer, to pull that damn shirt off of her. He carried her to the nearest piece of furniture, the table. It nearly killed him to end the kiss long enough to kick one of the chairs out of the way and set her on the table in front of him.

He kissed her again and slid his hands down the shirt, ripping it open, sending buttons pinging across the table and onto the floor. His greedy fingers spanned her narrow waist and moved across her warm, soft skin to the underside of her breasts. Perfection. No other woman had ever felt so right in his arms.

By Lena Diaz

EXIT Inc. series
EXIT STRATEGY

Coming Soon
NO EXIT

Deadly Games series
TAKE THE KEY AND LOCK HER UP
ASHES, ASHES, THEY ALL FALL DEAD
SIMON SAYS DIE
HE KILLS ME, HE KILLS ME NOT

LENA DIAZ

EXIT
STRATEGY

AN EXIT INC. THRILLER

AVONBOOKS

An Imprint of HarperCollinsPublishers

AVON BOOKS
An Imprint of HarperCollinsPublishers
195 Broadway
New York, New York 10007

Copyright © 2015 by Lena Diaz
Excerpt from *No Exit* copyright © 2016 by Lena Diaz
ISBN 978-0-06-234908-8
www.avonromance.com

First Avon Books mass market printing: July 2015

Avon Trademark Reg. U.S. Pat. Off. and in Other Countries, Marca Registrada, Hecho en U.S.A.

HarperCollins ® is a registered trademark of HarperCollins Publishers.

Printed in the U.S.A.

10 9 8 7 6 5 4 3 2 1

Thank you, Chelsey Emmelhainz,
for loving my "it's not a proposal."
Thank you, Nalini Akolekar,
for keeping everyone else from knowing how crazy
I can get (wait, did I say that out loud?).

This book is dedicated to all of my
www.KissAndThrill.com sisters
for your love and support. But thank you especially to
Sarah Andre, Carey Baldwin, and Gwen Hernandez,
who read this story at various stages and
offered tremendous insight and suggestions.
Thank you!

And finally, to my hero, George.
I love you.

Chapter One

Day One—11:00 p.m.

Sabrina crept into her moonlit living room and grabbed the arm of the couch for support. Her right hand, slippery with blood, slid across the cloth and she fell to her knees on the hardwood floor. A gasp of pain escaped between her clenched teeth before she could stop it.

She froze, searching the dark recesses of the room, squinting to try to bring everything into focus. If the intruder was within ten feet of her, no problem, she could make out every little detail. But any farther than that and he might as well be a fuzzy blob on the wallpaper.

Had he heard her? She listened intently for the echo of footsteps in the hall outside, or the squeak of a shoe, the rasp of cloth against cloth. But all she heard was silence. In a fair world, that might mean the stranger had given up and left the house. But in *her* world, especially the nightmarish last six months, it probably meant he was lying in wait around the next corner, ready to attack.

The throbbing burn in her right biceps had her angling her arm toward the moonlight filtering through the plantation shutters to see if the damage was as bad as it felt. Nope. It was *worse*. Blood ran down her arm from a jagged, two-inch gash and dripped to the floor.

She clasped her left hand over the cut, applying pressure and clenching her mouth shut to keep from hissing at the white-hot flash of pain. She had to stop the bleeding. But there wasn't any point in looking for something here in the living room to bind the wound. Only the couch and a wing chair remained of the antiques that she'd brought with her halfway across the country from Boulder, Colorado, to Asheville, North Carolina. She'd sold the other furniture, and even some of her sketches, to pay the exorbitant fees of the private investigators searching for her grandfather and the even more exorbitant fees of the lawyers.

She supposed the Carolina Panthers nightshirt that she was wearing might be useful as a tourniquet. But she didn't relish the possibility of facing an intruder in nothing but her panties. The nightshirt was definitely staying on.

If only she still had a shotgun. Even half blind, she was bound to at least wing her target with the spray of pellets. But convicted felons couldn't own guns. And thanks to her *loving* cousin's schemes, that's exactly what she was—a felon who'd brought shame to the great Hightower legacy. A felon who'd been forced through her plea bargain agreement to sell the gun collection that she and her grandfather had worked years to build.

Sabrina squinted again. She should have grabbed

her glasses before fleeing her bedroom. But she'd been startled from sleep by a sound downstairs and had flailed blindly in the dark, knocking everything off the bedside table: her glasses, her cell phone, and the lamp. It had broken into pieces and one of the shards had ricocheted off the floor, cutting her arm—probably the lamp's way of getting back at her for breaking it.

Still, she'd managed to make it downstairs without being caught, by sneaking down the front staircase while he went up the back stairs. But she hadn't even made it to the foyer before she'd heard him in the dark, and knew he was on the first floor again. So far she'd won the deadly game of cat and mouse. But she was running out of places to hide. It was time to make a run for it.

Easing to the doorway, she peered down the long hall. Was that dark shape against the wall just a decorative table? Or a man, hunched down, waiting? When no one pounced at her, she decided to chance it and took off, running on the balls of her feet to make as little noise as possible. The dark opening to the foyer beckoned on her right. She dashed around the corner and pressed against the wall, her pulse slamming so hard it buzzed in her ears.

Had he seen her? Where was he? In one of the guest rooms? The study? Keeping her left hand clamped over her wound, she hurried down the marble-tiled foyer.

The useless security panel mocked her as she passed it. For what she'd paid for the thing, it should have come with armed guards. But it hadn't gone off tonight, not even when she'd slammed her hand on the panic button in her bedroom.

A dull thump from somewhere around the corner had her stomach clenching with dread. *When had he gotten so close?*

She hurried to the door, flipped the dead bolt, and yanked the doorknob. The door didn't budge! She pulled harder. *Nothing.* She looked over her shoulder before double-checking the lock and trying again. The front door was stuck, jammed, as if nailed shut from the outside. A moan of frustration and fear bubbled up inside her but she ruthlessly tamped it down.

Think, Sabrina. Think.

She could run to the kitchen. It wasn't far, just on the other side of the foyer wall. There was a butcher block of knives on the marble-topped island. But the man she'd glimpsed from the upstairs railing when she ran out of her bedroom was built like one of those bodyguards her alarm system should have come with. What chance did she have against him in hand-to-hand combat? Especially with the cut on her arm? He'd probably end up turning the knife on her. The thought of being stabbed had bile rising in her throat. No thank you. Scratch the kitchen off her list.

The garage. Her Mercedes was inside. But her keys were in her purse. Could she sneak upstairs, get her keys, and make it all the way back to the garage without him hearing or seeing her? Even if she could, the garage door was slow and noisy—one of those irritating things she'd discovered shortly after moving in. Cross the garage off the list too. That was a small list. What other choices did she have?

She ran to the other end of the foyer and stood

looking across the hall to the dining room, with its floor-to-ceiling windows. *Heavy* windows that would be hard to raise even when she wasn't hurt. Her shoulders slumped as she accepted what she hadn't wanted to admit—the only way out was through a door, and the only other door was in the family room, which meant going *toward* that thump she'd heard moments ago.

Before she could think too hard and become frozen by fear, she took off down the long hallway toward the back of the house and didn't slow down until she reached the family room. She felt the rush of warm air a moment before she saw the broken pane in the French door. That must have been the sound that had awakened her. Glass littered the floor in a wide arc like a lethal moat. But if getting cut again was the price of escape, so be it.

Bracing herself against the imminent pain, she raised her foot.

Strong arms clamped around her waist, jerking her into the air. She let out a startled yelp, kicking and flailing her arms. "Put me down! Let me go!"

Ignoring her struggles, the stranger effortlessly tossed her onto his shoulder in a fireman's hold, his forearm clamped over her thighs like a band of steel. Good grief, he was strong.

Clasping her nightshirt with her good hand to keep it from falling down over her head, she tried to beat his back with her other hand. But with it throbbing and weak, her efforts were puny and laughable at best. Using the only other weapon she had, she bit him, right through his shirt. Or tried to. The cloth was thin, but he was wearing a thicker material beneath it. Kevlar. She blinked in surprise. Growing

up with a team of armed guards as reluctant baby-
sitters had taught her exactly what he was wearing
beneath his shirt, even if it was thinner than what
her guards had worn. Why was this man wearing a
bulletproof vest?

Sabrina twisted sideways to see what he was
doing. "What do you want?"

"I want you to be quiet." The slight Southern
drawl in his deep voice did nothing to dull its edge
of authority, as if he was used to giving orders, and
used to having them followed.

He crunched through the broken glass to the
door and reached up with his free hand. A wood
shim was wedged between it and the frame. Was
that why the front door hadn't opened either? Had
he wedged both doors shut? What was going on?

The wood shim creaked as he worked it loose.

"Please, *please*, let me go." She was shamelessly
considering offering *anything* if he'd just set her
down. But the shim popped free and he yanked
the door open. Her breath left her with a whoosh as
he jogged down the brick steps with her bouncing
against his shoulder. He skirted the long, rectangu-
lar pool, then sprinted across the lawn toward the
woods that bordered her yard and led into the foothills of the Blue Ridge Mountains.

She clutched his shirt during the wild dash to
keep her jaw from snapping against his spine. Every
jarring step shoved his shoulder against her belly,
forcing the air out of her lungs. Just breathing was
a challenge. She couldn't have screamed if her life
depended on it, and it probably did.

Her shirt slipped down farther to expose her

thong underwear to the humid air. Her face flooded with heat as she realized her nearly naked bottom was bouncing on his shoulder just inches from his face. Tears of humiliation stung her eyes. *No.* She blinked them back, refusing to let them fall. If she acted liked a victim, she would become a victim. No matter how much she was shaking on the inside, she couldn't let him see her as weak.

When they entered the woods, he didn't slow down. She expected the low-hanging pine tree branches to scrape against her exposed skin. But somehow, nothing did. When he finally stopped in a clearing, they were deeper in the woods than she'd ever been. She wasn't even sure whether they were still on her property or if they'd crossed into the nature preserve behind her rental. And now that she could finally draw a deep breath, there was no point in screaming for help. They were too far away for any of her neighbors to hear her.

Suddenly he stood her up and let her go. The blood that had rushed to her head while she'd dangled over his back now rushed to her feet, making everything spin around her. She staggered like a drunk. He grabbed her hips in a firm but surprisingly gentle grip, steadying her.

The feel of this stranger's hands on her bare skin sent a jolt of panic through her. Sabrina shoved him away, wobbling backward. A warm breeze against her belly had her sucking in a startled breath and looking down to see her nightshirt bunched around her waist. She jerked it down to hang mid-thigh and cast an anxious glance up at him. Thankfully he didn't seem interested in her state of undress. He was too busy checking what appeared to be a rather large watch on his wrist.

He towered over her. But then again, most people did. Dressed in black pants and a black T-shirt—like any good burglar or kidnapper should be—he had a solid, muscular frame she'd become intimately familiar with while plastered against him. His dark hair hung like a ragged mane to his shoulders and framed an angular jaw and cheekbones a camera would love. He'd probably look quite handsome in his mug shot. And thanks to the sometimes curse—sometimes gift of a photographic memory, she'd be able to pick him out of a future lineup without any trouble at all. She would even be able to draw his likeness to almost perfectly match the picture in her head. Her artistic skills were rusty, but she'd be happy to polish them up if it meant putting this man in jail.

Tall-Dark-and-Deadly.

That was the moniker that immediately popped into her mind to describe him. It fit perfectly, especially considering the bulky pistol holstered at his waist—a Glock 22, from the looks of it. She was a Sig Sauer girl herself, preferring the solid feel of steel over the "combat Tupperware" of a mostly plastic Glock. Just one more thing to hold against her kidnapper—his lousy taste in firearms.

"You're bleeding," he announced, snapping her attention back to his face.

He reached for her but she quickly stepped back and clamped her hand over her cut again. "Don't touch me," she ordered, trying to sound brave and unafraid in spite of the hysteria bubbling up inside her. If she was going to survive, she had to keep her wits about her.

Impatience etched itself on his forehead but he didn't move toward her. Instead, he checked his watch again, his mouth twisting with displeasure. "We need to get moving. We're behind schedule. If they suspect the mission has been compromised, they'll send someone else to kill you."

The blood drained from her face, leaving her cold. *Mission? Kill her?* Wait, he'd said "they" and "someone else." And he'd seemed concerned, if only for a moment, about her cut. Did that mean that he *wasn't* here to hurt her? Then he was, what, protecting her?

A shaky breath escaped between her clenched teeth as hope flared inside her. If this man wasn't the real threat, then who was? The only person that she knew of who hated her was her cousin, Brian. But kill her? No. That would only delay him from getting what he really wanted—their grandfather's money.

What then? Was Brian planning a worse stunt than his last one? Now *that* she could believe. Had her sister-in-law, Angela, found out that Brian was up to something and sent this man to warn her? Had this stranger misunderstood and thought she was in *physical* danger, and completely over-reacted?

"You said 'they.' Who are *they*?" she asked, trying to fit the puzzle pieces together.

He shrugged. Either he didn't know, or he didn't want to waste his precious time explaining.

"Did Angela send you? To warn me about Brian?"

She gave a nervous laugh. "He'd love for me to stop fighting him in court, but *kill* me?" She shook her head. "You've got this all wrong. He doesn't want me dead. That would just complicate things."

She couldn't help the bitterness and hurt that had crept into her tone. All her life she'd thought Brian loved their grandfather as much as she did. But instead of helping her find Grampy after he went missing, Brian was fighting to have him declared dead so he could cash in on the estate.

"I don't know any Brian or Angela. But someone is definitely after you." Tall-Dark-and-Deadly closed the distance between them and leaned down as if to pick her up again.

She jumped back and clenched her fists in front of her, steeling herself against the throbbing in her right arm. "Touch me and I'll kick your balls all the way up to your throat."

This time it was his turn to blink in surprise. His mouth tightened into a hard line, making her immediately regret her rash words. Angering a man with a gun was never a good idea.

Rushing to fill the tense silence, she said, "You keep saying 'they' and 'someone.' You're here to protect me, right? Someone *other* than my family is after me? *They* want to hurt me? Or maybe you got the wrong house, the wrong person." She latched on to that last thought with the desperation of a skydiver clawing for the secondary chute when the primary failed.

He shook his head as if she were daft. "They don't want to hurt you, *Miss Hightower.* They want you *dead.*"

She sucked in a sharp breath, the certainty in his voice and the emphasis on her name telling her there had been no mistake. A renewed stab of fear shot straight to her gut. "Why are you so sure?" she whispered.

"Because I'm the one they hired to kill you."

Chapter Two

Day One—11:20 p.m.

Mason shook his head as Sabrina Hightower tore off through the trees to escape him. Obviously, telling her that he was supposed to kill her wasn't the wisest thing he could have said. But *not* killing someone he'd been sent to terminate was a new experience and he was a bit out of his element.

He'd expected a tiny woman like Sabrina to be docile and scared, easily subdued, especially barefoot, in a nightshirt, and without the glasses that he'd pocketed when he found them on her bedroom floor. Most people in her position would have cowered before him instead of acting like a little warrior, trying to bite through his shirt even though he was twice her size. He'd had to work at not laughing when she'd threatened to kick his balls up to his throat. She definitely had spunk and courage, which—unfortunately—only added to her appeal.

When he'd carried her through her backyard, her sexy, round bottom bouncing so temptingly next to his face, a fog of lust had slammed into him until all he could think about was the feel of her soft thighs beneath his hand. He hadn't planned on stopping in the clearing. It had been an act of desperation, to put some space between them so he could reengage his brain. And then she'd ruined that plan by pelting him with questions while her nipples formed mouthwatering, tight peaks against her shirt. Add to that her arrow-straight, no-nonsense black hair that swished halfway down her back, and sassy bangs that framed her defiant blue eyes, and he'd been lost.

He swore viciously. He was a fool to have let her rattle him. The only reason she had was because Ramsey, his friend from his army days, had raised questions about Sabrina's guilt. Or, more accurately, the concerns of Ramsey's *friends*—a former enforcer and his wife who both believed Sabrina's EXIT order had been faked, even though they were still trying to prove it.

Mason had always been honored to work as an enforcer for EXIT, to bridge the security gap left by the traditional alphabet agencies. Killing, when he was called upon to do so, wasn't something he relished or enjoyed. But sacrificing one evil life in exchange for dozens, hundreds, or even *one* innocent life, was a trade he was compelled, and duty bound, to make. He couldn't stomach the idea of waiting for a heinous crime to be committed if he could stop it ahead of time. Inaction, allowing people to die when he could have saved them, was inexcusable.

But only if the target, the mark, was truly guilty of the charges listed in the EXIT order.

Mason was betting—*hoping*—that Ramsey's friends were frauds and they couldn't prove their claims. Because, if Sabrina was innocent, if her EXIT order was wrong, then other orders could have been wrong. Which meant that people he'd terminated in the past could have been innocent too. *That* prospect was too horrible to contemplate.

He checked the GPS tracker on the multipurpose unit on his wrist. The tiny transmitter he'd tacked onto Sabrina's nightshirt when he'd first picked her up gave a strong, clear signal. She was heading due west. Convenient.

After taking off in a jog, he noted the GPS coordinates on his watch and made a call on his cell phone. "Guide to base. Over."

The phone crackled. "Base here. Over."

"Tracking target. Heading your way. ETA ten minutes. Over."

"Tracking? You didn't *acquire* the target?"

Mason gritted his teeth. Having someone question his actions was another new and entirely unpleasant experience, especially since the person doing the questioning was a man he'd spoken to only once, in the rushed meeting Ramsey had arranged less than two hours ago. A meeting that had put him behind on his mission.

Since he hadn't called in and sent a picture as proof of death, EXIT had probably already dispatched another enforcer to terminate Sabrina. Which was why Mason had been in such a rush that he'd been sloppy, breaking the glass in her door to get in quickly and get her out of harm's way before someone else showed up. A decision that had ended up being a mistake since it had warned her of his presence and sent him on a time-eating search through the house for her.

Now he was risking his career—and his life—based on his friend Ramsey's trust in a former enforcer turned rogue whose past was shrouded in rumors and secrecy. Ramsey might have worked on dozens of EXIT missions with the rogue enforcer, but until tonight, Mason had never met the man. He had no shared history on which to base any trust. Still, he couldn't stomach letting Sabrina die if there was even a chance she was a victim in all of this, so he'd agreed to play along, for now.

"Just watch out for her," he snapped. "She'll reach the road before I do." He ended the call without waiting for Devlin Buchanan's reply.

SABRINA FELL OVER another log, landing hard on her hands and knees. Again. She pounded the ground in frustration and wished for the hundredth time that she'd taken an extra few seconds to find her glasses before running out of her bedroom.

She searched the dark line of trees behind her and drew deep, gasping breaths. What had she heard right before she'd fallen? Footsteps? She heard nothing now. Even the night birds and insects had stopped singing and chirping, as if they sensed the dangerous hunter on her trail.

If you want to kill me, Tall-Dark-and-Deadly, you'll have to earn it. I'm not going to make it easy for you.

Bracing herself against the shooting pain in her arm and bruised knees, she shoved to her feet and took off again. An agonizing few minutes later she glimpsed a break in the trees, and something else. A road? Maybe the Blue Ridge Parkway that snaked around the protected area behind her house? Hope spurred her forward in a wobbly lope.

She burst through the trees into the open. A dark ribbon of asphalt stretched out in the moonlight, boasting one of the familiar wooden Appalachian Trail signs a few feet away. *Yes!* She grabbed hold of the sign, leaning on it as she tried to catch her breath. Looking down the road, she willed someone to come along. She'd heard that tourists traveled this scenic highway at all hours.

Please, please, please.

Headlights flashed off to the right. A dark-colored vehicle seemed to appear from out of nowhere, barreling up the hill. Terrified the driver might pass her by, she ran out onto the road directly in its path, waving her good arm over her head.

Brakes squealed. The Hummer's nose dove toward the ground as it screeched to a halt just a few feet from her.

Sabrina ran to the driver's door and pounded on the glass. The man behind the wheel glanced at the woman sitting beside him before lowering the window. He rested his arm on the door, the dark shape of a tattoo on his massive biceps peeking out from beneath his shirtsleeve. The dashboard lights illuminated his face, though his eyes narrowed dangerously as they dipped to the blood on her arm.

His jaw tightened, giving him an angry, fierce expression that was so similar to the one Tall-Dark-and-Deadly had worn that it sent a spike of alarm straight to Sabrina's belly. Her would-be savior had some kind of high-tech binoculars on the top of his head, flipped up the way someone would wear sunglasses when not using them.

Why would someone wear binoculars at night?

Probably for the same reason someone would wear a Kevlar vest.

Trap! Her mind screamed the warning. She took a quick step back. Of *course* she hadn't been lucky enough to reach the road just as a vehicle came up the hill. The Hummer must have been *waiting* and only flipped its headlights on once she'd stumbled out of the woods. Because "luck" was never a word she associated with herself, unless she slapped the word "bad" in front of it. Could these be the same people who'd abducted her grandfather? And now they were after her?

"You look like you could use some help, miss," the man said.

Sabrina took another step back, shaking her head. "I, ah, thought you were someone else. Sorry. Please, go on ahead. The person I'm . . . waiting for will be here soon." She looked down the road as if expecting someone to come up the parkway any second and backed toward the side of the road.

A car door slammed. Sabrina jerked toward the Hummer.

The female passenger was rounding the hood, holding out her hands as if to show Sabrina that she meant no harm. Moonlight bathed her face, illuminating a smile so sympathetic and kind that Sabrina hesitated. Had she jumped to the wrong conclusion? Could these people really be harmless strangers, *not* in league with the man who was after her?

"Please," the woman said, opening the door behind the driver and waving Sabrina forward. "Let us help you. You've got blood all over your arm. We'll take you to the hospital."

Sabrina glanced at her cut, which was still oozing blood. When she looked back at the woman, she was staring at something over Sabrina's shoulder.

Sabrina whirled around.

Two strong arms grabbed her, yanking her back against a familiar hard body.

"No!" she screamed. "Let me go." She twisted violently, trying to get away from him. "Help me!" she cried to the woman.

The woman flushed guiltily.

Sometimes Sabrina hated being right.

She stomped her heels on top of her captor's boots and tried to wrench herself out of his arms.

"Stop it, Sabrina," a familiar Southern drawl ordered next to her ear. "You're just going to hurt yourself."

"It'll be worth it if I hurt you too," she spat out, trying to elbow him in the stomach.

His right arm tightened over her arms, beneath her breasts, crushing her against him, effectively immobilizing her except for her feet. She kicked and flailed backward, slamming her right heel into his shin.

He sucked in a breath and shifted his body sideways.

"I didn't want to do this. You've left me no choice," he bit out.

She could feel him reaching for something. His gun? Alarm spiked through her. She drew a deep breath to scream just as he pressed a cloth over her nose and mouth, the smell sickeningly sweet.

No, no, no! She tried to fight him, to hold her breath, but she could already feel a heavy lethargy flooding through her veins as whatever drug he was using began to take effect. She silently pleaded with her eyes for the driver and woman to help her.

The man's expression was stony. The woman bit her bottom lip and looked away.

"Stop fighting me," her captor's deep voice whispered near Sabrina's ear. "It's easier if you don't fight."

Said the spider to the fly.

Her lungs burned from lack of oxygen. Dark spots swam in her vision.

"Breathe," he ordered. "You've got no reason to fear me if you're innocent. Take a breath."

Innocent of what? She hadn't done anything wrong!

A wave of dizziness had her clutching his arm.

Is this what happened to you, Grampy? Did they do this to you too?

Grief slammed into her as she finally accepted the possibility that she might never see her beloved Grampy Hightower's face again.

"Sabrina, breathe," her captor ordered, a note of worry in his voice.

She jerked her face to the side, desperately taking a quick breath of untainted air. "Go to hell."

"Already been there." His voice held a tinge of bitterness as he clamped the cloth over her nose and mouth again.

Unable to fight the desperate need for air, Sabrina allowed herself one shallow breath. Her world went dark.

MASON CAUGHT SABRINA'S unconscious body in his arms and scooped her against his chest, more shaken than he'd been in a long time. She'd fought like a hellcat, defiant to the last. But even her curses couldn't conceal the bone-deep fear in the tone of her voice. Fear that he had caused. Had his other marks felt that kind of fear before their executions? He didn't know, had never cared to find out. Had never *cared*. Period. Because they deserved the punishment that justice had dictated. And it was killing *him* not knowing whether Sabrina deserved it too. For the first time ever, as he looked down at her angelic face and cradled her delicate body, he fervently hoped his mark was innocent.

Stop it. Enforcer Training 101: Never identify with the enemy. Never become attached. If Sabrina was guilty—and she probably was—he'd have to carry out his duty just as if she were any other mark.

He didn't understand what it was about her that tugged at his sympathies. But if he didn't get a handle on it now, he was going to make mistakes. And in his line of work, mistakes could be deadly. He drew a deep breath and forced himself to look up from the confusing woman in his arms.

"What the hell did you do to her?" Devlin Buchanan demanded from the open driver's window. "She's bleeding all over the place."

The censure in his voice had Mason bristling with anger, mostly because Buchanan was right. He should have taken better care of her, should have bandaged her arm as soon as he'd seen the cut. But to Buchanan, he said, "She's alive. Which is more than any of my other marks can say."

Buchanan's eyes narrowed.

His wife, Emily, a brown-eyed brunette several inches taller than Sabrina, waved toward the open door behind her husband. "We don't have time to argue. Put her in the car. *Please*."

Mason hesitated. Things might be going according to the hastily constructed plan they'd made at the cabin before he'd gone after Sabrina. But still, he barely knew these people and he wasn't entirely sure where their loyalties lay.

"Where's Ramsey?"

He jerked at the feel of Emily's hand on his arm.

She snatched her hand back and clasped her fingers together. "EXIT's firewalls and compression algorithms are more intricate than we expected. Ramsey's working with our computer expert to try to cover up the attempts we made to break into the mainframe."

"Then you *weren't* able to get the information?"

"No, I mean, yes, we did. Just not everything we were hoping for. We wanted to retrieve all of the EXIT orders from the past—"

"But you got the intel on Sabrina Hightower?" he interrupted.

"Yes. Ramsey dropped it off at the cabin. It's the only useful info we got before a security program closed the firewall again. Or something like that. I'm not the computer whiz. We probably won't be able to get back in again, and will have to physically break into an EXIT facility and go for the backups, maybe even paper files. Those won't be as protected because—"

"Enough." He tightened his arms around Sabrina. "What did you find out about Sabrina?"

She smiled, not at all put off by his rude interruptions. "You did the right thing, Mason. She's innocent."

Innocent. One little word with so much power—the power to save Sabrina, the power to destroy

Mason. His entire world was tilting on its axis. Everything was about to change—if the information was legit, something he had to confirm for himself. He'd been loyal to EXIT for six years. Turning traitor didn't sit well with him, not unless there was a solid reason to do so.

"Where is it? This so-called proof?"

"Still at the cabin. We stopped—"

"Headlights," Buchanan announced. "On the hill a quarter mile back. Let's go."

Mason glanced down the road. Whoever was behind them was coming up fast, far above the speed limit. Not a good sign. He hopped into the Hummer and settled Sabrina onto the seat beside him before slamming his door shut.

As soon as Emily's door was closed, her husband floored the gas and the Hummer barreled down the two-lane highway.

"Would you fasten Sabrina's seat belt please? And yours?" Emily asked.

He vaguely wondered if she was always this polite as he secured Sabrina. Emily glanced pointedly at his unbuckled seat belt. He had no intention of putting it on. Let her think he was being stubborn. Better that than to admit the real reason: that being restrained in any way would make him batshit crazy. Just the thought of being strapped down had phantom pain shooting through the ridged scars on his back and shadows of memories threatening to overcome him.

Wires crisscrossing over his back held him to the cot, biting into his skin. Sand and grit mixed with blood, setting his open wounds on fire. Mason watched as the Jackal smiled like an old friend, dipped his hand into his cup,

*and let the salt water dribble onto Mason's skin, stinging
like the bite of a hundred fire ants, burrowing through his
flesh.*

No!

He shook his head, ruthlessly forcing the memories back into the dark pit from where they'd come. Wear a seat belt? Not in this lifetime. He crossed his arms and defiantly returned Emily's stare.

She sighed and held out a white cloth as she flicked the dome light on overhead. "For the wound on her arm. She's very pale. Looks like she's lost a lot of blood. She can't afford to lose much more."

Sabrina's head had fallen against his shoulder. She *was* much paler than when he'd first seen her. Blood oozed from the deep cut on her arm, which must have happened as a result of the breaking glass he'd heard upstairs when he went into the house. There were dozens of other, shallower cuts on her arms and legs that hadn't been there when he'd first seen her. Since he'd been careful to keep the branches from brushing against her as he'd carried her through the woods, he could only assume she'd gotten those cuts while running from him. Had he really frightened her so badly that she'd run blindly through the underbrush, hurting herself?

"Mason?" Emily's voice was soft but insistent.

He hesitated, wary of touching the strangely appealing woman beside him again. He needed his wits about him right now, and touching her seemed to scatter his brain cells faster than a hurricane could rip the roof off a building.

"Just press the damn towel against her arm," Buchanan interjected. "It's not that difficult."

Mason didn't care one bit for Buchanan's tone.

But he didn't bother arguing. Taking care of Sabrina was his primary concern right now. He nodded his thanks to Emily and took the cloth, then tied it tightly around Sabrina's upper arm, careful not to let his fingers linger against her ridiculously soft skin.

Headlights flashed through the rear window. An engine roared behind them.

"That's not a tourist behind us, ladies and gentlemen. We've got company." Buchanan switched the dome light off.

Emily grabbed binoculars from the console.

Mason plucked them from her hand, ignoring her aggravated look, and swiveled around. "Huh. Haven't seen *him* around in a while."

"Who?" Emily asked.

"Another enforcer. I've only met him a couple of times. Mean son of a bitch. I think he calls himself Ace."

"Oh no." Her words left her in an anguished whisper.

Mason glanced back and saw some kind of silent communication pass between her and her husband. Obviously they'd had some kind of run-in with Ace before. Were the rumors true, then? Was Ace one of the enforcers Buchanan had allegedly tangled with when he'd gone rogue and turned against EXIT?

Rat-a-tat-tat. The sound of semiautomatic gunfire punctuated the night as bullets pinged off the body of the Hummer. The rear window exploded in a hail of glass.

Mason ducked down and unclipped Sabrina's seat belt before shoving her to the floorboard.

"Did you bring my bags from the cabin like I asked?"

"In the back," Emily said.

He reached over the seat and grabbed the one with his ammo and clothing, his go-bag, always ready for a quick getaway. He pulled out the small, lightweight Kevlar vest that he'd brought after Ramsey first contacted him, and tossed it on top of Sabrina before reaching for his other bag, the one with his crossbow. He could have used his Glock or the Sig Sauer P938 holstered on his ankle but firing a gun inside the confines of the Hummer would be too loud, so his crossbow was their best option.

"Get down!" Emily leaned over her seat with a .357 Magnum and fired several rounds toward the car behind them. Ear-splitting booms filled the Hummer, leaving both men glaring at her.

Mason jerked the gun out of her hand. His hearing would probably never be the same. She gave him a sheepish look and turned around in her seat.

The headlights behind them had swerved and dropped back but were still following them.

"Hang on, everybody. It's about to get bumpy." Buchanan switched the headlights off, plunging the road ahead into darkness. He flipped his night vision goggles down from the top of his head and jerked the wheel, taking the car off road down a steep hill.

There didn't seem to be any plan to Buchanan's twists and turns through the tree cover beside the road other than to try to lose Ace—who was still hugging their trail a hundred yards back, probably guided by the brake lights every time Buchanan was forced to tap them.

"You're not from around here, are you?" Mason shouted to be heard over the scrape of tree branches against the sides of the car.

"How'd you guess?" Buchanan threw back the sarcastic remark, then swerved to avoid something.

"You might as well use the headlights so I can help guide you through this mess," Mason said. "He's following your brake lights anyway."

Buchanan flipped on the lights and tossed his binoculars onto the console.

"Turn there, after that next stand of oak trees." Mason pointed up ahead.

"You sure?"

"I've lived here my whole life. These foothills were my playground."

Buchanan immediately slowed for the turn, then accelerated around the thick trees. The ground smoothed out and he was able to pick up some speed.

"Hard right," Mason yelled.

The Hummer took the abrupt turn on two wheels, then plopped back down, kicking up dirt as it dipped down an incline. Buchanan wrestled for control, then gave Mason a crisp nod. "Good call. We haven't lost him, but we've got a good lead now."

"Not enough. We'll run out of navigable woods soon and have to hit the highway. His car is faster than this tank. We won't even make it to the cabin before he overtakes us. And we've got the women to worry about."

Emily waved her gun. "Um, hello. Not exactly helpless here, guys."

"Sabrina is," Mason reminded her. "Pull over. I'll buy us some time." He slung his quiver of arrows over his shoulder and grabbed his crossbow. He still had his guns too, if he needed them. And a knife in his boot. But he preferred the crossbow for a situation like this. The intimidation factor of a lethal crossbow pointed in someone's face could turn the bravest enemy into a sniveling coward.

The car didn't slow. Buchanan's mouth was set in a firm, hard line.

Mason met his gaze in the rearview mirror. "I trusted you two this far. Trust me on this."

"If anyone goes after Ace, it's going to be me," Buchanan said. "I owe him payback, big time. He nearly killed my father, and sent my little brother to a burn unit. He's mine."

Buchanan's anguish struck a chord with Mason. He was intimately familiar with that deep-seated desire for vengeance against someone who'd gutted your soul and left a wound that could never heal. But he also knew that keeping a tight rein on that need for revenge was the only way to survive when emotions ran hot. So, instead of trying to talk Buchanan out of his justified rage, he appealed to a completely different set of emotions, using Buchanan's one obvious weakness against him. His love for Emily.

"You're going to leave your wife with me then? You trust *me* that much?" Mason challenged, already knowing the answer in the tensing of Buchanan's shoulders. Buchanan didn't have any intention of leaving his precious cargo in the hands of an enforcer, even if they were supposedly on the same side now.

"All right. You made your point. Hang on, Em."

She pulled her seat belt tighter and grabbed the

armrest. Mason braced himself against the seat in front of him.

Buchanan slammed the brakes. The Hummer skidded sideways and stopped just inches from another large oak tree.

Mason checked Sabrina. She was still out cold, but appeared to be okay. He hopped out of the Hummer and slammed the door. "Keep going south for another quarter mile, then head due west about three hundred yards. That'll get you to the parkway. I'll hike the rest of the way to the cabin and meet you there after I take care of Ace."

Buchanan still looked like he wanted to argue, but headlights flashed over the rise behind them. He glanced at his wife, as if to remind himself of what was most important, then he maneuvered the Hummer around the oak tree and floored the accelerator, rocks and dirt spitting up from beneath the tires.

Mason rested the end of his bow on the ground and cocked the string back into the firing position. Then he hefted up the bow, notched the arrow into place, and waited for his prey.

Chapter Three

Day Two—12:00 a.m.

M ason sprinted through the woods, arms and legs pumping. He leaped over a fallen tree and skirted around a boggy patch of ground more lethal than quicksand. Barely visible through a break in the trees off to Mason's right, Ace gunned the Chevy. The engine whined in protest as it chugged up an incline.

Headlights danced crazily through the bushes, illuminating an upcoming sharp curve that Mason knew would force Ace to slow down yet again. Mason pushed harder, faster, cutting across a ditch, back toward the car. With seconds to spare, he reached the turn ahead of Ace and hid behind a tree. Chest heaving as he drew deep breaths, he pointed his crossbow up at the sky and edged out just enough to watch the approaching headlights.

Closer, closer, almost there. Now!

He leaped in front of the car, dropped to his knees, and aimed the crossbow directly at the driver.

The car's brakes locked up. It skidded sideways,

hop-skipping to a halt as the tires slid, then held. Before the Chevy stopped bouncing on its springs, Mason was at the driver's side window, pointing the business end of the bow directly at Ace's head.

Ace blanched and slowly raised his hands from the steering wheel.

Feigning surprise, Mason frowned, as if he hadn't known that Ace was the one driving. He'd decided to play this very carefully, to keep up the pretext that nothing had changed, that he was still a loyal EXIT enforcer. After all, if the proof Buchanan had promised turned out to be bogus, Mason fully intended to go back to his life the way it had been. But that was only possible if he could convince Ace that he hadn't gone rogue, that he wasn't a threat to EXIT or the very people he was supposed to be saving. Because going rogue meant putting a target on his back, with every enforcer in the company gunning for him—not exactly the type of future he wanted.

"Lower the window," Mason ordered.

Ace complied then put both hands back in the air. "Point that thing somewhere else, Mason."

He kept the bow steady, his finger resting on the side of the trigger. "Not until you explain why you were shooting at me out on the parkway. And why you're following me now."

Ace's jaw tightened. "I'm just doing my job. You're the one who went off-mission and didn't call in. Miss Hightower should have been dead hours ago."

"Things happen. Missions get delayed. Are you telling me our boss sent you to terminate me, *because I'm late making a phone call*?" It was a legitimate question. Cyprian might send an enforcer to check on him, to *help* him if things had gone wrong. But it was unlikely he'd immediately assume the worst and declare war on Mason—not without some other reason.

Ace looked away, as if dismissing him.

Mason tapped the crossbow, regaining his attention. "Meet my lie detector. Unless you can duck faster than four hundred feet per second, you'd better tell the truth. Who sent you after me tonight?"

Ace's face reddened as if he were struggling to control his temper. But after another glance at the bow, he said, "EXIT. They sent me to check on you."

"Who specifically? Cyprian?"

He shook his head. "Bishop, Cyprian's assistant. What difference does that make?"

Probably none. Mason had heard of Bishop—Cyprian's replacement for Kelly who'd been killed a few months ago—allegedly by Buchanan. But he'd yet to meet Bishop. As a new assistant it was unlikely the man would make unilateral decisions about something as critical as a mission. Which meant that Cyprian personally knew that Mason's mission had encountered some kind of problem. But could he have known about Buchanan contacting Ramsey, and then contacting Mason?

He motioned with the crossbow. "Keep talking. I'm still waiting for that explanation."

Ace's eyes flashed with anger. "I saw your tracks behind the Hightower house," he snapped. "I figured your mark got away and you were chasing her through the woods. I drove behind the property and waited, thinking to *help* you. Then Hightower ran to the road, very much alive, and you put her in that Hummer and rode off with her instead of taking care of business. I knew Cyprian wouldn't want her to get away so I made an executive decision." His gaze fell and he lowered his hands to the steering wheel, one small act of defiance to let Mason know he couldn't completely control him.

The "executive decision" claim didn't ring true. One of Cyprian's few, written-in-granite rules was that enforcers couldn't kill other enforcers except in self-defense, or if an enforcer had been declared rogue. So, what was Ace's reason for firing at the Hummer? If any tourists had been on that parkway and heard the shots they would have called the police. Cyprian would be furious—to put it mildly—if any enforcers attracted the attention of law enforcement by doing something so blatant. No, something else was going on here. And unless Mason was totally misreading Ace's body language, the motive behind tonight's shooting rested squarely with Ace.

Mason studied him. With his short dark hair and tall, muscular build, Ace could almost pass for Buchanan—except for the eyes. Ace's were darker, almost black. If eyes were the windows to the soul, then this man's soul was an empty, dark crevasse. And right now, judging by the whitening of Ace's knuckles against the steering wheel, that crevasse was filled with hate and anger.

Why? Or, at least, why tonight? Mason tried to picture what Ace would have seen on the parkway. He'd probably parked his car back in the trees down the road but he must have had some high-powered binoculars. With the Hummer's headlights on, and the full moon, he should have been able to see fairly well. But when Sabrina collapsed into Mason's arms, could Ace have realized he'd only drugged her, instead of killing her? Doubtful. Mason could just as easily have given Sabrina a lethal dose of some toxin instead of putting her to sleep. Then what else could Ace have seen? What could have upset him so much that he'd reacted the way he had? Besides Mason, Sabrina, and the Hummer, there was just . . . *the Buchanans.* Of course. That was it.

If Ace realized the people driving the Hummer were the Buchanans, and not just some low-life thugs Mason had hired to help him out with the mission, then Mason's pretext of still being a loyal EXIT enforcer was blown all to hell. "Why didn't you ask me who was driving the Hummer?"

Ace's obsidian gaze bored into him. "What?"

"You said you saw me put Sabrina in the Hummer and *ride* away with her, not *drive* away. Why didn't you ask who was driving?"

Ace smirked, his mouth twisting savagely. His earlier mask dropped away and he was no longer even trying to hide his contempt. "Since when is she *Sabrina* instead of Miss Hightower? Is that something *Buchanan* taught you?" He spit out the name like it was a bitter poison he was trying to get out of his system. "To get cozy with your marks? To *care* about them? If you're going to kill me, hurry up and do it. But don't expect any more *explanations.* I'm done talking."

Mason tightened his hands around his bow, weighing his options. Killing Ace was the sensible thing to do. It would buy Mason some time until he reached the cabin and got the information about Sabrina. But killing Ace only made sense *if* the Buchanans were right, *if* Sabrina was truly innocent, *if* EXIT was *purposely* falsifying EXIT orders and hadn't just made some kind of horrible mistake with

Sabrina's order, and *if* Ace was in on all of this and knew about EXIT's deceit.

Those were a lot of "ifs" to consider when deciding whether to take a man's life. What if the Buchanans were wrong? What if Sabrina was everything her order claimed her to be?

Then killing Ace—even if he deserved it for the stunt he'd pulled back on the parkway—would be wrong, plain and simple. Mason wasn't judge and jury. That role belonged to EXIT's governing Council and to Cyprian. It was Mason's job to carry out their verdict, to protect others who would pay the ultimate price if he didn't act. The line between being a tool of justice and becoming a vigilante might sometimes be thin, but he'd always prided himself on carefully making that distinction with every action that he took. Tonight was no exception.

But even if that weren't the case, he couldn't help empathizing with Ace to some degree. The man fervently *believed* Buchanan had betrayed him. Rumors were that Ace had loved Kelly, and that Buchanan had killed her. And even though Kelly had left Ace for someone else—Cyprian, if the grapevine was to be believed—Ace still had a close friendship with her and despised Buchanan for his alleged role in her death.

His thirst for revenge had consumed him and caused him to make foolish decisions—like shooting at the Hummer. Mason too had been driven by a similar thirst for vengeance, after the other soldiers in his unit had been massacred by the Jackal, and the army wouldn't go after their killer because of political concerns.

If it hadn't been for EXIT recruiting him after

he'd quit the army, he wouldn't have survived the grief and bitterness that had sucked him into a black hole for months. His EXIT mentors and trainers had taught him that if he couldn't have justice for his men, and himself, then at least he could seek justice for others. He was one of the lucky ones. He'd learned to redirect his frustrations and had come out the other side with a new sense of purpose. Ace was still caught in the throes of darkness.

He lowered his crossbow to his side. "Go on. Get out of here. If you come after me again, next time I'll do my talking with a gun." He lifted the bow. "Or this."

The glare Ace gave him as he drove away left little doubt that Mason had just made a powerful enemy. As soon as the car was out of sight, Mason took off running, using his knowledge of the area and the constellations overhead to guide him on the shortest route to the cabin. He couldn't afford to waste any time, not with Ace sniffing after them like a great white shark scenting blood in the water. And once Ace told Cyprian that Mason was working with the Buchanans, Cyprian would likely declare Mason "rogue." Any enforcers in the area would be told to kill him on sight. This little section of the Blue Ridge Mountains had just become the most dangerous spot in the Carolinas.

SABRINA'S EYES FLUTTERED open and she blinked at the dark ceiling above her bed. It looked different, somehow. Alien, not what she was used to seeing when she woke up. Was she even awake? Everything seemed . . . off.

Her thoughts were sluggish, rolling around inside

her head, bumping against each other, then floating away, unable to form a cohesive picture.

Her tongue felt thick, her mouth dry as she tried to make sense of her surroundings. The room was dark, but she could still see the lone window on the far wall, and the silhouettes of furniture—a small nightstand, a rocking chair in the corner, a chest of drawers. Typical furniture for a bedroom.

But none of it was hers.

Panic jolted the fog from her mind, snapping everything into place: the break-in at her house, being carried into the woods, fleeing to the parkway and asking strangers for help—strangers who'd done nothing to stop her abductor from drugging her. They'd probably been in league with him all along. And then he must have brought her here. But where was *here*?

She tried to sit up, but all she managed to do was lift a few inches before collapsing against the mattress. Something was holding her down. She raised her head, her eyes widening at the thin rope crisscrossing beneath her breasts, over her hips, her legs. Instead of one of the nightshirts she normally wore to bed, she was dressed in jeans, tennis shoes, and a dark, oddly thick, button-up shirt with a high neckline. Not her clothes. Not her room.

The fog lowered again, scattering her thoughts. Tired. She was so tired. Her lashes fluttered closed. *No.* She forced her heavy lids open. *Wake up, Sabrina. Fight the drugs. You have to figure out a way to escape.*

She strained against the rope. Sharp pain radiated up her right arm. She sucked in a breath and squinted down at her body again. The silver flash of duct tape shined around her wrists, imprisoning them against her belly. A stark white bandage covered the cut on her right upper arm. She supposed that was a good sign. If her captor wanted her dead, he wouldn't have worried about her injury, would he?

The sound of muted voices had her turning her head on the pillow. The door to the bedroom was slightly ajar, giving her a limited view of another room. Without her glasses, she couldn't see much detail beyond the confines of the bedroom, but she could tell there were three people standing by a high-top table—two men and a woman. And there was no mistaking the guns each of them wore holstered at their sides.

One of the men turned her way, his dark brown, wavy hair brushing the tops of his broad shoulders. *Tall-Dark-and-Deadly.* He started toward her door. The woman hurried after him.

No! It was too soon. She hadn't figured out a way to escape yet!

Sabrina fought down her panic and did the only thing she could for now. She closed her eyes and regulated her breathing, pretending to be asleep just as they reached the door.

MASON HALTED BESIDE the bed, with Emily hovering by his side, watching him like a mother hen over her chick. He observed Sabrina's breathing. Was it too shallow? He'd expected her to be awake by the time he made it to the cabin and was alarmed when Emily had told him she was still asleep. Had he drugged her too deeply?

He wrapped his fingers around one of her slender wrists, checking her pulse. Relief eased some of the tension in his shoulders. Her pulse was strong. And fast. Much faster than he'd expect if she were sleeping. Her eyes were closed, but she was either in the process of waking, or was already awake, feigning sleep. He dropped his hand to his side as he noted what she was wearing and the bandage on her arm. More bandages, medical tape, a small pair of sewing scissors, and disinfectant sat on a TV tray near the headboard.

"I told you she was okay, Mason," Emily whispered.

"That you did," he whispered back, even though he was almost positive that Sabrina was already awake. "You stitched her arm?"

"I was going to but ended up not having to. It had finally stopped bleeding, so I cleaned it and covered it to keep it from getting infected."

"Thank you for taking such good care of her, and for changing her clothes." The last he'd added for Sabrina's benefit, so that she knew it was a woman who'd dressed her. He wouldn't want her to feel further violated than she probably already did, thinking that a man she didn't know had been that familiar with her body.

"It was no trouble. I wanted to make sure she was protected," Emily said.

Sabrina's brow furrowed, then quickly smoothed out. Awake then, and understandably confused by Emily's comment. Well, if she was going to play possum, he couldn't explain what Emily meant without calling Sabrina's bluff. He had to admire her resourcefulness. She'd already shown herself to be a fighter. Now she was showing herself to be clever as well, probably hoping her playacting would buy her some time so she could try to escape.

She was certainly proving to be one of the more interesting marks he'd ever met. Then again, maybe his fascination with her wasn't so much in his mind as in another part of his anatomy. Just standing this close to her had his blood running hot, as it had every time he'd been near her tonight.

Disgusted with his lack of focus, he motioned to Emily. They left the room and he closed the door behind them. While Emily hurried to her husband's side at the high-top table, Mason stopped across from him.

"Okay," Buchanan said, his tone impatient. "You've seen her like you *demanded*. Now tell me what happened with Ace."

Mason grabbed his two bags from underneath the table and set them on top next to the bow and arrows he'd left there before checking on Sabrina. As he stowed the equipment into one of the bags and checked the contents of the other one, he summarized his meeting with Ace.

Buchanan's jaw tightened after he heard the whole story. "After the savagery Ace inflicted upon my family, it was my *right* to finish him off. But, at your insistence, I trusted that duty to you so that I could get Emily to safety. And now you're telling me that you let him go? That my wife is still in danger? Why didn't you kill him when you had the chance?"

Mason arched a brow at Buchanan's tone.

Emily placed her hand on her husband's arm as if to try to calm him. She bit her bottom lip, glancing nervously between the two men.

Mason knew that Buchanan blamed Ace for what had happened to his family. And he'd seen first-hand tonight that many of Buchanan's decisions were driven by his concern for his wife. Mason understood Buchanan's anger, and imagined that he'd feel the same way in the same situation. So he kept a tight rein on his own temper and carefully modulated his tone as he responded to what amounted to an accusation.

"Judgment call. I gave Ace the benefit of the doubt. He believed he was doing his job when he fired at us. I warned him, and let him go. Maybe you would have done differently, but—"

"Damn right I would have."

Mason shrugged. "Understandable, given your history. But *I* don't have a history with Ace, or at least, I *didn't*. Until tonight. I expect our next meeting won't go the same way."

He set both bags on the floor, leaving the top of the table clear. "Rather than argue, I suggest we review the documentation you promised me and come up with Plan B. Staying in the cabin until the rendezvous tomorrow night is no longer a safe option."

"Only because you let Ace go."

Mason simply waited, keeping silent.

Buchanan seemed to struggle for composure, but after exchanging a long look with his wife, he blew out a breath and gave her a crisp nod.

Apparently his nod had been a signal. Emily crossed to Buchanan's black go-bag sitting on the floor by the door and pulled out a computer tablet. When she returned, she handed it to her husband and climbed onto the bar stool beside him. Buchanan pressed her hand in thanks.

"It's encrypted and password protected." He slowly typed the password, glancing at Mason to make sure he was paying attention.

Mason nodded to let him know he'd seen and memorized it.

Buchanan slid the tablet toward Mason and pointed at one of the document icons on the screen. "That's a copy of the EXIT order that you were given for Miss Hightower, listing the main charge against her, that she's funneling millions from the Hightower fortune into a cell of domestic terrorists in the Carolinas. Allegedly, that's the reason she moved here from Colorado a month ago." He tapped another icon. "This is a more in-depth background report, put together by someone who's helping me on this. You'll want to pay particularly close attention to the part about what happened to her parents, and the lawsuit. And when you compare the report to the information on the order, you'll see they bear little resemblance to each other."

Mason ignored the screen for now. "Your wife mentioned something earlier about a firewall, and that you might have to locate physical backups of any other data that you want. Does that mean that EXIT knows you broke into the mainframe?"

"My computer expert doesn't believe so, no. Just that there was a security audit about the time we retrieved our data and they decided to upgrade their security measures."

"Who's your security expert?"

"Next question."

"Wrong answer. You want me to trust you? Then you'd better start trusting me."

"It's not about trust. It's about limiting collateral

damage if things go wrong. I'm not giving up my sources, or how they get their information. Period."

Buchanan's answer rankled. But Mason understood his position, and respected him for it. If he protected others by keeping their secrets, then he'd protect Mason the same way if they were on the same team. Knowing that, made it easier to understand why Ramsey trusted Buchanan.

"How do I know your background report is accurate and EXIT's is false?"

Buchanan pointed to another icon. "Every fact is corroborated with a minimum of two sources. You can follow up on a lot of this on the Internet, but only if you know where to look. Whoever falsified the Hightower EXIT order did a remarkably thorough job of twisting innocuous information to make it look damning."

"Is Sabrina the only one?"

"The only one with a fake EXIT order?"

"If you're right about her order being fake, yes."

"I'm right," Buchanan assured him. "And so far it's the only one that we've *proven* is fake. But we've identified four others that are suspect. We're looking into them right now. It's all there, on the tablet."

Emily kept glancing anxiously toward the bedroom. Mason knew she was worried about what was going to happen to Sabrina. But he couldn't reassure her—not until he examined the evidence.

"Besides Ramsey and me, how many enforcers know about this?" Mason asked.

Buchanan cleared his throat, suddenly looking uncomfortable. "I've spent the past few months digging into backgrounds on other enforcers. When I worked for EXIT, I was tasked with pursuing enforcers who'd gone rogue. Because of that, I have extensive knowledge and information on every one who works for Cyprian. After weighing the data, I've identified specific men and women to target to convince to come over to our side. I've spoken to—"

"How many?" Mason interrupted.

"Cole, Bailey, and Graham. They haven't committed yet, but Ramsey is helping me in discussions with them. They've all given their word to keep our confidence and consider the facts."

"But they haven't joined your team. Not officially."

"No. Not yet."

Mason cursed. "You've started a war against Cyprian and an entire company of enforcers with just Ramsey at your side? And you're hopeful that I, and the others you listed, *might* join you?"

"And me," Emily added. "I've never been an enforcer, but I was a police officer—a detective, actually. I know my way around a gun and my investigative skills are an asset."

Since his ears were still ringing from Emily firing a gun inside the Hummer, Mason wasn't sure he agreed about her firearms skills. But he didn't belabor the point.

"And you," Mason agreed. "Still, that's a handful against, what, seventy, eighty enforcers trained in intelligence gathering, hand-to-hand combat, guerrilla tactics, and a dozen other specialties? Not to mention any backup the other alphabet agencies might supply if we can't convince the Council that Cyprian—or whoever within EXIT might be creating false EXIT orders—needs to be taken down."

Buchanan was shaking his head no even before Mason finished. "EXIT's strength is its secrecy, in the government's ability to deny EXIT's existence with no paper trail that can lead back to anyone outside the company. Even the Council's involvement is based on verbal, in-person communiqués. They're all completely shielded from anything to do with EXIT's missions. No way would the Council ever involve the other agencies. That's not a valid concern."

"Maybe, maybe not. You still should have waited until you had a bigger force, a realistic chance of winning before declaring war."

"If I'd waited, what would have happened to Miss Hightower?"

Mason swore again, hating that Buchanan was right—but *only* if Sabrina was innocent.

Buchanan stood and reached for Emily's hand. "I'd planned on a lengthy discussion and answering all of your questions. But as you stated earlier, we don't have the luxury of staying in the cabin tonight with Ace out there hunting for us. Plan B is that we get the hell out of here." He glanced at his wife before continuing. "Ace got far too close to Emily once. I'm not going to let that happen again."

Emily's eyes flashed with irritation and she patted the pistol holstered on her hip. "You keep forgetting that I can protect myself."

He swept her hair back from her cheek, revealing a puckered scar that appeared to be from a burn. Buchanan feathered his hand down the scar.

"Humor me," he said, his voice gruff.

Her shoulders slumped. Mason suspected this was an ongoing argument between the two of them. But Emily nodded, giving in for now.

"We'll split up to make it more difficult for Ace,"

Buchanan said. "Your Jeep is still parked on the side of the cabin. We'll take the Hummer and meet you at the rendezvous point tomorrow evening, at eighteen-thirty, sharp. I assume you can find somewhere to lie low for the night?"

"Of course. What about you? Ramsey told me you're from Savannah. Have you got somewhere to stay?"

"We're pretty much from nowhere these days. Don't worry about us. Since I left EXIT, lying low is all we've been doing. Emily and I will be fine." He gestured toward the tablet. "If you still have any questions after reading the documents, I'll address them at the meeting. Ramsey will be there too, assuming he shakes anyone on his tail before then. He said you offered one of your properties as the location for the rendezvous. Is that still good?"

"'Offered' isn't the word I'd use."

"Strong-armed you, did he?"

"More like begged. It was pathetic. I don't normally share that location with anyone. It's buried under layers of fake names and corporations. I expect complete discretion. You, Ramsey, your wife—that's it. No one else."

"Agreed." He pulled Emily to the door and grabbed his go-bag.

"Wait." Emily waved toward the bedroom. "We should take Sabrina with us if Mason hasn't decided yet whether he's going to join us against EXIT."

Buchanan studied Mason. "Regardless of your decision about the company, do I have your word that you won't harm Miss Hightower?"

"You have my word that I won't harm her, *as long as she's innocent* of the charges in the EXIT order."

"Good enough."

Emily tugged her hand out of his grasp, frowning at him. She unzipped the go-bag hanging off his shoulder and rummaged inside.

"Em, what are you doing?" Buchanan asked. "We have to—"

"Just a minute." She shot him an aggravated glance and grabbed something out of the bag before crossing back to Mason. "Here." She handed him some clothes. "I'm guessing you didn't think to grab her a change of clothing. I know how it is to be on the run. She might need those."

Mason felt awkward taking the clothes, especially since he didn't know what was going to happen to Sabrina yet. But he nodded his thanks.

Emily looked torn about leaving, but Buchanan didn't give her any more time to think about it. With a nod to Mason, he pulled Emily out the door and shut it behind them.

Mason shoved the clothes in one of his bags then locked the door before returning to the table. He still couldn't quite believe that Buchanan had left Sabrina with him, particularly with his wife expressing doubts. Obviously, Buchanan was convinced the evidence on the computer tablet would prove conclusively that Sabrina was innocent or he wouldn't have left.

In spite of tonight's confrontation with Ace, Mason held out hope that he could convince Cyprian he had *not* gone rogue, if the evidence didn't prove out the way Buchanan believed it would. Both Mason's future, and Sabrina's, were now at stake.

After changing the password on the tablet to one

of his own making, he clicked on the first icon, Sabrina's EXIT order. The green EXIT Inc. logo was printed on the top right, along with its subtitle, "EXtreme International Tours." The accompanying thumbnail of smiling tourists riding the rapids made his eyes roll, as it always did. Officially, EXIT was a company that specialized in planning extreme, and often dangerous, outdoor vacations and providing expert survivalist guides to ensure the clients' safety. But the name EXIT was far more appropriate for the company's secret, true mission than most people would ever realize.

He began reviewing the documents on the tablet. Long ago, when he first became an enforcer, he'd made a habit of verifying the data before going after each mark. He'd wanted to be absolutely certain—beyond *any* doubt—that the person judged guilty truly was guilty. Somewhere along the line he'd stopped bothering with the verification, because he'd never—not once—found any errors or cause for concern. Now he wondered if that had been a mistake. Particularly when he read the background on Sabrina and her family. Either she had the worst luck of anyone on the planet, or something else was at work here.

Three years ago she'd graduated with a BS in management from the University of Colorado, Boulder. She'd immediately gone to work for her grandfather as head of his philanthropy foundation, doling out millions in donations and grants to various charities. Judging by all the zeroes listed beneath her grandfather's net worth as owner and CEO of a global mining corporation, Sabrina hadn't even made a dent in his empire in spite of all the grants she oversaw.

Six months ago, her world fell apart.

Her brother, Thomas, was killed in a mugging, leaving behind a wife, Angela. That must have been the Angela she'd mentioned when she'd asked Mason who had sent him to help her.

Three months after Thomas's death, her grandfather—who by all accounts had raised her, because her parents were trotting around the globe all the time—literally disappeared. The police had no clue what had happened to him. Sabrina was the only one pressing to keep the investigation open and to prevent her grandfather from being declared dead, even though her cousin—Brian—wanted the courts to issue a death certificate and split up his massive estate. It appeared that Brian would get millions if that happened. But Sabrina would get *billions*. That was a hell of an incentive to want her grandfather dead. And yet she was fighting that possibility with everything she had.

Those twin losses of her brother and grandfather weren't the last of her family tragedies. Just two months ago, her parents had died in a zip-lining accident. Mason swore when he read the details. Buchanan had been right that they were interesting, to say the least.

The final notable event in Sabrina's bio: A little over a month ago she'd been charged with felony theft for taking some of her grandfather's collections of old coins and Civil War–era weaponry from his home. Her claim in court was that she was trying to protect them so her cousin, Brian, didn't sell them.

She believed he was behind the mysterious disappearances of other valuables from the mansion.

Mason was inclined to believe her since Brian was the one who had pressed charges against her for the alleged theft of the collections. In the plea bargain that Sabrina's attorney arranged, the court locked up the mansion—which prevented Brian from getting anything else—but Sabrina, in return for no jail time, had to agree to leave Colorado for a period of at least twelve months and just check in via phone to an assistant DA once a month. That seemed like a bizarre agreement and Mason could only speculate that her cousin had someone in his pocket in the prosecutor's office. Brian probably hoped that by getting Sabrina out of the way he could get the courts to move forward and declare his grandfather dead.

After reading the rest of the details in the background document, Mason clicked the Web site links that Buchanan had listed and read the supposedly corroborating information. But he didn't stop there. He'd cultivated an impressive collection of research sites over the years, sites that would make a private investigator envious. He used these now to delve beneath the surface and dig up everything he could on the Hightower family. By the time he was done, he was confident that he had an accurate picture of Sabrina's background and what she'd been doing for the past couple of years.

With everything laid out in front of him on the screen, the feelings of protectiveness and the inconvenient physical attraction he felt for Sabrina no longer mattered. The truth was what mattered.

After stowing the tablet into one of his go-bags, he secured the straps over his shoulders, backpack style. Then he drew his knife from the sheath inside his boot and headed to the bedroom. But when he opened the door, he froze.

The room was empty. Sabrina was gone.

Chapter Four

Day Two—1:45 a.m.

Sabrina stumbled, her slightly too large sneakers flopping on her feet, causing her to lose her footing on the slippery grass.

Officer Jennings, the supposedly undercover policeman who'd freed her and helped her climb out of the cabin window, grabbed her left arm, steadying her. "You okay, miss? Do you need me to carry you?" He kept his voice low, barely above a whisper, as they hurried through the mixture of grass and rocky soil toward the woods.

"No, I'm fine. Thanks." Sabrina tugged her elbow out of his grasp. His touch felt every kind of wrong and kicked off internal alarms that were already on high alert. She wasn't totally sure that he was who he'd said he was, but at least she wasn't tied up anymore and had three fewer bad guys to worry about. And the only alternative to going with him once he'd broken into the bedroom and cut her bonds would have been to yell for help. But the people who'd have come running weren't the kind of help she wanted.

As unobtrusively as possible, she inched her right hand down toward her pocket—the one with the sewing scissors in it. She'd managed to swipe them from a tray inside the cabin after he'd cut the ropes and tape on her arms, while he was occupied freeing her legs.

Had she just exchanged one bad guy for another? It really was nearly impossible to believe that an undercover cop was in the area just when she needed help. Even people who were fortunate enough to have good luck in their lives—which definitely didn't include her—couldn't be *that* lucky.

She glanced at the badge clipped to his shirt collar, the same badge that he'd pressed against the window before forcing it open and climbing inside. It looked real enough. But then again, she hadn't met any cops in Asheville and wasn't sure what one of their badges was supposed to look like. But, the questions that he'd whispered to her once they were outside all made sense.

Are you hurt?

Is the person who tied you up still inside?

Was anyone else taken captive with you?

Let's get you to safety first. Then I'll call for backup.

He'd said the things she'd expect a police officer to say, given the circumstances. He'd done nothing suspicious and had been polite and seemed concerned about her the whole time. But she still felt uneasy.

Maybe because she'd already been fooled once tonight. She had no intention of being fooled twice. Her plan, once they reached the woods, was to drop him to his knees with the same kick she'd threatened to deliver to the man who'd taken her from her house. Then she was going to run faster than if a swarm of horseflies were hot on her trail.

If he really was a cop, hopefully he'd understand and wouldn't arrest her later. If he wasn't a cop, well, then at least she'd have a head start. She'd do her best to hide. And if he caught her, she'd fight with everything she had, including those tiny scissors. Of course, it would make everything easier if he really was here to help her and her imagination was just taking her on a trip to nightmare land.

"Officer Jennings? How did you find me?" she asked, trying to sound curious instead of accusing. "Did one of my neighbors call 911? I, ah, wouldn't have thought they were close enough to even know that I was in trouble."

Was it her imagination that his smile seemed forced, fake?

Twenty yards to go. Twenty more yards and they'd reach the trees.

"I was working undercover in your neighborhood and heard the call-out about a vehicle driving suspiciously on the parkway. Out here a car can disappear into the mountains in no time and I was just a few minutes away." He shrugged. "Never saw the vehicle but I did see some fresh, muddy tire tracks leaving the road a few miles up and followed them to the cabin. I couldn't believe it when I looked through the window and saw you tied up. Thank goodness I took the call."

"Yes, thank goodness." Did undercover cops listen to police radios? Or carry badges on them? She knew more about police procedure than she'd ever wanted to, because of her arrest in Colorado, but that knowledge didn't extend to undercover cops. And the idea that Jennings was listening to a police radio seemed counterintuitive to the whole undercover premise.

She rubbed her right hand against the bulge of the scissors in her pocket and glanced at the pistol holstered on his belt. She quickly looked away and judged the distance to the woods again. Almost there.

As they reached the first tree, a good ten feet from the others, he suddenly grabbed her arm and jerked her around, forcing her back against the trunk.

Wincing against his hold, she said, "Officer Jennings, what are you—"

"Call me Ace." He reached behind him and pulled out a pair of handcuffs, the silver metal flashing in the moonlight. "And I'll just call you bait to get who I really want." He clipped one end of the cuffs to a small branch beside her head, obviously intending to chain her to the tree.

Sabrina dropped her legs out from beneath her, yanking her arm out of his grasp.

He cursed and grabbed for her but she rolled out of the way, digging for the scissors as she scrambled to her feet.

"Get back here, you little bitch." He closed the distance between them.

She slammed her foot toward his crotch as she swung the scissors at his neck. He brought up his knee, blocking her kick. But he wasn't quick enough to block the scissors. He let out a guttural roar as they punctured his neck.

Sabrina took off running toward the woods.

MASON DROPPED THE cut pieces of rope and duct tape onto the bed and ran to the bedroom window. The shouts he'd just heard sounded like a wounded animal, or a person in a great deal of pain. Moonlight revealed a man and woman about fifty yards away. The man writhed on the ground, clawing at his neck. The woman disappeared into the trees, her straight, dark hair bouncing past her shoulders, her white tennis shoes flashing in the dark—the same woman he'd just gone into the bedroom to cut free.

Sabrina.

The man on the ground tossed something away, lunged to his feet, and then took off after her.

Ace.

A sick feeling twisted Mason's gut as he saw the gun in Ace's hand.

He yanked his Glock out of his holster and vaulted over the windowsill.

DAMN HER SHORT legs. And curse her poor eyesight. Sabrina hunched down behind some bushes, trying to blend in with them. She'd run as fast as she could, but Jennings—no, he'd called himself Ace—had quickly caught up to her with his long strides. And even though she could see every ridge in the bark on the tree beside her, those dark shapes looming farther away could just as easily be bushes or a man with a gun getting ready to shoot her.

Where was Ace now? She'd heard him run by as she'd ducked behind some oak trees. But everything was quiet now, too quiet. As if he was stalking her, listening for the tiniest sound to give her position away.

Her hands shook as she pushed a low-hanging

branch out of the way and squinted into the darkness. She should go back toward the cabin. There had to be a road out front. If she could skirt around the edge of the woods, staying out of sight, and reach that road, she could find her way to the parkway and flag someone down.

The idea of asking another stranger for help was terrifying, but no worse than waiting here for the bad guys she already knew about—Ace, the man and woman from the Hummer, and Tall-Dark-and-Deadly. What had the woman called him when Sabrina was pretending to be asleep? Oh yeah—Mason. It was a nice name. Too bad it belonged to someone who was the opposite of nice.

She stayed as still and silent as she could, watching the shadows, ticking off the seconds in her head. When she reached sixty and hadn't seen or heard anything alarming, she stepped out from behind the bushes and headed in the direction of the cabin.

A shadow separated from the trees a short distance in front of her.

She froze, swallowing hard. It was Mason, standing with both hands wrapped around the grip of his Glock. But he was aiming it off to her left. She started to look in that direction when he suddenly swung the muzzle back toward her.

Bam, bam, bam!

The bullets slammed into her chest, stealing her breath in a white-hot burst of fiery pain. She dropped to the ground, writhing in agony.

Mason fired several more shots toward the trees as he sprinted past her without a glance. Answering gunfire and the thumping sound of someone running echoed back.

The noises quickly faded as pain became her world. Pain and the struggle to breathe. She lay like a fish on dry land, gasping for air, unable to pull blessed oxygen into her aching lungs.

A few moments later, the dark shape of a man entered her line of vision. The moonlight behind him left his face in the shadows. But she knew who he was because of what he held in his left hand pointing down toward the ground—a gun, the same one he'd pointed at her before he'd so callously pulled the trigger.

Mason holstered his pistol and crouched down. Funny, he didn't look like the evil man that she knew him to be. He looked . . . concerned, his handsome brow furrowed with worry lines. That made no sense. Why would he care about someone he'd just shot? Not that his reasons mattered. Not anymore. Very little mattered anymore.

Not the series of tragedies that had claimed the lives of her brother and parents.

Not the bogus felony conviction that had forced her to leave her home state.

And certainly not the struggle to clear her name and reclaim her legacy. Her cousin's twisted machinations would continue unchecked.

But that didn't matter either. What *did* matter was that, without her around to keep pressuring the Boulder police and to keep paying the private investigators, the search for her missing grandfather would stop. Everyone but her had already given up and thought she was crazy to keep hoping he might still be alive. Knowing that her death might mean Grampy Hightower would never be found hurt worse than the burning ache in her chest.

She gasped for air but the sharp pain in her ribs had her arching off the ground.

"Dying hurts," she bit out between clenched teeth.

Mason slid his fingers into the line of buttons on her blouse and ripped it open. Tears of pain and humiliation started in Sabrina's eyes. It wasn't enough that he was killing her, was he going to molest her as well?

She raised her hands to cover her breasts but was surprised when she touched cloth instead of skin.

"You're not dying. It only *feels* that way when .40 caliber rounds slam into a Kevlar vest."

"Kevlar?" She raised her head. Sure enough, the odd bulkiness beneath her shirt that she now remembered feeling back in the cabin was a bulletproof vest. But it was much thinner than the vests she'd seen before. And she hadn't even thought about what she was wearing while climbing out of a window and running for her life.

She gingerly lifted her hands, feeling the vest for herself, the holes where the bullets had flattened against the material rather than go through her. She looked up at him but he was staring past her, scanning the trees.

"I don't understand," she said. "You knew I was wearing the vest?"

He cocked a brow and looked down at her. "Of course. I'm the one who brought the vest in the first place. And I verified that Emily had put it on you back at the cabin. I would have had to go for a leg shot otherwise."

"A leg shot? I don't understand."

"Ace had you in his sights. He was going for a

headshot but he stepped behind a tree and I couldn't see him anymore. All I could do was shoot *you* so you'd fall down and he'd miss."

"You're saying that you shot me to *save* me?"

He nodded. "You don't need to be afraid of me anymore. I promise that I only want to help you."

"I'm not afraid of you," she lied.

"Uh huh." He didn't sound convinced.

She frowned and risked a shallow breath. It didn't hurt nearly as much this time, probably because her mind finally realized she wasn't really hurt. At least not as badly as she'd believed. She drew another, deeper breath. The pressure was easing.

"I don't understand," she repeated. "You're saying you aren't going to hurt me, but earlier you said you were hired to do exactly that."

He let out a deep sigh. "Yeah, that was a poor choice of words."

Everything he said only deepened her confusion. "Then . . . you *weren't* hired to kill me?"

"I wouldn't say that, exactly."

She threw her hands up in exasperation, then winced and grabbed her right arm. The cut had started throbbing again after she'd fallen to the ground.

"Just tell me if you're going to kill me," she demanded.

"Killing you is the last thing that I want to do now."

"Why? What's changed?"

"Now I know that you're not a terrorist sympathizer."

Her eyes widened. "Well of course I'm not, you dolt. What gave you the idea that I was?" She sucked in a breath, hoping her off-the-cuff insult didn't make him change his mind about hurting her.

He coughed behind his hand, his eyes suspiciously crinkling at the corners like he was trying not to laugh. "We'll continue this conversation later, after I get you to safety." He scooped her into his arms and held her tight against his very broad chest as he took off running toward the direction of the cabin.

Sabrina curled her fingers into his shirt, trying to steel herself against the pain that jarred her ribs with his every step. By the time he reached the cabin, she was a twisted bundle of raw nerves ready to beg him to put her down. But he didn't take her inside. He ran past the front door to the far side, only stopping when he reached a small, black Jeep—the kind with chunky steel roll bars and a canvas top. Except that the top was nowhere to be seen and the doors had been removed.

With far more gentleness than she would have expected, he leaned over the side and settled her into the passenger seat. She slowly let out a pent-up breath as he fastened her seat belt. Their eyes met and she almost blurted out, *Thank you* before she caught herself and averted her gaze. She'd be damned before she'd thank the man who'd kidnapped her. If he really had just saved her life, it was only because he'd put her in danger in the first place.

He ran around the hood and tossed two large bags into the back, then grabbed the roll bar and hopped into the driver's seat. The springs squeaked in protest as he started the engine.

"Brace yourself," he said.

Without an armrest to cling to, she was forced to

grab the edge of her seat. He floored the accelerator and they took off like a racehorse bolting from a starting gate.

Sabrina grimaced and changed tactics as the Jeep bumped across the uneven ground. She pressed both hands against the dash and marveled that Mason managed to stay in his seat without falling out even though he wasn't wearing a seat belt. She didn't even see a seat belt on his side. It was as if he'd removed it from the vehicle.

"Just a little farther," he said, checking his rearview mirror.

"A little farther until what?" she asked, dreading the answer.

"Until we can stop. I want to make sure Ace isn't following us first."

At his reminder about Ace, she looked in the side mirror. Even though the moon was full it was still fairly dark. Still, she didn't see any headlights behind them. Hopefully that meant no one was following them.

A few minutes later, Mason pulled the Jeep to a stop, seemingly in the middle of nowhere with trees closing in on all sides. He cut the engine and the headlights and hopped out of the car.

Sabrina wasn't sure if she was supposed to get out or not, but the decision was made for her when Mason unclipped her seat belt and then lifted her in his arms.

She automatically started to put her arms around his neck to hold on but she stopped herself and clasped her hands together instead. Mason was a *bad guy*. She had to keep reminding herself of that. Even though he looked like heaven and smelled even better, if it weren't for him she'd be lying comfortably in her bed at home instead of being carried.

Or would she? He'd implied something else a few minutes ago, but his confusing explanations were all scrambled up in her pain-clouded mind and she couldn't make sense of any of it.

He gently set her down on a fallen log then returned to the Jeep. Before she could even dredge up the desire to try to stand and run, he was back. He dropped a black bag at her feet and knelt in front of her. He pulled a shirt from the bag, along with some water, and a bottle of pills.

She eyed the pills with suspicion and mentally weighed the odds of grabbing his gun from his holster before he could stop her. Based on how stiff and sore she was and how he'd just sprinted through the woods carrying her without even getting winded, she figured her odds were pretty much nonexistent. But she wasn't going down without a fight.

He lifted the bottle of pills.

She held out her hands to stop him. "I'm not going to down some pills to make it easy on you. If you want me dead, you'll have to shoot me—for real this time."

He arched a brow. "You still think I'm trying to kill you? We're back to that?"

She tried arching one brow too but was pretty sure she'd failed when he coughed behind his hand as if to hide his laughter.

"Yeah, we're back to that," she snapped. "I know I should probably beg you for mercy and fall at your feet pleading for my life, but that ship sailed along with my patience about the time you unloaded a magazine into my chest and—"

"Three rounds."

She shoved her bangs out of her eyes. "What?"

"I shot you three times. A magazine would have been at least—"

"Yeah, yeah. Whatever. My point is that I'm sick of being afraid so I'm just plain done with it. I want answers. Who are you? Really? You said something about thinking I was helping terrorists? Are you some kind of government assassin or something? Who, exactly, hired you? Why is this Ace guy after me? Who was that couple in the Hummer?"

His eyes crinkled at the corners again and his mouth tilted into a grin that was as lethal as his gun. "Is that all? Are you sure you don't have any other questions?"

She studied his expression, trying to read him. She'd thought for a moment that something she'd said had made him stiffen, like she'd gotten a bit too close to the truth. But she'd spouted out her questions so quickly she wasn't sure which one had hit a nerve, if it even had. Because the way he was smiling now, he didn't seem concerned in the least.

"Those are all my questions, for now," she said. "Start explaining."

"Are you always this shy around strangers?"

She wagged her finger at him. "Stop trying to act charming and answer my questions."

He arched that infernal brow again. "You think I'm charming?"

"Don't twist my words around."

He looked like he was trying not to laugh again,

which only made her more aggravated. She glanced longingly at his pistol.

"Don't," he warned, his expression turning serious.

She shrugged innocently. "I have no idea what you're talking about."

"Right."

He held up the pills and bottle of water. "Based on all of the hisses and winces coming out of you, you obviously need these. They're prescription strength and will make you feel much better."

She eyed the pills like a starving man looking at a buffet overflowing with food but agonizingly out of reach. She wanted, no, she *needed* those pills, if they really were pain relievers. But no way was she going to willingly ingest anything from a man who'd already drugged her once.

"No thanks. I'll pass." She clutched her hands against the desire to swipe them out of his hand.

He tossed the pills and water back into the bag. "Suit yourself."

The cut on her right biceps seemed to throb in protest. Maybe she should have taken him up on his offer. Her shoulders slumped.

"Don't look so dejected," he chided. "Your night is about to get a whole lot better."

"Really? The police are about to burst into this clearing and arrest you?"

He coughed again. "Uh, not that I know of. But I *am* going to let you go. *After* you change out of that ruined shirt and take off the Kevlar. I can't take you into town with bullet holes in your shirt and a bulletproof vest underneath."

"Wait. You're saying that you're going to let me go?"

"I'm saying I'll drive you wherever you want,

after you take the vest off." He grabbed the fresh shirt and offered it to her.

Afraid he might change his mind if she hesitated, she took it. Thankfully it was a button-up blouse, because she was fairly certain that pulling a T-shirt over her head was beyond her current abilities.

"Turn around," she ordered.

He shook his head. "Not happening. I don't trust you any more than you trust me. If I turn my back, you'll try to run away, or grab my gun."

"I won't try to run away."

He arched a brow. "I notice you didn't mention the gun."

She batted her lashes. "Nothing gets by you, does it?"

"I'm not turning around. But I promise I won't look at anything you don't want to show me."

"That pretty much means all of me."

He stared at her a moment, then checked the chunky-looking watch on his wrist. "I wonder if Ace went back to check on you and was surprised not to find a body. If he had his car hidden close by the cabin and finds our trail—"

"Okay, okay. You win." She dropped the shirt in her lap and shoved the tattered edges of her ruined blouse aside. But when she tried to pull it over her arm, a fresh rush of agony swept through her, making her bite her lip to keep from moaning.

Mason's brows lowered but he didn't say anything.

She tried again, and again she had to stop. Her nails bit into her palms as she waited for the pain to pass.

"Sabrina, let me—"

"No. I can do this."

His jaw tightened but he didn't argue.

She managed to get the blouse off her left arm, but it got hung up on the vest underneath.

Without a word, Mason freed it, then lowered his hands again.

She grudgingly nodded her thanks and let the blouse slip off her right arm to the ground. Halfway there. Now for the hard part. The vest.

She locked her eyes with his. "No looking south of my chin."

"Promise."

That one word sounded like a solemn vow. She still wasn't sure she trusted him. But the way he'd spoken, and the way he was looking at her, she had no doubt that he meant what he'd said and that he would keep his word.

She swallowed hard and fumbled for the Velcro straps beneath her arms. But no matter what position she tried, she couldn't pull the straps free without her ribs violently protesting every movement.

Unshed tears blurred her vision. She was so tired of fighting. So tired of hurting. All she wanted was to go home. Drawing a shaky breath, she closed her eyes. A tear escaped and slowly slid down her cheek.

A feather-light touch beneath her chin had her eyes fluttering open. Mason gently tilted her chin up until she was looking right into his chocolate-brown eyes. He slid his hand from her chin to her cheek and gently wiped away her tear.

"Sabrina, let me help you. Please."

The warmth and concern in his voice started an ache deep inside her, an inexplicable longing to curl up against his chest and feel his arms tighten around her. It was a beautiful fantasy, to believe that this handsome stranger would protect her and keep her safe. And since she was so close to breaking down, she gave in—just this once.

"Okay," she whispered, her throat thick from the struggle to hold back her tears. "Go ahead."

He gently swept her bangs out of her eyes and feathered his hand down the side of her face. His touch was so gentle, so sweet, that instead of telling him not to touch her, she found herself leaning into his hand.

His breath caught in surprise. Embarrassed at her response, Sabrina pulled away.

Mason dropped his hand to the top of the vest and cleared his throat. "This might hurt a little, but I'll be as gentle as I can."

She nodded, and braced herself. But he was true to his word. He was incredibly careful, barely jostling her at all as he worked the Velcro straps loose.

He paused with his fingers beneath the edges of the vest, silently waiting for her permission.

Her face flamed hot. She was naked beneath the vest but there was no turning back now. She nodded.

His gaze locked on hers, never dipping down to her chest as he worked the vest free. She swallowed hard, staring into his warm brown eyes, amazed and confused at the same time that this incredibly gentle, considerate man was the same one who'd forced her from her home and drugged her. Which man was the real Mason?

It would be wonderful if he really was a good guy, and if he really cared what happened to her. It had been so long since anyone had.

"Sabrina?"

She blinked, her face flooding with heat. She'd obviously been staring for a while. "Um, yes?"

"Do you want me to button your blouse?"

She swallowed and looked down, stunned to see that he'd already pulled the new shirt on her and she hadn't even noticed. She grabbed the edges and pulled them together. "I've got it."

While she buttoned her shirt, he zipped up the bag and strapped it on his back. She smoothed the blouse down, and suddenly he was scooping her up in his arms again.

She blinked up at him. "I'm pretty sure I can walk."

"Humor me."

While she wondered what *that* statement meant, he carried her to the Jeep. Once she was buckled up and he'd started the engine, he looked at her expectantly.

"Where to?" he asked.

"You're serious? You'll take me wherever I want to go?"

"As long as it's somewhere safe, yes. I don't recommend that you go back home until you hire some bodyguards. The people who hired me, and Ace, won't stop once they realize you're still alive."

"Well, I guess you should take me to the police station then," she quipped, expecting him to immediately say no.

"You got it."

Chapter Five

Day Two—3:30 a.m.

Ace pressed his hand against the wound on his neck and kicked the French door open. Glass crunched beneath his shoes as he entered the Hightower house. It was the closest place nearby that he knew was empty so he'd come here to patch himself up after the close call with Mason. He still couldn't believe Mason had shot at him.

He swiped a vase off a table and slammed it onto the floor. It exploded into dozens of pieces, tinkling like rain on a tin roof as they scattered across the hardwood. Too bad he couldn't cut the Hightower bitch into little pieces just as easily. But at least she'd paid the ultimate price for that stunt with those scissors—she was dead.

He made his way down the hall to the first bathroom that he found and flipped the light on. The amount of blood on his neck and shirt had him cursing again. But when he slowly pulled his hand off the wound, he was relieved to see that it wasn't as deep as he'd thought and it was barely bleeding anymore.

After rummaging through the drawers and finding antiseptic and bandages, he tossed them onto the black granite countertop and wet a hand towel in the sink. As he washed the blood off, he couldn't stop obsessing about Hightower.

He couldn't picture her as the leader of a terrorist cell, concocting plans to blow up a mall or an elementary school. So what had she done to earn an EXIT order? Maybe she'd been a behind-the-scenes kind of coward, someone who funneled money to others to do the dirty work. She'd lounge in a silk robe, sipping some expensive, imported tea while she killed innocent people with the flick of a pen across a checkbook.

An agonizing memory formed in his mind: a small white church in the distance, rain clouds ominously forming overhead, a dark omen in contrast to the happy wedding going on inside.

Thunder clapped as he pushed his car to its limits. If he wasn't inside before the preacher pronounced his brother and fiancée man and wife, his brother would never forgive him. He floored the accelerator and then watched in horror through the windshield as the little church exploded into a fireball, destroying his world, incinerating everyone he'd ever loved in one swift, violent moment.

Because of someone like Hightower.

He cursed and threw the bloody towel into the sink. His chest heaved as a more recent, horrific memory came into focus. Another white building, this one a house in the middle of a sea of green grass. Inside, Kelly Parker, the woman he'd grown to care for, if not love. Dead. Just like the others. And the man responsible, along with his cop girlfriend, was the same person who'd assisted Mason tonight.

Devlin Buchanan.

He was at the top of a very exclusive list—Ace's *personal* hit list. Beneath Buchanan, a question mark that he hoped to replace with a real name someday, once he discovered who'd blown up that church and killed his family. And beneath the question mark? One more name, a name he'd added to the list tonight.

Mason Hunt.

But before he could pursue vindication, he had to report the results of his mission. What was he supposed to tell his boss? Everything had been a screw-up from the moment Bishop told him that Cyprian wanted him to check on Mason.

The truth—that he'd seen Buchanan on the parkway and had fired at him—would make Cyprian furious. If he admitted he'd grabbed Hightower to use as bait to lure Buchanan out of the cabin, that would only make it worse. And if he told his boss that he hadn't bothered to double back and take the proof-of-death picture of Hightower's body because he was worried Mason would be waiting to ambush him, that would make him look like a coward. Which he sure as hell wasn't. He'd just been more concerned with tending his injury than snapping a picture.

No, he couldn't tell the truth. He'd risk losing his post as Cyprian's personal enforcer—the one responsible for taking care of unexpected problems, like Mason going off the grid tonight.

Then what should he say? How could he perform the required check-in without making himself look bad? He supposed he'd just have to get creative and leave out the parts that Cyprian didn't *need* to know.

He pulled out his cell phone and called the hard line in Cyprian's office, knowing the fancy encryption software on the other end would ensure that no one listening in over the airwaves would be able to understand anything he said.

"Bishop," the voice on the other end of the line answered.

Ace hesitated, his distaste for Kelly's replacement leaving a bitter taste in his mouth. He'd much rather have spoken to Cyprian. "It's Ace. The mission was successful, but there were . . . complications."

"Complications?"

"Mason didn't kill Hightower until I basically forced him to. It was like he was . . . protecting her, by taking her from her house. But when I was about to kill her he stepped in, like maybe he didn't want me having credit for the kill. Then he went after me. I don't know what's going through his head. Definitely can't be trusted anymore."

"You're saying he's gone rogue. That doesn't make sense. We've never had any problems from him. Did something else happen tonight? Something that can explain why he'd suddenly turn against us?"

Yeah. Something with the initials D.B. "No clue. You'll tell Cyprian?"

"Of course. But I didn't see proof of death come across the network. You're sure the mark is terminated?"

"Like I said, Mason was shooting at me. It wasn't exactly a picture-taking opportunity. But, yeah, she's dead. I saw him blow her away."

The answering silence didn't surprise Ace. Bishop

didn't have a clue what to do about a mission that hadn't gone exactly according to plan. He was turning out to be no better as an admin than he'd been as an enforcer. Why Cyprian had kept him around this long was a mystery. Maybe Bishop had something on his boss, something that could ruin Cyprian if it ever got out. That was the only thing that made sense.

"Do you have anything else to add to your report?" Bishop asked.

Not a chance. "Nope."

"Excellent. Good night."

The call clicked and Ace shoved the phone in his pocket. Now that business was taken care of, he'd have to clean up any signs of having been in the house. But after that, it was time for pleasure. Time to go to work on that very special list. He needed to draw Buchanan out. But how? Since the events of two months ago, every member of Buchanan's family was under protection. His hometown of Savannah, Georgia, had been locked up tighter than a virgin's knees.

But not all of his family was in Savannah.

One particular family member was in Augusta. And maybe now that Devlin Buchanan had resurfaced, it was time to test the security there again. First, he'd make Buchanan pay for his treachery, for killing Kelly.

Then it was Mason's turn.

SABRINA HAD TO grudgingly admire Mason's cleverness. He'd parked the Jeep at the end of a parking lot beside an exit, catty-cornered to the front of the police station, which was just barely visible because of another building blocking it. He'd kept his word. He'd brought her to the police. But none of their security cameras would snap any pictures of him. There was no traffic on these back streets either, especially this late at night. Or early in the morning, really, according to the digital clock on the Jeep's dash. It was unlikely anyone would notice them.

He cut the engine and she unclicked her seat belt, still half in shock that he was letting her go.

"Wait. I'll lift you out." Mason hopped out of the driver's side and headed around the back of the car.

Sabrina hated to accept his help again, but her sore ribs had already protested the simple movement of unfastening her seat belt. Climbing out of the Jeep on her own would probably be excruciating.

When he reached her side, instead of scooping her up out of her seat like he'd done before, he grabbed a folded-up white cloth out of the back of the Jeep and unrolled it.

Moonlight glinted and Sabrina blinked in surprise at what he was now holding.

"You had my glasses all this time and didn't give them to me?"

She reached for them, but he pulled them back.

"Put them on after I leave. I kept them, hoping you wouldn't get a good look at any of us." He rolled them in the cloth and handed it to her.

She clutched the cloth, deciding it probably wouldn't be a good idea to mention that she could see perfectly well at short distances, or to mention her photographic memory. Every fascinating angle of his face, every bulge of muscle in his sculpted arms, was imprinted in her mind. But even without her special memory skills, she wasn't likely to forget his smoky, deep voice and that sexy Southern drawl.

Perhaps it was the proximity to the police station that had her fear burning away like fog in the morning sun and allowed her to see him, *really* see him, for the first time. And she liked what she saw. He had a rugged, wild, bad-boy charm that could melt away a woman's defenses with one well-aimed grin. And while Sabrina certainly wasn't immune to his particular twist on tall, dark and *handsome*, it was his quiet strength, his confidence, and the way he'd risked his own life to protect her that had her so confused.

He cocked a brow. "Sabrina? Are you okay?"

She slowly nodded.

He gave her a quizzical look and reached in to pick her up. But she grabbed his hands in hers, stopping him.

He froze, his face just inches from hers, his chocolaty eyes searching hers in question as he cleared his throat.

"Sabrina? What—"

"I can't figure you out. Are you really a bad guy, or a good guy?" She entwined her fingers with his.

His eyes widened and she could feel his pulse speed up. He swallowed, his Adam's apple bobbing in his throat, then gave a short, awkward laugh and gently disengaged his hands from hers. Gesturing toward the police station, he said, "I imagine once you tell the boys in blue what happened tonight they can answer that question for you. Now, I'm just going to pick you up and set you—"

"I don't pretend to understand you. I can't fathom how someone who would work so hard to help someone would have accepted a contract to kill them in the first place. But I do know one thing. It's because of you that I'm alive. You saved me. Several times tonight. I've been so scared and worried that I hadn't really thought it through. But looking at everything in black and white, evaluating exactly what happened without emotion clouding the facts, it boils down to one thing—if it weren't for you, I'd be dead." She held her hand out toward him. "Thank you."

He looked stunned as he stared at her outstretched hand, making no move to take it. "Are you . . . thanking me, for *not* killing you?"

"I guess I am. And for *not* letting Ace kill me. I mean it, Mason. Thank you."

With obvious reluctance, he shook her hand. But when she would have pulled her hand back, he held it tight, lacing his fingers with hers as the expression on his face turned deadly serious.

"You need to get this police business out of the way. Tell them whatever you want to tell them, but don't count on them to protect you. They can't. They don't have the manpower or the knowledge to go up against the kind of people I work for. I wasn't kidding earlier about you needing to hire a bodyguard. Don't leave the police station without contacting a personal security service. Hire them to send someone to escort you back to your house. Hire two, or three. Just don't go anywhere alone. Promise me."

The urgency in his voice, in the way his eyes bored into hers, sparked an answering fear inside her again, chilling her from the inside out and making goose bumps pop up on her skin. "What am I supposed to do? Live the rest of my life in hiding?

Can't you at least tell me who hired you so I know who my enemies are?"

He shook his head and tugged his hand out of hers. Before she could stop him, he'd scooped her up and lifted her out of the Jeep. She clutched the cloth with her glasses so they wouldn't fall out while he turned with her in his arms. He crouched down, gently lowering her feet to the ground before helping her straighten, his hands on her waist to steady her.

The tug on her sore ribs had her drawing several slow breaths until the pain eased.

"Better?" he asked.

She let her breath out slowly. "Better."

"I should have taken you to a hospital instead of the police," he said. "Promise me you'll see a doctor."

"I promise. Trust me. I want some good drugs for the pain."

He raised a brow as if to remind her that he'd offered some to her earlier. "I'm still waiting on that promise that you'll hire some bodyguards."

"I'm not an idiot. I'll hire someone to protect me. But how will I know when it's safe again? Will I ever be safe, Mason?"

His face softened with sympathy and he gently swept her bangs out of her eyes before fisting his hands at his sides.

"I honestly don't know. But I'm going to do everything in my power to straighten this out. The people who hired me never should have targeted you. I'm going to find out exactly what happened, and make sure it doesn't happen again." He gently turned her in the direction of the station. "Now, go. I'll watch over you to make sure you get inside safely."

Frustrated that he wouldn't give her the information she wanted, she turned to ask him again. But the gentle, caring man of just seconds ago was now the stone-faced stranger who'd abducted her from her house. His longs legs were braced apart and his left hand flexed near his hip, and near the pistol holstered at his waist. He was through talking and in full protector mode, his dark eyes scanning every potential hiding place between the parking lot and the police station. His jaw was tight and he was once again the predator she knew he could be. The shiver that ran down her spine this time had nothing to do with attraction.

She turned around and hurried toward the station.

MASON PULLED INTO a parking garage not far from the police station and cut the engine. The Jeep was registered under one of his many aliases, so even if the cops went searching for a Jeep to corroborate Sabrina's story and found this one, there'd be no reason to match it against his real name, Mason Hunt.

He grabbed his go-bag and the bag with his crossbow, strapped them on his back, and headed out. A short hike later he entered another parking garage. Halfway down the first aisle sat his pride and joy—the dark blue F150 pickup he'd been driving for the past six years. It might've been dinged and scraped and not much to look at, but the powertrain purred like a well-fed cat and had never let him down. It was also the perfect getaway vehicle since cops never looked twice at a good ole boy driving a beat-up truck. He snagged the Carolina Panthers ball cap out of the glove box and put it on—good ole boy transformation complete.

He couldn't help remembering how adorable Sabrina had looked in her Carolina Panthers shirt last night. At the same time, he couldn't understand anyone adopting a new team after living somewhere for just a month. Based on what he'd read of her background in the files on Buchanan's tablet, she'd lived in Boulder, Colorado, her whole life. Maybe she wasn't a football fan at all, or just didn't like her home team, the Denver Broncos.

Mason had been a staunch supporter of *his* hometown team since he was a kid and the NFL expansion had created the Panthers. His dad loved football too and had treated the entire family—minus sister Darlene who was in Germany with her navy husband at the time—to a trip to Houston, Texas, to watch the Panthers battle it out in their Super Bowl XXXVIII appearance. Damn the Patriots for winning that one.

His thoughts turned back to Sabrina as he drove out of the parking garage. A few minutes later he merged onto I–240, all the while reminding himself that he'd done his duty—protected an innocent woman and made sure she was aware of the dangers. Sabrina was intelligent, and in spite of how petite and delicate she looked, she was far from helpless, as evidenced by her escape from Ace. There was no reason for him to worry about her. She'd take the necessary precautions to keep herself safe.

Now that she was gone, he could focus on helping Buchanan figure out who was behind the chicanery at EXIT so they could bring them down. It would be much easier to concentrate without staring into those ridiculously blue eyes that had him hardening every time she looked at him beneath those sexy bangs.

She was tiny, barely five feet tall, if that, and far too thin. He preferred chestier women with more curves, and certainly taller ones to make it easier to kiss them without getting a crick in his neck. But there was something about her—probably her fire and sass more than anything else—that had him constantly wanting to pick her up and carry her to the nearest bedroom. He'd bet she was a real fire-cracker in bed, and he'd like to be the one to make her fireworks go off.

What was she doing now? Were the police treating her like the victim she was, or were they swayed by her felony record and treating her like a scam artist and a liar? His hands tightened on the steering wheel. It didn't matter. She was safe. That's what mattered. And if she didn't follow through on his bodyguard advice and got herself killed, well, that wasn't his fault either. She was a grown woman. She'd been warned. He'd given her a second chance. If she blew it, that was all on her.

Just three more exits to his turnoff. Like many other enforcers, he used a maze of aliases and paper-only corporations to hide his assets in various places around the country, ensuring he always had somewhere safe to retreat to if things went bad. The house he considered his true home was over an hour away, in a rural part of the state, surrounded by acres of pristine hunting land. But the one he was going to now was much closer, just a few minutes past the suburbs. It was more a base of operations than a home, but met his most urgent current requirement. It was close by.

If Ace believed Sabrina was dead, he might not have even told Cyprian everything that had happened so he could cover up his own rather questionable decisions. But it would eventually come out, one way or another, that she was still alive. And then EXIT would come looking for him. Which was why he was heading to one of the most secure homes he owned.

He could wind down, knowing his cutting-edge security system would alert him if trouble came calling. All he wanted to do right now was lie down and get some much-needed sleep. The rendezvous with Buchanan and Ramsey wasn't until this evening. He had plenty of time. He'd been up all night, on full alert, never letting down his guard. Constant vigilance could be exhausting, and he was ready to give in to the lure of a soft bed and a hot shower, not necessarily in that order.

He passed a green road sign announcing the last downtown exit was coming up in less than a mile. He'd have to take that exit and do some backtracking if he wanted to return to the police station to watch over Sabrina when she left. He could keep to parallel streets, watching whatever vehicle her hired guards drove. Tracking them without them noticing wouldn't be much of a challenge. How to tail a vehicle was one of the first skills he'd learned when training to be an enforcer. He could make it work, if he needed to. If he wanted to. Which he did *not*.

The off-ramp loomed on his right, fifty yards away.

She's not my responsibility.

Forty yards.

She's an adult. She's been warned and she has plenty of money. She can afford to hire the best security around.

Thirty yards.

Two more exits and a few turns after that and I'll be home. I'm not a babysitter. Why should I even care?

Her almond-shaped eyes swam in his vision, her delicate face pale with fright as she stared up at him in the parking lot.

Will I ever be safe, Mason?

Ten, nine, eight . . .

Damn. He jerked the wheel and barreled down the exit.

Chapter Six

Day Two—6:30 a.m.

Sabrina figured Mason would probably have liked Detective Harry Donovan. Because as soon as she'd gotten to the part of her story about getting shot and showed him the angry red circles on her ribs, Donovan had stopped the interview and insisted on driving her straight to the hospital.

But that was two hours ago. Even though she'd had a policeman with her, Sabrina hadn't been given priority over the others in the ER waiting room. And Donovan didn't want to question her where anyone could overhear. So they'd both sat for over an hour before she'd been taken to one of the tiny rooms to wait yet again—this time for someone to take her to radiology.

While a young nurse helped Sabrina change out of her shirt into a gown, the detective waited outside the door.

"There now, you're all covered up again," the nurse assured her. "Radiology should be up here with a wheelchair in a few minutes to take pictures of those ribs."

"I'm happy to walk. It will probably be faster. I'm not in much pain anymore."

"No, no. Sorry. Hospital policy, for your safety. You have to wait for a wheelchair." She tapped a buzzer hanging off the bed where Sabrina was sitting. "Just press that button if you need anything."

She rushed out the door and Detective Donovan stepped back in, his old-fashioned pencil and spiral notebook looking fragile and tiny in his large, calloused hands as he resumed his seat in the orange plastic chair across from the bed.

At the police station he'd been the epitome of kindness and empathy as Sabrina had recited her tale about her abduction. And in the ER waiting room he'd seen to her every need, keeping others from sitting too close to her, guarding the bathroom door as she freshened up, getting her a bottle of water and some crackers from a vending machine when her stomach started growling.

He'd made her feel safe, like he really wanted to help her. Now she didn't even need to wait for the words to come out of his mouth to know that something had changed. His expression had turned hard, suspicious. The same expression she'd seen on the faces of other police officers back in Colorado.

"You found out about the felony," she said.

"Yes. I did. Why didn't you tell me?"

"Because I knew it would change everything. That you'd be more inclined *not* to want to help me, and not to believe me once you knew. I'm right, aren't I?"

His faded blue eyes regarded her beneath his

bushy, gray eyebrows. "Knowing you're a convicted felon makes me more . . . cautious . . . about trusting you, yes. But it won't change the way I handle your case. I'm doing everything I can to corroborate your story. In fact, I just got off a call with one of the officers who went to your house. He confirmed a glass pane had been busted out of a French door. But so far we're coming up empty confirming anything else." He gestured toward her arm. "How did you say you cut your arm again?"

She absently rubbed the fresh white bandage the nurse had applied earlier after cleaning her wound and putting some antibiotic ointment on it.

"A lamp, in my bedroom."

"Right." He consulted his notes. "When you heard an intruder and you knocked the lamp over. Have you ever been known to sleepwalk?"

"No, why would you ask that?"

He tapped the notebook with his pencil. "The officer who went to your house found a garbage bag in the trash can in your garage. It contained glass shards, probably from the broken pane in your French door. But nothing else of note. No ceramic shards to prove you'd broken anything in your bedroom to explain the cut on your arm. The floors were clean, no extra glass anywhere. Everything was neat and tidy." He shrugged. "I've been doing this job for a long time, probably before you were born. Can't say I remember ever coming across an intruder who cleans up after himself and doesn't take any valuables."

She clasped her hands together, more unnerved that someone had gone back into her house and cleaned up the evidence than she was about the detective questioning her story. Would Mason have gone back there? Maybe, if he wanted to make sure there wasn't anything that could implicate him.

She shivered and rubbed her hands together. "I understand your skepticism, Detective. All I can tell you is that, as far as I know, I've never sleepwalked. And if I did, I can't imagine cleaning my house in my sleep. Besides, I was too busy being abducted and shot to do any cleaning. I haven't even been home since I was taken. Have your men looked for the cabin I told you about? There has to be something in that bedroom to prove that I was there."

"Some uniforms are looking for it, but I have to say, without an address or some kind of landmark, it's a nearly impossible task. There are all kinds of cabins in the foothills off the Blue Ridge Parkway. Do you remember anything that might narrow the search?"

She shook her head. "Nothing more than what I already said. I wasn't wearing my glasses, so I didn't get a clear view of any road signs until we got closer into town and the signs were much bigger." She clutched the mattress as another thought occurred to her. "I told you that Ace pretended to be an undercover cop. He called himself Jennings. He had a badge—"

He held his hand up to stop her. "I see where you're going. Don't worry. There is a Jennings in our department, but he's present and accounted for. He wasn't anywhere near your side of town when all of this went down. So this Ace character didn't hurt the real Jennings or even steal his badge. It's just a coincidence that he chose that alias."

A coincidence? Or had he planned that Jennings

alias long ago in case he ever needed it, basing the alias on the fact that there really was a Jennings in the police force here? Regardless, at least the real policeman hadn't been hurt, which had been her fear. She relaxed her death grip on the mattress. "That's a relief. Thank you."

He nodded and tapped his notebook again. "We ran a DMV search for the type of Jeep you described, which sounds like an old Wrangler to me. Tried using Mason as a first name and then as a last name."

"Let me guess. No hits."

"No hits. I'm sorry, Miss Hightower. I'm sure this is very frustrating for you."

She stilled. "You sound like you might believe my story."

"'Believe' is too strong a word. I believe in things I can see and touch, facts. And so far there aren't too many of those to support what you've told me. But I also trust my gut instincts, and how to spot someone in a lie. My gut says you're telling the truth, or what you *think* is the truth. And there's one key piece of evidence that I can't figure out how to explain away." He waved his hand toward her gown. "I've seen the marks that a bullet leaves when someone's shot wearing Kevlar. They look exactly like those marks on your ribs."

Her breath caught and then she let it out. "I never thought I'd be grateful for getting shot tonight. But if it means you'll keep looking into who's trying to kill me, it was worth the pain."

"Oh, I'll definitely keep trying to figure all of this out. Don't you worry about that. You said the man who allegedly abducted you was named Mason.

You're sure he never mentioned his last name? The others with him didn't either?"

She tried not to let his "allegedly" bother her. At least he wasn't discounting her story completely like the police in Colorado had.

"No, he didn't tell me his last name. The only other name I heard was Ace."

He wrote a note down. "The one you stabbed with the scissors?"

She winced. "Yes."

"Think carefully, did you ever hear anyone refer by name to the couple that you saw?"

"No. I've played it over and over in my head. I never heard their names."

A knock sounded behind him. A police officer stood in the open doorway holding Sabrina's purse.

Donovan thanked him and handed the purse to Sabrina. "It was in your bedroom, like you said it would be."

"Thank you so much." She smiled at the officer, who nodded and ducked back down the hallway. "Now I can fill out all of those insurance forms the administrator was pestering me about earlier."

"Once we're finished here I'd like to take you back to the station to work with a sketch artist. With any luck we can get a good enough description of the people you saw tonight to identify them, if they're in the system already."

She set her purse aside. "You don't have to wait. I can draw them for you."

One of his bushy brows rose as he handed her his notebook. "You're an artist?"

"I sold my drawings to pay my way through college, so, yeah, I guess so."

"Why would you have to work your way through college? I thought you were a millionaire. That's what the police in Boulder said when they told me about your police record."

"Yeah, well, I wouldn't say the Boulder police have ever worried all that much about accuracy. At least not where I'm concerned." At his admonishing look, she cleared her throat and continued. "My grandfather is the one who controls the Hightower fortune. He set up fairly complicated trusts for his grandchildren. I couldn't get a penny out until I turned twenty-one. Now I receive a monthly allowance, which increases every year. Once I turn thirty, I'll have access to all of it. But until then, I have to stick to a budget like anyone else."

"I bet that makes you resent him, or at least, until he disappeared not too long ago."

She bristled at the implied accusation. "Let me guess. The cops in Boulder told you they suspect me for my grandfather's disappearance too."

"Actually, no. They said you had an ironclad alibi for when he went missing. I was just asking a question, more out of curiosity I suppose. Comes with the territory."

Her face heated with embarrassment. "Sorry. I'm touchy when it comes to Grampy Hightower. I don't begrudge his decision to dole out his money the way he does. He wants his grandchildren to value hard work and understand how hard it is to earn a living, so we don't take it for granted. He learned that giving someone millions of dollars from day one creates self-centered people who care more about their next jaunt through Europe than the family they left behind."

She bit her lip, belatedly regretting her outburst.

"You're talking about your parents I assume?"

She picked the pencil up. "I'm finished talking for the moment. I'll work on the sketches now if you don't mind."

Another knock sounded. She looked up to see a man in lime-green scrubs pushing a wheelchair.

"I'm here to take you to radiology, Miss Hightower."

SABRINA CHECKED THE security alarm panel by the front door, again. Was this the sixth time she'd done that since getting home? The seventh? After last night, she definitely didn't trust the alarm—even though her new bodyguards had tested it and confirmed it was working. How could she trust it when she knew she'd set it last night but it hadn't gone off when Mason had broken in? And yet, when Detective Donovan had spoken to the alarm company to verify her story, they'd insisted that she *hadn't* set it. Once it was a decent hour, she fully intended to call them back and insist that they send someone to inspect the system. But first she needed to get some sleep. If she *could* sleep.

It didn't matter that she had three bodyguards to watch over her. She didn't think she'd ever feel safe here again, not until she could figure out who wanted her dead. But at least she had one person on her side: Detective Donovan. He might not buy her whole story yet, but he was intrigued enough to keep digging. It was refreshing to have a police officer not assume the worst about her for a change.

But just like Mason had warned her, the police couldn't offer protection—thus the security guards.

And since she was on unpaid administrative leave until her year of exile from Colorado was over, she couldn't really afford the guards. She couldn't have even afforded the nice home she was renting if it weren't for the bad economy. The desperate home-owner had slashed the price in order to get someone into the long-vacant house. But even with a cheap lease, she still struggled with too much month at the end of her money.

When it came time for another payment to the private detectives who were trying to find clues in her grandfather's disappearance, and to the lawyers who were pressing the lawsuit over her parents' deaths, she might be forced to let the guards go. It all depended on how quickly she could sell more of the expensive antique furniture her grandfather had gifted to her over the years, and how much money she could get for it. The furniture had sentimental value worth far more than its cost, but she'd give everything she had if it meant she could see Grampy's smiling face even one more time.

That was a bridge she'd have to cross later. For now, she was grateful to be home, even if she didn't feel nearly as safe as when Mason had been the one watching over her. Mason. Every time she thought about him she got more and more confused. So confused, in fact, that after giving Donovan sketches of Ace and the couple from the Hummer, she'd made dozens of starts and stops trying to draw Mason. She'd finally told the detective that she'd been so scared of Mason that she'd never really looked him full-on in the face and couldn't remember exactly what he looked like.

Donovan had readily accepted her lies, patting

her shoulder to console her, and assuring her that he'd do his best to get the local TV news station to broadcast the other sketches. Maybe someone would recognize Ace and the couple and would come forward.

Of course she hadn't forgotten what Mason looked like. She'd drawn him in a matter of minutes, while the detective was out of the room taking a smoke break. But she'd felt like a traitor at the thought of turning the picture over to the police. Her mind told her that was silly, crazy. But her heart kept telling her there was more to Mason than she knew, that he'd proven he was really a good guy over and over, that she owed him for saving her life. In the end, she'd folded the paper with his likeness and had shoved it into her jeans pocket.

She thunked her forehead against the wall beside the security panel.

"Miss Hightower?"

She turned toward the sound of the bodyguard's voice. Which one was he again? What was his name? He stood at the end of the foyer, in the opening to the main room at the front of the house, impeccably dressed in an expensive dove-gray suit. She hesitated, wishing her memory of what she'd *heard* was as good as her memory of what she'd *seen*. Was it really too much to ask that the bodyguards wear name tags?

"Vince," he said. "My name? That *is* what you were trying so hard to remember just now, right?"

"Vince Barton," she said, his full name finally coming to her as she headed toward him. "Sorry, it's late. Or, early, I guess?" She rubbed her temple to ease the pressure there. "What time is it?"

He checked his watch. "Not that early. Nine-thirty in the morning, ma'am."

She winced. "I've been up all night."

"If you want to go upstairs and get some sleep, I promise you don't have to worry about your safety." He patted the gun holstered at his hip. "I'm armed and dangerous," he teased. "No one's getting in on my watch. The other guards are taking turns patrolling the property and checking all the entry points down here. There will be at least two of us inside the house at all times. You're completely safe."

His high-wattage smile had her realizing how completely exhausted she must be. Because if a man as gorgeous and perfect-looking as Vince Barton had graced her with that smile at any other time, she'd have been blushing like a schoolgirl. Instead, she was just annoyed. He seemed too confident: of his looks, of his abilities, or both. She'd been extremely detailed in her description of what had happened last night and the people who'd abducted her. Shouldn't he be more serious, more alert, more . . . concerned?

Maybe tomorrow she'd hire a different security company, one whose guards weren't quite so polished or polite or . . . pretty. Maybe they'd send someone taller than Vince Barton, brawnier, with hair that was too long and unkempt, and a hard, angular face that needed a shave. A man who looked like he'd grown up on the wrong side of the tracks and had learned to fight without rules, using whatever means were necessary to survive.

A man like Mason.

She pressed her hand to her temple again.

"Miss Hightower? Do you need me to get you something? Aspirin? A glass of water?"

She forced her hand down. Okay, maybe this bodyguard, Vince, was more observant than she'd given him credit for. Maybe he wasn't just a pretty face. She *should* trust him and do what he'd suggested, get some sleep. She'd been up over twenty-four hours straight, and even with her glasses on, she could barely focus anymore.

"I've got everything I need upstairs." It was time for more pain pills anyway, for her bruised ribs. Luckily the hospital pharmacy had filled her prescription before she left.

"Good night, Vince. And thank you, and the others, for rearranging your schedules so you could take me on as a client without any advance notice."

"It's our pleasure, ma'am." Too-polite Vince stepped back to let her pass.

She headed up the front stairs. But even knowing the house was locked, that the temperamental alarm was set, and that three professional bodyguards had searched from top to bottom for intruders after Detective Donovan drove her home, she couldn't help the prickle of fear that skittered up her spine.

She reached the top of the stairs and headed toward her bedroom. Everything was neat and clean, like the rest of the house, as if nothing bad had happened. She'd studied the couch downstairs earlier, trying to find a trace of her blood from the cut on her arm, but it was clean, pristine.

When she saw the spot on the table by the bed where the now broken lamp used to sit, she started to shake. In spite of everything else some mysterious person had done to make the house look untouched, they'd been unable to fix the glass in the French door, or glue that lamp back together. For those small favors, she was grateful. It proved she wasn't going crazy.

Still, knowing someone had been here covering their tracks gave her a bone-deep chill. It proved how vulnerable she really was. She should leave, move out of this house. But where would she go? She couldn't just disappear. She still had to keep her investigators and lawyers pushing for answers regarding both her grandfather and her parents. Tomorrow. Or later today, really, she'd make some kind of decision about her future. But right now she needed sleep more than anything else. A shower sounded wonderful, but she was suddenly too tired to even think.

After swallowing some pain pills, she was about to strip down to her underwear and put on a night-shirt, but the thought of going to bed that way again made her feel far too vulnerable. Instead, she wadded up the shirt and jeans that weren't hers and tossed them in the bedroom trash. She grabbed one of her own shirts from the closet and her own jeans, put them on, and then slid between the sheets fully dressed.

The last thing she saw before she closed her eyes was the five-by-seven framed picture on her dresser, the one of her with her parents wearing the green T-shirts the tour company had given them. It had been taken just moments before her parents had plunged to their deaths over a gorge because of a faulty zip line.

Unbidden, hot tears coursed down her cheeks. That day had started out as one of the happiest of her life, one of the few times that her parents had actually wanted to include her on one of their adventures. But after the horrible accident, she was left bitterly regretting that she'd surprised her parents by purchasing them an anniversary trip package. She cursed the day she'd ever heard of EXtreme International Tours, Incorporated.

Chapter Seven

Day Two—5:30 p.m.

Cyprian Cardenas looked over the podium at the crowded lobby of EXIT Incorporated's newest location just outside of Asheville, North Carolina, carefully maintaining his smile for the reporters. His daughter, Melissa, had basically bribed every newspaper features editor or vacation magazine contributor within a three-hundred-mile radius to cover the grand opening. It was costing a fortune in free tours, but Melissa was a savvy businesswoman and Cyprian didn't doubt that the resulting press coverage would more than make up for the freebies.

The only true downside was that his work was piling up while he had to stand here answering the same lame questions the press asked at nearly every event Melissa put together. One of the more egregious of the reporters today, Kaysen Landry from the *Citizen-Times* newspaper, was waving her hand with yet another question, probably as juvenile as the last one. When all of the other reporters' questions were answered and the young woman was still waving her hand, he braced himself and called on her.

"Yes, Miss Landry?"

"Mr. Cardenas, can you tell me again what EXIT stands for?"

The pen in his hand snapped in two. Luckily his hand was hidden from view. What exactly had this woman been doing for the past half hour if she still didn't know what his company's acronym stood for?

"EXtreme International Tours."

The puzzled look on her face had him dreading her next question.

"But you're opening this facility here in Asheville, offering the same kinds of local tours other companies do—horseback riding, whitewater rafting, zip lining. How is that extreme or international when your only other office location is in Boulder, Colorado?"

"As I explained earlier," he reminded her, "our tours provide clients with a more intense experience than other companies. We cater to thrill seekers. We have unique tour experiences that will stretch each client to their physical and mental limitations. And as the 'international' portion of our name implies, we offer packages in sixteen countries across four continents through several satellite branches of EXIT Inc. If there's something you want to do in the wild outdoors anywhere in the world, we'll make sure you have a safe, exciting adventure."

He swept his hand to his right, indicating the six men and women in traditional green EXIT tour T-shirts sitting at the table beside the podium.

"The real experts of EXIT are right here and can answer—"

"Mr. Cardenas," the same reporter called out again.

Something about the barely contained excitement on Kaysen Landry's face put Cyprian on alert. What was she up to? "Yes?"

"You say that your guides ensure each client's safety. But there was an accident on one of your tours in Colorado just two months ago that claimed the lives of Mr. and Mrs. John Hightower. Their surviving daughter, Sabrina Hightower, is currently suing both you personally and your corporation for negligence. How can the residents of Asheville feel secure scheduling tours with your company when some clients have actually *died* on previous tours?"

The room grew silent and every eye focused on Cyprian. Even the greeters at the door and the security guards roaming the room had stopped to see how he would respond.

He noted Landry's smug look. She'd sandbagged him, making him think she was harmless, clueless, when she was actually quite clever. Her earlier questions had done exactly what she'd intended—made him careless, backed him into a corner, so he looked like a fool when she threw that zinger at him.

He cleared his throat. "Yes, well, that was a tragic loss, the details of which are in dispute and can't be discussed because of the ongoing litigation. However, just as someone wouldn't give up flying on airplanes because of one crash, I think we can agree that one regretful accident out of thousands of successful tours is an impressive record. Now, if you'll

excuse me, I have an appointment. Please treat your-
selves to the dinner buffet we've set up in the next
room, which includes an open bar. Thank you."

The near stampede to the other room drowned
out the further questions Kaysen Landry was
trying to shout at him as he left the podium. The
open bar had been his salvation, getting him out
of a difficult situation. He'd have to remember to
thank his daughter, Melissa, when he called her in
Colorado tonight. She'd specifically suggested that
he hold the press conference closer to the supper
hour so they could offer adult beverages. With the
free alcohol and food flowing, the reporters would
leave happy and hopefully feeling good about the
company. Melissa's suggestion had been just the
thing to divert everyone's attention from the unpleasantness of Landry's questions about the Hightower accident.

As he neared the door marked "private" at the
back of the room, it opened, held by Bishop, his
assistant. Cyprian stepped inside. Bishop immediately shut and locked the door, blocking out the
noise from the lobby. The barely perceptible nod of
his assistant's head told Cyprian that he needed to
discuss enforcer business.

Cyprian greeted various staff members while he
and Bishop headed down the long hall that ran the
length of the building. All of these people worked
to support the tour side of EXIT and thought he was
here to establish this new location to expand into
another market. While that was certainly true, he
had another, far more important reason for being
here—setting up redundancies and backups for the
company's critical enforcer network.

A mainframe mirroring the one in Boulder was now fully functional and operating in the tunnels beneath this office building, ensuring that if something happened to the Boulder location, EXIT's business would continue uninterrupted. The tunnels had been suggested by the contractor as a way of saving money on utilities, using the cooler temperatures underground to help keep the mainframe from overheating without having to spend so much on air-conditioning. And of course, Cyprian had immediately seen the benefit of using those tunnels for an entirely different purpose as well—one which his own *personal* contractor had seen to after the other renovations were complete.

As far as anyone who worked in the tour side of the business was concerned, there were just a few tunnels—the main one with the computer room opening off it, and some side tunnels with supply rooms. But there were several other tunnels accessible through a hidden panel that only Cyprian and a select few knew about.

To help him with that particular "purpose," he'd also brought his favorite pit bull enforcer, Ace, and his assistant, Bishop. Which had turned out to be fortuitous once he found out that Sabrina Hightower had followed him from Colorado to North Carolina. But even that was being dealt with. Everything had been going according to plan until that clever reporter had spoiled the press conference.

"I want Kaysen Landry banned from future media events." He kept his voice low so that only Bishop could hear.

"Done."

Bishop's quick response set Cyprian's teeth on

edge. He'd heard the same response before. But with Bishop, the outcome was always an uncertain proposition. Which was why Cyprian had been poised to fire him as an enforcer, and the sole reason Bishop was in Cyprian's office on that fateful day months ago when Cyprian had lost his customary control and gave an order he later regretted. Now, because of that order, he and Bishop were bound together by a shared secret. And everything Cyprian had done since then was about containment and damage control.

Hiring Bishop as his assistant after Kelly's death had been an easy way to keep Bishop close while they sorted out this Hightower situation. It had also been a way to keep Bishop employed—and quiet—while Cyprian tried to figure out how to end their association without risking Bishop telling anyone what he knew.

Because of EXIT's secret charter, any enforcer who was fired or chose to leave on their own was closely monitored to ensure that they didn't disclose any confidences about the company. But in Bishop's case, Cyprian couldn't just let him retire and then risk that someone monitoring him might learn Cyprian's secret. For that reason—and because it wasn't Bishop's fault that he was in this predicament—Cyprian was torn about what to do about him. Which meant, for now, tolerating him.

They turned at the end of the hall and headed into Cyprian's office. Or, at least, his *official* office. Enforcer business was conducted in a honeycomb of hidden, soundproofed rooms with dedicated phone and data lines between this location and the one in Colorado to ensure complete privacy.

Bishop locked the office door to keep the admins from wondering why no one was in the outer office after seeing the two of them go inside. Then he keyed the security code into the phone on the desk and a hidden panel slid into the wall. They both headed inside and the panel automatically closed and locked behind them.

Cyprian immediately strode to the bank of windows behind his massive desk—fake windows, because the walls were actually concrete. But if someone didn't know it, they'd think they were real, both inside and out. They were actually enormous monitors that could show anything he wanted, from his desktop computer to security camera shots to whatever was playing on TV.

Right now, the incredibly clear picture was a gorgeous, live shot of the Blue Ridge Mountains, courtesy of a camera on a piece of land that he'd purchased for just this reason. He could just as easily switch to a live shot of the Rockies. The illusion of real windows was what made it possible for him to spend hours cooped up inside this fortress without feeling like he was in a prison. And it was this "window," with its view of the mountains, that helped lower his stress when something like that reporter business set him on edge.

"Cyprian, we need to talk about Sabrina Hightower. She—"

He held up his hand, demanding silence. The Hightowers were going to be his ruination if he didn't get this ongoing fiasco resolved soon. And from Bishop's tone, Cyprian knew he wasn't going to like whatever his unwanted partner-in-crime was about to tell him. Which meant he really needed a moment, or he'd shoot Bishop right here and now. Which would just complicate everything enormously and force him to involve someone else in this mess.

He took in the view of the mountains for several more minutes, watching the leaves blow in the light breeze, finding his center and pushing past his irritation over the press conference.

Finally, he turned around. "Is she dead?"

"No, sir." Sweat broke out on his forehead. He waved to the bar on the other side of the room. "This is going to take a few minutes to explain. Can I . . . get you a drink first?"

Normally Cyprian wouldn't brook that type of delay once he was ready to discuss something. But a drink might be just the thing to help him stay calm. He couldn't afford to lose his cool. Again.

He nodded his permission. Bishop crossed to the bar and began mixing Cyprian's drink. In spite of Bishop's eagerness to see to Cyprian's every need, it did little to atone for his mistakes—and nothing to ease Cyprian's grief and sense of loss over the death of his previous assistant.

Of course, Kelly Parker had had other, considerable "talents" he'd fully explored, which made the loss much deeper. Even knowing that it was Kelly's eclectic . . . tastes . . . that had caused the other unfortunate problems, the ones with Buchanan a few months ago, he could never truly regret their time together.

Bishop handed him the smooth blend of Hennessy whiskey and soda on the rocks and they sat in the seating area in front of the bar. For himself, Bishop had simply grabbed a bottle of Heineken from the mini-fridge. Low class. Kelly would have shared the Hennessy.

When Cyprian was halfway through with his drink, he decided he was mellow enough to handle whatever news was about to be thrown his way. He set his drink on the granite-topped bar beside him. "Explain."

Bishop set his beer down and braced his forearms on his knees. He was a bear of a man, with meaty paws and too much bulk around the middle, which made it all the more telling when his legs began to shake.

Staring at his knees, Bishop said, "Because of what happened last time, I thought it might be better to get help with my assignment." He risked a quick look up. "I involved Mason Hunt."

"Excuse me?" Cyprian asked, very softly, trying to hold on to his temper.

The shaking traveled up Bishop's torso to his hands. "I . . . might have created a fake EXIT order to get Hunt to take care of Miss Hightower for me." He met Cyprian's stare and turned pale. "I thought there wouldn't be any harm. Mason's one of the best around. He'd take care of it. No one would be the wiser." He swallowed again, making a choking sound. "But something went wrong."

Cyprian stared at the other man for a long moment before he could trust himself to speak. "I'm sure I couldn't have heard you correctly. Because I know that I was extremely clear when I told you that I wanted no one else involved in this situation. Your first attempt to terminate Miss Hightower was disastrous precisely because you involved the tour side of the company. Plus you relied on too many variables. You rigged equipment, hoping a guide wouldn't notice you'd sabotaged it. Then you didn't take into account things that could go wrong, like the target getting sick and not completing the anticipated tour. This time you were supposed to keep it simple. You were supposed to shoot her in her home and stage it to look like a burglary gone wrong. Even the greenest recruit could handle something like that."

Bishop's complexion turned a sickly shade of gray. "I'm sorry, boss. I was trying to make sure that nothing could possibly go wrong. I thought my plan was failproof."

Well, it definitely wasn't *fool*proof. Cyprian pictured his hands closing around Bishop's neck as he pinned him to the floor, his knee digging into Bishop's stomach while he choked the life out of him. But he carefully composed himself, holding back his rage and letting none of those thoughts show. Instead, he flicked a piece of imaginary lint off his suit jacket as if he were more concerned with his appearance than the disaster unfolding in front of him.

"Do continue, Bishop," he encouraged, drawing the fly into the web. "I can't offer a solution without knowing all the details."

Relief flashed across the other man's face and he wiped the flop sweat off his brow. "Okay, okay. Obviously, I shouldn't have created the fake order. That was a mistake."

"Yes. Yes it was. Go on."

His head bobbed up and down like one of the great blue herons common to the area. "Ace called in to say the mission—"

Cyprian held up his hand. "How did Ace get involved in this?"

Bishop tugged at his collar, knocking his tie askew. "When Mason didn't call in to report that the mission was over, I sent Ace to see what had happened."

"Ah, I see. As we would do on any *legitimate* mission."

"Exactly," Bishop said, not catching Cyprian's sarcasm. "The thing is, Ace said the mission was successful. Mason shot and killed Hightower, but only because Ace forced his hand. They argued or something, and exchanged gunfire. But I gather neither of them was hurt. I asked Ace about proof of death but he said he hadn't had a chance to snap a picture because Mason was after him." He waved his hand as if he could wave the trouble away just as easily. "I tried calling Mason's company cell phone. Naturally I wanted to double-check everything."

"Naturally."

Bishop must have caught the sarcasm this time, because the sweat started up again, popping out on the sides of his face. "Uh, neither Ace nor Hunt are answering my calls at this point."

"Did you try tracking the GPS location of their phones?"

Bishop nodded. "Nothing came up."

"Then they've obviously removed the batteries on their company phones, or destroyed them altogether, and are using burner phones. Apparently neither Mr. Hunt nor Ace desire to be found." Had they both gone rogue, like Buchanan?

"I'm . . . I'm sure I'll be able to fix everything. It's just going to . . . take a bit longer."

"If you believed *that* you wouldn't have told me any of this."

"Right." Bishop's eyes widened. "I mean, no. I would have told you, eventually, once I knew Hightower was dead. I wouldn't want to worry you unnecessarily. I never . . . I didn't plan on . . ."

"Lying?"

Bishop shook his head back and forth, making the sweat fly and revulsion twist Cyprian's stomach.

"No, no, no. I would never lie to you, boss. I just . . . made a bad decision. I didn't want Hightower to get away like she did the last time. So I thought that by enlisting Hunt it was a done deal, no possibility of failure." His face turned a bright red and his Adam's apple bobbed in his throat.

Cyprian slowly rose to his feet and jerked his suit jacket into place. "You said that Ace saw Mason shoot Miss Hightower but that she isn't dead yet. Hopefully it's just a matter of time. If she's gut shot, it could take a while. Which hospital is she in?"

"Yeah, about that. It, ah, took a bit of trickery to find out where she was because of the privacy policies but I—"

"Did you find her or not?"

"She was treated at Mission Hospital and released early this morning."

"*Released?* Was she shot or not?"

"I'm still working on that. Maybe it was a flesh wound?" He tugged at his collar again. "She hired bodyguards. I have someone watching the house in case she decides to go anywhere."

Unable to remain still any longer, Cyprian began pacing in front of his desk. At least he could be grateful for one thing—that Bishop hadn't foolishly approached the house himself. The hospital would have filed a report about the gunshot wounds. The police might very well be watching the house. "You did say that Ace reported Hightower was dead?"

Bishop nodded. "Yes. But I'm not sure what happened. Maybe he didn't—"

Cyprian held up his hand to stop him. "I've heard enough. What *happened* is that you've made yet another mess for me to clean up. Mason Hunt is a lot like Devlin Buchanan—intensely moral, honest, idealistic. You know what happened with Buchanan after Kelly framed him and I foolishly tried to protect her. He's on his own personal vendetta to bring both me and EXIT down. So what did you think would happen if *Hunt* found out his mark was *innocent*?" He stalked to his desk.

"I . . . I didn't think—"

"Exactly. You didn't think." He stared suspiciously at his biggest failure. Bishop wasn't acting like someone who'd just confessed *all* of his sins. He was still nervous, too nervous, and kept glancing at the wall of windows behind the desk.

"What else haven't you told me?" Cyprian demanded.

Bishop winced as if he were in pain and retrieved the remote control from the top of the desk. "This came on TV a little earlier." He pressed a button and the Blue Ridge Mountains were replaced with a recording of the local news.

The first story was a short clip about the opening of the new EXIT office in town. It showed people touring the building last month as the final construction was being completed. Recording the news for the past few weeks had been one of Bishop's responsibilities so that any coverage about EXIT could be evaluated and sent to Cyprian's daughter, Melissa, to review. She would make marketing decisions about new strategies based on how EXIT was being portrayed by the press.

"Wait, pause the recording." Alarmed, Cyprian pointed at the screen. "That's Sabrina Hightower, in that last group. What was she doing here?"

Bishop shook his head. "Touring the building I assume, but I don't know why she'd want to do that."

Cyprian could well imagine one reason she might want to look at EXIT's headquarters: to look for anything that was further proof of the company's alleged negligence and carelessness. But was there another reason? Did she suspect anything? Was there any possibility she might have separated from the tour group and nosed around? That could be *extremely* problematic. He tapped his fingers impatiently against his thigh. "Continue."

Bishop pressed the start button. "*This* is the part that concerned me."

Stupid fool. What Cyprian had just seen was intensely important and very concerning. But Bishop wasn't adept at recognizing the significance of minor details, which was one of the reasons that Cyprian had planned on firing him before the Hightower fiasco had started. And then it was too late.

Cyprian watched the second news story, and his stomach dropped with dread. Black and white sketches of three people were displayed behind the TV anchorman, along with a request for information if anyone knew who they were or had seen them anywhere. The reporter stated that the three people shown, plus one more not shown, were being sought as potential witnesses to a crime that had occurred last night.

"Pause it," Cyprian snapped. He stalked closer to the screens, shaking his head at the amazing likenesses revealed by each of the sketches. "Devlin Buchanan, Emily O'Malley, and Ace. Who drew these?"

"I called a contact at the television station and put some pressure on her to—"

"Who. Drew. Them?" he gritted out.

"Sabrina Hightower, early this morning, for a Detective Donovan."

Cyprian swore and began pacing in front of his desk. Things were unraveling faster than he could patch them back together. He didn't need any magical tea leaves to know what those sketches meant. Buchanan was back, and butting his nose into EXIT business. Somehow he'd gotten wind of Mason's bogus mission and let him know that Hightower was innocent. Probably because of that fake EXIT order Bishop had created. That was the only explanation—documentation where there shouldn't have been any. Which meant the mainframe's supposedly infallible security had been breached. He didn't know why there wasn't a sketch of Mason too, but the anchorman had mentioned a fourth person, so he was likely part of whatever had happened.

And what role was Ace playing in this? Calling in to say a mission was successful even though the mark hadn't been terminated? Ace wasn't the type to care if his mark was innocent. The only reason he'd lie about a mission was to cover his own ass. With Buchanan back in the picture it didn't take a genius to realize what must have happened: Ace *knew* Buchanan was back, and he didn't want his boss to have a chance to reel him in before Ace had had his revenge for Kelly's death, and for his bruised pride. Buchanan had nearly killed him during their last encounter, and Ace had been forced to tuck tail and run. *That's* why Ace wasn't answering his phone.

Cyprian stopped pacing and flattened his palms against the windowsill, resting his forehead against the cool glass that protected the screens.

This had all started six months ago with one stupid, rash mistake. *His* mistake. Cyprian had no one to blame but himself. Because of a father's love for his only daughter, his love for Melissa, he'd acted out of anger, thinking to protect her. But all he'd done was make everything worse.

Now he'd been reduced to murdering innocent people like Sabrina Hightower. He was turning against truly good men that he genuinely admired—Buchanan and Hunt—to cover his tracks and keep EXIT's core charter intact. He despised himself for the things that he'd done, for what he still had to do. But there was no turning back now. He had to finish this. He had to eliminate all the loose ends. And equally important, he had to reinstate strict discipline among his subordinates.

He'd allowed them to take advantage of his distraction over his mistakes—starting with Kelly and continuing with Bishop. If he'd paid attention to what Kelly had been doing, the Buchanan incident would never have happened. If he'd paid attention to Bishop, Mason wouldn't have been dragged into the Hightower mire. Well, he was paying attention now. And it was time to stop the bleeding, to deal with each of his problems one by one.

Starting with Bishop.

He turned around and forced another smile. Sometimes he wondered that his face didn't crack. "Have you told me everything?"

Bishop's eyes darted to the side and he swallowed. "Y-yes, sir. Of course."

Liar.

"Good. What I need you to do right now is find Mason and Hightower. Can you do that?"

"Of course. Absolutely. I assume you want them both dead?"

Cyprian held back the sneer that threatened to curve his lips. Bishop kill Mason? He couldn't even begin to imagine a scenario where that was a possibility. Right now he wasn't even sure that Bishop could handle Hightower, let alone a skilled enforcer. But that wasn't the point. He wanted Bishop out of the way for a while, so he wouldn't get wind of what Cyprian was about to do.

"That would be excellent. Be sure to send proof of death. And use the cleanup crew to ensure the scene is sanitized. No mistakes this time. No loose ends."

"Of course. Of course. Thank you, sir. Thank you for being so understanding. And for giving me another chance to make it right."

"Everyone deserves a second chance." *But Bishop had already been given a second chance.* "I assume you'll want to start your assignment immediately."

"Yes, sir." Bishop gave him a pathetically grateful look and exited through the sliding panel. It swished closed behind him.

Cyprian moved to the wall of fake windows

again and pressed the remote, rewinding the news coverage until the picture of the tour group inside the new EXIT building was displayed. He ran his finger down the curve of Sabrina Hightower's face. She wasn't particularly beautiful, but she certainly wasn't ugly. And there was something about her that was compelling. The eyes perhaps? Startlingly blue, they were large, expressive, and hinted at an underlying curiosity and intelligence. It was that curiosity that had him concerned.

"What were you up to that day, young lady?" He studied the clip several times but didn't see anything amiss. Maybe a call to one of Bishop's local media contacts could get Cyprian the full, unedited tape.

His lip curled with distaste. Bishop. Who'd have thought he could screw up so badly? He punched the speaker button on his desk phone, then sat down and speed dialed a number in the Colorado office.

The line clicked. "Systems Security. How can I help you, Mr. Cardenas?"

"Good afternoon, Eddie. I have reason to believe that a data security breach has occurred. I'd like you to look into it, assess the damage, and report back to me. And I want this to stay confidential, just between the two of us. Understood?"

"Of course, sir. Is there something in particular that concerns you?"

"Yes. EXIT orders. And my assistant, Bishop. I want his access revoked. But I don't want him notified. He's on . . . temporary assignment, so he won't have reason to try to log onto the mainframe. I'm hopeful he won't notice that we've disabled his

ID." He heard the tapping of computer keys over the line.

"His ID is disabled. I assume you'll want a report of everything he's accessed. Do you have a time-frame in mind?"

"He was promoted to his current position two months ago. His clearance would have been too low to do any damage prior to that."

"Two months it is. Anything else, sir?"

"It would set my mind at ease if we perform an-other full-system security audit even though we just finished one. I have reason to believe some-one outside the company also accessed the EXIT order database, a former enforcer named Devlin Buchanan, although I have no clue how. This is all confidential, Eddie. I want you to do the work your-self. No delegating. And no sharing anything you find with anyone but me. I don't even want the Council to know about this until I review the data so I can make recommendations."

"I'll clear my calendar so I can work on this full-time, alone."

"Thank you, Eddie. I appreciate that. There is one more thing, though. Mason Hunt, an active en-forcer, has gone off the grid and I need to find him. Could you please supply me with a list of all of his real-estate holdings? Not the kind of list I could get from a property appraiser. I want the real list."

"Of course. That will take a bit more time, de-pending on how many layers of aliases and holding companies he might have created."

"But it can be done?"

"Of course, sir."

"Excellent. Notify me immediately once you have anything. And if you find even the whisper of a security breach of any kind, by *anyone*, I don't want to have to wait for a formal report."

"Yes, sir. I'll call as soon as I have any information at all."

Cyprian disconnected the call and considered his next set of problems, two very big problems.

Devlin Buchanan and Mason Hunt.

He sorely regretted having to add Hunt to his list of loose ends, but it couldn't be helped, not since he knew about the fake EXIT order. Cyprian could well imagine Hunt's outrage. It had been that moral outrage that had drawn Cyprian to him as a potential enforcer in the first place. One of his contacts in the army had alerted him about Mason shortly after Mason quit the army, bitter and disillusioned. Appealing to his burning thirst for justice had been the right strategy to get him to sign on with EXIT. But that same mindset was what made Mason a liability now.

He would be worried that other innocents were being targeted in addition to Hightower. Like a bloodhound, he'd keep digging until he turned over the wrong grave. He was far too dangerous to allow to go unchecked. And if he teamed up with Buchanan, the two would be a formidable pair. It would be far easier to deal with them separately.

What he needed was a diversion, a way to get Buchanan out of North Carolina and focused on something other than EXIT. Fortunately, he knew exactly how to do that. *Unfortunately*, it meant crossing a personal line that he'd never crossed before, breaking one of his own rules that he drilled into all enforcers—never go after an enforcer's family. That rule was in place as incentive when signing on new recruits. They needed assurance that no matter what, their families would be safe, that they wouldn't become targets for retribution if things went sour. It also was a quid pro quo—honor among thieves, as it were—to keep his own daughter safe if anyone broke with the firm. The rule was supposed to protect a family forever, even after the enforcer left the company.

But did it apply if the enforcer went rogue?

He blew out a breath and scrubbed his face. What choice did he really have? Weaken his authority by breaking his own rules, or risk EXIT being destroyed because he didn't act to put down the current rebellion? Or was there another option altogether? He clicked the remote, changing the scenery on the wall of windows, and swiveled in his chair watching the leaves, weighing the pros and cons. After he thought it through, a reassuring calm settled over him. He knew exactly what he had to do. And he knew just the person who could help him: someone without scruples, or a conscience. Someone who always followed orders, without question.

He flipped through his old-fashioned Rolodex, preferring the comfort of names and numbers on paper over the current fashion of having everything stored electronically. When he located the name he wanted, he keyed in the number. A moment later, the line beeped, letting him know the encryption software was preparing to scramble the line before placing the call, to ensure that no one could ungarble the conversation even if the call was intercepted.

As long as he spoke to someone on this particular

phone, it didn't matter what type of phone was on the other end. The contents of the call would be protected. It was an expensive, sophisticated upgrade that he'd insisted on when he'd purchased this old building and had it retrofitted. It made everything simple and secure.

Another beep signaled that the call was going through. After one ring, the line crackled. "Stryker."

"It's Cyprian. Where are you?"

"Athens, Georgia. Hunting."

"Will your . . . hunting . . . take much longer to conclude?"

"Actually, my prey is in my sights right now."

"I'll wait." Cyprian leaned back against the desk and adjusted the lapel of his charcoal gray suit. Less than a minute later, the sharp crack of a rifle echoed from the speaker. Then a pause, probably while Stryker snapped the required picture through the rifle scope. Pounding footsteps and heavy breathing followed. Another minute and the roar of an engine filled the room, and something that Cyprian imagined were tires kicking up gravel and dirt.

"Okay," Stryker said, sounding slightly out of breath. "Mission accomplished. What can I do for you, boss?"

"I need a favor."

"Name it."

"I want you to go to Augusta and pick someone up for me."

"Who?"

"Austin Buchanan."

Chapter Eight

Day Two—5:30 p.m.

Sabrina rinsed her hair beneath the jet sprays of the shower, relishing the feel of the hot water sluicing down her back. She couldn't believe she'd slept so long—it was almost the dinner hour. But the sleep had done wonders for her aches and pains. The bruises on her chest, just beneath her breasts, were an ugly dark purple now. Thankfully, they looked far worse than they felt. And her arm barely bothered her at all. *That* was probably due to the pain pills she was taking.

Thinking about her injuries had her remembering last night and everything that had happened. Her enjoyment of the shower faded and she turned it off. It was time to make some decisions about her future. She just wished there was even one person she could trust so she could discuss the pros and cons of her current predicament.

Six months ago, she'd had her brother, Thomas, to talk to. And Grampy Hightower, of course. She fought back the grief that always threatened to overwhelm her when thinking about either of them. Not even her parents' deaths two months earlier had the power to destroy her like the loss of Thomas and Grampy did. But then again, she'd never really known her parents. John and Jacinda Hightower were just the fun-loving, smiling strangers who visited her on Christmas. And, sometimes, on her birthday.

She towel-dried her hair and plopped down on her makeup bench, quickly putting on some mascara and eyeliner, but nothing else. She wasn't much for primping, but accentuating her best feature made her feel more confident, even if she didn't have anyone to primp for but herself. Confidence was definitely what she needed right now.

Her hair, as thin as it was, would quickly dry on its own and hang straight as usual. When she was younger, she'd hated her hair and had spent untold hours trying to curl it or follow the current fashions. But no matter what she did, within a few hours her hair would slide out of whatever style she'd arranged. So she'd given up the fight and had adopted straight, heavy bangs and allowed her hair to fall the way it wanted. As soon as she'd accepted her hair's foibles, she'd learned to appreciate how easy it was to take care of.

Sitting there thinking about hair and makeup wasn't going to make her problems go away. She had to face them head-on. And what, exactly, did that mean? Stay and hope the people who'd hired Mason and Ace didn't send another hit man after her? That held no appeal. She couldn't afford the three bodyguards she'd already hired. She certainly couldn't pay them long-term.

Leave, then? That seemed to make the most sense. She could rent someplace outside the city, use a fake name. Would someone rent to her without ID? She didn't know. How did a person assume a fake identity? She had no clue.

Wherever she went, she'd have to call in monthly to an assistant DA back in Colorado per her plea bargain agreement. She'd also have to check in with her lawyer and private investigators. And pay them. She wasn't sure how to work all of that out, but the thought of leaving felt right. The tension in her shoulders eased just knowing that she wasn't going to sit here waiting, hoping that some hit man didn't come looking for her. Well, if she was going to leave, she might as well do it right now.

She put her glasses on, hung up her towel, and hurried into the bedroom to get dressed and start packing.

She saw him a split second before he grabbed her. She drew a breath to scream just as he clamped his hand over her mouth, capturing her hands between them and pressing her against the bedroom wall.

Mason.

She wasn't sure who was more surprised. Her, because he'd managed to break into her home, again, in spite of *three* bodyguards. Or him, because she was naked.

One thing was for sure, he wasn't shy about enjoying the view. His dark gaze roamed leisurely over the upper swells of her breasts crushed against his chest, before he looked her in the eyes. The sudden pressure against her belly told her he wasn't unaffected by her nakedness.

Her face flamed and she tried to tell him to let her go, but her words came out muffled against his hand. His erection continued to harden against her belly, and since that's where her hands were trapped between them, she was literally getting a handful of him.

A flash of heat swept through her, making her lower belly clench and her toes curl against the floor. To her shame, her body was just as turned on as his, and the shiver that swept through her was just as telling as his erection.

His mouth curved in a knowing smile.

Damn him.

He bent down toward her. Was he going to kiss her? She hoped so. Because this time a Kevlar vest wouldn't save him from her bite.

But instead of kissing her, he pressed his lips close to her ear, his warm breath tickling the fine hairs on her neck.

"We need to talk," he whispered, his lips brushing against her skin, raising goose bumps. "I'm going to move my hand. If you scream and alert the guards downstairs, I may be forced to kill them in self-defense. Neither of us wants that. I just want to talk to you. That's all. Do you understand?"

He waited, his body pressed against hers so tightly that she could feel his heartbeat against her breasts. She didn't doubt what he'd said. If she screamed, he really would kill the men tasked with protecting her. She slowly nodded, letting him know she understood and that she wouldn't make a sound.

"Only whispers," he said. "We're going to have a calm, quiet conversation."

She nodded again.

He moved back, just enough to pull his hand away from her mouth.

She licked her dry lips.

His erection pulsed against her hands.

Part of her was so mortified that she wanted to crawl under the bed and hide. The other part, a part she didn't even recognize, wanted to stroke that impressive erection through his jeans just to see how he'd react.

"Please," she whispered, refusing to meet his gaze, afraid he'd see the confused jumble of fear and desire roiling inside her. "Let me get dressed."

Surprisingly, he immediately stepped back.

The heat in his gaze reminded her that she was still standing there, completely naked. She ran into the bathroom for a towel.

AFTER SABRINA, ALL covered up in a towel this time, retrieved some clothes from her dresser and disappeared back into the bathroom, Mason plopped down on the chair by the window. He let out a deep breath and adjusted himself to ease the pressure of his erection against the front of his jeans. With those cute glasses on her perky little nose, Sabrina had reminded him of a librarian. Who knew that librarians were his weakness? The wave of lust that had slammed through him had nearly driven him mad.

Damned if he hadn't wanted to drop to his knees right there and dip his tongue inside her, tasting and worshipping her, stroking her softness with his fingers while he suckled her until she sobbed his name and climaxed against his mouth. Then he'd wrap her toned legs around his waist and pump into her over and over, hard and deep until she screamed his name again and came undone around him. She'd collapse in his arms and he'd carry her to the bed. And this time, he'd take it slow and easy and enjoy every luscious curve.

He shuddered and scrubbed his face. Sabrina Hightower was dangerous, in more ways than one. He shouldn't have come back. Shouldn't have decided to check on her security one last time before heading off to the rendezvous. But he'd had to assure himself she was safe before he could focus on his new mission—finding out who was behind the fake EXIT orders.

But now that he'd seen how easy it *still* was to break into her house, he was so disgusted that he hadn't decided what to do. Those pathetic bodyguards she'd hired were too interested in watching the big-screen TV in the back of the house to even notice him sneaking inside and slipping up the stairs. A neighborhood thug would have no trouble breaking into this place, let alone an enforcer like Ace. She wasn't even remotely safe.

"How did you get in here?"

He looked up to see the object of his lust and consternation standing outside the bathroom again, her back to the same wall he'd pressed her against earlier. Unfortunately, instead of being naked, she had jeans and a shirt on. And her small, soft, perfect breasts were almost flattened to nothing in the utilitarian bra she wore. If she were his, the first thing he'd do was throw away that bra and take her to a decadent lingerie store to buy the type of underthings that would accentuate and reveal her for the beauty that she was.

"Mason? How did you get inside with the alarm set, and avoid the bodyguards?" Her brows drew down. The flash of anger in her eyes had him fighting a smile as usual around her. She had more spunk than women twice her size and didn't seem the least bit intimidated that *he* was *more* than twice her size and carried a gun.

Damn, he'd love to get her into bed.

He raised his hand and pointed to the watchlike unit on his wrist. "I programmed this last week to knock out your alarm through a wireless override. Basically, it fakes out the alarm so it doesn't realize it's been overridden. Then it scrambles the history so the alarm company thinks the alarm was never set."

Reluctant interest lit her eyes. "I didn't hear any breaking glass this time."

"I picked the lock. I was in too much of a hurry last time to bother."

"And the security guards?"

He shrugged. "Amateurs."

She looked past him toward the bedroom door.

"Sabrina?"

"Yes?"

"You've got no reason to fear me."

Her eyes widened. "I'm not afraid of *you*. I'm afraid of this whole situation. I thought I'd be safe with three bodyguards, at least for a little while. But if you could get in here that easily, I have to assume whoever is after me could do the same thing."

She closed the distance between them. "Due to my felon status, I don't own a gun. And in spite of how inept my guards appear to be, they refused the bribe I offered if they'd give me one of their guns. So, if you don't mind, I'd appreciate it if you'd share.

I saw the Sig Sauer on your ankle earlier. I prefer the Sig, since it's smaller. But then again, the recoil is less on the heavier Glock, so I'll take either. I hope you have some spare ammo too because, obviously, I'm fresh out." She held her hand out as if she fully expected him to give her one of his pistols.

He imagined he looked as stunned as he felt. Here he was, worried about her being helpless, and she was demanding a gun and citing calibers and manufacturer names like an expert.

"You're serious," he said, still a bit rattled.

She put her hands on her hips. "I have to defend myself. Look, if you're worried that I don't know how to handle a gun, don't be. Grampy Hightower took me and my brother target practicing in the Rockies all the time. I can shoot the eye out of a rattlesnake at twenty paces."

He shook his head. "That felony will get you thrown into prison if you're caught with a gun. Regardless of your reasons."

She gave him a droll look. "Seriously? The hit man is lecturing me about the law?"

He shoved out of the chair and towered over her. "I prefer 'enforcer' to hit man. And I do a lot more than kill people for a living. Or did. As for giving you a weapon, not happening. I came here to check on your security. It sucks, by the way."

"Obviously. Thus the need for a gun."

"*Thus* the need to hire better bodyguards and go somewhere else. Have the security company rent a house for you, under their company name. Pay for everything in cash."

She opened her mouth, probably to continue arguing, but he cut her off by holding up the picture from her desk, the one of her and two other people wearing dark green T-shirts that he'd noticed while she was in the shower.

He was pretty sure he knew who the two other people were in that picture, but he wanted to be certain. And then he was going to make sure she knew exactly how much danger she was in, and why she needed to fire her current guards and get out of Dodge. "Tell me about this picture."

Her blue eyes widened and she pressed her hand to her throat in a moment of unguarded emotion. But what that emotion was he wasn't sure—fear? Regret? Anger? She blinked and lowered her hand. "That picture is none of your business. Put it down."

"They're your parents, aren't they?"

Her jaw worked for a moment. "Yes. They died a few months ago. Why are you asking me about them?"

"They were on an EXIT tour when they died."

"Is that a question?"

"Were you with them? Was that picture taken on the same tour where they died?"

"They only went on one tour. Yes, I was . . ." She closed her eyes briefly. "I was with them. They died right in front of me, if you must know. Will you please tell me why you're so fixated on that picture?"

He set it down and grabbed her shoulders. "You moved to Asheville from Colorado because EXIT was opening an office here, didn't you? Since you're suing them for the wrongful death of your parents . . ." Her startled look made him pause.

"Yes," he continued. "I know about the lawsuit. It's one of many things I've learned about you in the past twenty-four hours. Did you think moving here would give you an advantage somehow, that it would help you pressure Cyprian and EXIT Inc. to admit their wrongdoings?"

She frowned and pushed his arms down. "Enough with the inquisition. If you're not going to give me a gun, then get out of here. I'll even open the door for you." She stalked past him toward the bedroom door.

He clapped his hand over her mouth and grabbed her from behind, pulling her against his chest. "Quit being so stubborn and listen for a minute."

Her teeth clamped down on his index finger.

He swore and jerked his hand back.

Sabrina whirled around to face him.

Mason blinked in astonishment to see his own Glock in her hand, the muzzle pressing against his stomach. "You little devil. You do know the gun is loaded, right?"

"I'm counting on it. Got an extra magazine on you? I'd be obliged if you tossed it onto the bed as you leave."

He sucked the blood welling up on his finger before waving toward his right front pocket. "Be my guest. I've got a full magazine."

She narrowed her eyes. "I've felt your . . . magazine, and while it's impressive, it's not going to do me much good in the Glock. Where do you *really* keep your spare ammo?"

He grinned. "I don't have anything *spare*, darlin'. I keep my gun cocked and loaded at all times. And I use it *all*."

She rolled her eyes. "I bet women fall all over you with those kinds of lines."

He lifted his hand toward her, ignoring the fact that she'd shoved the gun harder against his belly, and gently brushed the bangs out of her eyes. "There's only one woman that I want falling all over me right now." He leaned down, watching her incredible blue eyes grow wide with uncertainty. He parted his lips, angled his head, leaned lower, lower.

Sabrina's breath caught in her throat. She tilted her head up, ever so slightly, her lips parting.

Score.

Mason snatched the Glock out of her hands and jerked her toward the bed.

By the time she recovered from her shock he'd holstered the gun and was lying on top of her on the bed with her hands trapped against his chest. He covered her mouth with his right hand, careful to keep it cupped so she couldn't bite him again.

"As much as I'd love to kiss that angry expression right off of you," he said, "I don't have the time. No more games. Just the facts. Blink once for yes, twice for no. Will you do that?"

She glared at him, then blinked. Once.

"I know you're suing EXIT because you think they used faulty equipment that made your parents fall to their deaths on a zip line. Question: were you supposed to be *with* your parents on that zip line?"

One blink.

He swore. "I'm going to lower my hand. But, if you so much as move a muscle other than your lips I'll shove a sock in your mouth and tie you up. Promise me you'll behave."

She frowned but blinked. Once.

He lowered his hand. "Quickly, tell me why you weren't on the zip line when the accident happened."

"I was sick. I couldn't keep anything down that morning. I opted to stand on the platform and take pictures instead."

He rolled off her and pulled a piece of paper out of his pocket. He unfolded it and held it up.

She gasped. "Where did you get that?"

"I searched your room while you were in the shower."

He pitched the sketch of himself onto the comforter. "I saw similar sketches on the news. They were remarkably accurate. I assumed there was another witness somewhere since there wasn't a picture of me too. I wracked my brain trying to think of who might have seen Ace and the others, but not me. And then I saw that sketch just a few minutes ago. You're the one who drew the sketches."

"Yes."

"Why didn't you give the police the drawing of me?"

"I . . . wasn't sure I got it right."

He raised a brow. It was a perfect likeness of him, right down to the stubble. "How about now?" He turned his head left and right.

"Um, yes. Looks like I remembered you fairly well. Guess I should call the police and have them come pick up the last drawing. Can you hand me my phone?" She pointed to the side table.

He chose to ignore her sarcasm. "You need to destroy your phone. It can be traced. You should pick up a no-contract phone and pay cash, use a fake name." He pointed to the sketch. "Back to this. You're an artist. But no artist I've ever heard of could draw someone that detailed and accurately from memory, not unless they'd known the people for years. So, what, you have a photographic memory?"

"Yes." She sounded like she was used to having to defend her abilities.

"How does it work? Can you remember just the past few days, or weeks? Or can you remember farther back?"

"I have memories, just like anyone else, except that my memories are in pictures. As long as I can remember the event, I can see all of the details, just like the first time I saw them."

"That has to be it."

She frowned. "What has to be it? I don't understand. Why are you grilling me with questions?"

He glanced at the watch on his wrist. He was out of time. No, *screw that.* He would make time. He helped her sit up, but he trapped her hands in his so she couldn't do anything crazy like grab his gun again.

"Listen to me," he urged. "Your parents are the only people who have ever died on an EXIT tour—"

"How . . . how would you know that?" she interrupted, frowning up at him.

"Just listen. They died in a freak accident. But you were supposed to be with them. You'd be dead too, except that you were sick. Then, just a few months later, assassins are hired to go after you. Do you think that's just a coincidence?"

She clasped his hands so tightly they started to go numb. "You think . . . you think my parents were killed on purpose, but I was the real target?"

He thought there was a whole lot more to it than

that, but he didn't want to scare her so badly that she couldn't function. Or cause her additional grief if he was wrong. "I do."

"But how can you be so sure that my parents' accident . . . wasn't an accident?"

"Because no one dies on those tours. And the company that hired me to terminate you is the one that ran that tour. EXIT Incorporated."

She gasped.

"I don't know why they're after you. But I do know that if it's because of your photographic memory, they're never going to stop. You probably saw something and don't even realize it. You need someone who knows the ins and outs of the company. Someone who knows most of the other enforcers on sight. Someone who can protect you."

"Mason? Are you saying that you want to take me with you? That you'll help me?"

"Do you *want* me to help you?"

"Do I get a gun?"

"*Sabrina.*"

"Okay, okay. Yes. I want your help. I want you to take me with you. *Please.*"

"Then you have to agree to my terms."

She frowned. "What terms?"

He leaned down inches from her face to make sure she could see that he was deadly serious. "If you ever point a loaded gun at me again, I'll kill you. Understood?"

She swallowed, hard. "Understood."

He grabbed the Sig out of his ankle holster and handed it to her. "Pack light. We leave in five minutes."

Chapter Nine

Day Two—6:00 p.m.

After Mason had agreed to take Sabrina with him and she'd packed a small bag, she'd gone downstairs and fired her bodyguards. Once they were gone, she and Mason had headed out the French doors, in an eerily similar escape to the previous night. Except that this time she'd been jogging beside him instead of bouncing on his shoulder. He'd taken her through the same path in the woods, and when they were about twenty feet from the parkway behind her property, he pulled some branches off the top of a dark blue pickup truck hidden in the bushes.

"Yours?" she'd asked.

"Yes. Did you think I stole it?"

"The thought did occur to me. Detective Donovan mentioned he searched DMV records for a Jeep Wrangler registered under either a first or last name of Mason and didn't find any."

"That's because my Jeep is registered under an alias. It's bought and paid for. I didn't steal it."

"Touché. My apologies."

He grinned, and some of the tension in her shoulders eased. Ever since he'd told her his "terms" back in her bedroom, she'd been uncomfortably reminded that he really was a dangerous man. She tended to forget that when he was flirting and smiling at her. She still wasn't sure which side was the real Mason. Maybe they both were. But either way, she had no right to complain. It was that dark and dangerous side that she was counting on to help protect her. Although now that she had her own gun holstered on her ankle, she didn't feel nearly as vulnerable as before.

Half an hour later, Mason pulled up in front of a boxy, two-story, concrete house that Sabrina supposed was considered contemporary. She just considered it ugly. When he took her inside, her opinion was confirmed. From the stained concrete floor, to the fabric on the lone couch in the expansive living room, to the solid-surface countertop in the open kitchen, everything was decorated in varying shades of one depressing color: gray.

"This is . . . yours?" She tried not to let her distaste show.

"It is. Do you like it?" He leaned across the kitchen counter, propping his chin in his palms.

"It's . . . big. Modern. Um. Clean lines."

He glanced around as if seeing it through someone else's eyes for the first time. "Yep. That about describes it."

She clutched her bag on her shoulder. "What do we do now?"

"We wait. This is where the rendezvous is going to take place."

"Rendezvous?"

"We're meeting with the people you saw in the Hummer and a friend of mine, Ramsey. The three of them are the reason you're alive today. They realized you'd been targeted even though you were innocent and they stopped me from . . . carrying out my original mission."

She shivered and ran her hands up and down her arms. "Remind me to thank them."

He nodded. "We're going to talk about EXIT and how to keep what happened to you from happening to other people."

"You're including me in this meeting?"

"Of course. We're a team now. Right?"

"Right."

He winked, making her toes curl in her loafers. If she'd thought his sexy grin was lethal, that slow, lusty wink was a lady killer.

"Feel free to look around," he said. "The bathroom is at the end of the hall."

"Okay. Thanks."

As SOON AS Sabrina was gone, Mason grabbed his cell phone and punched in Ramsey's number. No answer. He called three more times before the line clicked.

"WTF, Mason? I was talking to someone. How many times were you going to call?"

"Until you answered. Where are you? You're late. And there's no sign of Buchanan or Emily." A long moment of silence followed. "Ram?"

"I'm at the airport."

Mason's hand tightened around the phone. "Say that again. Because it sounded like you said you were ditching me."

"I'm not ditching you. Plans changed. I've got to get to Augusta to help the Buchanans."

"The Buchanans? Oh, right. I remember them. They're those people who are supposed to be right here. Right now. With you."

"Sarcasm doesn't become you, Mason."

"Lying doesn't become you."

Ramsey blew out an impatient breath. "I didn't lie, not on purpose at least. I'd planned on being there. But Devlin's brother, Austin, was in a burn center in Augusta. He's been recovering from injuries sustained in a house fire. This morning, he disappeared. But no one reported it until a few hours ago. They thought he was sleeping in his room. When the nurse went in to check on him, he was gone."

"I'm guessing he didn't walk off by himself."

"Not likely. He had mobility issues before the fire. And now, well, he couldn't have left on his own. Devlin and his brothers are frantic. They're all on their way there now."

"All? How many brothers does he have?"

"Three or four I think. Doesn't matter. The point is that this has the earmarks of something Ace might have pulled. He and Devlin have a brutal history between them and this may be Ace's attempt at payback. I've got to help Devlin before it's too late."

"Hold it. If he's got all of those brothers why does he need you? I need you here. While the Buchanans are looking after this Austin guy, you and I can figure out our next steps against EXIT. If there are other marks being targeted, we can't afford to wait. Someone innocent will die."

"I know, I know. But Devlin needs someone else who knows how EXIT operates to help him figure out what they've done with Austin and to watch his back. Not to mention keeping an eye on his wife."

"She's a former cop. I imagine she can handle herself."

"Not against EXIT. Plus, you know the family won't be focused right now, not with their brother's life at stake. I can't abandon them. And before you say it, yeah, I know it seems like that's exactly what I'm doing to you. But this is different. You see that, right?"

Mason swore. "Yeah, I guess I do. Go. We'll have the meeting after you're done there. I'll do what I can to try to get information about EXIT, but without Buchanan's computer contacts, I'm not sure what I can do. One thing, though. Make sure you tell Buchanan and Emily that their pictures are being circulated on the Asheville news as potential witnesses to a crime."

"What? How did that happen?"

"If you were here, I'd tell you."

"Ouch. Guess I deserve that. I'll be back as soon as I can. We'll sit down, compare notes, and make stuff happen."

A final boarding announcement sounded over an intercom in the background.

"I have to go before I miss my plane. Good luck, Mason. I'll call when I can."

"Be careful, Ram. This could all be a trick."

"I know. Believe me, I know."

Mason ended the call and shoved the phone across the countertop.

"Bad news?" a soft voice called out.

He looked up to see Sabrina standing a few feet away. Her hair had been brushed out to a glossy sheen that made his fingers ache to touch it. Another part of him ached to do a whole lot more, but now wasn't the time or place, even if he was sure she'd be receptive to him. Which he wasn't. All that he was sure of was that his reason for coming here—the rendezvous—had just evaporated. And if EXIT was actively seeking the little band of rebels, then Mason preferred to be in a much more defensible position without any other houses close by that could hide an assassin waiting with a gun.

"The meeting was postponed," he said. "Something came up." He grabbed his phone again and shoved it into the holder on his belt. "Grab your bag. We're leaving."

Her eyes widened with alarm. "Is something wrong?" She looked toward the windows as if expecting someone to drive up.

He forced himself to relax, offering her a lazy smile he was far from feeling. "Nothing's wrong. I'm just taking you to my home."

"I thought *this* was your home."

"This ugly place? Not a chance," he teased. "Let's go."

THE SUN HAD set before they'd reached Mason's real home, an hour west of Asheville. Although this house was smaller—a two-bedroom, two-bath cottage that could fit inside her living room—it was cozy, welcoming, and much homier than the concrete monstrosity back in town. Best of all, it was on a farm, surrounded by acres of rolling hills, trees, and cornfields. She'd adored it on sight, or at least what she'd seen in the truck's headlights and the outdoor security lights as Mason had driven her up to the house.

He'd shown her to the master bedroom and told her to make herself comfortable while he whipped them up something to eat. More than a little curious what a man like Mason would "whip up," she quickly changed into a T-shirt and some shorts, her version of comfortable. She took another dose of pain pills and used the restroom. Then she hurried back into the kitchen just as Mason was pouring two glasses of milk.

She burst into laughter. "This is what you whipped up? Peanut butter and jelly sandwiches?"

He pressed his hand to his chest as if offended. "According to my seventh grade home economics teacher, these are *ribbon* sandwiches, thank you very much. They're also nutritious, full of protein."

"And the milk? Calcium, I suppose?"

"Strong bones are important."

"So, basically, you don't know how to cook."

"Basically." He picked up the two plates. "If you'll bring the drinks, I figured we could eat on the back porch and watch the lightning bugs."

"Sounds perfect." She grabbed their glasses and followed him outside.

The wooden porch wrapped around the entire house, its weathered-gray floor contrasting nicely with the whitewashed railings underneath the soft glow of the outdoor lights. Bright spotlights at the corners of the house illuminated the backyard and the edge of the cornfield directly behind the property.

Sabrina set the glasses beside their plates and took a seat at the table across from Mason.

"This is a big table. Six chairs."

"I have a big family."

She paused with her sandwich halfway to her mouth. "Family?"

He leaned toward her conspiratorially. "Did you think people like me don't have families?"

Her face flushed and she set the sandwich down. "Of course not. Well, honestly, I guess I hadn't really thought about it. So . . . they come here often?

"A couple of times a year, if I'm lucky. Darlene lives in Germany with her husband. My parents are there right now, visiting."

"Darlene?"

"One of my sisters. The baby, Suzie, is at UGA. And my brother, Zack, he's a firefighter back in Asheville. Whenever I'm out of town, which is a lot, and he has time off from work, he tends to crash here."

She'd taken a small bite of her sandwich and quickly swallowed. "Why would he come out here if you aren't home?"

His mouth quirked up. "Women. It's hard to socialize at the firehouse. And he rents the apartment above the garage at Mom and Dad's. So it can get a little . . . awkward . . . bringing home dates."

"Ah, I see."

He pointed across the waving stalks of corn that seemed to go on forever behind them. "See that barn out there, just past that clump of trees on the right?"

"Um hm."

"That's where Zack likes to hang out with his dates. There's a lot of hay in that barn."

The amusement in his eyes let her know exactly what his brother was doing in that hay. She cleared her throat. "If you have hay, you must have horses."

"Nope. I'm not here enough to take care of any animals. But it is a working farm. I've got a deal with the guy who owns the land adjacent to mine. He stores his hay in my barn and plants and harvests the corn, or some years, soybeans."

"Sounds like a good gig. He does all the work and you get to split the earnings."

He shook his head. "I don't take any money from him. Don't need it." He slid a glance at her. "And before you ask, yes, working for EXIT is quite lucrative."

She decided not to touch that comment, for now. "Then what do you get out of the deal you made with your neighbor?"

He waved his hand. "That gorgeous view."

The contentment in his eyes as he stared over his land was even more breathtaking than the fiery colors in the sky as the sun had set on the drive here.

Thomas would have liked Mason.

Sabrina blinked back the moisture in her eyes. Her brother had been a nature lover too. And she could easily imagine him enjoying that barn when he was younger, just like Zack.

After they finished eating, they went inside and washed the dishes. Once everything was put away, both of them stood in the middle of the kitchen, unable to ignore the elephant in the room any longer.

It was time to talk about EXIT, and figure out what they were going to do.

The acknowledgment was there in his eyes as he held out his hand. "Come on, Rina. You look like you'll explode if you don't ask me all those questions building up inside you. Let's get it over with."

She was still reeling from the cute way he'd shortened her name to Rina when he tugged her down onto the couch beside him in the family room.

"Go ahead," he encouraged her. "I'll answer what I can."

She folded her hands together. "All right. What exactly *is* EXIT?"

"At this moment, I'm not really sure." He scrubbed the stubble on his jaw. "Someone high up in the company is abusing their power, using enforcers for their own purposes."

"Enforcers. You mentioned that word at my house. But I'm not sure I understand what it means. Isn't it the same as a hit man? Or an assassin?"

He stared at her unblinking, unashamed. "When necessary, yes. But that's not all we do, not all *I* do. What I'm about to tell you is highly classified, and dangerous. I've never told anyone else outside of EXIT about my work, not even my family. I'm telling you this now because, after the injustices that have been done to you, you deserve to know the truth. But more importantly, you need to understand exactly what you're up against."

The deadly quiet quality of his voice had her almost regretting asking him about his work. But he was right. She did need to know what type of enemy was after her.

"EXIT is a privately held company, sanctioned by the government as a weapon of last resort. Its public face is the tour side, of course. But its true purpose is to train and deploy highly specialized operatives who can be called upon to protect our country and its people when the alphabet agencies have exhausted all traditional means of resolving an issue. We mostly operate domestically, but all of us rotate overseas every few years because of the conflicts our country is embroiled in around the world right now. In those cases we mostly gather intel and assist our military's special forces." He shrugged. "We do whatever has to be done."

"You mentioned alphabet agencies. You mean like the FBI, or CIA?"

"And many others. Those agencies have restrictions that we don't have. They can only go so far."

"Restrictions?"

"Laws."

The idea that an entire company could be sanctioned by the government without the restriction of laws was incredible, and terrifying.

"So, basically, as an enforcer you do the government's dirty work, things they would never admit to publicly, all in the name of protecting the country?"

The corner of his mouth lifted in a semblance of a smile. "I've never heard it put quite that way but I suppose that's an accurate description. More specifically, the major difference between EXIT and the other agencies is that they have to wait for a crime to be committed. We're more pro-active. We make selective, preemptive strikes to prevent loss of life."

Her stomach sank. How could she crave this man's touch, want his arms around her—even now—his lips on hers, when he spoke about preemptively killing people, all with a smile on his face?

"You sound like you still support EXIT's mission, that you think they're doing the right thing."

"That's because I do. If there's one bad apple

in the company creating fake orders, and we can eliminate him and preserve the company's main mission, that's the best-case scenario out of all of this. Unfortunately, I doubt the situation is that simple. Especially since we don't know yet whether Cyprian Cardenas, the CEO, is involved in the fake EXIT orders."

"Then, you're still okay with their business-as-usual way of doing things. You don't see that this is wrong? Mason, you talk about killing someone just because you think they *might* hurt someone else. But how can you know that? You can't know the future. No one can. You said it was wrong that EXIT went after me, because I'm innocent. But the people you kill are innocent too. You're assuming they'll go through with their plans. What if they change their minds? What if they realize what they were going to do is wrong? You can't really know what they'll do."

His earlier amusement disappeared. "Your situation is totally different. You've never funded a terrorist organization. That was the crime EXIT accused you of. The people I kill have usually spent their entire lives doing bad things, which makes future behavior easier to predict. I don't take what I do lightly. I only eliminate people I know are a threat to others. But enforcers don't sit around and wait for our marks to kill others first. We save lives by taking lives."

"But how can you be sure?"

He gave her an aggravated look. "Waiting for incontrovertible proof might sound great on paper, but in reality, it means people die who shouldn't have to."

Sabrina marveled at the conviction in his voice. Mason was obviously a man with his own moral code who truly believed that by breaking the law, by preemptively killing people that he believed were "bad," he was doing the right thing. But Sabrina just couldn't understand that mode of thinking.

The potential abuse of power within a company like EXIT was mind-boggling, and obviously the worst *had* happened—someone *was* abusing that power, using the company as their own personal weapon. And they needed to be stopped. It was just too dangerous for one company, or one person, to have the kind of power to decide who was good and who was bad, who lived and who died.

She held her hands out in a placating gesture. "I'm trying to understand. I really am. But I just don't see how your way is the right way. There has to be an alternative."

He stared at her a long minute. "Okay. Hypothetical. You're a cop, or an FBI agent. You have a nugget of information, a whisper of intel about an extremist cell planning on blowing up a school. But you have no proof, nothing that would hold up in court anyway. Tell me, Sabrina. If you're convinced a school might be blown up, but you don't know which one, and all you have is the name and address of a guy who *might* know, what would you do?"

She clasped her hands together. "I . . . I don't know. I guess I would . . . try to find out more information, get a search warrant."

He looked disappointed with her answer. "What if you're the parent of one of those kids? Knowing your child could die waiting on a warrant that might never come. *Now* what would you do?"

She swallowed against the tightness in her throat. "That's not a fair question. It would never happen."

He arched a brow. "Those types of scenarios happen more than you think. You sit there making moral judgments, but you refuse to face reality."

"Okay, fine. I'm the parent. I would . . . I would hope that I would have the strength of character to stand up for what's right. And, Mason, what's *right* is to work within the law. It's the only way to guarantee that people's civil rights aren't trampled. I know our justice system has problems. I've been a victim of that broken system myself. But that doesn't mean we should throw the whole thing out. We have to fix it. Going vigilante isn't the answer."

He stared across the room through the large picture window, watching the stalks of corn bending in the breeze. "'The only thing necessary for the triumph of evil is for good men to do nothing.'"

"I'm sorry, what?"

He sighed and looked back at her. "It's a quote, by Edmund Burke. What it means to me is that if I have the power to act to save someone, and I do nothing, then that's the most horrible sin of all." He searched her eyes, as if hoping to see something, but the disappointment in his expression told her he hadn't found what he was looking for.

He stood and shoved his hands in his pockets. "Based on your reasoning in my hypothetical situation, four hundred kids would be dead on your watch, all because you had to wait for the crime to be committed. Because it wasn't hypothetical. It happened, a month ago. I chose to act. I didn't wait. I busted into a guy's house and found bomb-making materials, but no bomb. No clue where the bomb that he'd made was planted. And when he laughed in my face and asked for a lawyer, I didn't call the police or follow due process. I pressed his cheek against a hot stove until he screamed in agony, until he screamed the location of the bomb, a middle school in downtown Asheville. Once I got that information, and the bomb squad confirmed it, I put a bullet in his brain."

Sabrina choked and pressed her hand against her mouth in horror.

Mason gave her a sad smile. "You think I'm a monster. Maybe I am. But because I did what needed to be done, because I acted like an animal and showed no mercy, I saved *four hundred innocent little kids*. And it only cost the life of one, deranged, sick terrorist. I haven't lost one bit of sleep over my decision. I'd do it again in a second. And for that, Sabrina, I make no apologies."

He strode out the back onto the porch, letting the door slam closed behind him.

Chapter Ten

Day Three—7:00 a.m.

Cyprian nodded with satisfaction as he approached the archway to his hidden office. Stryker, efficient as always, had corralled a resentful-looking Ace between him and Bishop in the row of chairs in front of the desk. Whether Ace wanted to or not, he was about to explain everything that had happened between him, Mason, and Hightower.

Cyprian was just about to step into his hidden office when the intercom on his official EXIT phone buzzed behind him.

"Mr. Cardenas?" his administrative assistant's voice called out through the speaker.

He frowned and returned to the desk. "Yes, Miss Evans?"

"There's a policeman here to see you, Detective Donovan."

Cyprian let out an impatient breath. After finding out yesterday that Hightower had gone to the police, he'd been expecting them to eventually question him to confirm her background, specifically the death of her parents on an EXIT tour and the subsequent lawsuit. But the timing could definitely have been better.

He signaled Stryker through the archway and closed the panel, hiding the other office from view. Then he settled himself at his desk, turned on his computer monitor, and pressed a remote to unlock the main door. "Bring him in, please."

The door flew open and a slightly heavy, balding, man well past his prime stepped inside. Before Cyprian could do more than look up from the screen to take in the rumpled, off-the-rack suit, Miss Evans hurried in, blubbering apologies.

"Mr. Cardenas, please forgive me." She was slightly out of breath and frowned her displeasure at the stranger who was now standing a few feet in front of the desk. "I told the detective to wait for me to bring him in. But he rushed by before I could even get up from my chair."

"Detective Harry Donovan, Asheville PD." He held his hand out toward Cyprian. "I hope I'm not interrupting. It was a long drive out here and I still have to face rush hour to get back in town on time for a morning meeting. I got a mite impatient."

Cyprian smiled warmly and shook the other man's hand. "Perhaps next time you could let me know that you're coming and I could arrange a better reception, croissants, muffins, bagels. Miss Evans would be happy to bring you some coffee if you wish."

"No need to go to any trouble on my account. This won't take long. I just have a few questions." He sat down in one of the chairs positioned in front of Cyprian's desk without waiting for an invitation. "I'm here about Sabrina Hightower."

The detective's shrewd, intelligent gaze zeroed in on Cyprian. This wasn't just about background information, not from the way Donovan was watching him. Was the detective digging to see if Cyprian might have orchestrated Hightower's abduction to avoid a costly court battle? Or had he stumbled onto something more damning?

Either way, if he was hoping for a reaction, Cyprian was happy to disappoint him. After all, he'd been running this company and keeping its secrets for years. He wasn't an amateur.

"I'm always happy to speak to Asheville's finest. Of course, I'm not certain what I can say in regards to Miss Hightower. Our lawyers won't want me to comment about anything related to the civil suit she's filed." He nodded to his assistant. "Miss Evans. Please close the door, won't you?"

Her face alight with undisguised curiosity, she seemed to leave with reluctance, slowly closing the door behind her.

"This isn't about the civil suit. It's about Miss Hightower's alleged kidnapping."

Cyprian hesitated. "Kidnapping? I do hope she's okay. But you said alleged. I'm afraid I don't follow."

"She came to the police station yesterday with some convoluted tale about a man breaking into her home. She described coconspirators and insisted that the man who'd taken her said she'd been marked for assassination, and that he was the one who was supposed to kill her. But the funny thing is, I guess the guy decided she didn't deserve to die, so he let her go. At the police station."

The police station? Not the hospital? He was beginning to wonder if Hightower had been shot at all. Maybe Ace had made up the story about seeing her shot to cover that he'd failed to even find Mason. And maybe the police had taken Hightower to the hospital just to have her checked out. That would certainly explain why she was released a few hours later.

"Well, that's quite a story," he said to Donovan.

"Yep. Can't say that I really believed her. But I can't explain away one particular piece of evidence. Someone shot her."

Cyprian blinked, genuinely confused. He'd just decided that she hadn't been shot, and now he was back to wondering what had really happened. "Pardon? She was shot? Then, she's . . . in the hospital? Recovering, I hope?"

"Last I heard she was home, safe and sound."

Cyprian curled his fingers into his palms. The detective was playing games. He wouldn't do that unless he suspected EXIT was involved. All of this went back to Bishop's failed attempt to kill Sabrina during their tour, which had resulted in her parents dying instead. Cyprian's guilt over involving Bishop in the very beginning was rapidly fading. He might have made one mistake, but Bishop's were compounding themselves and making everything far worse.

"That's quite an amazing recovery from being shot," he said, trying not to let his impatience show. He needed answers. And most of those answers were waiting for him just a few feet away in his hidden office. "A flesh wound, I'm guessing? She was very . . . lucky."

Donovan waved his hand. "No, no. Sorry. Didn't mean to give you the wrong impression. I took her to the hospital for X-rays. Turns out she had bruised ribs, nothing worse than that. You see, she was wearing Kevlar."

"Kevlar."

"Yup. Now ain't that just the darnedest thing? The guy that kidnapped her put a bullet-resistant vest on her. Saved her life. Kind of odd, don't you think?"

"Um. Yes. Very odd, indeed." He rested his forearms on his desk. "Detective, while I certainly wish Miss Hightower no ill will, I'm really not following why you feel compelled to speak to me about whatever happened, or didn't happen, to her."

Donovan tapped his meaty hand on the arm of the chair. "It's that due diligence thing, I suppose. You see, what bothered me when speaking to Miss Hightower was how forthright she sounded. I've been a cop for a long time and I can usually spot a liar a mile away." His gaze narrowed on Cyprian before he continued. "I spoke to her for several hours. Her story never wavered."

He leaned forward in his chair, resting his arms on his knees. "You seem like an important, busy man. So, I'll get to the point. I'm not so sure that Miss Hightower's abduction story was a lie." He reached into his suit jacket, pulled out three pieces of paper, and unfolded them on the top of Cyprian's desk. "These are copies of sketches that she drew of the coconspirators in her alleged abduction. Do any of them look familiar?"

The pencil drawings of Devlin Buchanan, his girlfriend—former Detective Emily O'Malley—and

Ace all stared up at him from his desk. They were the same drawings that had appeared on the news clip yesterday.

And obviously Sabrina Hightower had lost none of her artistic abilities since the last time he'd seen one of her sketches. Or that incredible memory that allowed her to recall every detail. But why wasn't there a sketch of Mason?

He studied the drawings closely, as if trying to jog his memory. In reality, he was trying to consider what facts the police might have before he stated whether he knew the people in the sketches or not.

Ace was strictly an enforcer for EXIT and had never worked on the tour side. On the rare occasions when they were together, it was always somewhere private, such as in the tunnels or in his hidden office. So there was no danger that anyone outside of the enforcer network would even know of their association.

As for Emily, Cyprian had never met her in person, so he felt safe in denying knowledge about her. But Devlin had worked as a tour guide off and on as part of his cover as an enforcer. Denying that he knew Devlin would make the detective suspicious if Donovan ever found out that Devlin had been employed as a guide. As much as it galled him to admit any tie between any of the people in the sketches and EXIT, his hand was forced. He'd just have to play dumb and hope for the best and deal with the fallout after the cop left.

He tapped the middle picture. "Those other two don't ring any bells, but this one looks an awful lot like one of our tour guides. Or at least, he was a guide off and on through the years. I don't think he still works for us anymore but I can certainly check our records." He tapped the picture again. "I'm trying to remember his name, if indeed this is even him."

"Does Devlin Buchanan ring any bells for you?"

He was careful to hide his surprise. Had Devlin gone to the police instead of trying to find his missing brother? Sending Stryker after Austin had seemed like a brilliant move. But it might have been too late.

"Yes, yes I think that's his name. If he's turned to a life of crime, that's certainly a shame. I assure you EXIT would never condone such behavior. If he's still one of our guides I'll begin termination procedures immediately. Assuming, of course, that he's guilty."

"Of course." Donovan gathered the papers and slid them back into his jacket pocket. "I sent those sketches to every major police department in the south in case our kidnappers had done this sort of thing before. I was grasping at straws, I suppose. But a detective in Savannah—Tuck Jones—recognized Buchanan and his wife."

"His wife?" Cyprian cleared his throat, chagrined that, in his surprise, he'd blurted that out. "I, ah, never knew he was married."

"Apparently it's fairly recent. Tuck used to work with Emily O'Malley, a fellow detective. He said that she married Devlin and the two of them have been off on their honeymoon for the past few months. He and Emily aren't exactly close anymore but he checks in with her family every now and then and they're the ones who told him about the marriage. When I asked Tuck why he and his former partner weren't still friends, he told me something very interesting. He said that Devlin Buchanan had been under suspicion at one time of possibly being some kind of hired assassin. Long story short, Tuck isn't sure what to think of Mr. Buchanan and he's not comfortable with Emily's choice of a husband."

Cyprian held himself very still at the mention of the word "assassin," careful not to even glance to the side. Police were experts at reading body language, and he'd learned long ago the types of "tells" they looked for to see if someone was lying or covering something up.

Donovan clasped his hands together over his knees. "What are the odds that a man who used to work for EXIT would be labeled as a suspected assassin, then a few months later, he'd be tagged as potentially being involved in a case where we have *another* suspected assassin? And tacked onto those coincidences, the victim in this case is one associated with EXIT. She took a tour with your company a couple of months ago and her parents were killed. And now she's suing your company. I don't know about you, Mr. Cardenas, but that's an awful lot of coincidence to swallow all at once."

The two of them studied each other from across the desk. And Cyprian knew he was in trouble.

"I'm not sure what to say." He shrugged. "I'm not a detective so I wouldn't really know if coincidences like that are unusual. What exactly can I help you with, Detective? EXIT Inc. is an open book for our law-enforcement friends. Are there records I can retrieve for you? Perhaps Mr. Buchanan's personnel file? I'm not going to stall and demand a warrant. If there's something you need and it's within my power, I'll provide it."

"How about Devlin Buchanan? Can you provide him?"

"If I knew where he was, I certainly would. As I said earlier, I'm not even sure if he still works for us. But I'll get my assistant to work with Human Resources and pull his file. I can have it delivered to your office this morning."

Some of the suspicion seemed to fade from Donovan's face as he stood, probably because he was surprised at Cyprian's full cooperation—which of course had been his intent.

They shook hands as Cyprian came around the desk to lead him to the reception area.

"Thank you for your time, Mr. Cardenas. I'll be looking for that file."

As soon as the detective left the reception area and stepped into the hallway, Cyprian closed and locked his door. He strode to his desk, keyed the code to slide the panel open, and hurried through the archway into his other office.

Bishop, Ace, and Stryker were still sitting in front of the desk. They rose as he entered. The handcuffs around Ace's wrists jangled against the chain that was being held by Stryker and there was a small white bandage on Ace's neck.

Ace's opinion of his current situation was no mystery. His eyes were narrowed and he looked like he wanted to kill someone. Well, join the club. Right now Cyprian wanted to kill quite a few people. But he was far more civilized than that. Killing was a last resort. But violence had its place, when necessary. And right now, it was definitely necessary.

Bishop opened his mouth to say something but Cyprian held up his hand to stop him. "Detective

Donovan is suspicious about EXIT's involvement in Miss Hightower's abduction. He's also under the impression that she's home right now. Since I'd sent you to find her and Mason, can I assume you've at least already verified that she's *not* home?"

"I've, ah, set up surveillance on the front of the house in case she goes somewhere and to watch for any activity through the windows. But I didn't break in to see if she was already home. I thought the police might be watching the house, so I didn't want to risk being seen."

Thank goodness for small favors. He was probably right about the police watching the place. "All right. I want you to check on the surveillance you set up. Make sure no one from EXIT approaches her house and that the surveillance is undetectable. Do you understand?"

"Yes, sir. Watch, don't approach. Got it."

"Then why are you still here?"

He gulped and hurried to the other side of the room, exiting through the archway that led into the section of tunnels that had nothing to do with the mainframe, and ended past the parking lot via a maintenance building. One problem solved—getting Bishop out of the way—for now.

"Pardon me, gentlemen," Cyprian addressed the two remaining enforcers. "I have to make one very important call before we can take care of our business." He punched the speed dial he'd used earlier in the day and picked up the receiver. "Eddie, yes, Cyprian again. Any luck with that property list that I requested?"

"I'm close to providing it, sir. Mr. Hunt seems more concerned about his privacy than most. The web of fake corporations is impressive. But I'll break it all down. No one can own property without a paper trail, no matter how hard they try. I'll figure it out."

"I need that information ASAP."

Cyprian punched the button to end the call. "Once we have that list, the three of us will work together to pare it down to the most likely places where Mason might be hiding. I'm betting that the good detective is wrong and that Miss Hightower is *not* home. If Mason believes she needs protection, he'll have her with him, wherever he is."

He noted that one side of Ace's face was swollen. But Cyprian didn't have to ask who'd done that damage, since Ace kept glaring at Stryker like he wanted to kill him. Then again, Ace could just be furious that Stryker was pointing a gun at him.

"Stryker," Cyprian said. "Has the entire matter that I assigned you been taken care of per my instructions? Once you took care of the . . . complication . . . that you mentioned over the phone?"

Ace's clenched hands told Cyprian what he thought of being called a "complication."

"It has," Stryker said.

"Wonderful. Excellent job. Ace, on the other hand, you've been a very, very, bad boy. Stryker tells me that you were already at the burn center when he arrived. If you'd managed to extract Austin Buchanan before Stryker got there, you could have ruined everything. You've made me an unhappy man."

Ace didn't look like he cared one bit if he'd upset his boss. He looked as if he wanted to strangle him, and he probably did.

Cyprian sighed and shook his head. He'd allowed Ace far too long to mourn Kelly's loss. It was time to rein him in. "You were assigned to back up Mason Hunt the other evening." He didn't add that the EXIT order had been faked or that he wasn't the one to request Ace to back up Mason on the mission. He had no intention of anyone ever finding out that Bishop had been that bold and had managed such a security breach without Cyprian even realizing it. If the Council found out how badly he'd lost control of his people, they might be tempted to replace him. And that he could not allow.

"You were supposed to make sure that Mason's mission was concluded per the EXIT order. Bishop informs me that you said the mark had, indeed, been eliminated."

He grabbed the remote from his desk and pressed one of the buttons. The screens lit up.

Ace paled when he saw the sketches.

"Tell me, Ace," Cyprian continued. "If your mission was successful, then how did Miss Hightower manage to go to the police station and provide sketches of Devlin and Emily Buchanan, and you?"

Ace's surprise at hearing the Buchanans were married was obvious when his eyes widened, but he didn't say anything. His lips compressed in a tight line of mutiny. What he needed was to be broken down, for something to get past that arrogance and resistance. And Cyprian knew exactly which button to push to accomplish that goal.

"I think it's time you explained to me exactly what happened during your mission the other night." Cyprian held his right hand out, and Stryker immediately put his gun in Cyprian's palm. Cyprian stepped closer to Ace until their bodies were almost touching. He pressed the gun hard against Ace's forehead and leaned in close so he could whisper in his ear. "Kelly was a great lay. We can *both* attest to that."

Ace cursed foully but didn't move, probably because he knew Cyprian would blow his head off if he did.

"Because of your feelings for her," Cyprian continued to whisper, "I've given you far more leeway than I would any other enforcer. But be warned. The time for leniency is over. One more screw-up and you're dead." He pressed the gun harder, certain it would leave a mark. "Do we have an understanding?"

Ace remained stubbornly silent.

Cyprian shoved the muzzle, knocking Ace's head back, but he still didn't say anything.

"Stryker?" Cyprian asked.

"Sir?"

"Ace seems to have forgotten his manners. Remind him." He set the gun on the desk and headed into the outer office. The panel slid shut as the screams began.

Chapter Eleven

Day Three—9:00 a.m.

Sabrina stretched out on Mason's king-sized mattress covered with soft, royal-blue cotton sheets that smelled like a summer breeze. The sun was just peeking in through the window blinds. She assumed that Mason had slept in the guest room, but she wasn't sure. She hadn't heard him come back inside after their conversation about EXIT.

She hated the way they'd left things. But she'd learned one thing after tossing and turning most of the night. Mason had gotten under her skin in ways no one else ever had. What had it been? Two? Three days now since he'd first carried her out of her house? How could he *matter* so soon, especially given how their short acquaintance had begun? All she knew for sure was that he *did* matter. He'd been all she could think about last night. And she wanted, more than anything, to move past their conversation of yesterday evening and get back to the way things had been before—when they'd shared the laughter and stories about his family on the porch while eating peanut butter sandwiches.

She padded into the bathroom and took a quick shower. Dressed in shorts again and a white button-up blouse, she headed into the hall. The door to the guest room was open but no one was inside. The bed was made, but she didn't know if that meant he'd made it this morning or hadn't slept in it at all. She hurried into the family room, but her shoulders slumped when she saw he wasn't there.

A bowl and a box of Frosted Flakes cereal were sitting on the kitchen counter. With a note propped up against the box. There wasn't much to it—it simply said to make herself at home, that he had a security monitor on so he'd know if anyone approached the house. She should watch TV and relax.

She wasn't hungry, but since she hadn't really eaten much since this had all begun, she forced herself to eat the bowl of cereal. After cleaning and putting the dishes away, she considered watching TV. But the lure of the beautiful outdoors beckoned from the large picture window. She put her tennis shoes on and headed out back.

Sun glinted off something in the distance. She shaded her eyes and realized it was Mason's blue pickup, parked beside the barn. He must have moved it this morning. It had been parked by the house last night. A whistling noise sounded from the direction of the barn, followed by a thump. She had no clue what the sound was, but since Mason wasn't running toward the house with gun drawn, there must not be anyone else around. Which meant he was the one making the noise.

She jogged down the porch steps and headed toward the barn.

MASON WAS ABOUT to pull the trigger on the crossbow when he spotted Sabrina rounding the barn fifty yards away. He slowly lowered the bow and watched her with the same awe that he'd felt when he'd seen her all dewy and wet and naked at her house. She was one of the most beautiful creatures he'd ever seen. And he could barely catch his breath watching the early morning sunlight glinting off her dark hair.

She waved when she saw him.

He waved back, but smiling was harder to come by this morning. He'd spent the night in the barn, mostly thinking about her, and trying to understand why it bothered him so much that she'd seemed so horrified over what he did as an enforcer. He hadn't come up with any answers.

She reached him and shaded her big, blue eyes from the sun. They lit with interest when she saw the paper targets tacked to the bales of hay at the edge of the nearest corn row.

"You're using your bow. I'd love to see you shoot it."

"Whatever the lady wishes." He lifted the bow, sighted the target in his scope, and squeezed the trigger. The arrow flew straight and true, puncturing the center circle and embedding itself deep into the bale of hay.

"Wow. Great shot."

His mood lightened with her praise. He motioned toward her ankle holster. "Want to practice with the Sig?"

Her quick nod and smile were infectious. In

no time, he was laughing along with her as if last night's conversation hadn't happened, and taking turns firing his Glock while she fired the Sig Sauer.

Half an hour later, Mason pulled another paper target off the bale and shook his head. All of Sabrina's shots had hit the mark, practically on top of the ones that he had fired. If she could shoot a moving target as well as a stationary one, she just might be a better shot than him. And that was saying something. He pinned a fresh paper to the bale and walked back to the three-rail wooden fence line where Sabrina was waiting with the Sig Sauer.

"Well?" she asked, trying to peer around him to see the target in his hand. "How did I do? Better than you, right?"

He handed her the paper and took her pistol so she wouldn't accidentally shoot him in her excitement.

She gave a squeal of delight, thumping the paper where he'd circled his shots in red before she'd taken a turn. "Two of mine are better than yours and the rest are so close they might as well be the same. I beat you."

Watching her take such enjoyment over something as simple as target practice was as close to pure joy as he could ever remember feeling. "Let's try something that requires a little more skill."

"The heavy, unwieldy Glock?" The grumpy look on her face told him she wasn't fond of that suggestion.

"No, the crossbow." He holstered his pistol and picked up the bow. "Her name is Lola."

"You named your crossbow?"

"We've been through a lot together. It seemed only fitting."

"Do you name your guns too?"

"Why would anyone name a gun? That's just crazy."

She rolled her eyes and leaned against the top rail while he put his gloves on. "It looks like a rifle with a bow stuck on the end. Why are you wearing gloves?"

"Makes it easier to draw the string back." He stood the bow on end.

"What are you doing now?"

"Getting it ready to fire. I put my foot in the stirrup to keep it steady, grab the string, and pull." He cocked the bow and lifted it to notch the arrow into place.

"It looks like a bumblebee."

He arched a brow in question.

She pointed at the arrow. "The yellow and black feathers on the end. Like a bumblebee."

"Watch out for its sting."

She groaned at his corny joke.

He lined up the target in the sight and readied his finger on the trigger.

"Pulling that string back looked pretty hard to do, even for someone as muscular as you."

He paused, his concentration thrown off as he thought about her watching his movements. He'd certainly been watching every movement of her tone, lithe body as she'd practiced with his gun. But he hadn't realized she'd been doing the same.

Pushing thoughts of sexy Sabrina out of his mind, for now, he lined up the target and squeezed.

The bolt exploded from the bow and flew across the space in a blur, burying itself deep into the bale, tearing a hole through the middle of the target.

"Wow," Sabrina breathed. "That was fast. And powerful. Can I try it?"

"If you can load it, I'll let you shoot it."

Five minutes later, after enjoying her struggle to pull the string far more than he should have, he went back to the truck.

"If you're giving up on me," she called out, sounding out of breath, "don't. I know I can do this. I just have to figure out how to get the right leverage."

"I'm not giving up on you," he said, when he returned. "Here, put this in your shoe." He held out a small pocketknife.

"My shoe? Why?"

"Because you're not wearing boots like me. And because it's more secure than in a pocket where it could fall out. The first rule of shooting a bow and arrow is to keep a knife handy. You might have to cut a string or make an adjustment to the arrow."

She shrugged and dropped the tiny knife in the side of her shoe. "What next?"

He held his hand out.

She eyed the cord with suspicion. "What is it?"

"A rope cock."

Her eyes widened. "You're totally making that up."

"I'm totally not. It cuts the force in half that you have to use to pull the bow string into firing position. You don't even need gloves for this. Here, I'll show you how to use the cock." He winced as soon as the words left his mouth.

Sabrina burst out laughing.

Mason leaned against the fence, unable to contain

his smile. When Sabrina quit laughing, she picked the crossbow up again and put her foot in the stirrup.

"Okay, show me how to load this thing. And no more dirty talk unless you're going to follow through." She winked, which had Mason's mouth watering. *If he could only be so lucky.* He'd love nothing more than to sink to the ground and make love to her. But the teasing twinkle in her eyes was just that—teasing—because there was no way she'd want to share herself with a man like him. Not after last night's conversation at least.

Even now he was already regretting what amounted to nothing but showing off by switching from the pistols to his favorite weapon—the crossbow. He used it when quiet stealth was critical and never in close quarters. Too impractical. And now that he'd have to essentially wrap his body around hers to show her the right way to load and fire the bow, he was about to enter a hell of his own making. Wanting, but never having.

"Mason?" The uncertainty in her voice had him forcing a smile.

"Pay attention to the master," he said.

She rolled her eyes. "Just one lesson is all I'll need to have you begging for mercy. Maybe I'll split your arrow right down the center like in *Robin Hood*."

"Whatever you say, Maid Marian. Step out of the stirrup and I'll show you how to load it, then you can try it."

He shoved his shoe in the stirrup, strung the rope cock on the line, and grasped the handles. "Pull straight up until it clicks." He pulled the bow up until the line snapped into place, then removed the rope. "Now for the arrow."

"I want a bumblebee one like you had."

"All of my arrows have black and yellow fletching."

"Fletching?"

"Feathers. Basically."

"Always yellow and black? Is that your trademark?"

He shrugged. "I suppose." He lifted the crossbow and positioned the nock into place, then set the bolt. "Done. Easy, right?"

"Didn't look too hard, as long as I'm strong enough to pull the string back like that."

"All right, Marian. I'll show you how to hold it."

"Anything you say, Robin." She held her hands up for the bow.

"Just remember," he said, all teasing aside, "this is a dangerous, lethal weapon. It's not like the bow and arrow you probably used as a child. It's just as deadly, and in some ways more so, than a gun."

She nodded, suddenly just as serious as he was. Good. He didn't want her treating this like a game and getting hurt.

He settled the stock at her shoulder and positioned her hands. He had to stand slightly to the side and behind her to get her set just right. Feeling the warmth of her so close, breathing in the flowery scent of her shampoo was the sweetest form of torture. His hand shook as he placed it on her right hip and adjusted her stance. For a moment, all he could do was stand there, frozen, feeling the soft, feminine curve beneath her shorts and wishing for more, so much more.

She looked at him over her shoulder, a question in her eyes.

He forced himself to drop his hand and he let out a long breath. "Have you ever used a sight before?"

"Yes, on rifles. This seems similar."

"It is. Just sight the target, make adjustments for the wind."

"There's a slight breeze blowing left to right," she said, and moved the stock, just barely, to the left. "Is that it? I just fire?"

"That's it. Just squeeze, slowly, no jerks. And be prepared for recoil. It's not as bad as most rifles but it has a kick." He stepped back to watch.

She took her time, made another adjustment, then squeezed. The arrow shot from the bow far left of the target and her arm kicked up as she stumbled back. He grabbed her hips again, to keep her from falling. But when he should have let her go, instead, as if his hands had a will of their own, he slid his fingers around her narrow waist, pulling her against him as he helplessly buried his face in the curve of her neck.

He expected a kick to his shin, or an elbow in the ribs. Instead, she slowly lowered the bow, and tilted her neck, ever so slightly, exposing her soft, silky skin. It was all the invitation he needed. He spanned his left hand up beneath her shirt, reveling in the feel of her warm, incredibly soft skin as he settled his mouth against her neck and lightly sucked.

The sexy catch in her breath had his lower body tightening in a hard ridge against her bottom. He couldn't believe she was letting him touch her like this, but he wasn't about to stop unless she told him to.

He slid his right hand down, down, slowly, giving her time to stop him. When she didn't, and his fingers touched her through the cloth of her shorts, she jerked against him and moaned low in her throat.

He kneaded her through the material as he tasted and stroked her neck with his mouth and tongue. Salty and sweet, just as he knew she'd be.

The crossbow dropped, forgotten, to the ground and she turned in his arms, angling her mouth up toward his. He slid his hand down her bottom and lifted her up, fastening his mouth to hers. The kiss was hot and wet and spoke of urgency and longing and was so damn sweet. But it wasn't enough. Not nearly enough. The craving to feel her body naked under his, to make love to her with his mouth before thrusting inside her, had been building since he'd seen her after her shower at her house. He was desperate to get her naked, now.

But soon she was pressing him back and breaking the kiss. He reluctantly let her legs drop and held her until she was steady.

"Wow," she breathed, blinking up at him.

"Wow yourself. Come on. We can clean the guns inside the tack room." He put the bow and arrows in a bag and tossed them into the truck bed before taking her into the little room in the back corner of the barn.

"You can sit over there and I'll clean both the guns and reload the magazines. It'll only take a few minutes."

"I know how to clean a gun."

"I'm sure you do. But I don't mind doing the work." He settled himself on a bale of hay so she could take the only chair at the desk in the corner.

She opened a drawer and rummaged around inside, picking up old coins and pencils and odds and ends then tossing them back.

"How long have you had this place?" she asked, as she opened another drawer.

He finished with the Sig and snapped it into her ankle holster before answering. "Five years or so. Bought it with my first big paycheck."

She shot him a look, as if she'd just remembered what he did for a living, then quietly went back to exploring the desk.

After finishing with the Glock, he holstered it, put the cleaning supplies in a tool box, and washed his hands at the sink by the outside shower. When he stepped back into the tack room, he froze. Sabrina was standing by the desk.

Holding a box of condoms.

He swallowed. Hard. "Uh, Sabrina. What are you doing?"

She flipped the box open and pulled out one of the foil packets as she lifted her gorgeous blue eyes to his. "I found this in the desk. I'm guessing they're Zack's?"

He slowly nodded, afraid to even breathe.

"Do you think he'll mind if we use one?"

His legs almost went out from underneath him. *"Sabrina."*

She crossed the short distance between them and slid one hand up the front of his shirt, a caress he felt all the way to his heart. In her other hand, she held the condom packet. She thumped him on the chest with it.

"I don't want a roll in the hayloft, Mason." She wrinkled her nose. "That's Zack's territory. But a cornfield, well, I've never tried that before." Her eyes twinkled with mischief.

"How are your ribs feeling?" he asked.

"I took my pills this morning."

He swallowed again. "And your cut?"

"I'm feeling no pain."

"Good." He swung her up and held her against his chest. "Let's tour the cornfield."

She giggled and put her arms around his neck as he snagged a blanket off one of the hooks on the wall. But instead of heading out of the tack room, he detoured to the desk, shuffled Sabrina in his arms, and grabbed the entire box of condoms.

CYPRIAN SHUT THE door to the room that housed the mainframe and pressed his code into the digital panel beside it. The electronic lock clicked, securing the steel door. With everything that was happening, he'd wanted to see for himself that the physical security to the computer room was still intact and that no one who shouldn't have been in this room had gained entry. He'd just spent the past half hour reviewing security videos and was pleased that no breach had occurred. At least *one* thing was going right this morning.

His phone buzzed and he took the call as he headed toward the mouth of the main tunnel that led into the hallway just outside his "official" office.

"Eddie, you have something more for me?" Eddie had already given him the list of Mason's properties. And now he also had the results of the searches he'd performed through the computer's logs. Cyprian listened with growing anger as Eddie explained exactly what Bishop had accessed and what he'd done. Eddie continued to list the particulars but Cyprian had already heard more than enough. Damage control was going to be dicey. He'd have to contact a handful of enforcers and give them a lame excuse to explain why he was canceling their EXIT orders, orders that Bishop had faked, just like the one he'd given to Mason. Unfortunately, some of the other orders that Bishop had manufactured had already been carried out. Innocent people had died.

If this were the only thing that had gone wrong on his watch this year, Cyprian would have immediately alerted the Council. But this could be the nail in his own coffin if it came to light. His only hope was to bury the evidence, at least until he got things back under control. If the Council found out what Bishop had done *after* everything was resolved, Cyprian might stand a chance of pinning everything on his assistant, *including* the Hightower business, if it came to that. But it would be much better if the Council never found out.

It would be less risky if he just allowed the pending executions to move forward. But he was growing weary of all the collateral damage that was racking up. It was leaving a bitter taste in his mouth and making him feel like a complete hypocrite when the entire purpose of EXIT was to save innocents.

As for Bishop, Cyprian felt no guilt now over his impending fate, which had been decided the moment Eddie began speaking. But he wanted to focus his resources on the Mason/Hightower problem first. For now, Bishop was still spinning his wheels performing surveillance on an empty house. Stryker had snuck into the back of the house to verify that it was empty, right after he'd taken care of Ace's punishment.

"Okay, Eddie. Thank you. If you can dig a bit

more, to see *why* Bishop might have faked the orders, I'd be most appreciative. And, again, utmost discretion." He hung up the phone just as Ace and Stryker stepped out of the door to the tunnel that led outside.

"Thank you for meeting me so quickly," he told them. He judged the swelling on Ace's face and arms from the beating Stryker had given him just hours ago. "Do we have any problems, Ace?"

Ace shook his head. "No, sir. We don't."

"Excellent. I've reviewed the list of Mason's holdings. He has homes in several strategic areas throughout the country. But there are four properties in and around Asheville, only two of which have homes on them. We'll focus on the local properties to start."

He pulled two pieces of paper out of his pocket, handing one to Ace and one to Stryker. "I split the list, two for each of you to cover more ground. If none of these pan out, we'll pick the next most likely locations. Gentlemen, I don't want to see or hear from Mr. Hunt or Miss Hightower ever again. Make it happen. Now, *go*."

MASON PRESSED SABRINA back against the blanket, their arms and legs tangled up in each other. The kiss was hot, wild, completely out of control. Someone whimpered. It might have been him. He rolled with her in his arms, desperate to get closer, to pull her shirt off her.

Her eyes were slightly glazed as she looked up at him. He imagined he looked about the same way. His fingers shook as he tried to undo the ridiculously tiny buttons on her blouse. For some reason, the task seemed beyond his mental capabilities right now. He slid his hands down the shirt, ripping it open instead, sending buttons flying across the blanket and the ground.

Sabrina laughed, then sucked in a breath as he spanned his greedy fingers across her narrow waist and moved across her warm, soft skin to the underside of her breasts. Perfection. No other woman had ever felt so right. He'd have ripped her bra off her if the hooks hadn't been so strong. But he soon had it removed and the full glory of her rosy-tipped breasts shined in the sun, demanding his attention.

"Mason, if we're going to do this, shouldn't I know your last name?"

"It's better if you don't."

"But—"

"I'm going to kiss you now. *Everywhere.*"

Her pupils dilated and her breath left her in a soft rush that had him tightening even more. They were suddenly a flurry of arms and legs and they both stripped out of their clothes. Mason quickly rolled the condom on, then covered her body with his. The feel of her sun-kissed skin was like coming home, so soft, so warm. He rose up on his forearms and slid lower, sucking one of her nipples into his mouth. She arched off the ground with a ragged moan, her legs moving restlessly beneath him.

She was so soft, so sweet, but it wasn't enough. He wanted more, so much more. And he couldn't wait another second. He slid down her body to the very center of her and dipped his tongue inside.

SABRINA ARCHED OFF the ground, digging her hands into the blanket. The pleasure Mason was giving her as he made love to her with his mouth was almost unbearable. Nothing had ever felt this right. He was a master, stroking her with his fingers, his tongue, exquisitely gentle, building the pressure inside her higher and higher.

Her pulse slammed in her ears as her belly tightened to one desperate center of need. She couldn't keep her legs still, drawing them up, her toes curling against the backs of his thighs. Just when she thought she couldn't go higher, he increased the pressure, his mouth and tongue worshipping the very heart of her, spiraling her higher and higher until her world exploded from the inside out. A tidal wave of pleasure swept through her and she screamed his name, her nails digging into the muscles on his shoulders.

He moved up her body, planting kisses as he went. Fire. She was on fire. From his kisses. From his clever hands stroking her everywhere. From the feel of his muscles rippling against her, beneath her fingers as she ran them down his arms, his chest, enjoying the springy feel of his hair.

His ragged breath tickled the hairs on her neck as he kissed her there, then captured her mouth in another, heady kiss. She clung to his shoulders, her tongue dueling with his. And then he took her glasses off, and set them aside. She hadn't even realized she still had them on. Everything seemed to fade away but him. He was the center of her world, the air she breathed. And if he didn't do something about this unbearable tension building inside her again she thought she might die.

As if sensing her urgency, he broke the kiss and stared into her eyes. And then he was pushing inside her. She sucked in a breath as he gyrated his hips, knowing just the right angle, just the right pressure to spiral all those delicious sensations out of control.

She moved with him, drawing her knees up, pulling him deeper inside. He groaned against her and clasped her to him as he plunged faster, harder inside her. The magic of his touch, of how perfect they were together, was so beautiful, so exquisite that her throat tightened with emotion.

She clung to him, wanting to draw him even closer. Sliding her fingers over his back, she tensed at the feel of dozens of rough, raised scars crisscrossing his back. She sucked in a startled breath. What could cause such horrible scarring? Burns? Knives? Horrified at the brutal treatment he must have endured to earn those marks, she feathered a shaking hand over one of the scars, wishing she could just as easily soothe away the hurt he'd suffered.

Mason froze above her, then swore and grabbed her hands. He tugged them down and pressed them over her head, his fingers threaded with hers.

Her heart lurched at the wary look in his eyes, and the horrible possibilities in her mind about what he might have endured. She tugged one of her hands free and gently cupped the side of his face. "Mason, the scars, what happened?"

"Don't."

Just one word, raw, ragged, but in it she heard everything. Pain, anger, *betrayal*. She wanted to ask him to confide in her, to tell her what awful things had been done to him, to hold him and help him work through the pain she sensed still deep inside him. But he covered her mouth with his and began to move again, easing in and out of her, fanning the flames to an exquisite pitch, making her forget everything but the feel of his body loving hers.

Using his hands, his hips, he urged her to match his rhythm, to touch him as he was touching her. Their bodies moved in perfect unison as the pressure spiraled inside her again, higher, and higher, until every nerve ending seemed to pulse with pleasure that couldn't possibly get better. And then it did.

Her climax caught her by surprise this time, the force of it bowing her back, shattering her from the inside out. As pleasure rippled through her, Mason pumped harder in a near frenzy, his hands clutching her bottom, pulling her up at an angle that had her crying out and climaxing all over again as he convulsed inside her. He pushed into her once, twice more, his entire body shuddering against her. And then he collapsed onto the blanket, rolling with her, one hand on her bottom and one on her back, locking her to him as he remained buried deep inside her.

They lay entwined for a long time, tangled in the blanket, with the bright sun shining down on them. As their heartbeats slowed and their breathing gradually returned to normal, the world around them began to come into focus again.

The green leaves on the corn stalks rustled against each other in the breeze, swaying gently and dipping like nature's dancers to music only they could hear. Crickets chirped. A crow's raucous cry called out from a nearby tree. And somewhere very far away, the dull roar of a tractor engine started up.

Mason gently pulled out of her and rolled her onto her back. He rose above her on his forearms.

His smile was sleepy, satisfied, and arrogantly male as he gave her a slow, lazy wink. Then he gifted her with one of his über-sexy grins that had her belly tightening all over again. He kissed her softly, then pulled back.

"So, what's your opinion of cornfield sex?"

She laughed and pushed at his chest. "Proud of yourself, aren't you? It was amazing, okay? I won't lie." She shifted her shoulders against the ground. "But it's starting to get a bit hard."

He cocked a brow. "Yes, it is." He shifted against her.

She blinked in astonishment as she realized exactly what he meant.

"Already?"

He held up the box of condoms and shook it. "There's an outdoor shower behind the barn. How do you feel about shower sex?"

She laughed and pulled him down for another kiss.

Chapter Twelve

Day Three—11:00 a.m.

Ace lowered his binoculars and idly ran his hand over the small, flesh-colored bandage on his neck that he'd finally been able to switch to instead of the larger white gauze from earlier. The cut seemed to twitch right along with the excitement sluicing through his veins.

Time for payback.

He scooted back down the ridge that overlooked the farm below. He rubbed his aching shoulder. Stryker was going to pay for that bruise. And Cyprian would pay for the rest. But not yet. Right now he had an appointment with Hunt and Hightower, two more people on his list.

Too bad he hadn't brought a rifle. He could have taken them out with two quick shots as they'd run naked from the cornfield to the back of the barn. No worries. He had plenty of firepower. He just needed to get closer.

He stood and jogged to his reliable, beat-up Chevy that no one ever paid attention to. The perfect car for assignments like this. Killing Hunt and Hightower was going to be pathetically easy, but immensely satisfying. He pitched his binoculars on the seat beside him, revved the engine, and headed down the road.

SHOWER SEX HAD turned out to be just as fun as cornfield sex. But Sabrina imagined that being with Mason would always be amazing, no matter the setting.

She tied the edges of her ruined blouse together, *sans* buttons, and sat on an old barrel beside the barn to pull on her shoes. Across from her, Mason pulled his shirt over his head. He'd just finished his Crocodile Dundee impression as he'd sheathed his knife in his boot, comparing it with her little pocketknife, saying, "Now this, this is a knife."

Who knew he had such a corny sense of humor, or that he was a devotee of old movies and could quote lines from so many of them? His favorites seemed to be sci-fi, particularly *Star Wars*. She decided not to admit she wasn't a fan and that she preferred *Galaxy Quest*, or the newer laugh-out-loud funny *Guardians of the Galaxy*.

She tucked the tiny pocketknife inside her shoe again. It seemed silly to keep it, but since Mason had given it to her it was more like a memento, and she couldn't bear to leave it. Their time together this morning was something special she never wanted to forget. And the past half hour they'd spent swapping funny and sometimes touching stories about their families had kept her fears at bay, at least for a little while. But no matter how cute, or silly, or sexy he was, it couldn't distract her forever from what she'd felt beneath her fingertips when she'd run them across his back.

"Mason, tell me what happened. Please." She didn't have to tell him what she was talking about. The knowledge was there in his eyes, in the way his smile faded.

"It's from my time in the army," he said, his voice quiet. "And it's why I can't wear seat belts. I can't stand to be constrained in any way."

He'd been tied up then. Had the ropes cut into his flesh? Her heart broke at the thought, but she didn't dare let it show on her face. He was talking now, about things she imagined he rarely spoke about, and she didn't want to do anything that would stop him from opening up to her. "You were in the army? When?"

He looked out over the fields behind the barn. "A lifetime ago. I joined right after graduating from UNC. I'd majored in physics and astronomy because they were easy, but I didn't want to work in those fields. The idea of being confined to a lab or a windowless office sounded like torture. But I had no real clue what I was going to do. Then I met Ramsey."

Sabrina couldn't imagine physics and astronomy being "easy." She'd struggled just getting a degree in management. "Ramsey, the enforcer who convinced you I was innocent, right? You went to school together?"

He shook his head. "No. I went to school with his younger brother. We were roommates. Ramsey was Special Forces in the army at the time. When he visited his brother, Ramsey and I talked about the army life and it appealed to me. So I signed up."

"I bet your parents loved that, after you spent all that time studying science."

His smile made a brief reappearance. "They definitely weren't thrilled, especially since they'd mortgaged their home to pay for my education." He turned toward her. "But I paid my debts years ago." His smile disappeared again. "All except one, and that one I can never repay, because the man I owed died before I found him again."

She curled her fingers against the barrel she was sitting on. "You're talking about the person who scarred your back?"

He nodded. "He was called the Jackal. But I wasn't worried about making him pay for what he did to *me*. I wanted to make him pay for what he did to my men, my unit." His lip curled in derision. "But the army wouldn't let me go after him. There was some kind of political tug of war going on, and killing the Jackal would have jeopardized the negotiations with some tribal leaders. As soon as my tour of duty was up, I quit, with every intention of going back overseas on my own to find him."

"The Jackal."

"Yes. But before I could go back, he was killed. And then I met Cyprian. Or rather, he met me. He sought me out, based on my history, I suppose. He knew I wanted justice for those who couldn't seek it for themselves. And then I mentioned Ramsey, and how he might like the same opportunity. The rest, as they say, is history."

He stared at the ground for a long time while Sabrina watched him. He still hadn't told her exactly how he'd gotten the scars. She hoped he would tell her someday . . . if indeed there would be a someday for them. If she even had a future. A shiver went up her spine and she couldn't help but feel that something very bad was about to happen.

"Come on."

Mason held his hand out toward her, with no signs of the darkness that had come over him just moments ago.

"I'll cook us a mean breakfast," he said, his Southern accent deliciously swirling the words together.

"I thought you already had breakfast? I had a bowl of cereal."

"I worked off all of those calories. I'm hungry again."

His sexy wink had her remembering exactly how he'd worked off those calories. She cleared her throat. "I also thought you couldn't cook."

He let out an exaggerated sigh. "Technicalities. I'm sure between the two of us we can figure something out."

They started to pass the truck on the way to the house, when Mason pulled his hand out of hers. "Wait, I left my watch in the tack room."

Because he'd taken it off for shower sex. She sighed dreamily. He winked, apparently knowing exactly why she'd sighed, and bent down to kiss her.

Bam!

The deep-throated bark of a gun shattered the morning. A shower of wooden splinters rained down from the side of the barn, right where Mason's head had been a half second before he'd leaned down to kiss her.

He swore and grabbed her, throwing her to the ground as more shots rang out.

"Where are they coming from?" she yelled, as he scrambled backward and yanked her behind the barn with him.

"The house." A beeping noise sounded from inside the tack room. "And that would be my perimeter alarm going off. Damn it. I screwed up. I shouldn't have taken off the watch."

"I'll try not to take offense at that 'screw up' statement since I'm the screw-up."

He winced and pulled her farther away from the corner as more shots cracked against the barn. "Sorry," he said, as he grabbed his gun. "Didn't mean that the way it sounded."

She raised her leg and grabbed the Sig out of her ankle holster. "You're forgiven, if you get us out of this alive." Another shot burst through the wood right beside her shoulder.

Mason grabbed her and pulled her down closer to the ground. "We've got to get out of here."

Another bullet whined by.

He scanned the area, but Sabrina didn't know why he bothered. There wasn't anywhere else to hide but the barn. The trees were too far away. She checked the loading on her Sig. "Will bales of hay stop a bullet?"

"I'd rather not find out. And we'll just get trapped if we hole up inside. He could prop the doors closed and burn us out."

Sabrina swallowed against her suddenly tight throat. Burning to death definitely wasn't an appealing option. "He? Did you see who was shooting at us?"

He nodded. "Ace. The son of a bitch is on my porch."

"Well, the nerve."

He grinned, then swore as another bullet tore through the wood a foot away. "All right. That's enough. I'm going for the truck. I need you to lay some cover fire."

"What? You're crazy. You don't have your Kevlar."

"Yeah, that's a bummer." He hefted his Glock. "Ready?"

"Don't you dare get shot, Mason."

"I'll try not to. You do the same."

He held up three fingers.

She wrapped both hands around the Sig, pointing toward the ground.

Two.

One.

Mason took off running for the truck, firing his Glock toward the house as he ran.

Sabrina crouched by the corner of the barn, firing as fast as she could toward the porch although she didn't see anyone there. Had Ace ducked for cover or was he on the move?

The truck door slammed shut and Mason started the engine.

Sabrina held her fire, puzzled at the silence coming from the house.

The truck's tires threw up dirt and gravel as Mason floored the accelerator and spun toward the barn. The tread grabbed hold and spit the pickup forward. He slammed the brakes and the truck nosedived to a stop behind the tack room. Mason shoved his driver's side door open.

"Get in," he yelled.

The sound of another engine, pitched high, had her looking back toward the other corner of the barn.

"Get in, Sabrina. Now!"

The urgency in his voice spurred her forward. She ran to him and he lifted her inside, shoving her into the passenger seat as he hit the gas again. The door slammed shut on its own as the truck swerved and barreled into the cornfield.

Sabrina was about to ask him why he'd done that when the answer plowed into the field almost on top of them. She instinctively ducked as the Chevy spun toward them, with Ace at the wheel, holding a pistol out the window.

Mason fired his Glock through his open window and jerked the wheel. Ace's windshield cracked in a spiderweb pattern as the car whipped past their rear left side, narrowly missing them.

"Get down," Mason ordered, as he pressed his foot all the way to the floor, making the pickup leap forward. *Thump, thump, thump.* The stalks of corn pounded against the sides of the truck and bumped against its underbelly.

Sabrina ignored his order and turned around in her seat. She slid the rear window open and shoved her arms through, aiming the Sig at Ace's car as it came up fast. *Bam! Bam! Bam!* She fired at the cracking glass pattern on the driver's side.

The glass shattered and fell mostly inside the car. She could hear Ace's curses as he hit his brakes, then swerved off to their left. He fired a parting shot that cracked through the glass, narrowly missing her.

"Get down," Mason yelled.

"Just drive. I've got this." She held the Sig Sauer as she hung farther out the back window, trying to lift herself high enough to see the stalks of corn being mowed down by Ace's car. She could hear the engine close by, but she still wasn't high enough to see the path he was taking.

She let out a squeak of surprise when Mason grabbed a handful of her shirt and yanked her back inside. She slid across the leather seat and plopped down on the floorboard on the passenger side.

Mason glared at her. "Stay down and hold on!"

She glared right back and tried to remember what exactly it was that she liked about him. She definitely didn't like being ordered around, particularly when she was a good shot and should be protecting both of them instead of lying in a floorboard.

The truck went faster and faster, the corn a green and gold blur as it hit the sides of the truck. Mason looked left, gritting his teeth. "Almost there."

"Almost where?" She clutched her gun, ready to do battle whether Mason wanted her help or not.

He didn't answer. He glanced left again, his jaw tightening. "Brace yourself. This is gonna be close."

Whatever he was planning couldn't be good. She shoved her gun in her ankle holster and wedged herself into a tight ball.

Another engine revved, impossibly close. Mason held his hand out the window, shooting over and over as he jerked the wheel. The truck kicked up dust and dirt as it jackknifed a one-eighty. It was all Sabrina could do just to hold on as her body was slammed back and forth.

"Ouch," she bit out as her head hit the glove box.

A shot rang out, followed by a sickeningly loud crunch of metal somewhere close by. Had Ace crashed his car? What would he have crashed it into out here in the middle of a field of corn?

Mason stomped the accelerator again and drove about twenty yards before he stomped the brakes and shoved the truck in park.

"Are you okay?" he demanded, finally sparing her a glance.

She rubbed the back of her head. "Just dandy."

"Wait here." He popped the door open and jumped out.

"No, *you* wait. I'm coming with you." She grabbed her Sig but by the time she unpretzeled herself from the floorboard, he was gone. The man was far too stubborn for his own good.

Without knowing exactly where he was, she couldn't risk going outside and possibly getting in his way. As much as it galled her to do nothing while he was risking his life for her, she settled down to wait. With her knees on the floorboard, she braced her elbows on the seat, watching the broken corn stalks through the open driver's side door. Except for the low hum of the engine, quiet reigned once again. But this time, even the crickets weren't chirping.

"Come on, Mason," she whispered. "What's happening?" A minute passed. Then another. That was it. She couldn't wait any longer. Mason must need her help or he'd have come back by now. And she wasn't the type to cower anyway. She'd rather go down fighting if she was going down.

She crawled out of the floorboard and slid across the seat to the driver's side. Aiming her Sig out the open door, she hopped out and headed toward the nearest stalks of corn that hadn't been obliterated by their wild ride through the field. Suddenly her gun was snatched out of her hand. She whirled around, kicking her legs in a circle to take out her attacker's knees.

Mason jumped to the side just in time to avoid a direct hit and glowered at her. "I told you to wait."

"And I told *you* to wait. I want to help you find Ace."

He let out what she could only think of as a growl and grabbed her around the waist, lifting and dumping her onto the bench seat. She barely had time to slide over to the passenger side before he was plopping down beside her. After slamming the door shut, he floored the gas, aiming the truck back toward where they'd come from.

"What happened? Where's Ace?" She held her pistol, watching out the back window.

Mason grabbed her and shoved her down onto the seat with her head in his lap. "Are you *trying* to get yourself killed?"

"Did you forget that I bite?" she snapped.

His eyes widened and he wisely let her go.

"What happened?" she repeated, shoving away from him but staying low in the seat this time. "I heard what sounded like a crash."

"I used Ace's temper against him. I lured him to the edge of the field and got him to chase us right into a tree. But when I checked the car, he was gone. I tracked him a short ways but he got into the woods. I couldn't risk him getting off a lucky potshot at me from there so I ran back."

"Then he could be anywhere."

"Pretty much." The cornfield ended and the truck raced across the backyard around to the side of the house. Mason pulled up beside the porch. "I'll be right back." He hopped out and ran up the steps, kicking the door open and disappearing inside.

A moment later he reappeared with both of their bags, although one appeared to be much fuller than it had been before, and tossed them in the back of the truck. Go-bags she remembered now. That's what he called them. Had he grabbed more guns, or ammo?

He hopped in and took off toward the road. The tires squealed as he barreled onto the little two-lane rural highway and headed south.

Sabrina straightened up in the seat and clicked her seat belt as she looked back toward the house. Sunlight glinted off something metallic. She drew a sharp breath as she realized Ace was at the edge of the cornfield on his knees, aiming his gun at them.

"Get down!" she yelled.

Mason leaned over with her onto the seat just as the passenger side window exploded. He cursed and sat up, jerking the wheel to keep the truck from going off the road.

Sabrina held her Sig out the window and fired off several rounds. She grunted in satisfaction when Ace dove back into the corn for cover. But unfortunately, she was pretty sure she hadn't hit him.

The truck squealed around a curve, and the house and cornfield dropped out of sight.

"ARE YOU SURE this is a good idea?" Sabrina scanned the neighborhood of average-looking houses from the concrete porch. She kept her back to Mason, trying to hide the fact that he was picking the lock. Her gun was at the ready, gripped tightly in her hand behind her. She wasn't about to get caught un-aware again if she could help it.

"Unless Cyprian has figured out that Ramsey is working with Buchanan and me, and he found out about the properties Ramsey keeps off the books like he somehow did mine, then it's probably safe. Emphasis on *probably*. We need to stay alert." He forced the door open and rushed inside.

Sabrina followed, closing and locking the door as she glanced at him. "That beeping. Is that—"

"A security alarm." He went straight to the keypad and punched in a code. The beeping stopped.

After assuring herself that no one was in the room ready to leap out at them, Sabrina pointed her gun down toward the floor. "This is Ramsey's house?"

"Yep."

"That explains the lock picking. How did you know the alarm code?"

"Ramsey's not the cleverest guy when it comes to remembering numbers. So he always uses the last four digits of the street address as his alarm codes."

"Hm. I wouldn't have thought of that."

"Trust me, any self-respecting burglar would. But since Ramsey's a light sleeper, I don't guess he worries about it all that much. Why he even has an alarm beats me. I'll change the code if we end up staying." With gun in hand, he went from room to room.

Sabrina didn't know why he bothered. She could see almost the entire house from where she was standing in the living room. To say it was tiny was an understatement. She secured her pistol in her ankle holster.

"Is this like your contemporary house in town? A front, not somewhere Ramsey really lives?"

He came back into the room, holstering his pistol. "You really don't like that house of mine, do you?"

"I didn't say that."

"You didn't have to. Your loathing was stamped all over your face when we were there. As for this place, surprisingly, no. It's not a front. It's the family home where Ramsey grew up. This is where he lives most of the time when he's not traveling. Keep an ear out for anything 'off'. I'm going to try to get him on the phone and get an update on his situation with the Buchanans."

"Okay, I'll just . . . look around."

He tilted her chin up and grinned. "You're a nosey little librarian aren't you?"

She frowned and pushed her glasses further up. "Librarian?"

"Never mind." He kissed her, then grabbed his cell phone and punched in a number.

Sabrina sighed, her lips still tingling. If it weren't for Ace going after them at Mason's farm, there was no telling what she and Mason might be doing right now. She really hated Ace.

The walls of Ramsey's house were filled with pictures, reminding her of her grandfather's study. He'd filled every available space with photos of her and Thomas and Brian, and her sketches of course. He was so proud of her sketches.

Her heart seemed to lurch in her chest. She missed her brother and grandfather so much. But she didn't have time to be sentimental, or emotional. She had to keep it together, keep an ear out, as Mason had said.

A car drove past the house. She listened to make sure it didn't stop, and continued to study the pictures. She recognized Cyprian in a couple of the photographs, the same smiling face that graced the EXIT brochures. She supposed it made sense for Ramsey to have his picture since he was his boss. But it still turned her stomach. Was he the one giving the orders against her family, against her and Mason? She didn't know. But it seemed almost impossible to believe that a man with his kind of power *wouldn't* know that his own company was after them.

One of the pictures appeared to be some kind of dinner party. She moved closer, and stopped. Her eyes widened. She grabbed the picture off the wall and held it closer.

"Ramsey's not answering his phone. I'll try again later."

She looked up at Mason who'd come up beside her without her even realizing it. "Who is this woman?" She held out the picture.

He shrugged. "I don't see Cyprian enough to know whom he might be dating. Smokin' red dress though."

Sabrina frowned down at the picture. "No, not the woman on his arm." She pointed to the brunette off to one side, in a black form-fitting dress. "That woman. Who is she?"

His dark eyes studied her intently. "Why do you want to know?"

"I've seen her before."

"Where?"

"At my brother's funeral, the graveside service. I knew most of his friends but I didn't recognize her.

And the way my sister-in-law was shooting daggers I thought maybe—"

"That Thomas was having an affair?"

She nodded. "He'd cheated in the past. So, yes. I knew it was possible. I went to confront her, to make her leave. But she took off before I could talk to her or find out her name. I guess I was angry, thinking that Thomas had hurt Angela again. I couldn't get that woman out of my mind. When I got home, I just sat down and drew her. Who is she? Why is she with Cyprian?"

"She's his daughter, Melissa." He put his hands on her shoulders. "You said you drew her. Did you show the sketch to anyone?"

Her eyes widened and her face went cold as the blood drained away. "Oh my God."

"Sabrina? Who saw that sketch?"

"My grandfather. I showed it to him and told him my suspicions about Thomas. He was as upset as I was. He took the sketch with him. Said he'd hold on to it in case he ever ran into the woman at any of the charity events or functions he went to. I . . . never really thought about it again."

"When? When did he see it?"

"This can't be related to his disappearance. That's what you're thinking right?"

"When, Sabrina?"

"Right after the funeral, three months before Grampy disappeared. If . . . if that sketch had something to do with his disappearance, why would someone wait three months?" She laid the picture on a side table and squeezed her hands together.

Mason led her to the couch and sat beside her. "Maybe it took three months for your grandfather to see Melissa and recognize her. But once he did, he confronted her and asked her about Thomas."

"Okay." She pressed her hands to her temples. "I'm trying to be objective, to look at all of these pieces, but I'm not seeing how they fit together. If we assume my brother was having an affair with Cyprian's daughter, so what? My grandfather recognized her from the sketch and confronted her at some party? And Cyprian was there and got mad? That can't be enough to justify him getting angry and . . . kidnapping . . . my grandfather." She refused to consider that Grampy might be dead.

He took her hands in his. "Explore all of the connections. See how they might tie together. To do that, go back to the first puzzle piece. Thomas's funeral. The background report that Buchanan gave me said your brother was killed in a mugging. Did the police ever catch the killer?"

She stiffened. "Please don't say it."

"I have to." He squeezed her hands. "EXIT's assassinations aren't always sophisticated. Staging accidents is one of the best ways to eliminate someone. A mugging is easy to stage and doesn't garner much media interest because it happens all the time."

She shook her head. "No, you're wrong. This one was all over the television, the newspapers, because of my family's social status in Boulder. Everyone heard about the mugging. Thomas's picture was flashed on TV so much that I was afraid to turn it on."

"Sabrina."

She tugged her hands out of his. "No. I don't want to talk about this anymore. Thomas was mugged. A random act of violence. So he was having an affair? Big deal. It happens all the time. It's not the social pariah type of thing people kill over."

"How about a father's love?"

She frowned. "What do you mean?"

"Cyprian adores Melissa. What if your brother hurt her somehow? Maybe he lied about being married, and she found out and told her father? Cyprian has an old-fashioned sense of honor. He'd be furious if Thomas tricked Melissa that way. He could have confronted him and accidentally killed him. Or maybe he had someone do it for him. That may not what happened, but it's possible. It's one explanation."

"No," she insisted. "I don't believe it."

He studied her for a long minute. "What did your grandfather say about the mugging?"

"What *didn't* he say? He was furious that the police didn't have any leads. He pressured them all the time, saying they had to keep digging, keep trying to find out who'd killed him. He wouldn't let it go." Her breath caught.

Mason tilted her head up. "He wouldn't let it go. And then he disappeared."

She searched his eyes for the truth. "You think Cyprian, or EXIT, killed my brother. And when my grandfather kept pressing the investigation, that they . . . killed him too. And then when *I* started pressing the investigation to find Grampy, they tried to kill me, not caring that my parents were caught in the middle. And now they're still trying to finish the job. I put the puzzle pieces together like you told me to. Is that how you see it? Is that what you think happened?"

"I never said that I thought your grandfather was dead."

Her shoulders slumped.

Mason pulled her onto his lap and cradled her against him. She wasn't weak. She didn't *need* him to hold her. But she *wanted* him to. For just a few minutes, she gave in to the desire to let him shoulder her burdens for her, to let him protect her while she clutched his shirt and tried not to let her fears and her grief overwhelm her.

"EXIT destroyed my family," she finally whispered, her throat tight.

"I believe so. Yes."

"Then I'm going to destroy EXIT. And you're going to help me."

His look turned wary. He lifted her off his lap and set her beside him. "How do you propose to do that?"

"We're going to break into EXIT, the building here in Asheville."

He laughed, then sobered. "You're serious."

"Deadly. Think about it. Ace and whoever else your boss has running around trying to find us would never think to look for us there."

"I'll give you that. But what would be the point of breaking in?"

"To find something incriminating against Cyprian. Something on a computer, or in a file, or even a picture. I'm not sure. We'll know it when we see it. But there has to be something there we can use against him. There have to be all kinds of secret documents in that building, things that could ruin him if they got out."

"I'm sure there are. Missions are run out of that

office just like the one in Boulder. Which is why the security is tight. The computers will have many levels of protection, both physical and virtual. And there will be security guards. And cameras. And alarms."

"That's where you come in. You knock out the cameras and alarms and *drug* the guards." She pointed her finger. "No killing."

"Well, gee, you had me until you said the 'no killing' part. That takes all the fun out of it."

"Stop kidding around. I'm serious."

He blew out a breath. "Okay. Serious. You've got my attention. I like the idea of going on the offensive. Especially since I can't reach Ramsey and don't know when he and Buchanan will be back in the picture. But what you're proposing would take weeks of careful surveillance and planning. We don't have that kind of time. Once Cyprian realizes that Ace failed, he'll send someone else after us. Then someone else after that. Since we can't risk going to any of my properties, we'll probably end up moving from cheap motel to cheap motel, constantly on the move until we can figure out something more permanent or until the heat is off."

"And when will that be? What happens while we wait? You said the EXIT order against me was fake. What if your theories about Cyprian and my family are wrong? What if he's going after others, issuing more fake orders? If we sit around and do nothing, innocent people will die."

He winced, and she knew she'd found the one thing that might sway him—his moral code, his drive to protect others. He was a man of convictions, with a strong sense of honor. She admired him for that, even though she didn't agree with his views. The words he'd told her last night about why he did what he did for a living had made her toss and turn. She'd heard them in her head so many times that they'd formed a picture. Now she brought that picture to the forefront, and ruthlessly used it to her advantage.

" 'The only thing necessary for the triumph of evil is for good men to do nothing.' That's an Edmund Burke quote. A very wise man told me that last night."

His eyes narrowed. "You're not fighting fair."

"That wise man also told me something else: 'If I have the power to act to save someone, and I do nothing, then that's the most horrible sin of all.' "

"Sabrina."

"I'm sorry. But I need your help. And apparently I'm not above using guilt to get it."

His jaw set. "Okay. You win. I'll break into EXIT and see what I can find. But you're not going with me. It's too dangerous."

"I *am* going with you. I'll have your back. Just like I did earlier when I warned you before Ace shot out the truck's side window."

"Sabrina—"

"I took a tour of the EXIT office building here in Asheville when it was being renovated."

"And?"

"And doesn't it make sense that Cyprian would need a suite of secret offices to conduct meetings with enforcers? Offices the public, and the tour side of the company, don't know about?"

"Possibly. Hell, probably."

"Do I have to remind you that I have a photographic memory? I've got the layout of that building imprinted in my mind, the way it looked during construction. If there are any hidden offices, you might walk right past them and not know it. But I can walk those halls and compare them to the pictures in my mind. If a wall is too far out or not where I remember it was, that's a good indicator that something might be hidden behind it, right? I can help you find the real offices, the ones that will have the information we want, not the glossy, brochure-filled offices the public gets to see."

He frowned, obviously not happy with what she was saying. But not denying that it made sense either.

"You need me, Mason. Admit it." When he didn't answer, she tried another approach. "I know that I can't break into EXIT without you. So if you won't help me, I'll just have to go back to Colorado."

"The hell you will. Why would you want to do that?"

"Because Colorado is where all of this started, and most likely where Cyprian's holding my grandfather, if he hasn't killed him already. Maybe I can find the guide who took my parents and me on that tour. Maybe he knows something and doesn't even know that he knows it, something that can point me toward where my grandfather is being held." She threw her hands up. "I know that doesn't sound like much, but what other leads do I have? I'm sure the investigators I hired have already spoken to the guide, but they didn't know about the secret side of EXIT. Or about Ace. So they wouldn't have known the right questions to ask. I'm certainly not going to hide and do nothing if there's some clue I haven't followed to at least try to find Grampy."

He narrowed his eyes at her. "You're trying to blackmail me with that Colorado threat."

"Is it working?"

He swore and stood up, then crossed to the door. "Since I couldn't get in touch with Ramsey, I'm going to assume the worst—that Cyprian knows he's helping us. Which means we're not staying here after all. We'll find a motel outside of town where we can hunker down for a bit."

She hurried to the door he was holding open. "Are we breaking into EXIT together? Or am I going to Colorado?"

"You're definitely not going to Colorado. But don't look so smug," he told her. "You might have just signed both of our death warrants."

Chapter Thirteen

Day Three—9:00 p.m.

Mason glanced at Sabrina lying on her belly on the ground beside him. She was keeping low like he'd instructed, her head barely visible above the ridge that looked down onto the EXIT building. Another quick look behind them reassured him that his truck was completely hidden, obscured by trees and bushes. If anyone inside EXIT looked across their parking lot, they wouldn't notice him and Sabrina, or the truck.

He settled back down, resting his elbows on the dirt as he peered through his infrared binoculars at the newly renovated three-story building. Most of the windows were dark, and uncovered by blinds, which gave him an unobstructed view. He'd been able to catch heat signatures passing the windows at regular intervals and had determined they were security guards.

One of them would come outside the side door every forty-five minutes and make a circuit of the parking lot, shining his flashlight into the trees and bushes near the building. The route took fifteen minutes. Then he would go inside and head upstairs to the next level. Another guard would go downstairs on the far side of the building and tour the lower floor, then go out the side exactly thirty minutes after the other guard had come inside. Like clockwork, for the past three hours, that was the routine.

"What do you see?" Sabrina whispered beside him.

"The building looks empty, except for three signatures on infrared—the security guards. What bothers me are the three cars parked by the maintenance shed right below us."

"Why does that bother you? Three guards, three cars. Doesn't that confirm the building is empty, except for the security guys?"

"Probably. Makes sense. But the company they work for may bus in new guards each shift and takes the others back to town since it's such a long drive out here."

"I've never heard of a company doing that."

"I have."

She sighed impatiently. "But you haven't seen any other heat signatures."

He tapped the side of his binoculars. "No. I haven't."

"So . . ."

"So I'm not worried enough about the cars to cancel, if that's what *you're* worried about. This late at night even a Type A like Cyprian should have gone home."

"Great. Now, what do you plan to do about the guards?"

The worry in her voice had him lowering the binoculars. "Per your instructions," he said drolly, "I'm not allowed to kill them. So I'll drug the guard at the side door when we go in. The others we'll avoid if possible. But if not, I'll take care of them too."

She leaned in and kissed him. Not a little peck but a full-blown, getting-him-rock-hard-and-wanting-her kiss. When she pulled back he was aching.

"What was that for?" he bit out, none too happy to be sporting a hard-on when he wasn't in the position to do anything about it.

"It was a thank-you."

"Hm. You're welcome," he grumbled, shifting his legs and trying not to think about how good it had felt to make love to her.

Focus. Concentrate.

He shoved the tiny pair of binoculars in one of his jacket pockets. It wasn't chilly, but he needed those pockets to hold everything for the mission. He pulled out the map the two of them had made of the lower floor while they were at a motel outside of town. She'd drawn the location of the executive offices, which apparently made up one-half of the building. They had a lot of searching to do.

Because of so many unknowns, he'd decided they would *only* explore the bottom floor. As far as he was concerned, this was a one-time deal. If nothing came of it, he'd take Sabrina somewhere—out of the country if he had to—so she couldn't come back and try to get into EXIT on her own.

The jammer he'd brought for the alarm system would probably buy them at most forty-five minutes. That was the time from when one guard went outside on patrol to when the next one reached the side door. They'd have even less time if the guards deviated from their routines.

As soon as one of them reached the side door and saw the alarm panel light was disarmed, they'd call the security company and go on full alert. Mason wanted to ensure that he and Sabrina were out of the building and far down the highway before that happened, so he was limiting them to thirty minutes for their search.

"The jammer freezes the cameras connected to the security system," he explained. "As long as there isn't much of a breeze, the guards should be fooled. They wouldn't expect to see tree branches swaying on their screens."

"Sounds like you've done this a few times."

"A few. Usually with a lot more preplanning. Are you sure you want to do this? You can wait out here."

She shook her head. "No. I've got your back, Mason. And I'm supposed to tell you if the layout doesn't match the picture inside my head. I'm going with you."

He sighed and used his regular binoculars to scan the parking lot. Still empty. But Cyprian was known to be a bit paranoid about EXIT's safety. What if he had another entrance to the building that couldn't be seen from here? Built into the side of the hill, an underground tunnel? That was the kind of thing Mason would have looked for if he'd taken days or weeks to case the building before planning an entry. Going in without that kind of intel had him nervous as hell.

He looked at Sabrina. Dressed all in black like him,

she was using some binoculars he'd given her earlier to study the building as if she were seeking out every little detail. As if her life depended on ensuring their mission was a success. In a way, he supposed it did. If something happened to him and she was on her own, would Buchanan or Ramsey be able to find her before Ace or another enforcer carried out the EXIT order? He'd tried to reach both of them before driving out, but neither had answered his phone. He'd fired off encrypted e-mails, letting them know about his plan, but still hadn't received any replies.

Sabrina lowered her binoculars. "Shouldn't we move closer to the side door so we can be ready as soon as the guard comes out?"

He sighed. "Yes. We should. All right, mini-enforcer. Let's do this."

She put her binoculars in one of her pockets.

A few minutes later they were in position. As soon as the guard came out, Mason would press the jammer to freeze the cameras and block the alarm.

"Sabrina?"

She was intently watching the side door and didn't seem to hear him.

"Sabrina?"

She frowned. "What?"

"It's Hunt."

Her brow furrowed in confusion.

"What?"

"My last name. It's Hunt."

Her brow smoothed out and she gifted him with the most beautiful smile he'd ever seen.

Man, he was in trouble.

The door opened and a security guard stepped out.

"Here we go," Mason whispered. "Wait until I disable the guard, then run inside."

She nodded, looking far too excited. Stoked. Like a kid at Christmas. He belatedly worried that he might not have impressed the danger and seriousness of the situation on her enough.

"What are you waiting for?" she whispered.

"Damned if I know." He pressed the remote to jam the system and took one of the filled syringes out of his pocket.

"You used a cloth when you drugged me," she reminded him.

"And you were out far longer than expected. I can control the dosage better with this. Ready?"

"Ready. Be careful."

"You too." He yanked the protective cover off the needle, and took off toward the guard.

SABRINA FOLLOWED MASON into another office and tapped him on the shoulder. She held up five fingers, letting him know they only had five more minutes before the thirty-minute mark. He gave her a thumbs-up, then hurried to the desk and sat down to search the drawers.

Following the routine they'd established in the first office they'd searched, she went directly to the filing cabinets along the wall. So far, everything they'd found seemed completely legit, only mentioning real EXIT tours. One of the offices they'd searched had all kinds of legal documents. But they had to do with land grants and permits and agreements with various landowners, even the federal government, to allow tours on their property or in national parks.

As Sabrina rummaged through the last drawer of the filing cabinet, she was coming across more of the same. Nothing that would give her and Mason any information on the private side of the company. No secrets. No EXIT orders. Nothing to prove they were anything but the EXtreme International Tours company they claimed to be. And nothing personal on Cyprian. Her shoulders slumped and she closed the drawer before heading to the desk to see if Mason was having better luck. But something was off. She slowed, then stopped and turned around.

At the door, she peeked out to make sure there were no guards before stepping into the hall. She turned in a complete circle, putting herself back to the day when she'd taken the tour. It took a few tries, but finally she could see the building the way it had been. She stepped through the doorway, the memory of the wood two-by-four walls superimposed over the sheetrock and paint before her now. She looked down the long hallway, counting doors, mentally measuring the distances between each office.

It was definitely off.

She hurried down the hallway to the office they'd been in last, then slowly walked forward as she'd done the day the walls were still being built. The next door she stopped at was the janitor's closet they had skipped. That was it. She hurried back into the office just as Mason appeared in the doorway, a fierce scowl on his face.

"What are you doing?" he demanded. "You're not to leave my side."

"I figured it out. The janitor's closet is a ruse. It takes up too much space along the wall between the offices. The two offices beside it should be bigger, or—"

"There's another office in between them, behind the janitor closet, with a concealed entrance."

"Yes!" She belatedly clamped her hand over her mouth, realizing she'd been too loud.

Mason looked down the hallway for guards and hurriedly pulled her into the office. They both headed to the far right wall.

"This wall shouldn't be here," she whispered. "It's several feet too far out into the room."

Instead of the excitement she expected to see on Mason's face, he shook his head, a look of worry in his eyes as he glanced at his watch.

"We have to go," he said. "We've already been here one minute longer than we should have." He grabbed her elbow and pulled her toward the door.

"Wait, don't we have some wiggle room?" she whispered as she pulled back, trying to slow his progress. "You said it takes forty-five minutes for the guards to make their full rounds. We can take five more minutes to see if we can figure out what's behind that wall and still be out of here before the next guard goes outside."

He stopped in the middle of the office to face her. "Sabrina," he whispered harshly. "This isn't a game. It's too dangerous to stay any longer. Time's up."

"It most certainly is," a voice called out from the doorway.

Mason shoved Sabrina behind him as the lights flickered on overhead. He whipped his Glock out and squeezed off two quick shots, the sound terrifyingly loud in the small space.

Before Sabrina could reach for her weapon, some-one grabbed her from behind.

Mason whipped around.

"Look out!" Sabrina screamed.

He jerked back but it was too late. The man behind him slammed his pistol against the side of Mason's head, sending him to the floor in a crumpled heap.

Sabrina tried to run to him, but the man holding her yanked her back and held her immobile. *Please let him be okay. Please let him be okay.*

Another man lay writhing on the floor not too far away from where Mason had fallen. He must have been the man Mason had shot. And beyond him, a man looking impeccable in an expensive dove-gray suit frowned down at the floor.

"Really, Bishop. Do stop being so dramatic. You're wearing Kevlar. There's no reason to act like you're dying."

His obsidian gaze rose to Sabrina and his mouth curved into a delighted smile as if they were about to be introduced in the middle of a dinner party. "Miss Hightower. What a pleasure to finally meet you in person. I'm Cyprian Cardenas."

Chapter Fourteen

Day Three—10:00 p.m.

S abrina strained against the rope tying her to the chair in the back corner of Cyprian's *real* office, the one hidden behind the wall that she and Mason had found right before they'd been caught. The man who'd tied her—Bishop—had pulled her arms so tightly that there was no way she could break free. She didn't even have the pleasure of being able to tell her captors what she thought of them because of the gag over her mouth. She tugged again at the ropes around her wrists, wincing when they bit into her flesh. The ropes didn't budge. She collapsed against the chair and watched helplessly as Mason was half dragged to face Cyprian in front of his desk.

A wall of obviously fake windows lit up the room behind him, displaying what she assumed to be a recording of the sun setting over the Rocky Mountains. He held court like a king, his thugs, Stryker and Bishop, standing on either side of Mason with their guns trained on him, his hands cuffed in front of him.

Mason had fought against those handcuffs like a madman when he'd first awoken, as if he'd lost his mind. And even with his hands cuffed, he'd fought valiantly while Stryker had kicked and beat him into submission. But in spite of how strong and determined he was, with his head bleeding and his arms behind his back, he'd been unable to defend himself anymore. It had been heart-wrenching to watch, and Sabrina's hatred of Cyprian and his men had increased a thousandfold seeing their brutal treatment of Mason.

Cyprian had ordered him stripped down to his underwear to remove the Kevlar vest and any weapons he might be concealing. When Mason's shirt had been removed, and Sabrina saw the spiderweb of scars on his back for the first time, her heart felt like it might break. He'd suffered far more than she'd realized when she'd felt some of those scars beneath her fingertips. Now she understood why the handcuffs had driven him nearly insane. When the Jackal had restrained him in the past, the bonds had been so tight they'd cut into his flesh. She couldn't imagine the pain he must have had to endure. That he was alive was a testament to his stamina and determination. It was so unfair that he was being treated so horribly yet again.

No amount of willpower could save him if he was so injured that he couldn't even try to protect himself. And based on the amount of blood that had seeped from his head wound and was now drying on his neck and shoulders, time was running out. He swayed on his feet and shook his head as if trying to focus on Cyprian. The act of remaining upright after the beating he'd taken was sapping his strength.

The only solace for Sabrina was in knowing that the man named Bishop was probably in almost as much pain as Mason. She remembered how much being shot had hurt, even with a bulletproof vest on. She'd thought she was dying. Every time Bishop moved, every time he breathed, his chest probably felt like icy hot needles were being jammed into his flesh. It was the least he deserved for what he'd done.

Cyprian snapped his fingers. "Mason." He clapped his hands. "Mason, there you are. Eyes open. You wouldn't want to pass out before I decide your fate and the fate of Miss Hightower, now would you?"

Even from Sabrina's vantage point she saw the deliberate raising of Mason's head, the straightening of his shoulders even though the room had to feel like it was spinning around him. She despised Cyprian for treating him this way.

"There we go," Cyprian said, satisfied. "I have to say, Mason. I'm very disappointed in you. It appears that you're in league with a former enforcer who went rogue, who turned traitor against this very organization—Devlin Buchanan. Tell me. What would make a loyal operative such as yourself go against years of training and close ranks with the likes of him?"

Mason's mumbled reply didn't carry very far. His head dipped to his chest and he swayed on his feet again.

Stryker punched him in the stomach, doubling him over.

Sabrina shouted against her gag and renewed her struggles against her rope.

Mason managed to shove Stryker away before straightening. But when Stryker would have retaliated, Cyprian held up his hand.

"Enough. I need him conscious. Now speak up, Mason. Why did you side with Buchanan? What are the two of you planning? More importantly, is anyone else helping you?"

He lifted his head again. "Screw. You."

Cyprian's nostrils flared. He looked at Stryker and nodded.

Stryker slammed his fist into the side of Mason's ribs.

Sabrina screamed with rage against her gag as Mason staggered against Bishop. Bishop let out a howl of pain.

Cyprian rolled his eyes. "Enough. You hit him too hard with that pistol, Stryker. He's useless to me right now. Lock him up in the tunnel and we'll try again later. Bishop, follow behind them. One wrong move and he's dead."

"Yes, sir," Bishop gritted out between clenched teeth as he held his ribs.

"And Mason," Cyprian added. "Be mindful. If you try anything while Stryker and Bishop escort you, remember that I have Miss Hightower with me. If Stryker doesn't call back that you're secured below in ten minutes, Miss Hightower dies. Understood?"

Mason didn't move.

Stryker grabbed a handful of Mason's hair and yanked his head back, forcing him to look at Cyprian. "Answer the man."

"If you hurt her," Mason bit out, "I'll kill you."

Cyprian's face turned a mottled red. "Get him out of here."

Sabrina watched with growing panic as Stryker grabbed Mason by the shoulders and shoved him through an archway on the other side of the room. Stryker hit a spot on the wall and a string of overhead lights came on, showing a concrete floor that sloped down—the tunnel Cyprian had mentioned. What were they going to do to him? She struggled anew against her bonds, steeling herself against the pain as the ropes chafed and bit into her skin.

The door to the tunnel slid closed, leaving Sabrina alone with Cyprian. He turned his dark-eyed gaze on her like a snake getting ready to strike.

She strained harder against her ropes. Were they loosening or was that her imagination?

"Well, well, now." Cyprian stood, jerked his suit jacket into place, and rounded the desk. "It's just you and me, Miss Hightower. Sabrina, isn't it? You don't mind if I call you Sabrina, do you? Oh, wait. How rude of me. We can't exactly have a conversation if you can't talk, now can we?" He mercilessly ripped the duct tape from over her mouth and yanked out the gag.

Her face stung like it was on fire from the tape. But she remained rigid, refusing to cower before him.

"What? No recriminations or accusations? I expected you to at least yell at me about Mason's treatment, based on the daggers you were glaring earlier."

"You're a bastard. Is that what you want to hear?"

He sighed. "Such language is not becoming of you. But at least you're talking." He grabbed a chair and tugged it a few feet closer before sitting down.

"I really am sorry that you've been caught up in all of this. It was never my intention for you or your family to be hurt. What has happened is . . . regrettable."

"Regrettable? You killed my brother, my parents, probably my grandfather, and now you're going to kill me. Yet you sit there in your suit pretending to be a civilized man and call all of that regrettable? You make me sick."

His perfectly plucked brows rose. "My, my, my. What interesting accusations you make. Tell me, dear. Where did you come up with these theories? Whom have you been speaking to?"

"I notice you aren't denying my theories."

He shrugged. "I'll neither confirm nor deny. Neither would serve me. What I wish to know is who you and Mason are working with and what you're planning. I already know about Buchanan. But I expect there are others. I want their names."

"I don't know any names."

"Hm. I doubt that. But I suppose it's possible that you've seen some of the rebels and don't know their identities. Not a problem. You've already proven you're adept at drawing faces. I'll just get you a pencil and paper and see what we come up with." He stood.

"You mean like the sketch I made of Melissa? The one my grandfather showed you?"

He turned to face her and slowly sat back down. Sabrina immediately wished she hadn't goaded him. She'd wanted him to admit what he'd done, to tell her his role in her brother's death and her grandfather's disappearance. But she feared she might have just awoken a sleeping dragon.

"It appears, Miss Hightower, that you know quite a bit more than I realized."

"I don't know anything," she hedged. "Like you said, they're just theories."

"Perhaps. But sometimes it's amazing how accurate theories can be. As you may have guessed, I'm in the process of performing damage control. But I can't be sure I've covered all my bases without knowing all the details. I want you to tell me everything you know, or think you know, about EXIT and about me."

"And if I refuse?"

He clucked his tongue. "That would be . . . disappointing. And I don't like to be disappointed." He rose from his chair with the grace and polish of a world-class gentleman, but what he retrieved from his bottom desk drawer had nothing to do with being civilized.

Sabrina clamped her jaw shut to keep from whimpering as he drew near.

"Are you sure you wouldn't rather do this the easy way, Miss Hightower?" He sat across from her again and pulled a decorative table next to her chair. "All you have to do is tell me everything you know about EXIT, and describe anyone who has been helping you, Mason, and the Buchanans."

She tried to answer him, but her throat was so tight her words came out in an unintelligible rasp.

"Could you please repeat that?" He leaned closer, turning his head to the side as if to hear her better.

"Go. To. Hell," she bit out.

He sat back, his eyes narrowing with displeasure. "I believe I mentioned earlier that your language was offensive. I have a feeling you'll realize the error of your ways very soon."

He plopped the heavy battery onto the table and attached the electrodes, leaving them to dangle next to the chair. Sabrina's hands started sweating so much she could barely keep her grip on the arms of the wooden chair where she was sitting.

"Although I'm loath to cause you any pain," Cyprian said, "I will do what is necessary." He stood again. "I'm going to give you some time to think about this. Hopefully, when I come back, you'll have made the wise decision and we can both avoid this bit of unpleasantness."

Relief swept over Sabrina as she watched him go through the archway that led to his official office. The door slid shut behind him. She couldn't believe he'd given her a reprieve. And she certainly wasn't going to waste it.

All the straining and tugging on her ropes had definitely loosened them. If she could just get one hand free, she could lift her foot up and go for the pocketknife tucked inside her shoe.

What if she couldn't break free? She glanced at the battery and shuddered. No, she refused to consider the possibility of failing. Because if she failed, who would help Mason?

She renewed her struggles, clenching her teeth together as the ropes bit through her skin.

MASON SHOOK HIS head, trying to clear the buzzing in his ears. The darkness was absolute and he wasn't sure where he was. His last clear memory was of warning Sabrina that they needed to leave. After that, only fuzzy images and pain drifted through his mind, but those small glimpses into what must have happened scared the hell out of him.

Because it meant that Cyprian had Sabrina. *If she was even still alive.*

No, he couldn't think like that. Sabrina was strong, a fighter. She would do whatever it took to survive. She would know that it was her duty, to stay alive until he could come for her.

Fight, Sabrina. Don't let them win.

He traced the long chain threaded between the handcuffs. The links ended at a heavy lock that fastened the chain to a thick metal loop in a concrete wall. That loop was his enemy now, the only thing stopping him from getting to Sabrina. He focused all his rage, all his hatred on that one piece of metal, bracing his feet wide apart against the wall, wrapping the chains around his arms, and grasping them with his wrists.

After two short breaths, he inhaled deeply and pulled. He pushed with his feet at the same time, every muscle in his body straining and working together against that one little loop. He gritted his teeth, his head beginning to pound from the effort. Sweat slicked his hands, making the chains slippery, but he couldn't give up. His muscles began to burn and sting. He kept pulling, tugging, pushing with his feet. His arms and legs started shaking from the strain until they finally gave out like limp noodles and he fell back, the chain sliding out of his sweaty grasp. He lay on the cold concrete floor, gasping for breath.

Again. He had to try again. He couldn't give up. Sabrina was counting on him.

When his muscles stopped shaking, he sat up, wiped his sweaty palms on his boxers, and wrapped the chains around his arms again. For a brief moment, the feel of those chains on his arms started a bubble of panic deep inside him. He could almost feel them cutting into his flesh, biting into his muscles, the sting of salt water being poured over his open wounds.

No, that was a long time ago. You're at EXIT. Sabrina needs you. Don't give in to the panic.

He wrapped the chains around his wrists to try again. Cold steel. Biting. Tearing into flesh. *No. I'm in the tunnel.* He yanked the chain.

Did you really think you could escape me that easily, soldier?

"Face me like a man," he yelled into the darkness.

The Jackal laughed.

Mason lunged toward the sound and jerked up short as the chain pulled taut, making him fall down onto the concrete.

The whip lashed, flaying open his skin.

The agony of a thousand burning suns seared his flesh. He bit his tongue, trying to stay silent.

Don't let him hear you scream.

The Jackal laughed again. The whip cracked down.

Pain and rage burst past Mason's lips in a guttural roar at the dark sky above.

SABRINA JERKED HER head toward the archway that led to the tunnels, the animalistic cry sending goose bumps across her skin.

What are they doing to you, Mason?

She sawed the tiny pocketknife harder on the

thick rope tying her right wrist to the chair. How much time did she have left before Cyprian returned? Where were his men? Had they remained in the tunnel with Mason? Or left to perform some other chore their boss had given them?

The last of the rope broke and fell to the carpet. *Yes!* She closed the knife and shoved it in her pocket as she jumped up and ran to the pile of Mason's clothes and vest on the floor beside the desk. She gathered them up in her arms, then searched the desk drawers as quietly as possible, looking for a set of keys. Cyprian had mentioned chaining Mason. And she didn't think her pocketknife would be much use against a chain.

Yes! A ring of keys was in the middle drawer. She grabbed them and ran to the tunnel. The door was closed, but she focused on the picture in her mind of Stryker and the others as they'd left. Then she put her hands on the wall in the exact place where they had. A button clicked. The door slid open and lights flickered on overhead.

Another guttural yell sounded from below.

I'm coming. Hold on.

She ran down the sloping floor, clutching Mason's belongings. It would have been perfect if Cyprian had left their guns, but of course, he hadn't. She'd worry about that later, after she found Mason. They'd just have to hope that they didn't run into any of Cyprian's thugs.

She rounded a curve in the tunnel and stopped. Although the tunnel continued on to some unknown destination, there were three doors in the wall to her left. They were solid steel and each of them was secured with a heavy-duty padlock. She fumbled with the key ring, looking for a key that might fit. Without knowing where Mason was, she had no choice but to search each of the rooms.

She glanced around, although she wasn't sure what she'd do if she saw anyone. There wasn't anywhere to hide. After trying several of the keys on the first door without success, she finally found a key that fit snugly into the lock. She was about to turn it when she heard Mason's anguished shout again.

From behind the farthest door.

She yanked the key out of the lock and ran to the last door. "Hold on," she whispered. "I'll get you out, Mason." Luck was with her for a change. The first key she tried was the right one. She turned it, cringing at the loud click that echoed against the concrete walls. She pulled the lock off and tossed it onto the floor.

Clutching the keys and Mason's clothing in one hand, she yanked the door open, flipped on the light, and ran inside. Her shoes squeaked on the concrete as she stopped inches from his outstretched hand. Silver handcuffs circled his wrists connecting to a long, thick chain which looped around his back and chest. The length went all the way to the wall to a large metal loop embedded in the concrete.

Mason was breathing heavily, his dark hair matted with blood, his eyes wild as he stared up at her.

"My God, Mason." She palmed the ring of keys from Cyprian's desk and threw everything else down as she dropped to her knees beside him. "Here, let me—ooof!"

He clamped his hand over her mouth and grabbed her, throwing her to the floor. Her head slammed against the concrete and she cried out against his hand. He covered her body with his, and leaned down close to her face.

"I've got you now, Jackal," he spat, his white teeth bared menacingly. "You'll never hurt anyone else again."

The insane light glinting in his eyes had her stomach sinking. He didn't really see her. He thought she was his enemy.

He shoved his hand against her ribs as if he were stabbing her. The Kevlar softened the blow but she still lost her breath and had to struggle to draw in air. He punched her again.

Her bruised ribs shot a fiery arc of renewed pain up her chest. Oh God, he was going to kill her if she didn't get away from him.

"Mason," she tried to say against his hand.

"Shut up," he growled, pressing his hand flat against her mouth.

She chomped down on his finger and brought her knee up at the same time, slamming it into his crotch. He yanked his hand back and twisted to the side, yelling his rage as he doubled over.

Sabrina tried to scramble away from him but he roared and grabbed her leg, yanking her underneath him again as he raised his arm as if to backhand her.

"Mason, don't! It's me! Sabrina!" She threw her hands up over her head and closed her eyes, bracing herself for his blow.

"Sabrina?" an anguished voice choked.

She slowly lowered her arms and looked up.

Mason stared down at her in horror, his hand still raised to strike. "Sabrina." His voice cracked. "Oh my God. What have I done?" He slid his hands beneath her and pulled her onto his lap, cradling her and rocking her against him.

He smoothed her hair back and pressed his cheek against the top of her head. "I'm so sorry," he whispered. "I'm so sorry. I'm so sorry. I'm so sorry."

MASON TUGGED HIS clothes on while Sabrina listened at the door for Bishop or Stryker returning from wherever they'd gone after chaining him up. He still couldn't believe he'd almost hit her. One blow of his fist could have shattered her delicate jaw, or worse. And instead of being angry with him she'd been more concerned with the laceration on his scalp and whether he was feeling well enough to be able to make it out of the tunnel.

He was pathetic. He'd known for a long time about his . . . issue . . . with being restrained. But he'd never once thought it could put someone else in danger. He didn't know if he could ever make this up to Sabrina, but getting her as far away from this building as possible would be a good start. He just wished he wasn't seeing two of everything.

He shook his head, trying to clear his vision, but it only made his head throb worse.

"Mason?" Sabrina was suddenly by his side, pressing her hand against his chest and looking up at him with concern. "Do you need to sit down for a few minutes?"

"I'll be fine. We need to get out of here."

"I'm sorry I couldn't get us some guns. I don't know where Cyprian put them."

He tilted her chin up. "Do *not* apologize to me for anything. You're the bravest woman, hell, *person* that I've ever met—standing up to Cyprian, then coming down into these tunnels to find me. Don't you dare say you're sorry again." He took her hand in his. "Come on. We'll just deal with whatever happens when it happens. Staying here isn't making either of us any safer."

He strode to the door, pulling her with him. It took a ridiculous amount of effort just to keep from wobbling on his feet. The blows to his head had left him disoriented and probably with a concussion. He didn't even remember what had happened in Cyprian's office and had to rely on Sabrina's accounting to piece the events of the past hour together.

He peered up and down the tunnel. "Seems clear," he said, keeping his voice low. "We'll go left, follow the downward slope. It probably goes beneath the front parking lot. With any luck, we'll come out fairly close to the ridge where my truck's hidden."

"Don't bring luck into it," she whispered as they jogged side by side. "Luck and I don't mix very well."

He squinted, still trying to bring the fuzzy images around him into focus, to no avail. He dug his keys out of his pocket and handed them to Sabrina. "You'll have to drive. I can't see worth a damn."

She shot him a worried look and tightened her hold on his hand. For the first time that he could ever remember, his face heated with embarrassment. This was so screwed up, her worrying about him when he was the one who should be strong and keeping her safe.

A few seconds later the tunnel stopping sloping and leveled out. The string of lights ended as they entered a gaping, dark hole.

"What is this?" she whispered.

He pulled her behind him, pausing to let his eyes adjust. Everything was blurry, but he could see well enough to identify shovels, rakes, and other equipment stacked against the wooden walls.

"We're in the maintenance shed we saw from the ridge. This must be how Cyprian disguises the mouth of the tunnel. There should be a door at the other end."

He let her hand go and hurried the last few yards, making his way around the stacks of pallets and bags to the other end. Sure enough, another steel door like the ones in the tunnel secured the entrance, or in this case, the exit. He turned the knob and inched the door open a fraction to look outside.

Bishop, Stryker, and Ace stood about ten feet from the door in a heated discussion. Ace was the one doing most of the talking, and cursing. And Mason's name came up enough times for him to figure out exactly what Ace was mad about. But it was Stryker's crude comment about what he'd like to do to Sabrina that had Mason struggling to hold himself in check. The only thing that stopped him from running to Stryker and slamming his fist against his jaw was that all three men had pistols holstered on their belts. With the element of surprise, Mason might be able to take one of them out. But the others would most likely get off several shots before Mason could neutralize them.

He quietly eased the door shut.

"What did you see?" Sabrina whispered.

He pulled her to the side where the door would hide her when it opened. "Bishop and Stryker are outside. And it looks like Ace just got here, because he's yelling at them for not telling him earlier that we'd been captured. He's mad that he's spent the past hour searching for us instead of being here and having some 'fun.' Oh, and they're also arguing about who gets to put a bullet in my brain after they interrogate me."

Her indrawn breath had him squeezing her hand. They were trapped, with few options. If they went back into the tunnel, there'd be nowhere to hide if the men came inside before Sabrina and Mason reached the other end. And since Cyprian was probably still on that other end, with guns, that wasn't a palatable option anyway.

No, their only hope was for him to use the element of surprise when the men came inside. He'd have to distract them and give Sabrina a chance to escape.

"Just hunker down behind the door. As soon as I attack them, get out and run up the ridge to the truck. You still have the keys?"

"They're in my pocket. But—"

Voices sounded from right outside the door.

Mason shoved Sabrina behind him. He wobbled on his feet and had to put his hand on the wall to brace himself against the dizziness.

"Mason," Sabrina hissed as the doorknob turned.

He ignored her and shoved away from the wall, his fists raised and ready.

Sabrina grabbed him and yanked him back toward the wall behind the door. He shoved her hands away and lurched toward the door. She lifted a tarp and threw it over the top of him and shoved him toward the wall again just as the door opened. She yanked his arm, pulling him down to the floor just before she ducked under the tarp with him.

He glared at her but doubted she could see him. It was pitch black under the heavy material. All he could do now was be as still as possible and try not to make a sound, and hope that no one noticed the two of them under their covering.

Footsteps echoed on the concrete, then quickly faded. Unbelievably, Ace, Stryker, and Bishop hadn't noticed them—probably because they were so busy arguing with each other.

Mason threw the tarp off and grabbed Sabrina's shoulders. "What were you thinking? You could have been killed."

She shoved his hands away. "Did you learn nothing from Harry Potter and the cloak of invisibility?"

He narrowed his eyes, not at all amused.

She sighed. "I was *thinking* that you can barely stand and it didn't make sense for you to try to fight them when we could both hide. Besides, if we have to fight, I'm fighting *with* you," she snapped, "not cowering in a corner or running away."

He didn't waste time arguing. It would have been far better for him to go down fighting if it meant giving her a chance to get away. If those men had found them beneath that tarp, Sabrina could have been killed right along with him. That thought had him feeling sick to his stomach.

They hurried out the door and ran up the hill, with him leaning on her far more than he wanted to admit, even to himself. By the time they got to the truck, he was ready to pass out. But he used the last of his strength to make sure she was safely inside before he got in on the passenger side and she started the engine.

A shout sounded from down the ridge.

"Go, go, go," Mason urged.

She floored the accelerator. The truck fishtailed on the dirt and leaves. She let up on the gas and took off more slowly. As soon as the tires grabbed, she gunned the engine again and the truck leaped forward.

A HANDFUL OF hours and one very tiny, cheap, but thankfully clean motel room later, Sabrina sat on the side of the bed closest to the wall watching Mason sleep on the bed by the door. It wasn't a restful, healing sleep like he needed. His forehead was wrinkled as if he were in pain, and every once in a while he would twitch or say something, but she couldn't make out the words.

They'd both taken showers and she'd used the medical supplies in the go-bag from his truck to clean his cuts—which thankfully didn't need stitches. But he'd refused to take any pain medicine, saying he needed to stay sharp and that he'd be fine after a couple of hours of sleep.

Would he be fine? Maybe. Hopefully. But if so, it was only on the surface. There was a darkness inside him that she'd seen back in the tunnel, when he thought she was the Jackal, that absolutely terrified her.

She rubbed her hands up and down her arms as she allowed herself to finally think back to that moment in the tunnel when Mason had been ready to slam his fist into her face. She shivered at the memory of that bottomless well of fury in his eyes as he'd stared unseeing at her. What would have happened if she hadn't gotten through to him? If he hadn't come back from wherever his mind had gone? Would he have stopped with just one punch? Or would he have continued to hit her until . . . She shied away from that thought.

Across the room, on the table beside the TV, sat her purse from her go-bag. And next to that sat Mason's burner phone. A few minutes ago she'd decided to go it alone, that since last night's attempt to break into EXIT had failed so spectacularly, her only remaining option was to go to Colorado to speak to the tour guide. So she'd booked a flight to Colorado. For one.

All she could seem to think about was that bitter anger in his eyes and his fist drawing back. Could she really trust him again after that? In his right mind, he would never hurt her. Of that she had no doubt. But if he was tied up again, what exactly was he capable of? And where did that leave the two of them?

Days. They'd only known each other for a handful of *days*. Not weeks. Not months. *Days*. And yet the thought of going off on her own, without him, was breaking her heart. How was it possible to feel so connected, so dependent on another person so quickly? How could she care about him so much that the thought of never seeing him again seemed as scary as the thought of staying? They'd shared so many emotions, so many intense life-and-death situations in such a short amount of time that it was like they'd already lived a lifetime together. So how could she even think of leaving him?

"You look like you're trying to solve the world's

problems." Mason's searching gaze belied the teasing note in his voice. He looked . . . unsure . . . worried . . . vulnerable, as if he knew the decision she'd been struggling with.

"I'm scared," she whispered.

"Of me." A statement, not a question, in a hollow, empty voice.

"Honestly, yes. I'm scared of what could have happened back in that cell, and of what could happen in the future."

"I'm so, so sorry." His face was lined with misery.

"I know. Stop apologizing. You didn't do it on purpose."

He didn't answer. He didn't need to. They both knew what had happened, and why, and that it could happen again.

She fisted her hands in the bedspread. "Since there doesn't seem to be anything else we can do here to search for clues about my grandfather, I've decided to go back to Plan B. I'm going to Colorado to talk to Rick Stanford, the guide from my parents' trip. Assuming the accident was on purpose, I have to believe it was an enforcer who organized it, right? If I can ask the guide who had access to the equipment, maybe he can tell me—"

"You're not going to Colorado."

She stiffened. "Yes. I am."

"Rick Stanford isn't in Colorado. He's one of the guides Cyprian brought to start up the office in Asheville."

She blinked. "How do you know that?"

"Because I live in Asheville and I pay attention to the news. EXIT has been running all kinds of ads about the new location and Stanford has been in several of them."

"Okay. That's good. Then I . . . I mean . . . *we* . . ."

"You can't decide whether you want me with you now or not, can you?"

"I'm . . . not sure. I guess. I just . . ." She shook her head.

"Stanford is one of the guides for the rafting and zip lining leg once the tours officially start up in a few weeks," Mason said, filling the silence. "Again, based on the TV ads. He's probably there now running equipment tests and getting the outpost set up. Or just doing paperwork."

"Will you . . . take me there?" she asked, already regretting her earlier indecision. She'd hurt him. She could tell by the look in his dark eyes. And she hated that she'd done that. The decision she'd struggled with moments ago now seemed clear. "I'd like your help. If you feel well enough, and still want to help me."

"Of course I'll help you." His voice was tired, resigned, the events of the tunnel still putting far more space between them than the two feet separating the beds. "But it will be on my terms. I want a full day of surveillance, maybe two, before we make a move this time."

She winced. "I guess it's my turn to apologize. I pushed you to go into that building too soon. I know you wanted to watch longer. If you had, we might have seen that Bishop and Stryker were there."

"And now it's my turn to tell you not to apologize. I'm a grown man, Sabrina. You can't force me to do anything I don't want to do. I weighed the odds last night and I thought it was a low-risk situation to go in. What happened is no one's fault. It just . . . happened."

"Okay, well. If I'm not going to Colorado, then I guess I should call and cancel my flight."

"You booked a flight?" The rest of his question went unsaid . . . *You booked a flight without me?*

"Yes. But I used the burner phone."

"What name did you use to make the reservation? And what credit card?"

"Mine, but there's no reason for Cyprian to think I'd book a flight. It's not like he's monitoring the airports."

He scrubbed his brow, looking incredibly tired. "Not only is he probably monitoring airports, he's got tracers on rental car companies, bus stations, you name it. I don't think you understand exactly how powerful EXIT Incorporated is. They have ties into everything." He dropped his hand. "If you wanted to go to Colorado, why not just ask me? I could have gotten us a private jet without leaving an electronic trail."

"Us?" she whispered.

"Did you think I'd want you to go by yourself? It's too dangerous." He searched her face, then briefly closed his eyes, looking pained. "But you still think *I'm* too dangerous now."

"No," she said fiercely, taking his hand in hers. "No, I don't. Not unless there's a . . . trigger. I trust you."

He pulled her hand toward him and pressed a soft kiss against the backs of her fingers. "I'm so sorry—"

"Stop. I told you not to apologize anymore."

"No amount of apologies will ever be enough. Ramsey or Buchanan will have to call in soon. When they do, I'll arrange to hand you off to them to protect you until we figure out something more permanent, a way to ensure that you don't have to keep looking over your shoulder. There has to be a way to get EXIT to leave you alone. I won't stop until I figure out how to make that happen. All I ask is that you stick with me a little longer, until I can get you better protection."

She wanted to reassure him, to remind him that she wasn't helpless, and that they made a good team. She wanted to tell him she wasn't afraid of what could happen the next time—if there was a next time—when he was tied up and the darkness took over again. But she was afraid. And she didn't want to lie to him. He deserved better than that.

But he also deserved not to keep beating himself up over what had happened.

She rubbed her palms against her shorts and noted the time on the digital clock between the two beds. The sun would be coming up in about four hours. What would that new day hold for the two of them? Would the tour guide be able to tell them anything that would lead to her grandfather? Would she find him alive and well? Or would she find out that he'd been dead all this time? She shivered and rubbed her hands up and down her arms again.

"Rina?"

"I'm just . . . thinking about . . . tomorrow. I know you have a Glock for each of us in your go-bag since you grabbed extra guns and ammo at your house when Ace was after us, but I really preferred the Sig and Cyprian took it and—"

"Sabrina."

"—I don't like the recoil of a Glock and it's too big for an ankle holster and I—"

"*Sabrina.*"

She pressed her lips together to stop her nervous chatter.

"I'll keep you safe," he said.

"I know. That wasn't why . . . I know." She gave him a lopsided smile. "Maybe it's a good thing that I booked that flight since I won't be on it. Cyprian will send his thugs there while we're talking to Stanford."

"Maybe. It's late. Or early. We've got a long day ahead of us. We should get some sleep."

She nodded and rose to get into the other bed. But then she looked back at Mason, and just thinking that today might be their last day together changed her mind. She turned back to his bed.

"Scoot over."

His brows rose in surprise but he moved back and lifted the covers. She lay down on the mattress, her back to his chest with her head pillowed against his arm. He put his other arm around her and pulled her tight against him.

Chapter Fifteen

Day Four—9:00 a.m.

Cyprian donned his gloves in the backyard of Bishop's rental home, while Stryker and Ace disarmed the security system and jimmied the lock on the door. The house was a bit overblown and gaudy for Cyprian's tastes, but the acres of trees blocking out the nearest neighbors were convenient for his purposes this morning.

After last night's . . . disappointment . . . with Mason and Miss Hightower managing to escape, he'd realized his crucial mistake—not killing them when he had the chance. He'd wanted to keep them alive long enough to get information out of them about what Buchanan might be planning against EXIT. A valid reason, perhaps, but it had resulted in them getting away. That, and the fact that Bishop was the one who'd tied her up. One more mistake on top of so many others was the final straw, and the last time Cyprian would tolerate any more mistakes from him.

The door popped open. Cyprian's men quietly

entered the home. He followed a few moments later, giving them time to make sure everything was secure. The kitchen he stepped into was clean, tidy. Much more appealing than the overlarge pool out back with its tacky, naked mermaid statues.

When he passed from the kitchen to the dining room, an archway opened into the ostentatiously large family room. And standing in the middle of the shiny marble floor, with Stryker and Ace flanking him, was Bishop. His face was pale, his eyes wide with apprehension. Good. If he was frightened then it wouldn't take long at all to get him talking. Although Cyprian trusted Eddie to have given him everything he found, there was always the possibility that he'd missed something. It certainly wouldn't hurt to double-check at the source. He needed to know *everything* Bishop had done so he could clean up the evidence and get things back on track.

Buchanan's family had made waves with the Council a few months ago, through Devlin's contacts and one of his brother's FBI contacts, complaining about Cyprian abusing his power. But the Council had accepted Cyprian's explanations and hadn't intervened. This new, fake EXIT order situation could give Buchanan—and those helping him—the ammunition they needed to get the Council to step in. That was something Cyprian could not allow to happen. It was looking more and more like he'd have to involve the Council at some point or look bad for not contacting them. But he wanted to be the one to contact them so he'd look like the good guy.

"Good morning, Bishop. I must apologize for intruding on the start of your weekend. But this

Mason-Hightower problem needs to be taken care of before things get out of hand."

Bishop cast a wary glance at the men beside him before answering. "Of . . . of course. I didn't realize you wanted me at the office today or I'd have gone in. I'm happy to do whatever you need me to do." He waved toward a grouping of couches and recliners. "Why don't you all have a seat?"

"Not necessary. This won't take long." Cyprian stopped a few feet away. "It's a shame that Mason's been caught up in this . . . situation and has to be eliminated, because he's exactly the kind of man I want working for me."

Bishop blinked nervously.

"He likes to help the downtrodden," Cyprian continued. "And because he was assigned to kill Miss Hightower, he now feels obligated to protect her. He'll want to help her figure out who targeted her and why. I'm making a logical leap that he and Hightower broke in last night for that very reason: to find evidence pointing to who was behind her assassination order. Of course, you and I already know the answer to that."

He stared at Bishop, noting that sweat had broken out on his forehead. "Tell me, Bishop. If you were Mason, what would your next step be?"

Bishop shifted his stance and used the pretense of scratching his head to wipe the sweat away. "I . . . ah . . . would probably start at the beginning. The tour where her parents died?"

"Excellent. That mirrors my own thoughts as well. I believe they'll want to speak to the guide from that tour, Rick Stanford. Lucky for us, he's here, in Asheville. That should make it quite easy to catch Mason and Hightower when they make their move. Ace, Stryker, I want you to work out a plan to keep an eye on Stanford. If you need assistance, get some local trash to help you."

"Yes, sir," they said in unison.

"Do you want me out in the field or assisting from headquarters?" Bishop asked.

"Actually, I need some information."

Bishop's earlier nervousness faded and he puffed out his chest like a self-important peacock.

"I've been speaking to Eddie in the Boulder office," Cyprian continued. "He's head of system security. Did you know that?"

"Ah, no."

"He's been digging into our security logs. You see, any time a file is created or updated on our system, the ID of the person performing that access is recorded. When I requested a list of those who've accessed the EXIT order for Miss Hightower, well, we've already had that discussion haven't we?"

"And . . . and I'm really sorry. I shouldn't have done it. It won't happen again."

"You're right of course. But what else do you suppose Eddie found when he looked at the rest of those security logs?"

"I . . . I . . . I—"

"You have a bit of a gambling problem, don't you, Bishop?"

The sudden change in topic seemed to throw him. He glanced beseechingly at his associates, but they offered no sanctuary. *Nor would they.*

"Enough," Cyprian said, wearying of the game. "You've been selling the services of *my* enforcers to the highest bidder. Haven't you?"

Bishop was sweating so hard now that Cyprian could smell his stink. He wrinkled his nose in distaste and signaled Ace and Stryker. They drew their weapons and trained them on their doomed peer.

Bishop made a whimpering sound.

"You owe your soul to loan sharks. Tell me, how have you managed to fend them off this long?"

"I . . . I paid them from my missions. But it wasn't enough. I was desperate. I put my house in Colorado up as collateral for my gambling debts. If I don't pay them back in the next two months I'll lose everything. It was just one EXIT order, *one*. Please, give me another chance."

Cyprian roared with rage and slammed his fist into the side of Bishop's jaw. He flew backward and skidded across the marble, slamming into the side of a couch. Bishop whimpered and held his hand against the cut that had opened up on his cheek. That would make staging the scene a bit more . . . complicated. But it could still be done.

Normally Cyprian exercised better control, but hearing the lies pouring out of his assistant was more than he could take. He stood over him, no longer bothering to hide his contempt.

"The truth will set you free, Bishop. You've been faking orders ever since you became my assistant. You've probably raked in enough money in the past two months to pay your gambling debts twice over. This isn't about saving your home. This is about paying for pools and disgusting mermaid statues. Do not dare to lie to me again. How many EXIT orders have you faked?"

"I don't know," he blubbered. "Five, ten."

"*Twenty-three*," Cyprian spat. "If the Council ever finds out about this, it could ruin me, you idiot."

He drew deep breaths until he'd calmed down, then straightened his suit jacket. "Get up, Bishop."

Bishop whimpered as he climbed to his feet.

"Ace, Stryker, give us a moment."

They immediately crossed the room and waited by the dining room opening.

"Bishop, I want to thank you."

"Wh-what?"

"When Melissa told me she was dating Thomas *Worthington* and never could manage to get our schedules aligned so I could meet him, I asked you to investigate. And you did a thorough job. I thank you for that. If it weren't for you, I wouldn't have known that Melissa's beau was actually Thomas Hightower and that he was married, cheating on his wife, and *using* my daughter. And in my anger, I ordered you to kill him. I'm not proud of that. It was a mistake that has led to an entire host of problems. But you were only doing your job when you arranged the 'mugging.' And it's certainly not your fault that Melissa saw his obituary in the paper, or that she went to the funeral and was seen by Sabrina Hightower."

He smiled sadly. "It's not your fault either that Miss Hightower was curious and drew Melissa's sketch and gave it to her grandfather. Or that he did his own digging into my background and accused me of arranging Thomas's death. And when Mr. Hightower informed me that he had evidence proving my culpability in Thomas's death, it certainly wasn't your fault that I reacted without thinking, abducting him without a plan in place. And, finally, it's not your fault that the torture you and Ace have inflicted has yet to yield the location of the evidence he insists he has against me, evidence that could come out someday and ruin me. I just wanted you to know, that in spite of everything that has happened, that I accept my responsibility in all of this. And I appreciate and acknowledge the work that you've done for me. Thank you." He headed toward the archway where Ace and Stryker were waiting.

Bishop called out from behind him. "Boss? Does this mean that you forgive me?"

Cyprian turned around. "Of course not. Whatever would make you think such a thing?" He shook his head in disgust and crossed beneath the archway. "Ace, Stryker, I notice the stove is gas. Accidents happen. And I can't have an ME seeing the cut and bruises on his face. Take care of it please."

"No!" Bishop screamed.

Cyprian hummed to tune out the screams as he washed Bishop's sweat off his gloves in the kitchen sink.

CYPRIAN SIPPED HIS Hennessy in the back of the limo, parked several blocks down the street from Bishop's home. Even from here, the wide lawns, hills, and tall trees kept him hidden from view. Perhaps he should look for a home in a neighborhood like this instead of the condo he was renting, if he ever decided to move permanently from Boulder to Asheville. He had to admit, North Carolina with its lush greenery did have a distinctive beauty that was refreshingly different from his home state. But then he doubted his daughter would want to leave the only place she'd ever lived. Melissa loved the stark beauty of the Rockies. And Cyprian couldn't stomach being away from his only remaining family for long periods of time.

Losing his beloved wife and sons in a terrorist hijacking over twenty years ago had been almost more than he could bear. Dark depression had sunk its talons into him for months. And if it hadn't been for little Melissa, needing her daddy, he'd have given in to the urge to end it all. But Melissa had been his one shining light, the only reason left to smile. She'd saved him and given him the courage and desire to go back to work, to the touring company he and his wife had begun several years earlier.

The idea to use EXIT as a weapon against terrorism, to save other families from the trauma and loss that he'd suffered, had been put forth by an army general who'd just taken an EXIT tour and wanted to meet with Cyprian. The general had been extremely impressed with the quality of men Cyprian employed, comparing them favorably to special elite forces in the military. After swearing Cyprian to secrecy, he'd explained a radical idea the government was considering. EXIT's enforcement arm came into being a mere month later.

Had innocent people died through the years, collateral damage from EXIT operations? Yes. But that happened in all wars, and this was definitely a war. Cyprian was keenly aware of his own loss and made every effort to keep his men and women under tight control, to protect innocents whenever possible. He was proud of his record. And he wasn't about to let Buchanan or Mason or even Sabrina Hightower destroy what he'd worked so hard to build, even though he could empathize with their plights.

He couldn't stomach the idea of hundreds or thousands of Americans dying at the hands of terrorists because a few bleeding hearts worried about a handful of mistakes over decades of service. His fascination with Kelly Parker had weakened him, had blinded him to what she was doing on the side. And by the time he'd realized Buchanan was the innocent scape goat in her games, it was too late. Buchanan had become an enemy and had to be eliminated. But Buchanan had disappeared. Not even Eddie's attempts to locate his properties had yielded success. Which of course had prompted Cyprian to make Eddie rework his programs to yield better success the next time—which it had with Hunt.

Now, Buchanan had come back. Yes, he'd been temporarily sidetracked by the Austin diversion. But that wouldn't last. And in his place he'd left Mason Hunt to bring EXIT down. Well, it was time to eliminate all of Cyprian's enemies. Then he would rebuild, make his empire stronger, better, with tighter controls in place so this could never happen again. Because what he did *mattered*.

He never wanted to have to look into Melissa's eyes and tell her that he hadn't done everything he could to make the world safer and better for her and the family she'd start one day. He owed it to his wife, his daughter, his sons, to keep EXIT viable in the war against terrorism.

No matter the costs.

ACE KNOCKED ON the limo's darkened window. The window lowered, revealing Cyprian reclining on the luxurious leather seats, calmly sipping a mixed drink while his minions once again cleaned up a mess for him. It was all Ace could do not to let his disgust show on his face while Stryker related the details of what he and Ace had just done.

From the moment that his boss had stolen Kelly away, Ace had been biding his time looking for the right opportunity to make him pay. And thanks to Bishop's marble-floored home that carried sounds better than a concert hall, he now had the information that might very well bury Cyprian. Fake EXIT orders? The Council wasn't likely to ignore something like that, especially once they knew that Cyprian had covered it up. For now, Ace would keep the information to himself. But when the time came, he'd use it to his advantage.

If by some miracle, Cyprian escaped the wrath of the Council, well, Ace knew another secret even *they* couldn't ignore. All he'd have to do was retrieve a certain patriarch of the Hightower family and present him to the Council. Then Cyprian's dictatorial reign would be over.

"The kitchen will blow in ten or fifteen minutes," Stryker concluded.

"Excellent work." Cyprian set his drink in the holder on the door. "Stryker, you're going to be in charge of eliminating Mason and Miss Hightower."

Stryker nodded and glanced at Ace, as if to judge whether their boss's favoritism had struck a blow.

Ace focused on keeping his expression blank. Let Stryker gloat. He was on Ace's short list too. Before the week was out, Ace was going to slit Stryker's throat from ear to ear to pay him back for every bruise.

Cyprian pulled a piece of paper out of his pocket and handed it to Stryker. Ace made no secret of reading it over his shoulder. It was an army report that detailed Mason Hunt's PTSD and how it was triggered by being tied up, and described the torture he'd endured that had brought on the PTSD. Ace couldn't help admiring this Jackal person for his ingenuity. Salt water in open wounds wasn't something Ace had tried but sounded like a rather useful technique. Simple and effective.

When Stryker was finished, he handed the paper back to Cyprian.

"Do whatever it takes to eliminate Mason and Hightower," Cyprian instructed. He waved the report. "Now that you know Mason's weakness, you can exploit it if necessary. I hope that's helpful in your quest." He pulled two more sheets of paper out of his pockets and gave one to each of them. "Those are the maps we give to the local EXIT tour guides. They detail every zip line, every storage building, and path we've carved into the foothills around here. Use whatever you need. The codes to any electronic locks are also noted."

"Thank you, sir," Stryker said.

Ace didn't bother thanking his benevolent boss. He just stuffed the map inside his jacket.

Cyprian's lids drooped as if he'd noticed Ace's breach in manners. But Ace wasn't in the mood to lick anyone's boots right now. He stared right back, as if he didn't have a clue why his boss was pissed.

"While I fully expect Stryker to be successful in his mission," Cyprian finally said, "I can't afford not to be prepared if something . . . unexpected . . . occurs. I need a backup plan, leverage, to bring Mason to heel if that happens. You, Ace, are my backup plan."

Excitement sent the familiar tingle of anticipation that he felt before any mission through Ace's body. "You want me to help Stryker kill them?"

"Only if Stryker asks for your assistance."

Ace let out an impatient breath.

"But of course, all of this is moot if we don't know where they are," Cyprian said. "I'm hopeful that they'll try to speak to Stanford. But I also have information that Miss Hightower booked a flight to Colorado." He handed another piece of paper to Ace. "This is the flight information. Make sure she doesn't board that plane."

Chapter Sixteen

Day Four—5:00 p.m.

Sabrina fanned herself with a piece of paper she'd taken out of Mason's glove box and rested her head against the seat back. Even though he'd parked his beat-up truck in the shade of mature oaks, ten feet back from the road where heat radiated off the asphalt, it was still humid and muggy. Not to mention more boring than watching grass grow, which she was pretty sure she'd witnessed since they'd been here all day.

She rubbed her tank top to stop the itchy trickle of sweat between her breasts and hopped out of the truck. Frowning at the unwieldy Glock 22 she was forced to use since Cyprian had taken the Sig Sauer, she shoved it in the right front pocket of her shorts, but the thing was so bulky she had to keep a hand on her pocket to keep it from falling out. Too bad Mason didn't have extra holsters in one of those bags in the truck bed.

Following Mason's earlier warnings, she gently

clicked the door closed so no one would hear it shut. Not that there was anyone around *to* hear. This place was so isolated that no one came near it.

"Much better," he said when she joined him by the small rise where he was lying on his stomach, peering through his binoculars. "I didn't hear the door that time."

"Yay, me. I know how to close a door without slamming it." She plopped down beside him on her back, staring up at the glimpses of the blue, nearly cloudless sky that she could see through the bower of branches overhead. She would have rather been on the other side of the road where she could lie on her belly and look over the cliffs to the gorgeous, glass-smooth river below. Just thinking about the water made her feel cooler—not that she'd ever get in it of course. But she could see herself sitting on the bank, dipping her toes. "I thought we were going to *talk* to Stanford, not act like voyeurs."

"It's called surveillance. I'm not a peeping Tom."

"So you say," she teased, once again trying to get him to smile like he had before the disaster last night. She plucked a long blade of grass and idly started pulling the little sections apart and tossing them aside. "What's he doing anyway? The canoes are still chained up. Wouldn't he have taken them down by now if he was going to inspect them or whatever he does until the first EXIT tours are scheduled?"

"Don't know. Haven't seen him."

She turned her head to the side. "You haven't seen him *lately*?"

"At all."

Her eyes widened. *"All day?* You haven't seen him even once?"

"Nope."

A prickle of alarm skittered up her spine. She rolled over on her stomach, blowing out an impatient breath when she had to adjust the gun in her pocket so it didn't hit her hipbone. The little hut was a good distance away, down the hill. Even squinting she couldn't see it that well. Too bad she didn't have a pair of binoculars too. This stakeout was seeming more and more lopsided since Mason had all the fun gadgets—and a holster.

"Do we even know if he's inside?" she asked.

"We would if we'd gotten here early, like I'd planned, so we could watch for his arrival."

"You needed your sleep, to heal."

"I needed the alarm that I'd set before going to sleep, precisely because I was too tired to wake up without it. You shouldn't have turned it off."

She shrugged. She certainly wasn't going to apologize for protecting him. The rest had done both of them a world of good. He was back to his usual self, minus the smile. She propped her chin in her palm.

He looked through the binoculars again. "My point is that he might be there, he might not be. The cliffs prevent me from being able to maneuver to see the parking spaces on the other side of the hut. I figure if he's there, he's got to be leaving in the next hour."

She put her hand on his shoulder. "Thank you. I know you didn't want to come here. But I really do appreciate it. I couldn't have forgiven myself if I didn't explore every option before giving up on finding Grampy." She dropped her hand and stared down the hill. "You don't . . . you don't think Cyprian would . . . do something to Stanford, do you? One of his own tour guides?"

"A week ago, I'd have said no way. Now"—he shrugged—"I don't know what to believe anymore, or what my former boss is capable of." He glanced down at her again and frowned. "Why aren't you wearing the dark-colored shirt you were in this morning? That white tank catches the light too easily. It's not good for surveillance." His frown deepened. "And why aren't you wearing your vest?"

"Why aren't you wearing *yours*?"

He hooked his finger in his collar and pulled it down, revealing his vest beneath his shirt. "I repeat. Why aren't you wearing your vest? I know you're not hiding it under *your* shirt."

"It's like eighty-five degrees out here. I left it in the truck and changed my top into something cooler. We've been out here all day without anyone else in sight. It's not like I need Kevlar."

His brows drew down in a harsh line.

"Okay, I'll put it on in a minute," she assured him, feeling a bit foolish for being so hung up on how uncomfortable she was when he was out here sweating in his Kevlar without a single complaint.

"You'll put it on now."

"Okay, okay. When did you become so bossy?"

"Waking up late does that to me," he grumbled. He looked through the binoculars again.

Sabrina was about to push herself up from the ground when something vibrated against her bottom. She jumped, and Mason was immediately there, gun drawn, half on top of her, looking around.

"Did you hear something?" he whispered.

She lifted her hips against him, enjoying the startled look he gave her. Then she pulled his phone out of her back pocket and handed it to him. "I think someone wants you. Other than me."

He gave her an exasperated look and put his gun away before sitting up and checking out the screen. He punched a button and took the call. "Mason."

Sabrina sat up and dusted grass and leaves off her. Mason had let her play games on his phone earlier. She'd forgotten she even had the thing in her pocket.

He listened for several minutes, giving one- and two-word answers through most of the call. Whatever the caller was saying must be good, because Mason gave her one of his trademark slow, sexy grins.

The way her heart sped up made her realize just how much she'd missed the old Mason.

"Okay," he said, still on the phone. "I'll call you back in an hour to see where you guys end up. No, Stanford hasn't shown. Yeah. Okay. Talk to you soon." He ended the call and slid the phone into his jeans pocket.

"That was Ramsey. They found Austin Buchanan alive and well. He'd been moved to another burn unit under an alias. They figure it was a diversion to get Devlin out of town, which is why he and Ramsey are heading back here soon. His father and one of the brothers is staying with Austin for now, and arranging better security. Some of the other brothers, and a friend of theirs named Logan, are coming back with Ram and Devlin. They want to help us fight EXIT."

"Wow, that's encouraging."

He nodded. "They haven't exactly been twiddling their thumbs during all of this either. They're pressuring the Council to act against Cyprian, trying to force an emergency meeting. Ram says it looks like they just might agree to it. The hope is that they'll remove Cyprian from power."

"Can they do that? I thought he owned the company."

"He does. But part of the deal that he made with the government was to follow any rulings by the Council, up to and including his removal as CEO. He would still own the assets but couldn't make any decisions."

"Doesn't sound legal. But then again, it's not like he can complain to anyone about it."

"I say we call it a day. We'll meet Ram and Dev back in town in the morning. We'll figure out a new strategy." He gently swept her bangs out of her eyes. "It's going to be okay. We've got a fighting chance now. I'm not giving up on finding your grandfather. And you shouldn't either."

She put her hand in his so he could help her stand. "Thank you, Mason. I don't know how I would have gotten through all of this without you."

He framed her face in his hands. "Somehow I have a feeling you'd have done just fine. You're an incredibly strong woman, a survivor. And way too sexy for your own good." He winked and pressed a soft kiss against her lips. But he pulled back far too quickly.

"Suddenly I want to get back to a crummy, cheap motel as soon as possible," he said, sounding hoarse.

"Suddenly I feel the same way."

He grabbed his binoculars and they headed toward the truck.

A loud boom cracked through the trees. A small hole appeared in the passenger door inches from where Sabrina had slid to a halt.

Mason swore and shoved her to the ground as another boom echoed through the woods. Sabrina's shocked brain slowly registered that someone was shooting at them. She'd thought they were totally safe up here away from everything else. She'd never expected they'd be found.

"Come on!" Mason grabbed her around the waist and yanked her up, half carrying her around the front of the truck as another crack sounded. This one slammed into the front bumper right beside Mason's leg at the same time that a bullet pinged against the hood.

"There's more than one shooter." He yanked her around the other side of the truck and pulled her down in a crouch. The windshield exploded, raining glass down on both of them.

Mason covered Sabrina's body with his as much as possible and returned fire with his Glock. *Bam, bam, bam!* He shoved her down farther, then jumped up.

Sabrina grabbed her own gun and rolled away from him, aiming underneath the truck back toward where the shots seemed to be coming from. She fired several rounds, ignoring Mason's dark look as he shot toward the same trees and bushes.

He reached over the side of the truck bed and grabbed one of his black bags, dropping it to the ground. He reached over the side for the other bag but dove down just as another bullet slammed through the side of the truck.

Sabrina fired twice more at where she'd seen the last muzzle flash. The cowards who were shooting at them wouldn't show themselves and she didn't even know if she was hitting any of them.

Mason gave up trying for the second bag. "There are too many of them." One of the front tires blew with a loud pop and hiss. The truck bounced on its springs, leaning at an awkward angle. He grabbed the one bag and slung the strap over his shoulders, wearing it like a backpack. "Come on. We have to run for it." He grabbed her hand and pulled her up with him.

"Run?" she yelled. "Where?"

But he either didn't hear her or was too busy returning fire to respond. He popped the magazine out of his gun, slammed another one home, then shoved her toward the road. "Go, run. I'm right behind you!"

She took off running across the road, half turning to return cover fire for Mason, but he was too close and she couldn't risk taking a shot. He was on her like glue, spraying bullets as fast as he could squeeze the trigger while urging her to run faster.

Sabrina saw the cliff and suddenly realized what Mason was about to do. She desperately tried to stop but he wrapped his arm around her waist and pulled her forward with him.

"Mason, no, I can't swim!"

His eyes widened with alarm but it was too late to stop their momentum. Sabrina screamed as her feet met open air and they plummeted over the cliff toward the river below.

MASON KICKED HARD and swam upward as fast as he could, holding his gun out in front of him as he breached the surface with an enormous splash. He'd made as much noise as possible, hoping to draw any fire away from where Sabrina might be. But a quick look around revealed no sign of her.

I can't swim. Her last words had cold fear congealing in his chest.

Shots rang out and bullets zipped into the water beside him. He whirled around, shook his Glock to make sure the firing chamber was empty of water, and aimed up at the cliff above. He fired three quick rounds at the gunman standing silhouetted against the sky. The man screamed as one of the shots hit him in the neck. Blood sprayed out around him as he fell like a limp marionette into the water before bobbing back up, curled over facedown like a dead fish.

Another shot cracked from high above, but Mason didn't return fire. He had to find Sabrina. How long had she been under water? Thirty seconds? If she couldn't swim, would she even have thought to grab a lungful of air before she went in? He shoved his gun into the holster, took a deep breath, and dove under the water.

He pulled himself forward with powerful strokes, looking for the telltale flash of Sabrina's white tank top. The water was cool and fairly clear, probably spring-fed in this section of the river. He should have seen something, but there was nothing, nothing but rocks and plants growing on the riverbed. He swam back toward the cliff, desperately turning his head back and forth, looking for her.

Nothing.

A bullet cut through the water so close the concussion knocked him back. He shook his head to clear it and lost the rest of his air. Lungs burning, he swam toward the edge of the river directly under the overhanging cliff, hoping the shooter wouldn't be able to see him when he came up for air. His vision started to blur. He had to take a breath soon or he'd pass out.

He swam up, up, breaking the surface and gasping for air. He was about to take another breath and dive back down when a flash of white caught his attention about ten feet away, near the rocky incline in the tall grasses at the edge of the river.

Oh God. No!

He kicked forward, lunging through the water. That flash of white was Sabrina's tank top catching the light, her partially submerged body hung up in the weeds.

Facedown in the water.

When he reached her, he rolled her over, bracing her head on the grassy stalks behind her. Her eyes were open, but unseeing. She wasn't breathing. *God, no, Rina.* He checked her airway, then pinched her nose shut and blew three quick, deep breaths, filling her lungs. He held his fingers against her carotid. *Yes.* Her pulse was weak, but her heart was still beating. He pinched her nose again and covered her mouth with his, blowing air into her lungs.

"Come on, Rina. Breathe. Breathe." He continued

breathing for her and checking her pulse. Her eyes still stared up at the sky, glassy.

The sound of voices had him looking down river, toward the building he'd been watching all day. Two men with rifles slung over their shoulders stood talking and gesturing toward the river and the woods surrounding it. Even from this distance, he could tell one of them was Stryker. He didn't recognize the other. Mason quickly submerged almost all the way, pulling Sabrina's limp body with him, holding her nose and mouth out of the water.

Kicking his legs underneath the surface, he worked Sabrina and him back, using the vegetation as cover while he continued to blow deep breaths into her lungs. He lifted his head, peering between the grasses, trying to locate the men again. There, by the edge of the water, they were getting into a canoe.

Three quick breaths, wait, see if she's breathing. Three more. *Come on, sweetheart! Breathe, damn it. Breathe.* Suddenly, Sabrina arched against him. He turned her on her side as a lungful of water rushed out of her mouth. She started coughing and convulsing against him, her eyes wide with panic as she instinctively struggled against his hold.

"Sh, sh. You're okay. It's Mason," he whispered, trying to keep her from splashing and drawing Stryker and his partner's attention. "You're okay. You're okay." He whispered soothing words, trying to stave off her panic and focus on the gunmen downstream when all he wanted to do was grab her and hold her close. *She'd almost died. He'd almost lost her.*

She stilled, finally focusing on him. "Mason?" Her voice came out a raw croak.

"Yes, it's me, sweetheart. It's okay."

She started coughing and gagging.

He turned her again as another rush of water left her lungs. He knew, even before he looked downstream, that Stryker and his partner had to have heard her this time. Sure enough, both men were staring straight toward them. Stryker grabbed for the rifle on his shoulder while the other man hopped into the canoe.

Ah, hell. "Deep breath, Rina." He didn't have time to explain. As soon as he saw her chest rise with an indrawn breath, he clamped his hand over her nose and mouth and dragged her under water.

The look of sheer terror on her face as he pulled her deeper was nearly his undoing. But there was nothing he could do to reassure her now. She jerked against him, obviously desperate for air. He kicked off the bottom, angling toward a spot on the bank a good twenty feet from where he'd pulled her into the water. It wasn't much, but it might be enough to give him a chance to get her out of the water before Stryker saw them, and before they both drowned.

Sabrina sank her teeth into his hand. Damn it, he should have expected that. He jerked his hand back and immediately covered her mouth with his own while pinching her nose shut. He blew his breath into her lungs and she suddenly clung to his shoulders like a greedy child, wanting more. But he had no more to give and was fighting the urge to gulp in a lungful of water himself.

He clamped his hand back over her mouth but he knew she'd gotten some water in her lungs again by the way she was panicking and fighting him. The bank was five feet away, four, three. He burst from the water, carrying her in his arms, clasped against his chest as he lunged into the cover of some bushes and trees. He twisted mid-air, trying to pillow her with his body as they fell to the ground.

He landed on something hard and unforgiving in the bag on his back. He hissed and arched away from it, cursing a blue streak. His crossbow. Which unfortunately meant his bag with extra ammo and other supplies was the one he'd been forced to leave in the back of his truck.

Sabrina coughed and pushed against him. He rolled off her and turned around, peering between the branches of a shrub. The canoe was on the other side of the river now, the same side as him and Sabrina. And it was empty.

He whirled around and yanked his shirt off over his head.

Sabrina hugged her arms to her chest, her eyes still unfocused, confusion marring her brow as he jerked the Velcro straps loose and pulled off his Kevlar vest. He started to lower it over her head but she ducked away and pushed at him.

"Rina, stop it. Let me put—"

"Put the vest back on yourself, Mason." She coughed violently and wiped her mouth. "It's my fault that mine is back in the truck. There's no way I'll let you give me yours. Besides, yours is too big for me."

He looked over his shoulder. "It's better than no protection at all. We don't have time to argue about this. There are at least two men heading our way." He tried to lower the vest onto her again, but she hunched over, making it impossible.

She scrambled away from him and stood, using a

nearby tree for support. "You're wasting time arguing." Without waiting for him, she took off in a jog through the underbrush.

Good grief, the woman was stubborn. Letting his bag dangle from his arm he sprinted after her, tugging the shirt and vest on as he ran. He quickly realized that if he hadn't seen where she'd headed he might not have known which direction to go to follow her. She was doing a good job of sticking to firmer ground that didn't show footprints easily. And he hadn't seen any small broken branches on any of the shrubs or saplings she'd passed.

When he caught up to her, he gave her a grudging nod of approval. "You've got experience in the outdoors. You're not leaving much of a trail."

"I used to play hide and seek with my brother when our family camped in the Rockies. I was the champion."

"I believe it."

A rifle cracked from somewhere behind them.

They both turned, looking back toward the river, which was no longer visible from their vantage point.

"Do you think they saw us?" Sabrina squinted at the trees behind them.

She'd lost her glasses. He hadn't even thought about them until now. They must have come off when he pulled her off the cliff. But he couldn't regret that, even though she'd nearly drowned. Because if they'd stayed by his truck, they'd both be dead by now.

"That was a test shot," he said, answering her questions. "They were hoping to flush us out of hiding if we were near them."

"How do you know that?"

He shrugged. "It's what I would do. Where's your gun?"

She automatically reached for her pocket, then shook her head. "I had it in my hand when you threw me off the cliff. I must have dropped it."

He shoved his gun into her hand. "I pulled you with me off that cliff. I didn't throw you."

"Semantics. I don't want your gun. How will you defend yourself?" She tried to give it back to him but he shook his head and pulled the bag off his back.

He unzipped it and took out his crossbow and quiver of extra arrows and strapped both of them on. "Don't fire unless you absolutely have to. We need to conserve our ammo. Let's go."

They'd gone only about fifty more yards when another shot rang out. *Close. Way too close.* Mason pulled Sabrina behind a tree. He held his finger to his lips, signaling her to be quiet. She nodded, letting him know she understood. She looked more angry than frightened as she watched the woods around them.

"Just how bad is your eyesight?" he whispered, as he turned his head slightly, listening, watching the shadows behind her.

"I can see just fine for about ten feet. After that, things start to get blurry," she whispered.

He pulled his crossbow off his shoulder, eyeing the trees about thirty feet away as he cocked and loaded the bow using one of the arrows clipped to its base.

Her eyes widened. "There's someone behind me, isn't there? Take the gun," she whispered.

He shook his head and held the crossbow down

in front of him. "When I tell you to duck, I need you to drop out of the way."

"Are you sure you don't want the gun? Or just tell me where to aim. I can—"

"*Duck*."

She dropped to the ground. Mason brought his crossbow up and squeezed the trigger. It slammed into his target's throat, throwing him back against a tree before he fell to the ground.

Mason immediately cocked the bow, ignoring the burn of the string against his palm, and notched another arrow. "*That's* why I use the crossbow," he whispered. "It doesn't make much noise. Be as quiet as you can. I wouldn't be surprised if there are several more men out here looking for us. I can't imagine Stryker would come after me with only one other guy. And by now he's probably calling in more reinforcements."

"You're that good, huh? Just how many men do you think it takes to bring Mason Hunt down?" she teased.

He gave her a quick, hard kiss. He should have known Sabrina wasn't the type to wilt and cower in the face of danger. She was as courageous as she was beautiful. He kissed her again before hurrying over to the dead man.

The arrow had done its job, severing the man's vocal cords, crushing his windpipe, and burying itself in the base of his skull. He'd died instantly, his hand still clutching the Colt nine millimeter he'd been aiming at Sabrina when Mason had sent the arrow slicing toward him. This wasn't Stryker, or anyone Mason knew. From the amateurish-looking tat on the man's shoulder, he figured him for an ex-con, probably some local muscle Stryker had hired.

Sabrina dropped to her knees beside the body. Mason was about to console her, thinking she'd finally broken down, when she pried the man's pistol out of his hand. She popped the magazine, checked the loading, then slid it back into the gun. Like a pro, she searched his pockets, coming up with another magazine, and put that in her pocket. "You can have your Glock back now," she announced, holding it out to him.

A twig cracked behind them. He whirled around, squeezing the crossbow's trigger, sending the arrow flying toward the sound. A pained grunt preceded a dull thump. The black and yellow feathers at the end of his arrow pointed straight up about twenty feet away. Mason didn't need to see the body to know he'd gotten lucky and had managed to take out the target. But with two men finding them in the span of a few minutes, he knew their luck was about to run out. They had to get somewhere more defensible.

Mason slung the bow over his shoulder and took the Glock. It would be easier to run without holding the crossbow. If he saw another gunman he'd just have to shoot him and hope he could take out any others who heard the shots.

He studied the woods around them, listening intently. He didn't hear anything, not even the sound of insects or birds. That was a very bad sign.

"If you have a plan, this would be a really good time to use it," Sabrina whispered.

"I do have a plan."

"What is it?"

"We're going to run like hell." He grabbed her hand and pulled her with him in a sprint through the trees.

A crashing noise sounded behind them, perhaps fifty yards back. Shouts sounded off to their left and right. They were nearly surrounded.

They both fired their guns toward the sounds as they made a mad dash around bushes and ducked beneath low-lying branches.

Answering gunshots rang out. A bullet whistled off to their right. Mason yanked Sabrina lower, almost in a crouch as they continued to run.

"Get in front of me and stay low," he yelled, trying to shield her from behind. "Don't stop. Run toward that break in the trees up ahead."

He fired off several shots, hoping to slow the men behind them. He heard the roar and immediately recognized the sound. He holstered his gun just as Sabrina skidded to a halt and jerked around. She must have just realized what the sound meant because her face was white with fear. It nearly broke his heart knowing what he was about to do.

"We have to go back! We have to go back!" She tried to rush past him, back toward the gunmen.

Mason grabbed her around the waist without breaking his stride, steeling himself against her terrified screams as he carried her with him over the waterfall.

Chapter Seventeen

Day Four—6:00 p.m.

Sabrina knelt on the ground beneath a towering oak tree, coughing up water. Beside her, Mason aimed his pistol toward the top of the waterfall, watching for signs of pursuit. Although, with the sun low in the sky, it would probably be hard to see anyone now even if they were standing at the top trying to find them.

Right now she didn't care if an entire army of assassins came after her. She'd gladly surrender if it meant not going back in that cursed river ever again. At least this time she hadn't passed out and nearly died. This time Mason had managed to keep her next to him as they entered the water—probably because she'd clung to him like glue. She was only under water for a few seconds before he was pulling her to the surface.

Mason must have decided no one was brave enough, or stupid enough, to ride that waterfall down to the river after them, because he holstered his gun and joined her by the tree.

"Sabrina, I'm—"

"Sorry, yes, I know. You've only told me that a hundred times already. I'm alive. So I forgive you. But only if you swear you will *never* do that again."

"I'll never do that again."

She wasn't sure she believed him, but she was perfectly happy pretending, because she certainly didn't want to nearly drown again. After shoving her dripping hair out of her face, she reached for her Colt, only to realize it wasn't there. Great. "I've lost another gun."

"You probably can't see well enough to shoot anything anyway," he reasoned.

"I can't *see* because I don't have my *glasses*. I don't have my *glasses* because you threw me off a *cliff.*"

"You're not going to let that go are you?"

"Nope."

He sighed and looked down river. At this point it was nothing like the calm, clear water farther upstream. This section had boulders and steep drops that formed the beginnings of rapids. He eyed her, as if contemplating throwing her in. She immediately backed away.

"Don't even think about it. I barely survived in clear, calm water. What do you think would happen if you toss me in those?"

"I wouldn't *toss* you, exactly. EXIT probably has more of those outposts along the river, with rafts and lifejackets. If we happen upon one—"

"We'll walk right by it and keep on going."

"Now, Sabrina. Let's be reasonable. We have an indeterminate number of gunmen after us. The river is the fastest way out of here."

"No."

"My phone was destroyed in the first dunking. We don't have any way of calling for help."

"No."

"Ramsey might come looking for us when I don't call him like I said I would. But that might be too late. And it's getting dark. If Stryker and the others have infrared binoculars, we're at a considerable disadvantage."

"I'm not going back into the river. Come up with another plan." She crossed her arms and looked around. They were in the foothills of the Blue Ridge Mountains. Trees and thick bushes covered nearly everything in sight except for the horrible river. She could well understand Mason's desire to use the river to escape, but she couldn't try that again. She just couldn't. There had to be another way.

She shaded her eyes against the setting sun, still looking around, squinting to try to focus. "How many men do you think are after us?"

"Based on the shouts and the direction of the gunshots earlier, I'd say at least four. But that number's bound to go up substantially now that Stryker knows where we are. I'm sure he's got reinforcements on the way."

Four heavily armed men—so far—against one not-so-heavily armed man and an unarmed woman, because she'd dumped her second gun in favor of clinging to Mason when he pulled her over the waterfall. Her shoulders slumped. "I don't want to go into the river."

He pulled her against him, wrapping his arms around her and resting his cheek against the top of her head. "I know."

She slid her arms around his waist, reveling in

his strength and that he stayed calm no matter what was going on around him. If he'd shown any sign at all of panic or fear, she probably would have fallen apart by now.

"Sabrina, look." Mason pulled back and pointed up at the sky. "Can you see it?"

She reluctantly lifted her head from his warm, cozy chest and squinted. "I don't . . ." She squinted harder. "Wait, there's some kind of straight line, above the trees." She sucked in a breath and shook her head, stepping back. "No, no, no. That's worse than the river. No, Mason. Don't ask me to do *that*. My parents *died* on one of those things. I saw them die."

He followed her until she was backed against a tree with nowhere else to go then framed her face in his hands. "Sweetheart, we need to get to the other side of the river to buy us more time. There are only two ways to do that—by water, or by zip line. Your choice."

"Can't we just hike for a while before making a decision?"

He shook his head. "We don't have time."

"That's because we're wasting time just standing here. We need to get moving." She started past him but he grabbed her shoulders and turned her around.

"We can't outrun rifles. Our only chance is to get on the other side of the river and find somewhere to hide."

"Why can't we stay on this side of the river?"

He sighed heavily. "Look at the terrain. What do you see?"

She studied the trees around them, the gentle rise

and fall of the hills. Then she looked across the river. The forest was much thicker there. The ground steeper, rising up toward the mountains. There were cliffs, what looked like caves, even steep drops that appeared to be canyons. She'd explored enough mountainous terrain in her lifetime to know why he felt it was so important to get across the river now. And as much as she hated admitting it, he was right.

"There aren't any good hiding places on this side, and it's mostly low ground. The other side would be easier to find a defensible position, or even just hide. With lots of cover, rocky places that can stop a bullet," she said, echoing his earlier words.

He nodded, and waited for her to say the obvious. "Okay, okay."

He cocked a brow, still waiting.

"The zip line. We'll cross the river on the zip line." She tried not to let the fear show in her voice, but the sympathetic look on his face told her she hadn't fooled him any more than she was fooling herself.

SABRINA HELD THE stitch in her side and plopped down on the dirt beneath the zip line platform, her lungs laboring as she tried to catch her breath. Once Mason had gotten her to agree to his plan, he'd urged her to run with him just inside the tree line as fast as she could go. It was probably a good quarter mile to the platform and she'd been gasping for air and thinking about begging him for mercy shortly after they'd started the insane run. But the tension in his face and the way his left hand had hovered near his holster told her that their pursuers were probably a lot closer than he'd let on.

He must have seen something, or heard something, to be so worried. So she'd suffered in silence and was a bit surprised she'd actually made it the whole way without collapsing. Mason, of course, didn't even seem winded. Which had her grumpily considering tossing him in the river. It would serve him right after tossing *her* into the river, twice. But she was too busy holding her side to make the effort.

A dull thump had her turning around to see what he was doing. The sun had set during their mad dash to the zip line tower. And with only the light of a nowhere-near-full moon, she couldn't see much at all except the dull flash of Mason's knife as he struck something, making another dull thump.

She shoved to her feet and trudged over to him, still holding her side.

A thick padlock secured the door on a small building that was little more than a shed. But it was brand new, so the structure was solid. Still, they needed harnesses for the zip line, so they had to get into it.

She supposed he could have shot the lock off, but that would have given away their position. Besides, Mason wasn't trying to break it. Instead, he was using his knife to pry the wooden molding away from the door where the lock was positioned. A few more thumps, some prying, and the wood where the lock was set suddenly broke away. The door sagged open, and he hurried inside.

Sabrina held the door open, hoping what little moonlight was available would filter inside to help him. Standing outside without any trees nearby, and hearing the river rushing over the rocks, was an eerie feeling. Was Ace out there looking for them? Or Stryker? Or that other man, Bishop? How many men had Cyprian sent after them? And more importantly, would they stop for the night or would they keep coming, never allowing her and Mason a moment's rest?

He came outside, carrying an assortment of harnesses, gloves, and two helmets. Kneeling down on the ground, he sorted through his haul, then waved her over.

He knows what he's doing. There's no reason to freak out over helmets and harnesses. What happened to Mom and Dad isn't going to happen to us.

She wished she really believed that.

She snagged the helmet he handed her while he put the other on. Once he adjusted his chin strap, he checked hers, wiggling the helmet.

"Too tight?" he asked.

"No. It feels good."

He tightened the strap. "How about now?"

She shoved his hand away. "Now it's too tight."

He surprised her by shoving her hand away when she would have loosened the strap. "No, now it's going to protect you if you don't stop fast enough on the other side and run into the platform wall. Leave it."

"I don't suppose anyone has ever accused you of being bossy?" she grumbled.

"Never." He went back to sorting the harnesses. He seemed to find one he liked and he held it up against her.

"This should work. Stand up."

"I am standing."

His answering grin told her he was teasing. "Hold on to my shoulders and step into the harness, like you're putting pants on."

"I know how to do it. I've done this before." As soon as the words left her mouth, the image of her parents falling sucked her breath away. She started to shake.

He cupped her face and pulled her down for a soft kiss. "It's going to be okay. I know what I'm doing."

"You've zip lined before?" she asked, embarrassed at the wobbliness in her voice.

"Many times. Trust me."

She forced the images of her parents out of her mind and let Mason take over. She lifted her legs when he told her to, stood still while he tightened the straps around her thighs, her waist. He checked her helmet again, then handed her a pair of gloves.

"What are these for?" she asked. "I didn't have gloves last time."

"Just a precaution. In case there's any reason to touch the cable. There won't be a guide on the platform to help us so it's best to be prepared."

Her earlier panic started taking hold again, but she swallowed hard and put the gloves on. They were too big, so he exchanged them for a smaller pair that fit better.

After putting on his own equipment, he used his knife to sever the remaining harnesses. She knew what that was for—so if anyone followed them, they wouldn't have equipment to use the zip line.

He sheathed the knife in his boot and settled his crossbow and quiver over his shoulders. Then he led her to the ladder that would take them up to the platform.

"You first," he said. "I'll be right behind you."

To catch her if she fell?

She shuddered and started up. The ladder was

thick and solid and secured to the platform at several points, making it sturdy. When it didn't even wobble as she climbed, she became more confident. Especially since it was too dark to see much below her if she did look down. But once she stepped through the gate onto the three-sided platform, and saw that dark maw that opened out onto emptiness and the rushing river below, she started shaking again.

A pair of warm, strong arms circled her from behind as Mason joined her on the platform and pulled her against him. He kissed her cheek, then the side of her neck, as he hugged her.

"Tell me about them," he whispered, before kissing her cheek again.

She shivered as his lips moved down the side of her face. Suddenly it seemed as if his earlier urgency was gone and all he cared about was holding her.

"Rina? Your parents. What were they like?" He nuzzled her earlobe, sending a streak of sensation straight to her belly.

She tried to remember what he'd asked her. Her parents. What were they like? Not an easy question to answer. She tried to think of a way to explain them without him misunderstanding, without him thinking they were bad people. Yes, the way they'd abandoned her and her brother was selfish, and she'd always resented it, but she'd also understood to some degree. But it was difficult to concentrate, to find a way to explain with Mason's hands roving over her belly, down to her hips. She shivered again, her eyes closing.

"They . . . they loved me, in their own way. I didn't . . . get to see them very often. They were free spirits who lived for adventure. But I always knew they'd come back and settle down, eventually."

He gently turned her in his arms and pressed a soft kiss against her lips. So short and so sweet she couldn't stop the moan that bubbled up in her throat. He captured the sound with another, lingering kiss, but pulled back all too quickly.

"They traveled a lot?" His body began to sway as he moved her back on the platform in a slow, sexy dance.

"Yes. Grampy Hightower took care of me whenever they were gone." She snuggled against his chest, her body swaying with his, moving across the wood. "But Mom and Dad always made it home for holidays, and sometimes my birthday. They brought special presents from exotic places. Homecomings were always such fun."

He stopped their dance. There was a slight tug against her harness and a loud click. She opened her eyes and looked up in confusion. But he wasn't in front of her anymore. There was only open space, and the river, the white frothy rapids flashing in the moonlight as the water rushed and gurgled past them.

She gasped and tried to back up, but Mason was behind her, a wall of muscle, his arms on hers, his chest pressing against her back.

"Let me go. I can't—"

"Yes, you can. You survived the loss of your brother. The loss of your parents. Your grandfather's disappearance. Most people couldn't live through all of that and come out so strong, so grounded. But you have. You're a very special woman, Sabrina. You've been through so much. But you've never given up, have you? And you're not going to give up now. You're strong, resilient, determined. I know you can do this."

He leaned over her shoulder to meet her gaze. "Thomas wouldn't want you to give up. And neither would your parents. Do this for them. The harness is secure. The pulley above you is new, strong. The clip holding the harness to the pulley is solid steel. I've double-, triple-checked everything."

He gently lifted her hands and placed them on the strap above her, which she knew connected to a pulley on the cable.

"I'll be right behind you," he continued, his deep voice so soothing, so confident, that it was hard to be fearful anymore. "Ten seconds, fifteen at the most. The line dips near the other side of the river then goes back up. It's designed to slow you down before you reach the other platform. You can't see it from here, but it's there. As soon as you reach the other side, put your hands out in front of you to stop yourself at the back wall. Then just unclip the carabiner from the cable and move to the side. When the line goes slack, I'll know it's clear and follow you over. All you have to do is take one step. And trust me."

"I trust you." She tightened her hands on the strap and stepped into space.

MASON QUICKLY CLIPPED his carabiner to the next pulley and put one hand on the cable, waiting for the tension to slack. He hated sending her over without him, but he didn't have a choice. The cable was plenty strong enough to hold both of their weights, but he could crash into her at a high speed if he didn't make sure she was off the line first.

And now he was getting more and more agitated waiting for his turn. While he'd been trying to keep Sabrina calm and convince her to face what had to be one of her worst fears, he'd heard something. A night creature foraging for dinner in the nearby underbrush? Maybe. It could have been the creak of the wood in the tower, contracting in the cooling temperatures now that the sun wasn't baking the wood anymore.

Or it could be one of Cyprian's men, working his way up from below.

How long had it been since Sabrina had stepped off this platform? Twenty seconds? Twenty-five? He didn't think the line was all that long, based on the curvature he'd noticed when he'd spotted it back by the waterfall. If that was the lowest point in the line, it had to curve up just enough to slow the zip liner so they wouldn't hit the inside back of the platform box. It couldn't be more than twenty feet past the tree line. So why hadn't the tension in the cable eased yet?

Just then the line bounced and went slack. Mason blew out a deep breath, relief easing the knots in his shoulders. She'd made it to the other side and remembered to unclip her harness from the cable. So far, so good. He grabbed the strap above him and shoved off the platform.

The line was new and strong and gave a smooth ride across the river. With Mason's greater weight, he covered the distance much faster than Sabrina would have and he quickly reached the line's low point on the other side of the river. The cable arched up, slowing his speed. The dark platform came into view exactly where he'd guessed it to be, about twenty feet back from the tree line.

He landed on the platform, grabbing the cable overhead to steady himself as he came to a stop and unclipped the carabiner. He turned around, searching for Sabrina in the dark.

The platform was empty.

Chapter Eighteen

Day Four—8:00 p.m.

S abrina blinked against the fluorescent lights overhead and poured all her anger into the shriveling glare she aimed at the man across the room. The same man who'd been lying in wait for her on the zip line platform. He'd gagged and bound her before he'd cut her harness strap and released her from the cable. Then he'd tossed her on his shoulder in a fireman's hold and hopped off the platform in a heart-stopping slide down a rope to the ground.

She'd done her best to struggle and slow him down as he'd jogged into the woods with her, but the way he'd bound her arms behind her, any movement caused sharp, agonizing pain in her shoulders. He'd brought her here, left her gagged and tied up, sitting on what seemed to be a cold, stone floor. Now that her eyes were adjusting to the light, she could verify that it was indeed stone. She was in a large rock cavern, cut into the side of the mountain. There were no windows, so the lights overhead and a steel door on the entrance kept any light from leaking outside.

It appeared to be a storage room for equipment for the EXIT tours. Boxes of supplies—bottles of water, helmets, even a pair of rafts up against one wall—filled about a third of the room. The rest was empty, except for her.

And Ace.

He was dressed head to toe in green camouflage. His pants were tucked into army-issue black combat boots. A pistol rode in a holster on each hip and a rifle was slung across his back. But in his right hand was a large, lethal-looking knife. He held it down against his side as he strolled across the room and stood over her.

"Hurts, doesn't it?" He gestured with his knife toward her arms, pulled tight behind her. "That's nothing, though, compared to what Mason's been through. I assume you're lovers. Did he tell you about those scars on his back? It happened when he was in the army. Did he tell you about it?"

He squatted down in front of her. "Happened years ago. Apparently he was held captive for weeks in the desert, tortured, tied up with steel wire that cut into his back. They called the guy who tortured him the Jackal. He rubbed salt water into Mason's wounds every day while he tried to get information about his unit. I hear Mason never cracked, never told him anything." He shrugged. "Didn't matter. All the men in his unit still died. The Jackal got his information some other way. Ironic that Mason ended up being the lone survivor."

He ran the edge of his knife under her chin. "Cyprian dug that information out of reports in Mason's personnel file. Apparently your lover goes nuts when he's tied up. Some kind of PTSD thing from his time with the Jackal. Did you know that?"

She looked away, dismissing him the only way she could. Her heart broke for the horrible torture that Mason had suffered through, but she didn't want to give Ace the satisfaction of thinking he'd found her main weakness—her feelings for Mason.

The sharp edge of Ace's knife pressed against her cheek, forcing her to look at him.

His eyes narrowed dangerously. "Don't turn away from me when I'm talking. You don't want to make me mad. I could cut you up into little pieces and enjoy every minute of it." He tilted his head as he ran his knife blade along the column of her throat, forcing her to tilt her head back. "If I had more time, maybe I'd try to see just what Mason finds so fascinating about you. *Then* I'd carve you up. But there's no need to wait to pay you back for that little nick you gave me with those damn scissors." He suddenly pricked her skin with the knife, laughing when she jerked back with a moan against her gag. The cut stung and warm blood ran down her neck.

"Don't worry," he crooned. "It's just a little cut. You won't bleed out. *Yet.*" He pulled the knife back, letting her lower her head. His callous words had her heart pounding double-time. The blood rushed in her ears and her lungs starved for oxygen as if she'd just run a race.

"You're hyperventilating." He laughed. "Guess I still have the power to strike fear into a lady, huh?" He half stood, bending over her with the knife.

She tried to lean away from him, but her shoulders tightened as if they were about to pop out of socket, making her arch back.

The cloth that was tied behind her head, keeping the gag in her mouth, slackened and fell away.

He squatted in front of her again, keeping the knife in his right hand as he grabbed the edge of the cloth in her mouth and yanked it out.

She coughed and worked her tongue to moisten her dry mouth, then drew her first deep breath since he'd captured her. When the searing pain in her shoulders eased enough so that she could breathe normally again, she straightened against the wall behind her.

"Before you kill me, will you at least tell me if you know whether my grandfather is alive?"

He cocked a brow. "Don't you want to know the whole story before I tell you the ending?" He shrugged. "You're in luck. I happened to overhear Cyprian discussing your family with Bishop, right before I stuffed Bishop's head into a gas oven." He laughed when she recoiled from him. "Seems like Cyprian used Bishop as his little lapdog back in Colorado, to kill your brother because he was using Cyprian's daughter."

Sabrina drew a sharp breath. Mason had been right.

"I guess it snowballed from there. Your grandfather saw some sketch you drew of Melissa Cardenas and he pieced it all together. He was stupid enough to threaten Cyprian. Then again, maybe not that stupid. The old coot supposedly locked some kind of evidence away somewhere that proves Cyprian had your brother killed. At least, that's what he claims."

He leaned so close she could feel his hot breath

against her cheeks, but she forced herself not to flinch or turn away.

"I knew part of the story, of course, since Bishop and I were the ones looking after that old man and torturing him. But I didn't know all of it until today. No amount of torture seems to work, though."

Sabrina's chest tightened. *Grampy is alive. He's alive. Oh God. But he's being tortured.*

"Where is he?" she demanded. "Where's my grandfather?"

"What? You want to see him? My pleasure. I just love family reunions." He pulled a cell phone out of a holder at his waist, tapped the screen a few times and then held it up for her to see. "There you go. Say hello to Grandpa."

Tears started in Sabrina's eyes. There, in living color, in what appeared to be some kind of live webcam, was her grandfather. He was chained to a wall, sitting on a bed, his bare toes curled against a sloping concrete floor. There were bruises up and down his arms, but he was alive. He was *alive*. She frowned. Something about the video seemed familiar. Why?

"Where is he?" she asked.

Ace pushed a button on the phone and put it away. "Not far from here."

"He's not in Colorado?"

"What do you think 'not far from here' means?" he said sarcastically. "I couldn't exactly torture him long-distance. We brought him with us when we moved out here for the new office."

She winced at the word torture. "Why are you holding him? Why would you torture an old man?"

"It's called following orders," he spat. "Your grandfather has my boss convinced that he's hidden some kind of incriminating evidence that could destroy Cyprian." Ace rolled his eyes. "Trust me. If your grandpa knew something like that he'd have told me by now. He's just yanking Cyprian's chain." He shrugged. "Actually, I kind of admire the old man's spunk. He's smart. He made up a story that sounded real enough that it convinced my boss, which bought Hightower some time. If it weren't for his lies, he'd have been dead long ago."

That sounded just like her Grampy. A shudder of relief swept through her. There was still time to save him.

He idly pressed the tip of his knife against the stone floor and spun it in a circle, catching it before it fell and spinning it again. "Cyprian's cleaning house right now. I'm not exactly on his favorites list, but I do know where enough bodies are buried that he's probably nervous about getting rid of me. I'm playing my cards, waiting to see what happens."

"What's any of that have to do with me?"

"You're one of my cards. Stryker's out here searching for you. If I kill you outright, he'll claim he's the one who killed you. I can't have that. I want him to go running back to Daddy with his tail tucked between his legs. Then I'll be the one to bring you in and kill you right in front of Cyprian. Clever, huh? And if I catch that lover of yours by using you as bait, and bring both of you in, all the better." He shrugged. "Then again, maybe I'll just kill both of you here and not bother bringing you back to Cyprian. Huh?"

He pushed her bangs out of her eyes, much as Mason tended to do. But where she welcomed Mason's warm, gentle touch, the tiniest brush of Ace's fingers had her fighting the urge to gag and shrink away from him. Antagonizing this man wouldn't help her out of her current predicament. And it wouldn't help her figure out a way to find Mason and warn him that both Stryker *and* Ace were gunning for the two of them now.

He twirled the knife again. "You know, I don't think I've talked this much to a woman in over a year. You're easy to talk to."

She wasn't quite sure what to make of his confession. "Where is Stryker now?"

He shrugged. "Not far from us, actually. He has men on both sides of the river and he's got all the right equipment to follow you, or anticipate your next move. Shouldn't be a surprise. Stryker's Cyprian's favorite at the moment, which means he gets all the fun toys." His lips curled with menace. "I was supposed to sit at the airport all day and wait for you. But I knew Mason wouldn't let you go back to Colorado by yourself. It had to be a decoy. So I came back here, figuring you two would be looking for Stanford." He leaned forward as if sharing a secret. "No need to keep looking, by the way. I sliced his throat before lunch."

This time Sabrina couldn't keep from gagging. She turned her face into her shoulder.

Ace flicked her hair again. "Squeamish, huh? Did I mention that Stryker was just seconds away from that platform when you landed? He anticipated you two would cross the river near there and he beat you to it. Lucky for you, I saved you before he could get there."

He shrugged. "I'm sure Mason wasn't quite so

lucky when he got there. But I figured, given the choice, he'd have wanted me to get you out of the area before Stryker attacked. Mason will put up a good fight. He's one of the best. If he makes it through the gauntlet, he'll find us. Actually, I'm counting on it. If he takes out Stryker, and I take *both* of you out, I become Cyprian's favorite again. I might hate the son of a bitch, but being favored has its perks."

He ran the knife down her jaw. "Actually, I have something special planned for a dear, dear friend of mine. Devlin Buchanan. Something quite spectacular actually. But my original plan to draw him out didn't work. So I have a new plan now. Your boyfriend is going to give me Buchanan. Right after *you* give me your boyfriend."

Sabrina glared her hatred at him. If she ever got the chance to shoot him, she wouldn't hesitate.

MASON HELD HIS knife in his left hand, balancing on the balls of his feet as he turned back and forth on the hard ground, trying to keep an eye on his adversaries. Bodies littered the pine needles at the base of the platform tower behind him. He'd lost count of how many he'd fought off but they kept coming. He'd unloaded his pistol into half a dozen of them, but without more ammo, he was left with the knife and his bare hands. One on one, not a problem. Dozens against one, *big* problem.

Stryker stood behind the others, out of Mason's range. Mason wanted to demand Stryker tell him where Sabrina was, but he didn't want to admit that she was even out here if she'd somehow realized the danger and hid in the woods before Stryker and the others had converged on the tower.

If she was still alive—and he refused to consider that she might not be—then she was still in danger. He needed to find her and get her to safety. But he had a lot of men to mow through before he could go looking for her. The only thing giving him an advantage right now was that they weren't using their guns. Stryker seemed to want to take him alive and had forbid them to fire. That gave Mason hope, because it might mean Sabrina really had escaped and Stryker wanted to capture him and force him to give up her location. He'd gladly endure torture by pretending that he knew where she was but refusing to tell them, if that meant giving her more time to escape.

Stryker's men were paying a high price for Stryker's decision, though, as evidenced by all their fallen comrades. And fewer and fewer of them seemed willing to brave Mason's knife.

One particularly large fellow suddenly lunged forward, swinging his own knife toward Mason's neck. Mason did a backflip to avoid it, slamming his shoe against the underside of the man's chin as he flipped over. He whirled around and followed his adversary's body to the ground, digging his knife into the man's soft belly with an upward twist that dissected his vitals. The man screamed and gurgled, then fell silent. Mason slowly wiped his knife clean on the man's pants as he eyed the others.

"Who's next?" he taunted. "I can do this all night."

Stryker shrugged, not seeming particularly concerned with the death of his latest lackey. The whites of his eyes shined in the moonlight as he glanced upward.

Mason tensed and whirled around just as a heavy

rope net fell on top of him from the platform above. A cheer went up from the men. Mason slashed in a blind fury at the ropes. Someone kicked his arm. The knife went flying somewhere behind him in the bushes. He twisted and yanked the ropes as they tightened around his body, and the world around him began to fade. *No, no, not again. No.* He bucked against the hands that were suddenly all over him, pulling the ropes until they burned his skin through his clothes. The air seemed to seize in his chest.

The weight of the men and the burning agony of the ropes brought him to his knees.

"Tie him to the tower," someone yelled. Stryker?

Mason tried to focus on the men holding him down, kicking out as they dragged him backward. He kicked one of them in the jaw so hard he heard his neck crack. The man fell away into a limp heap on the ground. But another quickly took his place. The sheer force of that many men, binding and tightening the ropes, was too much.

He roared with rage as he was tied against the wooden posts of the tower.

"Good grief, he's strong," someone yelled. "Grab his foot. There. Tie it down."

The grunts and curses faded beneath the buzzing in Mason's ears. He twisted and bucked and fought the blackness settling over him, hissing at the burn of his bonds. The boards behind him seemed to be on fire too, stinging where they touched his back. The pain was so intense, bone deep, that it had him hissing and arching forward. He shook his head.

It's not real. The rope isn't burning. Focus. Don't give in!

One of the ropes jerked tight, pulling his arms up over his head. He tried to kick but his legs were

yanked hard behind him. Sharp pain radiated up
his body, settling in the raw ridges crisscrossing
his back. A thousand bees sank their stingers deep
into his skin. The blackness dipped down over him
again, and this time he didn't fight it.

Mason.

Someone called to him in the darkness. There
was no pain there. He liked the darkness.

Mason.

He frowned, shook his head. No. He didn't want
to wake up. It was always worse when he opened
his eyes.

Mason!

His eyes flew open. He blinked against the
yellow light of the cheap candle dripping wax in
its holder a few feet away. He was naked, lying on
his stomach in his cot. Outside the tent the wind
whipped sand against the thick material. No matter
how tightly the flap was zipped, the sand always
worked its way in until everything was coated with
it. Including him.

A face swam into his vision, kneeling down
beside him, his robes brushing against the sandy
floor.

The Jackal! No!

Mason tried to jump up, but the wires over his
back held him to the cot, biting into his skin. Sand
and grit mixed with blood, setting his open wounds
on fire. The Jackal smiled like an old friend, dipped
his hand into the salt water in his cup, and let the
water dribble onto Mason's skin.

A guttural scream filled the air. Shame washed
over Mason when he realized that he was the one
screaming. He clamped his jaw shut and bit down

on his lip. The metallic taste of blood filled his mouth.

"It's been three weeks, soldier," the Jackal said. "Twenty-one days. No one, not even you, can hold out much longer. Tell me where your men are hiding and I'll spare your life."

Spare *his* life. Not *their* lives. No way.

He turned his head to the side, working his mouth.

The Jackal leaned in close to hear him.

Mason spit a stream of blood and saliva in his face.

The Jackal jumped back, cursing Mason in his native tongue and swiping at his wet face. His eyes flashed. He grabbed the cup of salt water and threw all of it onto Mason's back.

Stinging agony burned across his nerve endings. He went rigid, biting his lip nearly in two to keep from screaming. His world went black.

He drifted in and out for a while. Every time he moved toward the surface, up toward the light, pain slammed into him, stealing his breath. He shied away from the light. Darkness became his friend.

"Soldier, open your eyes. Soldier?"

Hands clapped next to his ear.

"Open your eyes, Hunt. That's an order!"

He pried his gritty eyelids open. He was on his stomach again, but there were real walls around him. No sand. And no Jackal. His commanding officer stood over him beside a medic and others Mason didn't recognize.

"Sir," he slurred. "My men?"

His CO shook his head. "Sorry, son. They're all . . . gone."

No! Twelve men—good men, with girlfriends, wives, sons, daughters. No!

"The Desert Jackal, sir," he gritted out. "He killed them?"

"We believe so, but we have no proof."

"If they're dead, he's the one who did it," Mason insisted.

"Without proof, there's nothing we can do."

Mason steeled himself against the agony of the wounds on his back and pushed himself up on his forearms. "Sir, we need to take him out. He killed my men. I know it. We have to stop him. *Before* he kills again."

The medic gently pushed Mason's shoulders. "You need to lie down, sir. Your wounds are bleeding again."

Mason shook his hands away. He had to make his CO understand. "He's dangerous. You have to stop him."

"I'd like nothing better than to put a bullet in his head, son. But that's not how we operate. Without proof, there's nothing I can do. We can't go around killing people because we think they might hurt someone in the future. That's not how it's done." He patted Mason's shoulder. "I'm here to thank you for your service. On behalf of our country, thank you for the tremendous sacrifice you made to try to protect your men. It's not your fault what happened. You survived, son. And you've paid your dues. You'll be issued a Purple Heart. And if I have anything to say about it, the Medal of Honor. Relax. Let your injuries heal. You're one of the lucky ones. You get to go home."

"But, sir. The Jackal—"

"Will be brought down, once we have proof of his crimes, not a moment before. Let it go, soldier. There's nothing else you can do."

The blackness shifted again. Another dark room, this one in a hospital back in the States. A man in a suit in the corner, a newspaper in his hands.

This time, Mason was lying on his back. The pain was a dull ache now. "Who are you?"

The man stood, adjusted his suit, and approached the hospital bed. "I'm your new best friend." He plopped the newspaper on Mason's lap.

Mason lifted it, his jaw clenching in fury as he skimmed the front page.

Over two hundred troops feared dead at the hands of suicide bomber at U.S. Embassy. Bomber was known in the region as the Jackal.

The man in the suit held out his hand. "Mason Hunt, it's an honor to meet you. I'm Cyprian Cardenas."

OUTSIDE, DIRT AND rocks crunched under shoes. Ace grabbed Sabrina and pulled her behind one of the upright rafts against the wall. He pressed his knife to her throat while circling his other arm against her stomach, locking her to him.

"Don't make any noise," he whispered. "Or I *will* cut you."

The door to the cavern burst open and slammed against the wall.

"Put him over there." Feet shuffled and something was dragged across the floor.

Sabrina recognized Stryker's voice. And she was very worried that she knew who the "him" was. She tried to lean around the raft to see what was going on but Ace yanked her back and pressed the knife harder against her skin. She sucked in a breath when the blade bit into her neck.

"Is he dead?" an unfamiliar voice asked.

"No, but he will be," Stryker gritted out. "The crazy idiot killed half our men. When he wakes up I'll make him tell us where Hightower is. Then we'll kill him. Make sure he's secure. I don't want him getting loose. There's another fool running around out here somewhere. Watch your backs. His name is Ace and he's just as crazy as this one. I'm pretty sure I saw him skulking through the trees when we crossed the river."

"What do you want us to do if we find him? Tie him up and bring him back here?" one of them asked.

"No. I've never cared for that sniveling trouble-maker. It's too bad he wasn't inside that church that our boss had me blow up all those years ago to help recruit Ace to the cause."

"Church?"

"Never mind. Don't try to catch him. If you see him, kill him."

Ace stiffened against Sabrina and his breath rattled next to her ear. She had to tilt her neck way back to keep the knife from cutting her again. Every muscle in his body had tensed at the mention of the church.

Shoes clomped across the floor as the men filed out. The sound of the door slamming shut echoed inside, followed by the click of an electronic lock.

Ace's arm went slack. "Son of a bitch," he whispered. "He's the one I've been searching for all this time. Son of a bitch."

Sabrina scooted away from him and was surprised when he didn't go after her. His arms dropped to his sides and the knife skittered across the floor, forgotten. Sabrina kept expecting some kind of trick. But he stared unseeing at the raft in front of him, his face a mask of hatred and grief.

She scooped the knife up and worked it sideways, cutting the ropes that bound her hands together. A few more slashes and the ropes fell away from her legs. With one last glance at Ace, she rushed around the raft.

"Oh, no," she breathed. Mason was lying on the floor, his entire body encased in a rope net with more ropes tied around it. His face was ashen, his eyes closed.

Dropping to her knees beside him, she began sawing on the ropes.

MASON FOUGHT HIS way through the layers of darkness. Wires still burned his back, but part of him knew this wasn't real. There was something important he had to remember.

Sabrina.

He groaned, the tightness against his chest bringing back the fiery pain. The net. The ropes. The wires. No. The wires were a long time ago.

Sabrina. He had to fight for her. He had to help her.

He drew several deep breaths and focused on what his senses told him. The smell: musty, damp. The air: cool, but no breeze. Was he in a cave? Bright lights shined against his closed eyelids, but not bright like the sun.

He lay very still, breathing deep and even, fighting his mind's attempts to drag him back to the horrors of his past. The rope holding his right arm dropped away. He tensed, ready to spring. The bindings slackened on his other arm, then dropped. Sweat rolled down the side of his face as he kept fighting the darkness, focusing on staying in the here and now in spite of the ropes that still bound his chest and his legs. Slow, deep breaths.

The moment he was free, he opened his eyes and grabbed the hands above him, one with a very large knife.

"Mason, stop," Sabrina rushed to say, but he was already letting her go.

The visible relief on her face shamed him. Thank God he hadn't hurt her. *This time.* His gaze dropped to the smear of red blood on her neck and his stomach dropped. *Or had he?*

"What happened? Are you okay? Did I . . . did I do that?" His hand shook as he reached toward her. Suddenly she was jerked backward.

The knife was tugged out of her hands and pressed against her throat. Mason lunged forward. He froze a foot from her, looking down the barrel of a gun.

Ace narrowed his eyes from behind Sabrina. "Back off, Hunt."

Mason slowly raised his hands and inched back on his knees. "Let her go. It's me you want."

"You're right. You're both on my short list, but not at the top. Not yet. Back. Up." He pressed the knife harder, forcing Sabrina's head back.

Mason immediately backed up a few feet, still on his knees, ready to launch himself the moment he saw an opening.

"You didn't cut me, Mason," Sabrina rasped, risking getting cut to reassure him.

Relief flashed through him that he hadn't been the one to hurt her. But it quickly burned away beneath his growing rage. The red smears of blood on Sabrina's neck had him aching to get his hands around Ace's throat. This time, he would show no mercy. The second Ace had put his knife to her throat, he'd sealed his fate.

Ace motioned with his gun. "I need you to make a phone call."

"I don't have a phone. It was ruined when I jumped into the river."

Ace frowned with displeasure. "My phone is clipped to my belt, left side," he told Sabrina. "Get it, toss it to Hunt. Make a wrong move and I shoot him. Hunt, make a wrong move and I slice and dice your girl."

A few tense moments later, Mason had the phone.

"Now what?" he asked.

"You're going to call Buchanan and convince him to personally come here to help you." He listed the GPS coordinates of their precise location.

"And once he's here, then what? You're going to kill him?"

"Bingo. You don't have to call him, of course. But if you don't, she dies."

"I'll call. But only if you lower the knife."

Instead of lowering it, he pressed it against Sabrina's cheek. "You're not in the position to make demands. Call him. Now."

Mason dialed Ramsey's number.

"Put it on speaker," Ace ordered.

Damn. He pressed the speaker button.

"This is Ramsey, who's this?" a voice came through the line.

Ace's eyes widened and he jerked Sabrina's hair back, holding the knife against her carotid artery. Sabrina arched her back, twisting her head to the side.

Mason held his hands up in a placating gesture, trying to get Ace to stop. "Ram, it's Mason," he said quickly. "I don't know Buchanan's number and I need to talk to him. Quick, I'm in a hurry."

"Okay, just a sec. He's right here. Hang on."

Some interference clicked on the line, then, "Mason? It's Devlin. What's going on?"

Ace eased the knife away from Sabrina's throat just a bit, and let go of her hair. If Mason wasn't so worried right now he'd have laughed at the spitting mad look on Sabrina's face. She looked like she'd scratch Ace's eyes out if she got the chance. Mason absorbed all the variables around him, judging distances, angles, probabilities, as he spoke to Buchanan.

"Sabrina and I are holed up in the foothills and need some help. Stryker and his men are prowling the woods looking for us. You've always been there when I needed you, buddy. Can you help us out?" He gave Buchanan their GPS location.

"Uh, yeah. We're driving in from Florida. We stopped in the panhandle to pick up Logan Richards, a friend of my brother, Pierce. By the time we get up your way into the mountains it might be first light. How desperate is your situation? Can you hold out that long?"

Mason raised a brow at Ace.

Ace didn't look too happy, but he nodded.

"I guess we'll have to. Thanks buddy. I knew I could count on you."

"Yep. Just hold out until dawn. We'll be there."

The line clicked. "Now what?" Mason asked.

"Now, I shorten that list of mine. By two."

Mason dove at Ace's knife arm, yanking it away from Sabrina's neck just as Ace got off a shot. It slammed into Mason's Kevlar, stealing his breath. Sabrina dropped underneath Ace's arm and tried to get away but he grabbed for her. Mason rolled toward him to grab his gun arm but Sabrina got in the way by accident.

The three of them became a flurry of arms and legs. Another shot went off, slamming into the wall. The knife skittered across the floor. Mason, still trying to catch his breath from the gunshot to his vest, slammed his fist down on Ace's gun arm. The gun flew through the air and hit the wall, then slid back toward him.

Mason lunged for the gun and brought it up just as the door slammed open and Ace ran outside. Mason ran to Sabrina, who was sitting on the floor, shoving her hair out of her face, breathing hard.

"You okay?" he asked.

"Fine, yes, I'm fine. Go."

He ran to the door and looked outside. Ace was gone. But way down at the bottom of the hill, just over the next rise, a handful of men were running toward the cavern, probably alerted by the gunshot. As he watched, they disappeared because they were blocked by the last hilltop.

"We have to get out of here. Now." He turned around, but Sabrina was already at his side holding his crossbow and quiver of arrows. "Where—"

"They were behind the door. I guess Stryker brought them in when they put you in here."

He handed her Ace's gun and took the bow and arrows. "I didn't see where Ace went, but Stryker's men are coming up the ridge. We'll have to make a run for the trees to our right and hope we make cover before his men top the next rise and see us."

"We just can't catch a break, can we?" she grumbled

"You're alive," he said, as he slid Ace's knife into his boot to replace his own. "That's the best break I could have hoped for." He gave her a fierce kiss. "Let's go."

Chapter Nineteen

Day Five—6:45 a.m.

Sabrina lay on her belly behind a fallen, rotten log, clutching the pistol that Mason had taken from Ace last night. Mason lay to her right, holding a Glock that he'd taken from one of Stryker's men after catching him trying to sneak up on the two of them. With his crossbow at his elbow, and his quiver of extra arrows on his back, Mason aimed his gun in the same direction Sabrina was pointing hers, at the woods down the hill.

It had been one of the longest nights of Sabrina's life, but they'd both survived, which was saying something. Now, if Ramsey and the others would just get here before Stryker figured out where she and Mason were currently hiding, they just might survive the day.

The sun was just starting to come up, its rays lightening the long, dark night into gray, and finally to a beautiful, soft blue that would have been gorgeous to look at any other time. But right now Sabrina was more focused on watching the trees for any signs of Stryker or his men. Or Ace.

"It's a shame we didn't think to look for Ace's phone before we left the cavern," she said. "We could have warned Buchanan that Ace is gunning for him, that the call was a trick."

"No need to warn him. He already knows."

"What? How?"

"Because of what I said on the phone. I acted like we were longtime friends and he'd helped me out of a few scrapes."

"You aren't friends?"

"I met him the same night I met you. He realized something was up. I'm sure that he planned for it."

"How can you be sure?"

"Because he said they were in the panhandle picking up Logan Richards, and that they couldn't make it until sunrise. Ramsey told me yesterday that Logan was already with them. They didn't have to go to Florida to get him."

She lowered her gun and stared at him. "Then where are they?"

"My guess is they reached Asheville several hours ago and have been working their way toward us in the dark, one thug at a time. They should be able to pinpoint our exact GPS location, as long as they're tracking us. We'll probably see them soon."

"Tracking?"

He tapped his watch. "It's a multipurpose unit, and waterproof, thankfully, with a GPS tracker. Ramsey has the frequency."

"It would have been nice if you'd shared all of this

with me last night," she continued. "I've been worried that Buchanan was stepping into an ambush and we couldn't warn him."

"He *is* stepping into an ambush. Ace is out there, somewhere, gunning for him. But at least Buchanan knows to be on alert, even if he doesn't realize that it's Ace, specifically, who's after him."

A loud boom sounded in the distance.

"Wait. Was that a . . . mortar?" Sabrina asked.

Mason slowly nodded. "Sounded like it to me."

She glanced at her nine-millimeter and shook her head. "We need to find more of Stryker's guys and take their guns and ammo to give us half a chance. Come on." She pushed up from the ground, ready to hop over the log and run to the woods, but Mason pulled her back down.

"Hold on, little storm trooper. I don't think Stryker's the one with artillery."

"Really, *Skywalker*? What makes you say that?"

He arched a brow. "You get points for getting the *Star Wars* reference. But you went negative calling me Skywalker."

"My bad. I should've called you Chewie, with all that wild hair hanging to your shoulders."

He narrowed his eyes. "You'll pay for that, my pretty."

"Nuh, uh. You can't switch metaphors in the middle like that. It's against the rules."

His answering laughter lightened her spirits like nothing else could have done. It felt good being silly, as if this were a normal day, even if only for a moment.

Something white flashed down the hill. She

tensed and squinted, trying to see what it was. "Um, Mason? Is that a . . . white flag? Is Stryker *surrendering*?"

He shook his head. "I forgot how blind you were. That's not Stryker. It's Ramsey. He's waving his T-shirt on a stick so we don't shoot him." He put his fingers in his mouth and let out a shrill whistle.

Sabrina hated not being able to see clearly. It certainly made defending herself challenging when she wasn't sure what she was shooting at in the distance. Right now she'd trade her trust fund for the spare pair of glasses in her desk drawer back home. "How do you know it's Ramsey?"

"Because Ram eats and breathes NASCAR. He's got the number eighty-eight painted on the shirt."

"Eighty-eight?"

He pressed his hand over his heart and gave her an incredulous look as if she'd just insulted him and everyone in his family tree. "You don't know Junior's number?"

"Sorry? Who?"

He slowly shook his head. "When Ram gets here, don't mention that you didn't realize number eighty-eight is Dale Earnhardt Junior's number. He may never speak to you again."

She leaned toward him conspiratorially. "Will he forgive me if I call him Han Solo?"

"Probably. But *I* won't."

She laughed and watched Ramsey running toward them up the hill. As he neared, she realized he was only wearing jeans and a Kevlar vest with the number eighty-eight in white letters so big that she could see them even without her glasses. And since he wasn't wearing a shirt at all, when he got closer she got an excellent glimpse of sculpted biceps and a gorgeous golden tan.

"Close your mouth," Mason snapped. "You're drooling."

"Just enjoying the view."

He gave her an annoyed look. When Ramsey reached them, he hopped over the fallen log and slid into position beside Mason, aiming his pistol down the hill as if they'd planned this rendezvous all along.

"Glad to see me?" Ramsey asked.

"That depends. Got any extra ammo? Forty caliber for mine, nine mill for Sabrina."

He took a magazine out of his pocket and handed it to Mason. "Nine millimeter for the lady."

Mason handed it to Sabrina.

She leaned past him and shook the magazine in the air. "Thanks."

"My pleasure."

"You can put your shirt back on now," Mason reminded his friend.

Ramsey chuckled. "It's shirts and skins today. Only way to make sure we don't kill each other with all those annoying mercenaries running around in the woods. Hard to tell us apart otherwise." He leaned past Mason and waved at Sabrina. "Miss Hightower. We haven't been formally introduced. I'm Ramsey Tate."

She reached in front of Mason to shake Ramsey's hand. Mason chose that moment to edge his gun higher, pushing her hand away.

"What took you so long to bring the cavalry?" Mason asked, as if he hadn't just intentionally prevented her from shaking Ramsey's hand.

Ramsey didn't look concerned about Mason's bad manners. "It took a while to drive here and then we had to hunker down through the darkest hours because we were worried we'd lose your trail."

"What's the sitrep? Who brought the mortar?"

Ramsey laughed. "Logan Richards, one of the most serious guys I've met, until he teams up with his best friend, Pierce Buchanan, and plays war games. He's having the time of his life down there. Our guys are coming up behind Stryker and his men, trying to work their way toward us in a flanking maneuver."

"Who exactly is this Richards guy?" Sabrina asked.

More gunshots sounded, still far away, but nowhere near as loud as the mortar. The "cavalry" must be exchanging fire with Stryker's men.

"He's the chief of police in a little Podunk town in the Florida panhandle. He was helping the Buchanans find their missing brother and decided to come with us to help you two out. Used his contacts to convince some retired police guy here in Asheville to loan us a few goodies from his surplus military equipment collection, no questions asked."

"Handy friend to have," Sabrina said, even though she was amazed that someone in law enforcement would be told anything about EXIT or would want to involve himself in the dangerous craziness that had become her world.

Another shot sounded, closer than the others.

"How many are with you?" Mason asked, scanning the woods, all signs of frivolity gone as the sounds of fighting got closer.

Ramsey became more focused too. "Besides me and Logan, there's Devlin and his brother Pierce."

"What's Pierce's background?" Mason asked.

"FBI. Used to hunt serial killers."

Sabrina's spirits plummeted. "Only four? That's six total, against how many?"

"We managed to pick off a few last night. I figure maybe twenty more are lying in wait. Those aren't bad odds, ma'am, considering that we do this kind of stuff for a living and most of those guys are crackhead criminals. It'll be all right."

"Ace is out here, somewhere," Mason said. "He came up here on his own, not with Stryker. I imagine he brought plenty of firepower and stashed it somewhere. And Buchanan is his favorite target. You'd better warn him."

"I really hate that guy." Ramsey pulled out a phone to call Buchanan.

"Trust me. I hate him more," Mason gritted out.

"It's worse than that," Sabrina said, remembering what Ace had told her in the cavern. "Last night Ace said he had something 'special' planned for Buchanan. I have a feeling it's really bad."

Ramsey nodded and relayed her information over the phone, then ended the call. "They're in position. Things are about to get interesting."

Mason leaned over and whispered something to Ramsey, who didn't look like he was happy with whatever was being said. After a heated exchange, Ramsey appeared to give in.

"Don't forget," Ramsey said. "We're skins."

Mason eased up and pulled his shirt off over his head, leaving him in his Kevlar. Sabrina wasn't sure why she'd even glanced at Ramsey's biceps. He certainly didn't make her mouth water like the sight of all those muscles on Mason. The man was a living work of art that would have made the masters drool with envy.

"What about me?" Sabrina asked. "Am I supposed to run around in my bra?"

"I wouldn't mind," Ramsey offered.

Mason shoved him, hard. "Our guys know you're out here. They'll know not to shoot any women."

"Gee, that's comforting. I hope they can tell I'm a woman from a distance."

He raked her with a steamy glance. "Trust me," he said, keeping his voice low and intimate. "They can tell."

Her face warmed. She watched the play of sunlight over his golden skin and didn't even try to hide her interest. What would have been the point? If she was going to die in the next few minutes, she didn't want to die wishing she'd looked her fill. She sighed, remembering the last time they'd been together.

"Eyes to the front, Rina."

"Why?" she asked. "You keep telling me how blind I am."

He pulled her in for a kiss, his mouth lingering against hers, making her toes curl. He groaned deep in his throat before pulling back.

"You're dangerous," he whispered.

"You're amazing."

He smiled and focused on the tree line. Sporadic gunfire broke out every few minutes, though not as much as Sabrina would have expected based on the number of men Stryker supposedly had.

"How do we know when to leave our position?" She kept her gun steady on the trees, hoping she'd get a chance soon to join the fray. Hiding behind a log while others risked their lives for her totally sucked.

"We wait for the signal," Ramsey said.

"What signal?"

"You'll know it when you hear it."

A few minutes later, a loud boom made Sabrina start.

"And that would be the signal," Ramsey added.

Mason suddenly leaped over the log and ran toward the trees, his pistol aimed in front of him, his crossbow and arrows on his back.

"Wait." Sabrina started to jump up.

Something cold and hard clamped around her wrist, pulling her up short. "Sorry, ma'am. I can't let you do that."

She blinked in surprise at the handcuffs on her right wrist. They dangled from a small chain that led to another handcuff around Ramsey's left wrist. She jerked the chain, tugging on Ramsey's arm. "You're clever, and fast. I'll give you that. But if you don't unlock those cuffs right now you're going to regret it. I promise you that."

He dipped his head as if he were a cowboy tipping his hat, except that he wasn't wearing one. "I imagine you can make good on that promise, but keep in mind I'm just following orders. Mason doesn't want you in the middle of a gun battle. And if he's worrying about protecting you the whole time he's out there, it'll just distract him."

"If he's really that worried about me, why didn't he stay with me while you went with the others?"

"I asked him the same thing. He feels it's his duty to put his life on the line since everyone else is risking their lives."

"I couldn't agree more. And that's precisely why *I* should be out there fighting." She jangled the chain between them. "Take these off, Ramsey. It's not right for me to sit and do nothing. I've got a gun and I know how to use it."

"Sorry. I really am. But I'm more worried about what Mason would do to me if I let you go than what you'll do to me if I don't. Like it or not, we're stuck together until this is over."

MASON STEADIED HIS crossbow and squeezed the trigger. The arrow zipped through the trees in a beautiful, straight line, slamming into his target. The man screamed and fell to the ground. In spite of the arrow embedded in his back, he twisted around, bringing up his gun. But Mason had already notched another arrow. He let it fly. His aim was true. The gun dropped from the man's lifeless hand.

A twig snapped behind him. He whirled around, raising his pistol.

"Hold up, Mason," a voice called out as a man ducked behind a tree. "It's Devlin."

Mason lowered his gun. "Next time announce yourself *before* you sneak up on me."

Buchanan stepped from behind the tree and strode over to him. "I was about to call out when you drew your gun." He nodded toward the dead man, the black and yellow feathers on the haft of the arrow ruffling in the breeze. "Good shot. I always wanted to learn to use one of those things."

"It's handy if you don't want to make noise and have time to reload. What's our status? Any casualties?"

They stood beside each other, an oak tree at their

backs. Mason slung his crossbow over his shoulder and kept his pistol trained slightly to the right while Buchanan kept his trained slightly to their left. They both kept an eye on the trees around them.

"A few cuts and bumps but so far our team is intact. The tide is turning in our favor. I got three of the bastards. You?"

"Four."

"Overachiever. We got a handful more when we got here, a few since. It's hard to find the little cowards. They won't come out and play face to face. We've spotted some of them running away, abandoning ship. Don't be surprised if you see some of them handcuffed to trees here and there."

Mason half turned. "Handcuffed to trees?"

Buchanan winced. "That would be Pierce and Logan's doing. They both brought cuffs and chains with them. They prefer the catch-and-release method." He shrugged. "What can you expect from a chief of police and an FBI agent? They're really touchy about using lethal force."

"You have some odd friends."

"Since one of them is my brother, it's not like I can dump them. They got the idea when I told them about EXIT's cleanup crews. They figure Cyprian will have to sweep these woods when this is over so none of the tourists or local LEOs stumble across any evidence that might point back to EXIT. The crew can deal with letting the fellows go, after we're long gone. You ready to find a few more of these cowards?"

Mason popped the magazine out of his pistol and checked the loading. "I'm almost out of ammo. Been using my bow and knife mostly, to conserve rounds."

"I'm getting low myself. Ramsey might have some."

"He's watching over Sabrina."

"Good. I wondered where she was. I'm sure Logan has plenty of ammo to go around. He's the epitome of being overprepared. We'll have to keep an eye out for him. If we don't run into him you'll have to go all Robin Hood on anyone we see. Or we can do some hand-to-hand."

"Either is fine by me. You heard about Ace?"

Buchanan's jaw hardened. "I'm keeping an eye out for him. I sincerely hope we run into each other."

"Has anyone gotten Stryker yet?"

"No. He's like an oiled pig. Keeps slipping away. We've only caught glimpses of him here and there, trying to rally his troops. Last I heard he was heading due north, which seems odd since that's deeper into the mountains and he'll just be trapped that way."

Mason stiffened. "North? *Exactly* where was he when you saw him heading in that direction?"

"About five hundred yards southeast of this point. Why?"

Mason did a quick mental calculation of the possible destinations Stryker might have in mind, then swore and took off running.

Buchanan took off after him. "What's wrong?"

"Stryker's heading to the cavern."

"Why do we care about a cavern?"

"That's where I told Ramsey to take Sabrina."

SABRINA KICKED ONE of the rubber rafts against the wall and aimed an irritated glance at Ramsey on the other side of the cavern. "I appreciate that you took the handcuffs off me, but I'd appreciate it even more if you let me out of here. We should both be helping everyone else instead of hiding."

"Sorry, ma'am."

She put her hands on her hips. "You say that you're sorry but I don't see you unlocking the door."

"No, ma'am. Mason's orders. I'm to keep you here until it's safe to go back outside."

"Can we ditch the *ma'ams* please? If I had to guess, I'm about five years younger than you but you're making me feel ancient."

"Yes ma— ah . . . Miss Hightower."

"Sabrina. And why are you taking orders from Mason anyway? Aren't you an enforcer like him?"

"He's my best friend. Has been since he joined the army. A lifetime ago, before EXIT. I'd do anything for him."

She nodded, fully understanding his loyalty. "I'd do anything for him too. I'd probably do it much better if I still had my gun—which you took—and if I was out there fighting alongside him."

"Sorry, m— Sabrina. He told me to take your gun or you'd probably shoot me trying to get away. And I'm sure he can fight much better not worrying about you out there in the crossfire," he reminded her.

She sighed. He had a point. She certainly didn't want to distract him and get him hurt. She didn't know how she and Mason had slipped into such an easy relationship so fast. And she had no idea what to expect down the line. All she could hope for was that they survived. Then she'd take everything else one day at a time.

Since there weren't any chairs, she was about to slide to the floor when a knock sounded on the door.

In the space of a breath, Ramsey's entire demeanor changed. Instead of the laid-back, light-hearted rogue he'd been since she'd met him, he was suddenly on full alert, his face grim, his pistol out and aimed at the door.

He motioned for her to back toward the cavern wall. Obviously he didn't believe that whoever had knocked was Mason. Maybe the two of them had agreed on a specific signal instead of a regular knock.

The lights went out.

"Get down!" Ramsey yelled.

Sabrina lunged to the floor just as a gunshot boomed through the cavern, sounding impossibly like it had come from behind her. An answering shot echoed from where Ramsey had been standing, the muzzle flash illuminating his taut face like a macabre strobe light. More flashes lit the back of the cavern where a dark hole had appeared in place of the wall that had been there moments earlier. Sabrina covered her ears and scrambled away from the muzzle flashes behind her.

A grunt sounded from Ramsey. The sound of his body falling against the door and slumping to the floor was almost as terrifying as the complete silence now that the gunshots had stopped. She had to get to him, see if she could help him. And if she could retrieve his gun, maybe she could keep both of them alive. But where was the shooter?

She ducked down, her hands out in front of her so she wouldn't run into a wall as she hurried toward where she believed Ramsey had fallen. The room was pitch black and as quiet as a tomb. No, wait, there—a slight wisp of sound, a shaky breath, coming from in front of her toward the floor.

Ramsey, it must be. She dropped to her knees and crawled until she bumped into him.

Running her hands up his torso, the rise and fall of his chest beneath his bulletproof vest reassured her that he was still alive. The dents and tears in the fabric told her he'd been hit several times, but it seemed as if the vest had protected him. That left only one terrifying possibility for why he was now unconscious. He might have been shot in the head. She shied away from that thought and focused on what she had to do—try to protect him until she could get help.

She listened intently for the gunman, trying to locate him while gently sliding her hand up Ramsey's neck, searching for injuries. With her other hand she patted the floor, trying to find where his gun might have fallen.

When her hand touched his scalp, it came away wet and sticky. *Oh no, Ramsey.* She pressed her palm to the wound to staunch the bleeding and ran her hand on the rocky floor all around him. *Where is that gun?*

The lights switched on.

"Looking for this?"

She jerked her head up and stared into the dark maw of a pistol muzzle just inches from her face. But it wasn't the pistol that terrified her, or even the familiar face behind it that had her shaking so hard that her teeth were chattering.

It was what he held in his other hand.

Chapter Twenty

Day Five—8:30 a.m.

Mason slammed his body against the door to the cavern again. Pain radiated up his shoulder but he refused to give up. The steel door wasn't going to break but the door frame would have to give way eventually, even if it had been reinforced. Buchanan was off trying to find another way in, but Mason didn't remember seeing another exit when he'd been inside.

Neither Ramsey nor Sabrina had answered when he'd done the special knock that he and Ramsey always used, so he knew something must have gone wrong. Though what that could be with the door still locked, he didn't know. He just knew that he had to get inside, as quickly as possible, to check on Sabrina. And Ramsey, of course.

"Sabrina," he called out again. "It's Mason. Sabrina? Can you hear me?"

He backed up to charge the door once more.

"Hold up," Buchanan yelled, jogging through the trees to stop beside him. "I found another way in."

They took off running. A few minutes later, after a steep climb up some rocks and then a sharp descent on the other side, they were at the hidden back doorway to the cavern.

Buchanan waved at the body lying just outside the open doorway partially obscured by a rock wall and thick bushes. "I probably never would have found the opening because it blends in with the rest of the mountain except that I saw the white of Stryker's sneakers poking out. Looks like he was stabbed multiple times before his face and throat were mutilated. Overkill. This was personal. Whoever did this knew him, and hated him."

Mason pushed past Buchanan into the cavern, sweeping his pistol out in front. His insides went cold when he saw Ramsey lying near the front door, a pool of blood beneath his head. He steeled himself against the sharp pain of grief and sorrow that slammed into him. Later. He would grieve for his friend later. Right now he had to keep his focus. He had to find Sabrina. When a quick search of the cavern didn't reveal her lifeless body, relief swept through him—but only for a moment. Whoever had killed Stryker and Ramsey now had Sabrina.

A groan had him whirling back toward Ramsey. To Mason's surprise, his friend was blinking his eyes and trying to push himself up off the ground. Mason shoved his gun in his holster, grabbed Ramsey beneath the armpits, and hauled him into a sitting position against the wall. He probed his head wound, trying to see how bad it was.

Ramsey hissed in a breath and knocked Mason's hand away. "Save the torture for the bad guys, will ya?"

Mason crouched in front of him, swallowing against the thickness in his throat. He squeezed his friend's shoulder and had to take a moment before he trusted himself to be able to speak. "Looks like you got lucky." His voice was hoarse. "The bullet grazed your scalp." He flicked Ramsey's dented and torn vest. "You were in a hell of a shootout. What happened? Where's Sabrina?"

Buchanan joined them, swearing softly before heading to the boxes and supplies stacked on the other side of the room.

"Sabrina's missing," Mason said, lightly shaking Ramsey. "Tell me what happened."

He blinked, looking glazed and pale. "I'm not sure. I don't . . . We were waiting for you. I took off the handcuffs and she wanted me to open the door but I wouldn't. That's . . . that's all I remember." He looked around. "My gun. Where's my gun?"

Buchanan returned with a handful of the bright green EXIT T-shirts that they passed out to clients. "I know it sucks to use one of these but this is all I could find to bind your head wound." He pulled out a knife and proceeded to cut up strips of the cloth.

"He must have lost consciousness, doesn't remember what happened." Mason let out a shaky breath and whispered a silent prayer of thanks that Ramsey was okay as he pushed to his feet. "Whoever took Sabrina had to have gone east, downstream back by the river. It's too rocky here to head deeper inland. And any other direction would have taken them back toward us and the others."

"It has to be Ace," Buchanan said. "None of those mercenaries would have been able to get the drop on Stryker. And it's unlikely any of them knew him well enough to have some kind of vendetta. But what did Ace have against Stryker? I always thought of Stryker as a lone wolf kind of guy. He doesn't associate with any other enforcers that I know of."

"I'm not really sure. But Ace was bruised up like someone had beaten the pulp out of him. Maybe Cyprian thought he needed a lesson and ordered Stryker to be his teacher. I don't give a damn. I just want to find Sabrina."

Buchanan wrapped a long strip of cloth around Ramsey's head and tightened it into a knot. Ramsey hissed with pain.

"Sorry." Buchanan reached for another piece of cloth.

"I can't wait around here. I have to find Sabrina." Mason hefted his pistol, remembering he was almost out of ammo. He spotted Ramsey's gun and took it, along with an extra magazine from his pocket. He decided to take Ramsey's phone too, since his own phone had been ruined in the river. He spun around and headed toward the back exit.

"Wait," Buchanan called out. "I'll get the others to help us search for her. Don't go looking on your own. It could be a setup."

He paused at the doorway. "Of course it's a setup. But I can't wait around here while Sabrina's out there alone with a psycho like Ace."

"What makes you think she's even still alive?"

He winced. *Because he couldn't bear the thought that she might be dead.*

"If that was Ace's only goal he'd have killed her and left her body in the cavern with Ramsey while he hightailed it out of here. He's definitely got something else planned. And I have to find him before he does whatever sick, twisted thing he's probably wanted to do all along. I have to find him before he gets holed up somewhere." He started to turn away, but hesitated. "If I don't find a trail to follow, I'll head toward the river. Tell the others to head that way too and I'll meet up with you if I haven't found her. But you should stay here with Ramsey."

"I'm not a baby," Ramsey muttered. "Give me a gun and I can help too." He tried to push himself up but Buchanan shoved him back down.

"Save the heroics for the ladies," Buchanan said. "You don't need to impress us. You aren't in any condition to go anywhere." He looked back at Mason. "You're just worried that Ace will be gunning for me."

"If he gets you in his sights I can't imagine he'd miss the opportunity to end your feud once and for all. Like I said, you should stay here."

Buchanan shook his head, clearly exasperated. "You're not worried about Ace hurting me. You're worried about *me* hurting *him*. You want to make sure that *you* get to take him out."

Mason narrowed his eyes. "Can't I be worried about both? I'm going to save Sabrina. But after that?" He clenched his jaw. "I guarantee Ace won't live to see another sunrise." He headed out the back of the cavern, ignoring Buchanan's shouts to come back.

SABRINA STOOD ON the zip line platform, wearing the vest Ace had been holding in the cavern. She was also harnessed and attached to a pulley hanging from the cable. She would have looked like a typical tourist except for the duct tape around her hands and over her mouth. She wasn't sure if Ace had gagged her to keep her from screaming for help or just to keep her from cursing at him anymore. She certainly hadn't left him with any doubts about how much she despised him for what he was doing, and what he'd done to Ramsey. But there was no way she'd even think of screaming.

Because she didn't want to draw Mason or the others into Ace's trap.

While Ace stood on the railing a few feet away, taking one of his "little surprises" out of his backpack and tucking it under the eaves, he didn't have to worry about Sabrina trying to get away. The vest ensured that. She was afraid to even move.

A trickle of sweat ran down the side of her face. She'd have liked to pretend it was just from the humidity and summer heat. She wanted to be strong, to face what Ace had in store for her with dignity and poise. She didn't want to give him the satisfaction of knowing that inside, she was terrified of what was to come.

Please let me die quickly. And please, please don't let Mason find me until it's too late. Keep him away. Keep him safe.

Ace jumped off the railing onto the platform and eased her closer to the edge, careful only to touch her shoulders and not the vest he'd put on her. She was tempted to throw herself against him and end it all right now. At least that way he would die too. But he must have read her intent because he quickly stepped back, out of her reach, his eyes narrowing in warning.

Instead of getting behind her, to push her down the zip line, he got in front of her and hooked another pulley to the cable—a pulley that looked very different from hers. Next went a spacer bar onto the cable between the two pulleys; obviously to make sure she wouldn't run into him on the line. He was certainly careful about his own safety. She glared her anger at him, but it was wasted. He was too intent on his work.

Finally, he attached his harness to the pulley and pulled a strap with carabiners on each end out of his pocket. He connected one end to his harness and one to hers, attaching the two of them together at the waist, just beneath the edge of her vest. She couldn't figure out why he was doing that, or why he was going out on the cable with her. Wouldn't it have been easier just to send her down the zip line by herself to the other platform? She certainly wouldn't have been able to escape, not all trussed up and taped up like she was.

"Ready for some fun?" He laughed and eased off the platform, one gloved hand on the pulley above him and the other on the cable.

The tension in the strap connecting them pulled her off the platform after him, and they immediately started down the cable. But instead of the fast descent she'd expected, this descent was much slower, more controlled. The squeak of his pulley had her looking up, finally understanding why it looked so different. It had a hand braking system. And as soon as they reached the middle of the line, he stopped them both.

She sucked in a breath as she swayed and looked down at the vest he'd put on her, then down farther at the sharp boulders at least thirty feet below, and the water rushing around them, plunging over the largest waterfall she'd ever seen up close.

She was going to die.

There was no way around that. She just prayed that it happened quickly, and that it didn't hurt too much.

"Careful, little Hightower. You're shaking like a leaf in a hurricane. If you shake too hard, well . . ." He leaned in close. "Boom."

She jerked away from his hot breath and got a little thrill of enjoyment from the startled, worried look on his face at her sudden movement. He turned a light red, whether from embarrassment at his reaction, or anger, she didn't know. But he was suddenly all business, through playing around. Using a pair of needle-nose pliers he'd taken out of his pocket, he went to work on her pulley.

Her stomach lurched. Was he going to make her drop to the rocks below?

"You know," he said, in a conversational tone, "what you're wearing was supposed to be for my friend Buchanan. But he's a slippery SOB and I never could get to him. Once I thought about it, this will work even better. You're the perfect bait to lure all of them into my trap. I really couldn't have planned it better." He laughed, like they were sharing jokes at a dinner party.

Sabrina called him every foul name she could remember her brother ever saying, including words she'd never used before. Too bad the duct tape kept him from hearing any of them.

With a quick twist and a jerk, he let go of her pulley and removed the spacer bar from the cable.

Instead of sliding forward with gravity toward the other zip line tower, she stayed right where she was. The sides of the pulley had been smashed against the cable, locking it in place.

"And this, sadly, is where we must part." He shoved the pliers in his pocket and disconnected the strap between the two of them, leaving it to dangle from her waist. "I wish I could stay to watch the fireworks. It should be very exciting." He laughed again and released the hand brake on his pulley, quickly sliding down the cable away from her to the other platform.

Sabrina hung like a cocoon from a branch, suspended over the rocks and the water rushing below. On the far platform, Ace unhooked himself from the cable and tossed the pulley and his harness into the river. After taking off his backpack, he unzipped it and slipped another of his little surprises under the eaves on the second tower just like he had the first one. He was nothing if not thorough. A few minutes later he was on the ground, emptying the storage room at the bottom of the tower, tossing all the harnesses and pulleys into the river.

When he pulled his gun out of his holster and raised it over his head, Sabrina breathed a sigh of relief and closed her eyes. He must have changed his mind about using her as bait. He was going to kill her now. Her torture was about to be over. And Mason would be safe.

The gunshot rang out, echoing against the rocky sides of the riverbank.

Her eyes flew open. She was still alive. He hadn't shot her. Then what had he shot?

Then she heard it—shouts in the distance, the

sounds of people running through the woods on the other side of the river, following the sound of the gunshot.

No. No, no, no!

Ace saluted her with his gun before taking off into the trees.

For the first time since Ace had dragged her out of the cavern, tears slid down her cheeks.

Please, Mason. Don't come for me. I can't bear it if you die because of me.

But a few minutes later, in spite of her prayers, a group of men burst from the trees beside the zip line platform where she'd been just minutes ago. And in the middle of the group, leading the charge, was Mason.

She shook her head back and forth, trying to warn him not to help her. But to her horror, he cupped his hands around his mouth and shouted.

"Hold on, Sabrina. I'm coming for you."

MASON WAS ALMOST to the ladder to the zip line tower when someone slammed into him, knocking him to the ground. He roared with rage and jumped to his feet, gun in hand. But it wasn't Ace or any of Stryker's thugs who'd attacked him. It was Buchanan.

"What are you doing?" Mason demanded as he holstered his gun and headed toward the tower again.

Buchanan shoved him away and blocked the ladder. "Saving you from being stupid. What are you going to do, blindly climb down that cable without assessing the situation?"

Mason was about to shove him out of the way

when Pierce and Logan flanked him, like three giants blocking his way.

"If I have to shoot the three of you, I will. Sabrina has to be terrified out there. Her parents plunged to their deaths right in front of her on a zip line. She's tied up and she's helpless."

"She's helpless for a reason," Buchanan argued. "She's bait. If you can't see that, it's because your feelings for her are clouding your judgment."

"My *feelings* are none of your business and my *judgment* is just fine. Move," he growled.

"Wait. We can all agree that Ace is the one who put her out there on that line. What do you think he'll do if you climb out there? He's probably on the other side of the river ready to shoot you. Or me. Or any number of us. If we don't take a minute to plan, some of us may die, including Sabrina."

Mason forced himself to back down and rein in his temper. Buchanan was right. He wasn't thinking clearly. If he didn't use his training, Sabrina would pay the price. "All right. A plan. I'll need zip line equipment—a pulley, a harness, gloves. They'll be in a storage room under the tower."

"I've got this." Pierce hurried to the tower.

"Logan, we need to make sure Ace can't ambush us. I remember we passed a bend in the river a bit upstream. The rapids were only ones and twos there. You should be able to wade across and circle back. Look for Ace and make your way to the other tower."

Pierce rejoined them, holding a pair of gloves in each hand, his face mirroring his disgust. "This is all he left—gloves and helmets. He must have taken the other harnesses and pulleys with him, or thrown them into the river."

Mason took the gloves, shoving one pair down the front of his vest for Sabrina just in case. He eyed Buchanan, who was still blocking the ladder. "I'm fresh out of any other plans besides crawling down the cable and getting her pulley working. Unless you can magically produce another harness and pulley for me."

"You might need rope."

"I might. Got some in your pocket?" Without waiting for a reply to his sarcasm he shoved Buchanan, hard. He stumbled a few feet, giving Mason the opening he needed. He hurried up the ladder to the platform.

Buchanan cursed him from below, then called up, "Hold it."

Mason looked over the railing. "You're not stopping me this time."

"Just let me check on Logan first." He pulled out his phone and made a call.

Mason looked out the opening of the platform, pulling his gloves on, anxious to get to Sabrina. She was too far away for him to see the fear that must be on her face. She kept staring in his direction, shaking her head. Leave it to kindhearted Sabrina to be worried about his safety when she was the one dangling from a zip line with nothing but sharp boulders directly below and a big-ass waterfall that probably had her terrified after her previous experiences with this river.

Buchanan held up his hand. "Just one more minute." He listened to the phone for what seemed like an eternity, then replied and hung up the call. "Okay, Logan's already across and he picked up a trail. It has to be Ace, heading back toward the access road, probably has his car parked there. Logan's in pursuit. If he doesn't catch him, at least he can follow his trail to make sure he doesn't double back and try to shoot you while you're on the cable."

Mason nodded and was about to climb out when Pierce called up to him. "I remember a footbridge not far from here when I was chasing some of Stryker's men earlier. The handrail is just rope looped through poles. I'll cut a good length of it in case you need it."

"Sounds good," Mason said. "But I'm not hanging around here waiting for it." He tugged his gloves into place, grasped the overhead cable, and pulled his legs up, locking them at the ankles on top of the zip line.

He pulled himself hand over hand toward Sabrina. He went slower than he preferred because he didn't want to bounce the cable with her suspended from it. But the closer he got to her, the more concerned she looked. She didn't stop shaking her head either, continuing to silently warn him away.

When he reached her and saw her harness, relief swept through him. The straps looked solid, new. She might be terrified at being suspended above the rocks and water, but she wasn't in danger of falling. All he needed to do was get her pulley working and use gravity to get her to the tower on the downhill side.

Keeping his ankles locked over the cable and one gloved hand holding on, he used his teeth to pull off the glove on his right hand. He stuffed it under the top of his Kevlar vest then grabbed the edge of the duct tape on Sabrina's mouth.

"Sorry, sweetheart. This is going to hurt." He tore the tape off as fast as he could, bracing himself for her cry of pain.

"Don't touch me, Mason," she said in a rush instead of crying out. "Don't touch me. Ace strapped—"

"I see them." His blood ran cold as he leaned down farther and took a good look at her vest. "My God. Don't move," he whispered. "There must be eight grenades taped to the inside of your vest." He studied it more closely. "The pins are all tied together with a spider web of fishing line. One wrong tug and they all blow."

She swallowed hard as he confirmed what she'd already suspected. "The pulley is broken too. He used pliers on it."

Mason pulled himself up and examined the pulley. The soft metal guides had been crushed around the wheel assembly onto the cable. There was no way she'd be able to slide down the zip line using that equipment.

"Sabrina, what exactly did Ace do when he brought you to the platform? Don't leave anything out."

As he listened to her, he looked back at the tower. Buchanan stood in the platform opening, watching them. When Sabrina finished telling him everything Ace had done, Mason pulled out Ramsey's phone and pressed the speed dial for Buchanan.

"Ace spent a few minutes up under the eaves just past the platform opening," he told Buchanan when he answered. "He strapped grenades all over Sabrina, so be careful when you look up there."

"Got it. Give me a second." He set the phone down

and climbed out onto the railing to look up at the eaves. Even without the phone, Mason could hear Buchanan's cursing as he climbed back down to the platform. He grabbed the phone and stared down the cable at the two of them. "I've got good news and bad news. The good news is that there aren't any hand grenades up there."

"The bad news?"

"Our friend left us a bomb."

Chapter Twenty-one

Day Five—10:30 a.m.

Sabrina clung to the strap on her harness that suspended her from the pulley. Mason had cut and removed the duct tape around her wrists so she had freedom of movement, but of course she couldn't move, not with little bombs strapped all over the inside of her vest, and another, bigger bomb strapped to the zip line platform that held up the cable she and Mason were hanging from.

Devlin was currently working on the bomb on the tower, trying to figure out how to disable it without setting it off. His first hope had been to simply remove it and toss it over the waterfall. But Ace had thought of that. He'd used some kind of heavy duty adhesive to bond it to the wood. It wasn't going anywhere.

Mason had carefully cut two grenades from under her vest so far and was currently working on a third. With each one that he removed, he pulled the pin and threw the grenade over the waterfall. The sound of the rushing water muffled the explosions but didn't lessen her worry that he'd pull the pin on the next one too late and would blow himself up, not to mention her.

She looked past him to where Devlin was working on the bomb. A shadow suddenly appeared at the top of the ladder. A man with a gun ran onto the platform toward the edge, toward Devlin. Devlin clawed for his gun but Sabrina was already grabbing Mason's Glock from his holster. She fired off two quick rounds. The gunman screamed, his gun falling from his bloody hand as he fell off the platform onto the rocks below. The sudden silence had her looking up into Mason's wide-eyed stare, his mouth half open.

"Told you I was a good shot," she said.

"I never doubted it." He slowly lifted his hand to show her the grenade he was holding. "Luckily I got the pin with this one right before you grabbed my gun."

"Oh my God." She could feel her face go cold.

Mason pulled the pin and tossed the grenade down the river. Sabrina flinched from the explosion and handed him the gun so he could put it back in his holster.

"I'll, ah, try not to move suddenly again," she said.

He very carefully pulled her closer and gave her a soft kiss. "You did great. You saved Buchanan's life. I'm sure he'll thank you later when he's not trying to dismantle a bomb."

He shuddered from the close call but immediately went back to work, trying to free the next grenade. Sabrina couldn't quite believe he was risking his life like this for her. But the whole thing just seemed hopeless.

"Please, Mason. Just leave me here. It's too dangerous."

"I'm not going anywhere without you. Stop asking."

His gruff voice didn't disguise the underlying concern. It warmed her heart to realize he cared as much about her as she did him, but she'd much rather that he didn't—because maybe then he wouldn't be putting his life on the line for her—literally. He was hanging upside down, his knees hooked over the cable above him in a precarious position that had her holding her breath every time the air stirred around them.

If it had been a windy day he'd have fallen long before now. Seemingly unconcerned with his dangerous position, however, he continued working on gently easing the edge of her vest back to get to the next grenade without pulling any pins out. A moment later, he had the grenade free and lobbed it away from them.

It boomed from below the waterfall.

"Mason," Devlin called out, just as Pierce climbed to the top of the platform, holding a length of rope in his hands. "I got the cover off the bomb and I can see the next layer of wires. It's on a timer. If we can trust it, you've got fifteen minutes to free Sabrina *and* get out of here before it all blows. So hurry up."

"Working on it," Mason grumbled beneath his breath.

"You should—" Sabrina began.

"No," Mason interrupted, before she could tell him to leave her again.

She let out a deep sigh. "Is there at least something that I can do to help?"

"Yeah. Don't move."

A light breeze bounced the cable, pushing her a few inches. He swore and grabbed her shoulders, then let out a shaky breath and moved on to the next grenade.

When Sabrina's heart stopped pounding so hard from that near disaster, she focused on holding on to the harness and doing what he'd said—not moving.

His face was so red from hanging upside down that his head had to be pounding, but he hadn't complained once or stopped working since he'd seen the grenades.

"What did he mean?" Sabrina asked, very softly, making sure not to move. "Devlin said we had fifteen minutes, 'if we can trust it'?"

He grew still for a second, then started working again. "Buchanan saw a timer, but it might not be the one that triggers the detonator. It could be a false one, to make us think we have more time than we do."

"Great. Is Pierce the one who's holding the rope?"

"Um hm."

"*Why* is he holding a rope?"

"Just in case."

She swallowed hard and risked another quick glance down. Ropes meant climbing. There wasn't anywhere to climb from here but down. Onto razor-sharp boulders. With intense rapids rushing over them. She'd rather blow up than get shredded on those rocks. At least she'd die quickly and wouldn't feel anything. Or so she hoped.

Mason had been splitting the seams and working the vest off her a little bit more with each grenade that he freed. He'd said his goal was to remove the vest entirely and then get them both to the receiving platform, where hopefully Logan would be soon to help them. But if they only had fifteen minutes, at the rate Mason was freeing the grenades, that didn't leave much time to maneuver down the cable, especially without a working pulley.

Even if she could start across the cable right now, Sabrina didn't think she had the strength and speed to make it to the platform and then run far enough away that she'd be safe when the bomb exploded. Basically, she was out of time. But Mason wasn't. She had to make him leave. Now. While he could still get away.

"Mason, fifteen minutes—or probably thirteen now, if the timer is even right—isn't very long."

"Nope." He looked past her and she followed his gaze.

A man was standing on top of the other platform, the one Ace had climbed down after leaving her stranded on the cable. He climbed up on the railing and started looking under the eaves.

"Logan," Mason called out. "Did you catch Ace?"

"I almost had him. He took off in a four-by-four pickup on a service road not far from here. I managed to put a few bullets in the back window but he went around a curve."

Mason ripped the seam another few inches. "What about the zip line equipment? Any usable pulleys?"

"Everything's gone. Just like the first tower. Mason, there's a bomb here too."

"I figured," he called out.

Logan reached up under the overhang, taking pictures of the bomb with his phone.

"Why's he taking pictures?" Sabrina asked.

"Probably because he doesn't know anything about defusing bombs. He'll text the pictures to Buchanan to analyze."

"Same kind of bomb," Devlin called out from the other platform as he looked at his phone. He was still standing on the railing, holding on to the eave with one hand, flipping his thumb across the screen with the other as he studied the pictures. His head snapped up. "Mason, stop playing around and get out of there. That other bomb is set to blow in five minutes."

Sabrina gasped.

Mason stopped, his knife poised in one hand as he looked at Logan. He looked back over his shoulder at Devlin. "Any chance you can disarm the one on your side, Buchanan?"

"If I had the right tools, and another ten minutes, maybe." He'd put his phone away but in spite of his gloom and doom, he was still tugging at the wires.

Mason's jaw firmed in a tight line as if he was thinking through all of the possibilities.

Sabrina let go of the strap that suspended her harness from the cable. She didn't need to hold on anyway. The equipment held her upright like a chair. She'd only been holding on out of fear. But now that fear had given way to acceptance. Everything that had happened over the past few days had led her to this point. And for the first time since this had all begun, she knew exactly what she had to do.

She cupped Mason's face in her hands, urging him to look at her. When he did, she carefully leaned forward and pressed her lips to his. It was a quick kiss, because they didn't have time for more. She pulled back and let him go.

"You have to go back to the platform right now," she told him. "You did your best. And I thank you for that. But we both know there's no way I can climb down the cable, get down from the platform, and run fast enough to make it. We also both know that you, however, *are* fast enough. So, go, Mason. Please. I don't want you to die for me."

"Four minutes," Logan called out from his platform. "Get out of there, Mason. There's nothing else you can do."

"See," she said. "Even your friends know I'm a lost cause. Save yourself."

His eyes narrowed. He suddenly reached down. Before she could figure out what he was up to, he'd attached the strap from her waist to his harness.

"What are you doing?" She reached down to unclip the carabiner.

He grabbed her hand and held it tight. "Stop trying to say good-bye. This is *not* good-bye. You need to trust me. We'll face the future together, whatever it holds." He lifted her hand and kissed her palm before letting go. "Logan," he called out. "Get out of here before your tower blows."

Logan yelled at Mason to get to the platform, but he didn't wait around. He slid down the ladder to the ground.

Mason went back to work on Sabrina's vest, sawing like a mad man, splitting seams, tearing fabric.

"There are only two more back here. With the other grenades gone, I've been able to split most of the seams now. That should make it possible to get the vest off before it blows."

"Should?" she choked.

"Will. It will. Trust me. When I say three, I need you to raise your arms. The pins will pull out as soon as you do and we'll only have a few seconds to get the vest off. Are you ready?"

"Oh my God, oh my God."

"Rina." He grabbed her chin. "You can do this."

She nodded. "Okay."

"One, two, three!"

She raised her arms, feeling something give behind her, probably the tension on the fishing line and the pins pulling out. Mason yanked the vest. It didn't move. He cursed and ripped his knife down another section. He yanked it again and this time it pulled up over her head. He split the last seam and pulled it from around her then heaved the vest toward the waterfall. He grabbed her, pulling her face against him and cocooning her body with his arms.

The twin explosions were close and nearly deafening. Water splashed up at them but no debris.

"Three minutes on that other platform," Devlin yelled across to them from his side. "When that tower goes, the cable goes."

Mason reached up and hooked an arm over the cable above them. "Throw me that rope, Pierce!"

It took three attempts. Obviously Pierce had never roped a steer or lassoed anything before, but finally the end of the rope fell close enough that Mason was able to grab it. As he reeled it in, he yelled at his two friends still on the top of the first tower. "Get out of here!"

They didn't waste time arguing. They hurried to the ladder.

"What are you doing?" Sabrina demanded. "Go! You might make it in time before the other platform explodes and you'll still be able to get into the woods before the second bomb goes off."

He shook his head as he looped the rope over and through itself around the cable and tied a thick knot at the end before dropping it to dangle over the rushing river. "Do what I say and quit arguing. We don't have time for it." He tugged on both of his gloves and climbed down onto the rope, using his shoe to loop the rope around his legs, using it like a brake. For the first time since he'd slid down the cable to her, he was upright but his face was still bright red.

"Put your arms around my neck."

She frowned in confusion. Did he want her to hold him as they died together? It was a sweet gesture, but a stupid one. "No, you're not staying here to die with me. Go on. Get back to the platform."

"Two minutes," Devlin cried out from farther upriver now, his voice barely audible.

"*Now*, Rina. Put your arms around my neck. Hurry."

His voice brooked no disobedience. She flung her arms around his neck.

"Tighter, hold on."

She tightened her arms, laying her head on his shoulder, finally accepting the inevitable. "I'm so sorry, Mason."

"Put your legs around my hips and lock your ankles around me."

She immediately complied. Being wrapped around Mason as she died wasn't exactly a hardship. She was finally right where she wanted to be. And she realized, it was where she *always* wanted to be. She just wished she'd realized that before it was too late.

"One minute," Devlin called out.

"Whatever you do, don't let go," Mason whispered against her neck.

"I won't let go. I love you, Mason Hunt." She pulled back to look at him. "I love you."

His eyes widened, then narrowed. "You're giving up, Sabrina Hightower. Stop it. Lay your head back down and hold on."

"Whatever you say." She tightened her hold and clung to him.

His hands were both above her holding onto the rope, while his legs were entwined in the rope below. He reached up and she felt his shoulder jerk, then the harness around her went slack.

She sucked in a breath, instinctively clinging harder to him. "Mason?"

"Hold on." He moved his legs and she felt his arms moving on the rope above them. Suddenly they were slipping down, dropping lower and lower until they were near the end. She could see below and he twisted his foot around the last part of the rope using the knot as his guide to know how much rope he had.

His shoulders flexed as he moved his hands on the rope above them again.

"Thirty seconds," Devlin called out.

Mason pushed against the rope, his entire body constricting. The rope began to swing back and forth.

Sabrina's fingers tightened so hard against her

forearms behind his head that she could feel her nails cutting her skin. "What are you doing?"

He pushed and pulled against the rope, swinging them over the brutally sharp rocks below, then toward the edge of the deadly waterfall.

"Rina, honey? Remember when I promised you wouldn't have to go into the water ever again?"

She suddenly realized what he planned to do and gasped against the side of his neck. "No, no, I can't. Please. Just let me go. Let me drop to the rocks. Don't do this."

"Ten seconds!"

"Take a deep breath right before we go in the water and hold it," he said against her ear. "We're tethered together, remember? Even if you let go, I'll still have you. I'll pull you to the surface."

Her tears wet his neck. She was so scared she couldn't even answer him.

"Rina, say it again."

"Five seconds!" Devlin and Pierce yelled together.

"Say it," Mason demanded.

She didn't have to ask what he meant. She knew. "I love you."

The rope swung toward the edge again. Sabrina closed her eyes as he reached above them and sliced through their lifeline. They dropped with a speed more frightening than any roller coaster.

"Hold your breath," he yelled.

She gulped in air as an enormous explosion sounded from overhead. They both plunged beneath the surface of the water as fiery chunks of wood rained down from above.

Chapter Twenty-two

Day Five—8:00 p.m.

Sabrina sat on a wooden bench, flanked by Pierce and Logan, just inside the expansive hallway of a mansion on the outskirts of Asheville. Due to considerable pressure by the Buchanan family, and threats to go national with information about EXIT's secret mission, the infamous Council had agreed to an emergency meeting to hear the evidence against Cyprian. And they were currently holding that meeting behind a set of double doors at the end of the hall.

It was surreal to think that only six hours ago she and Mason had plunged over a waterfall just seconds before one of the zip line platforms holding their cable exploded. The strap that Mason had attached to both of them had held, and true to his word, he'd pulled her from the water before her air had run out.

And now, here she sat, with Pierce and Logan sporting pistols on their hips, keeping her safe, while Mason, Devlin, and Ramsey—with his head bandaged—were facing the evil of EXIT Incorporated without her. With few exceptions, the Council refused to let anyone other than enforcers inside, not even Sabrina, even though most of what had happened centered around her.

Cyprian Cardenas was also inside that room at the end of the hall. It galled Sabrina to think of him in his pristine suit sitting in a comfortable chair, when he should have been sitting in a prison cell for everything that he'd done.

"Have they found Ace yet?" she asked no one in particular.

Pierce shook his head. "Not yet."

"Will the Council make a ruling about him too? Even if he isn't here?"

"I don't know." His face was drawn with worry, probably because his brother was behind those closed doors with people all of them considered to be the worst kind of evil.

Sabrina curled her fingers around the edge of the bench. Even though she despised Ace, she wanted him here. He was the only one she was certain knew what had happened to her grandfather. If Grampy was even still alive. Mason had assured her that he would press the issue, insist that the Council get Cyprian to speak to what had happened to her grandfather. But there was no way to predict the outcome of the meeting.

Footsteps echoed hollowly against the wooden floors as a man with two armed escorts walked past them toward the same double doors where Mason and the others had disappeared an hour earlier. Sabrina blinked in surprise as she recognized Detective Donovan. He looked equally surprised to see her and stopped as if to talk to her. But the men with him waved him forward. As if on cue, the double doors opened and he stepped inside. But they closed before Sabrina could see any details in the room.

Logan had retrieved her spare pair of glasses from her house, and she shoved them up higher on her nose, relieved to see the world clearly once again.

"Do either of you know why that man went in there? He's a detective, the one I spoke to the night . . . this all began."

Pierce answered her again, while Logan remained silent. Maybe since Pierce was Devlin's brother, he knew more about EXIT, and how it operated.

"It's probably damage control," Pierce said. "The Council works through many legal channels too, to oversee EXIT's secret charter. They'll most likely pressure the detective to drop any kind of investigation that he's been pursuing."

"They can do that?"

"They can. They will."

"You aren't optimistic about the outcome of this meeting are you?" she asked.

"Unfortunately, no. I'm not. I don't think anything's going to change without *us* changing it."

She twisted her hands together. "You have to be wrong. Cyprian can't get away with what he's done. The body count has been enormous. Just look at all of the men who died today while trying to kill us in the mountains. Surely they can't ignore that kind of carnage."

His mouth twisted bitterly. "Thugs. Ex-cons. Why would a company that does the type of work that EXIT does care about them? They'll hide all the evidence. No one will ever know what happened today."

She sank back against the bench. She prayed he was wrong. The Council, as Mason had explained to her, was formed to prevent any abuse of power within EXIT. How could they hear about everything that had just happened and not condemn Cyprian for his crimes?

Another hour passed. The sounds of chairs sliding back and raised voices from behind the double doors made Pierce and Logan stand up. When she would have stood with them, they both put a hand on her shoulders and shoved her down onto the bench. Then, as one, they stepped in front of her, guarding her, shielding her as the doors opened and people began to emerge from the other room.

Shoes echoed hollowly on the wooden floor as people walked by, heading outside. Sabrina tried to see who they were, but the wall of men in front of her wouldn't budge. Finally, when the commotion had died down, they stepped aside.

Mason stood in front of her, with Ramsey and Devlin off to his sides. She jumped up and threw herself against his chest, hugging him tight. He put his arms around her and squeezed her so hard that she could barely breathe and her sore ribs protested. But she didn't care. She was just glad to see him standing there, alive and well. No matter how many times he'd assured her that he'd be okay before he went in to see the Council, she'd been secretly terrified that he might never come back out those doors.

Mason gently pulled her arms from around his waist and took a step back as the others circled around him, Devlin, and Ramsey.

"Well?" Pierce urged. "What happened?"

"The Council ruled against us."

Sabrina looked at the stony-faced men surrounding her. "Wait, what does that mean?"

Mason took her hands in his. "The Council believed us about what happened, but they drew a different conclusion about the intent and who was responsible. Essentially, they blamed a dead enforcer—Kelly Parker—for what happened to Austin and the Buchanan family a few months ago. And they blamed another dead enforcer—Bishop, who conveniently committed suicide—for what happened to your family, and to you. They also blamed Ace, saying he'd orchestrated much of this with Bishop. He's been declared rogue. He'll be terminated once he's found. But Cyprian was . . ."

His arms tightened around Sabrina and she could feel the anger in the tension of his body. "Cyprian was reprimanded for not keeping a tighter rein on his people and is basically on probation. The Council is going to appoint someone to look over his shoulder for an indefinite amount of time, to double-check everything he does, every order, every piece of paper he signs. They'll review the overseer's reports monthly until it's deemed that EXIT is back on track and all of the rotten apples have been dealt with. Cyprian won't be able to get away with anything for at least the foreseeable future. For now, EXIT will be run like it's supposed to be run, and innocent people won't be harmed."

"That's a Band-Aid. You know that."

He nodded. "I do. I also know that EXIT can't be allowed to continue the way it has, with so much power concentrated in one person. It's too dangerous for everyone. You taught me that."

"What did Cyprian say about my grandfather? Where is he?"

His mouth tightened. "Cyprian claims not to know anything about your grandfather's disappearance."

She sank back down onto the bench, her legs threatening to collapse beneath her. "And . . . Detective Donovan?" she whispered, determined to hear it all out before she gave in to the grief threatening to overwhelm her. "I saw him go by. What was that about?"

"He was still looking into your claims about the abduction and had followed the bread crumbs to EXIT and Cyprian. Thanks to pressure from authorities very high up in the police department who are under the influence of EXIT, he's dropping that investigation. He wasn't happy about it, but when his pension was threatened, he backed off. Especially since he saw you out here and realized you were okay."

She stared down at the floor, thinking about everything he'd told her. She was vaguely aware of talking, whispering, of footsteps going down the hall, the sound of the outside door opening. But the noises faded away as she ran everything through her mind, looking at the pieces, evaluating them. Trying to think of something else she could do, some avenue she hadn't explored.

"You're still worrying about your grandfather, aren't you?" Mason said, his warm hand taking hers. He knelt in front of her.

She blinked and looked around. "Where is everyone?"

"They left five minutes ago. Are you ready to leave?"

"Yes. I mean no. I don't understand. How can the Council just do nothing?"

"This was a long shot to begin with, going through the Council. But it's not over. I promise you that. Devlin, Ramsey, and I will continue the fight. We'll have that long overdue rendezvous and figure out our next steps. Cyprian will be watched very carefully for a while. He won't risk doing anything to change the Council's mind. So you'll be safe. You don't have to worry about him coming after you again. He has nothing to gain, and everything to lose." He gently swept her bangs out of her eyes. "You can go back home without worrying about looking over your shoulders. Hopefully you can return to Colorado someday, if that's what you want. Whatever you decide, I hope you'll be happy. You deserve that."

He cleared his throat. "I'll, ah, take you home now. Like I said, there's no reason to be afraid. There isn't an EXIT order on you anymore. If something were to happen to you now, the first person they'd look at is Cyprian, so he wouldn't dare—"

"What are you doing?" She narrowed her eyes.

"I'm letting you know you're safe and I'm happy to take you home. You can forget all of this ever happened, move on with your life." He cleared his throat.

"Seriously? That's the way you're going to play this? You hope I'll be happy? I should move on?"

He looked away. "You're a wonderful person. You deserve to be happy. What's wrong with me saying that?" He stood and held his hand out to her. "Come on. You have to be tired and it's a long drive to your house."

She swatted his hand away. His eyes widened in surprise.

"Don't suddenly treat me like a stranger and give me platitudes," she snapped. "Just a few hours ago we were dangling from a cable, about to blow up, and you demanded that I tell you that I love you one more time. If we didn't make it, if we died, you wanted that to be the last thing that you heard. You wouldn't have done that if you didn't love me back. Don't try to pretend that none of that happened."

He raked a hand through his hair, then, as if resigning himself to an unpleasant task, he took her hand in his. "You're a wonderful woman, Rina. And I will always cherish every word you've ever said to me, every gesture, and the way you gave yourself to me so beautifully, so completely. I've never met anyone like you—"

She rolled her eyes and jerked her hand out of his. "Oh, stop it. Just stop it."

"*Sabrina?*"

"I don't want to hear it."

"I'm trying to—"

"I know what you're trying to do. And I don't accept it. I *love* you, Mason. And I know you love me. How do I know? You could have easily made it to safety but you chose to stay with me to the end. I noticed that Logan, Pierce, and Devlin didn't choose to stay." She poked him in the chest with her finger, emphasizing each word. "You love me, Mason Hunt. Don't deny it. Don't lie to me. I deserve better."

"Yes. You *do* deserve better. And you're right. I do love you, Sabrina. And I didn't think I could love anyone. Especially not this quickly. I love your sass, your strength, those sexy glasses." He briefly closed his eyes as if he were in pain. "But you deserve a man who could never hurt you. A man who can put a damn seat belt on without breaking out into a sweat. A man who won't wake up in the middle of the night in the throes of a nightmare and wrap his hands around your throat."

He shuddered and pushed to his feet. "It's *because* I love you that I can't be with you. I couldn't bear it if I ever hurt you again, like I did in that tunnel. I was chained to a wall like an animal and I *became* that animal. If it happened once it can—"

"Oh my gosh!" Her eyes widened and she jumped to her feet, shoving him out of the way. "That's it! The tunnels. That's where he's keeping him." She pressed her hand against her throat as a horrible realization swept through her. "When I unlocked the door to get you out, there were two other doors. I even had my key in one, but I didn't open it."

His brows lowered in confusion. "What are you talking about?"

"My grandfather. Ace showed me a webcam of my grandfather, sitting on a bed, chained to a wall. I can see it in my head, every detail. I thought it looked familiar, and now I remember why. It was the same type of chain, the same hook in the same gray concrete wall as when you were chained up in the tunnels. Even the floor was concrete with that same downward slope. Mason, he's in one of those cells, like the one where you were held, in the tunnels underneath EXIT!"

Chapter Twenty-three

Day Five—9:30 p.m.

Mason gunned his borrowed truck up another hill, going as fast as he dared on the winding road. His own truck was all shot up.

Behind him, Buchanan and Ramsey rode his bumper hard, keeping pace. Thankfully when he'd called them after Sabrina realized where her grandfather was being held, they'd still been close by and had immediately turned around.

Sabrina nervously tapped her shoes on the floorboard. "Can't you go any faster?"

"If I do I'll roll us into a ditch. Just hang on. We're almost there."

The truck's tires squealed as Mason steered into another curve. He topped the last hill, and swerved toward the entrance to EXIT's parking lot.

Sabrina clutched her seat. "Oh my God. Mason, the fire trucks—"

"I see them."

He hit the brakes, drastically slowing down to avoid the police cars, and steering toward the far end of the lot, stopping as close as he could to the maintenance building before one of the firemen waved at him to stop.

The light bars on over a dozen police cars flashed red and blue, and the orange lights on the fire trucks added to the chaotic atmosphere. Policemen stood in groups or ran back and forth shouting orders.

"The door's open on the maintenance building. They're going into the tunnel." Sabrina's voice came out in a choked whisper. She hopped out and started running toward the tunnel entrance.

Mason swore and ran after her. He grabbed her around the waist, lifting her and yanking her behind a tree as Buchanan and Ramsey ran over to them.

"Let me go," Sabrina yelled. "I have to find my grandfather."

"Just a minute." He noted where the policemen were and yanked his T-shirt out of his jeans, covering the pistol holstered at his waist. Buchanan and Ramsey did the same.

"I don't see any smoke," Mason said. "I don't think there's a fire. Someone must have pulled the alarm." He studied Sabrina's taut face. "I don't suppose you'll stay here if I tell you to?"

"Not a chance."

He gritted his teeth. "All right. Stick by my side and do what I do. Act like you belong here and we'll probably be able to run right in. Once we slip past any police, I'll give you my backup gun. Ramsey, Buchanan, there are secondary tunnels off the main. I assume her grandfather will be in one of those. We'll split up, check every door. Be careful. This has all the hallmarks of one of Ace's traps."

"You got it," Buchanan said.

Sabrina was so nervous she couldn't keep still. "What are we waiting for?"

Mason grabbed her hand in his, anchoring her to him while he waited for an opening. "Okay, now." They all took off for the maintenance building that concealed the entrance to the tunnel.

A flash of white just inside the opening had him pulling up short. He jerked Sabrina back just as two firemen jogged past them with a gurney, carrying a body covered with a sheet.

"Oh noooooo," Sabrina cried. She jerked her hand free from Mason's and took off running.

"Sabrina, wait. That's not your grandfather!" Mason yelled. But she must not have heard him and she'd been too distraught to notice the bulge of the pistol holstered at the dead man's waist. She kept running.

"I'll watch over her," Ramsey said. "Find out what's going on." He nodded toward the tunnel where another group was hurrying up the slope and took off after Sabrina.

Mason started after him, intent on reaching Sabrina, but he froze when he saw the group of men coming out of the tunnel. Firemen flanked an old man, holding on to his arms as he stepped out into the open. Another fireman followed, dragging an empty stretcher. Judging by the stubborn set of the old man's shoulders, Mason had no doubt the stretcher was supposed to be for him and he'd refused to be carried.

He was just as stubborn as his granddaughter.

"I'll be damned," Devlin said. He looked over to where Ramsey and Sabrina had disappeared into the throng of policemen and firemen on the other side of the parking lot. "Do you think Grandfather Hightower somehow killed Ace? Is that who was on the stretcher?"

Every muscle in Mason's body went rigid when he saw the man emerging from the tunnel, surrounded by Council members.

Cyprian.

His obsidian gaze met Mason's, and he stopped a few feet away with his entourage in tow.

"Mason, you'll be relieved to hear that Mr. Hightower is alive and well." He waved toward where the firefighters were pulling the older man toward an ambulance. "After hearing all those awful things at this evening's Council meeting, I suspected that Ace may have been the one behind his disappearance." He waved at his peers. "We arrived just in time to find Ace pulling Mr. Hightower out of one of the rooms below. It was quite shocking. I'm afraid I was forced to shoot him, to keep him from harming Mr. Hightower."

"You lying son of a bitch." Mason slammed his fist into Cyprian's jaw, flinging him backward onto the ground. He lunged to hit him again but someone grabbed his arms and jerked him back. Buchanan.

"Let me go," Mason growled.

"For God's sake, look around you, man. You're about to get shot."

The haze of anger clouding Mason's mind lifted and he realized two policemen were standing off to the side, their pistols trained on him. He slowly straightened and raised his hands in the air.

The councilmen helped Cyprian up and he

thanked them, assuring them he was okay as he dusted off his suit and jerked his jacket into place.

"Gentlemen, officers, please, no harm done," Cyprian assured them. "Mr. Hunt and I have had a . . . disagreement of sorts. I'm sure he regrets his impulsive actions."

"The hell I do."

Cyprian's nostrils flared but he maintained his smile. "Regardless, I'm sure we can clear this up without the intervention of our fine officers."

The police kept their eyes on Mason, but stepped back.

"Mr. Hunt. A moment?" Cyprian crossed to a spot about twenty feet away from the others and calmly waited, as if they were about to have a board meeting.

"I'm going with you. I don't trust that bastard," Buchanan whispered.

Mason nodded and they followed Cyprian, stopping right in front of him. Cyprian aimed a disgruntled look at Buchanan but didn't say anything to him.

"What kind of game are you playing now, Cyprian?" Mason demanded.

He turned his back to the Council members and his smile vanished. "No games. I don't want this . . . feud . . . to continue any more than you probably do. It's dangerous." He flicked his gaze toward Buchanan. "For all of us."

"Feud? You call this a feud? You destroyed Sabrina's family. If you think I buy that bullshit you told the Council about Bishop and Stryker being the bad guys, or that you were forced to kill Ace tonight to protect Hightower, you're even more deluded than I thought. Everything you did was to protect yourself."

"Everything I did was to protect my *daughter*," Cyprian bit out, his eyes flashing. He blinked, as if realizing he'd said too much, and glanced back toward the Council, as if to make sure no one had heard him. "One day, if you're ever blessed to have children, you'll understand that a father's love can make you do anything if it means keeping your children from being harmed. I made a mistake, Mason. And then I lied to cover it up, and then it got out of control."

"Why did you kill Thomas Hightower?"

Cyprian straightened his shoulders. "I never said that I did."

"Sure you did. You said you made a mistake, and everything else happened after that. Everything that happened can be traced back to Thomas's death. The way I figure it, you killed him, or had him killed because he lied about being married and had an affair with your daughter. That's the mistake you tried to cover up and it snowballed. But what I can't figure out is why you were so worried about the truth coming out that you kidnapped an old man. Or why you didn't just kill him outright if you thought he was some kind of threat. Care to share that little nugget?"

His eyes narrowed dangerously.

There were only two reasons to keep a mark alive: either to extract information, or to keep information from coming out if they were killed. Mason cocked his head and studied Cyprian.

"You were afraid to kill him. Because he knew you'd killed Thomas. Ace told Sabrina that, earlier today. Looks like he wasn't lying. Hightower had you convinced that if you killed him some kind of proof would come to light, something that would destroy you. But after the Council decided to assign an Overseer to watch you, you realized you couldn't risk holding Hightower anymore. You had to let him go and hope the old man was lying. Am I getting warm?"

"You're obviously not going to drop this," Cyprian said. "I don't know why I bothered to try to reason with you. We're done here."

He stepped past Mason, but Mason swung him around. "We're far from done."

Cyprian shoved his hand off his shoulder, then walked back to the waiting Council members.

Buchanan stepped in Mason's way. "There's nothing you can do about him. Not today, anyway."

Mason gave him a curt nod. "I know. Tell me, Buchanan, if Sabrina's grandfather had information that proved Cyprian killed her brother, why would Cyprian care? With the power of EXIT behind him, he could make something like that go away, just like he made Detective Donovan go away."

He shrugged. "I have no idea. But Cyprian did say that all of this started because he wanted to protect his daughter."

"That might be how it started," Mason said, as enlightenment dawned. "But I think it changed into something else entirely. He wasn't protecting his daughter. He was protecting himself. He doesn't want her to know that he killed Thomas because she was in love with Thomas, and she'd never forgive her father for that."

Buchanan crossed his arms and stood beside him as they watched Cyprian and the Council members getting into a limo. "Melissa is his world. I think you might be right."

"Maybe. Not that it matters. It doesn't change anything."

"No. It doesn't. Not today. But you never know when information like that can prove useful." He gave Mason a thoughtful look. "But there *is* one good thing to come out of all of this."

"Yeah? What would that be?"

"You're looking at her."

Mason stared at Sabrina, sitting in the back of the ambulance, holding her grandfather's hand.

"What are you waiting for? It looks like they're about to close up the ambulance doors."

Mason shook his head. "She's better off without me."

"Don't you think that's for her to decide? Looks to me like she's already decided."

Sabrina was standing in the back of the ambulance now, waving for Mason to come with her.

He shouldn't. They'd already said everything that needed to be said. Prolonging their good-bye would only make it worse. He clenched his hands into fists at his sides as he agonized over the wisdom of joining her.

"Would you just go already?" Buchanan shoved him, hard.

Mason shoved him back, then took off running toward the ambulance, with Buchanan's laughter ringing in his ears.

AFTER A QUICK, tearful reunion with her grand-father, Sabrina had been relegated to sitting with Mason in the emergency room waiting area. That was two hours ago. They'd finally just been briefed by his doctor. Hightower was dehydrated, slightly malnourished, but other than a few bruises he was going to be fine. He was suffering more from ex-haustion than from anything else. He'd be trans-ferred to a hospital room for further observation as soon as a bed became available.

When Sabrina had asked her grandfather what had happened, he'd confirmed what they'd already suspected—that he'd recognized Melissa Cardenas from Sabrina's sketch. But what they hadn't realized was that he suspected Cyprian of having Thomas killed, and deliberately baited him, telling him that he had proof even before he was kidnapped. Ace, however, was the one who'd taken Hightower, and the only one, besides Bishop, he'd ever seen the whole time he was held. So he couldn't even say for sure if Cyprian had ordered his capture. Once again, Cyprian was getting off on a technicality, the very type of thing that EXIT had been created to prevent.

"Well," Mason said, still holding Sabrina's hand as he sat beside her in the waiting room, staring at her reflection in the glass doors. "It's been a long day. Hell, it's been a long week."

"Yep. Looooong day." She met his gaze in their reflection and blew her bangs out of her eyes. "I forgot to tell you, after I spoke to my grandfather back there, I borrowed a nurse's phone and called my cousin, Brian, to let him know Grampy was still alive."

"The same Brian you mentioned when I . . . first met you?"

She smiled at his description of her abduction. "Yeah. The same. All this time I thought he wanted our grandfather declared dead just so he could get his hands on the estate. But I don't think that's the case. He totally broke down on the phone. He was shocked, but in a good way. I think Brian just thought I was drawing out his pain over the loss of Grampy by keeping the investigation open. Turns out he's just as happy as I am that our grandfather is alive and well."

"Did he change his mind about the felony conviction too?"

"We didn't talk about that. Maybe that will come in time." She shrugged. "I'm not too worried about overturning my conviction anymore. It gives me street cred to be a felon, now that I hang out with badasses like you."

"Badass, huh? Is that supposed to be a compliment or an insult?"

"Definitely a compliment." She laced her fingers with his, enjoying the warmth and strength of his hand on hers. "Brian and my sister-in-law, Angela, are booking a flight. They'll be here tomorrow."

His smile faded. "Good, good. You'll have your family again. I should, ah, probably go."

She shrugged. "If you want a boring life without cornfield sex, be my guest."

His lips twitched.

"You know they have this new thing that helps with PTSD," she said, nonchalantly.

"Oh? What's that?"

"It's called T-H-E-R-A-P-Y."

His lips twitched again, and the corner of his mouth lifted. "I've heard of that, actually. I think the person I heard it from was called a S-M-A-R-T-A-S-S."

"She sounds like an intelligent woman to me."

He nodded. "Yes. She is."

"And pretty."

"Beautiful, actually."

"And kind, and sweet, and—"

"You're pushing it, Rina." He squeezed her hand.

"You know, the way I figure it," she said, "as long as we don't do any kinky tie-each-other-to-the-bed kind of sex, we're probably in the clear on this PTSD stuff."

He choked and coughed to cover it as he looked around the waiting room. "Excuse me?"

"You heard me. As long as you get the help you need, aka see a therapist—a male, ugly one, by the way—you'll figure out a way to get past this post-traumatic stress stuff. So we don't get to tie each other up. Big deal. We can always do the actual sleeping in separate rooms if you're really worried. And there are other kinds of kink we can enjoy."

"Good grief," he whispered, looking around again. "Wait, what kinds of kink?"

She laughed, then sobered. "I heard something else today, from a very wise man. Want to hear it?"

"Do I have a choice?"

"Nope. This very wise man, who's also warm, generous, handsome—"

"Sexy?"

She smiled. "This wise, *very* sexy man said, 'Stop trying to say good-bye. This is *not* good-bye. You need to trust me. We'll face the future together, whatever it holds.'" She slowly turned to face him. "I haven't given up on you. You shouldn't either."

He cupped her face with his hands. "I'm scared, Rina," he whispered. "I swear I've never been scared before, but ever since I met you I've been terrified the whole time, terrified that something would happen to you. And I don't know what to do. I'm afraid that I'll hurt you if I stay. I'm afraid of hurting you by leaving. But I'm petrified about facing a future without you."

She kissed him, then pulled back, her mouth just inches from his. "Do you know what I'm even more afraid of, Mason?"

"No. What?" he asked sadly.

"I'm afraid of facing a future without cornfield sex."

His eyes widened and he made a strangling noise in his throat. "That's your plan? Tease me with sex to make me change my mind?"

She batted her lashes. "Is it working?"

"Yes." He growled and pulled her to him for a hot, wild kiss. He only stopped when someone cleared their throat from the other side of the room, loudly. When he pulled back, he was grinning. "I love you, Sabrina Hightower."

"I love you too, Mason Hunt. And you're not ever going to leave me."

"Apparently not."

She put all of her joy and love into her smile, but for some reason Mason suddenly shifted in his seat, looking like he was in pain.

"Are you okay?" she asked.

He winced, shifting again. "I could be. That is, if you help me out."

"Anything. What do you need?" She searched his eyes in concern, wondering if he'd been hurt after all and hadn't told her.

"Have you ever had hospital sex?"

She burst out laughing, finally understanding why he looked so pained. It was a good kind of pain. "No. Is it as good as cornfield sex?"

"Even better."

They grabbed each other's hands and ran down the hallway, laughing.

The thrills don't stop here . . .
Keep reading for a sneak peek
from Lena Diaz's next
heart-stopping EXIT Inc. novel

NO EXIT

Coming January 2016 from

AVONBOOKS

Jace tapped his brakes, allowing an extra car length to open up between his pickup and the sleek, silver Jaguar in front of him. As he slowed even more for one of the sharp curves on the two-lane road that wove through the Rocky Mountains, he checked the dashboard clock.

Showtime.

The roar of an engine announced the arrival of a white panel van, coming up fast behind him. The headlights flashed, then the van whipped around him, passed the Jag, and cut right in front of it, slamming its brakes.

The Jaguar nose-dived and skidded sideways. Jace braked hard and steered toward the shoulder. But the Jag kept sliding toward the steep ditch on the right side of the road. His stomach sank. *Let up on the gas. Steer into the skid!*

The car slammed lengthwise into the ditch with a sickening crunch, the hood crumpled and the windshield shattered.

By the time Jace brought his truck to a stop twenty feet behind the wrecked car, the van was sitting in the middle of the road, parallel to the Jaguar, and the side door was already sliding back on its rails. A man wearing a dark hooded jacket and a ski mask hopped out of the door, waving a handgun and running toward the car.

The ruined car's driver, a young woman in her mid-to-late twenties, stared wide-eyed at the man running toward her as she frantically pushed her air bag out of her way. She looked back at Jace, her face starkly pale, her frightened eyes begging him to help her.

He popped his glove box open and grabbed his pistol before sliding out of the passenger side of the truck, ducking down to keep the pickup between him and the gunman. He scrambled to the front bumper and gauged the distance between him and the Jag. Ten feet with no cover.

The gunman was just a few yards from the car, too close for Jace to shoot without risking hitting the woman. So instead he pointed his gun at the trees by the ditch and fired two quick warning shots.

The gunman ducked down and reversed direction, backing toward the van as he waved his gun back and forth in front of him. He must have seen Jace peering around his front bumper because he suddenly leveled his gun, aiming directly at him. Jace ducked just as a bullet slammed into the asphalt in front of his truck. He waited a few seconds, gulping in air as he listened intently for more gunfire. When nothing else happened, he duckwalked back toward the bumper, keeping his body shielded by the pickup, and peered around the front of the truck again.

The gunman was gone. The door on the van slammed closed and the van immediately took off, its tires squealing as it raced away. Jace dropped to a crouch in the road, firing several rounds at the fleeing van before it rounded a curve and disappeared.

He held his position, waiting to see if the van turned around and came back.

Another engine sounded behind him. He whirled around to see a black limo screeching to a halt beside his truck. Two men in black suits hopped out of the back doors, aiming guns at him.

Ah, hell.

"Drop your weapon!" one of them yelled.

Jace pitched his gun on the road and raised his hands in the air.

The men ran toward him as another man in a dark gray suit got out of the limo.

"Wait, stop!" a feminine voice cried out.

Jace glanced toward the sound, careful not to make any sudden moves that might get him shot. He was surprised to see the driver of the Jag running toward him, her long, brown hair flowing out behind her.

"Stay back," he yelled in warning.

She shook her head and ran right in front of him, using her body as a shield. "Leave him alone!" she yelled at the two gunmen as the man in the suit jogged to catch up.

Jace swore and shoved her behind him just as one of the gunmen reached them. He slammed his fist against Jace's jaw in a sucker punch that knocked him to the ground.

"Stop it, he was protecting me! Leave him alone!" the woman ordered, sounding angry now.

Two beefy arms grabbed Jace and hauled him to his feet. He twisted away and swung his legs in a circle, knocking the other man's feet out from underneath him. The man fell with a satisfying shout of pain as his head slammed against the asphalt. Jace jumped in front of the woman again, facing the second man who, unfortunately, was now pointing a .357 Magnum in his face.

This was not going well.

"Enough." The woman stalked past Jace to the man in the gray suit who'd stopped a short distance away. "Daddy, call off your goons. This man just saved my life. A van ran me off the road and a gunman was coming after me until this gentleman intervened. He risked his life protecting me. We need to thank him, not hit him or point a gun in his face."

The man pulled his daughter against him and gave her a fierce hug before letting her go and heading toward Jace and the others. The man Jace had knocked to the ground climbed to his feet and looked like he wanted to kill Jace. But Gray Suit held up his hand, signaling him to wait.

His eyes narrowed as he studied Jace from a few feet away. He glanced at the Jaguar in the ditch, then the pickup, before meeting Jace's gaze again.

"You saved my daughter?" he asked.

Jace glanced at the incredibly beautiful woman who'd just come up to stand beside her father. He shrugged. "I don't know if I saved her or not."

Gray Suit studied him for a full minute. Then he waved at his men. They both holstered their weapons and moved back.

"What's your name, son?"

He eyed the two gunmen to make sure they weren't trying to sneak up on him before answering. "Jace Atwell."

"I'm Cyprian Cardenas." He held out his hand.

Cyprian Cardenas. CEO of EXIT Incorporated, Fortune 500 outdoor tour company, front to a secret, brutal organization of professional killers who were supposed to protect innocent people by taking out terrorists but who, too many times, ended up killing the very people they were supposed to protect.

Jace knew all about EXIT Incorporated. Their collateral damage had gone on far too long and it was time someone stopped them. In particular, it was time someone stopped the man at the top, the man who wielded the assassins as his own personal killing machines, eliminating anyone who stood in his way. The man standing right in front of him.

Jace forced a polite smile and reluctantly shook Cyprian's hand when what he really wanted to do was wretch as soon as he touched him—or put a bullet in Cyprian Cardenas's brain to make the world a safer and better place.

"And this is my daughter, Melissa," Cyprian announced.

The woman offered her hand and Jace didn't hesitate this time. Based on numerous reports that he'd read, he was confident that she was a true innocent to EXIT's secret charter. She was clueless about the clandestine life that her father led, and all the people he'd killed over the years. Her skin was soft and warm, her grip surprisingly firm. And she smelled as sweet as sin.

He tipped his head. "Ma'am."

She winced. "I'm still in my twenties, younger

than you, if I guess right. Certainly not old enough to be called ma'am." She smiled as if to soften her words. "Please call me Melissa. I'm the president of EXIT Incorporated. My father is CEO. Daddy, give him a business card. My purse is in my car."

Her father took a card from his suit jacket pocket and handed it to Jace. "We're both in your debt, Mr. Atwell. If there's ever anything that I can do for you, name it."

Jace studied the card. "EXtreme International Tours, huh? I think I've heard of that. You take tourists whitewater rafting up and down the Colorado River, stuff like that?"

"Quite a bit more than that actually. But yes, we specialize in extreme adventures. I'd be happy to give you a tour package on the house."

Jace shook his head. "Thanks, but I don't have much leisure time these days. I'm too busy looking for a job. Actually, I'm on my way to an interview." He winced. "Or I was. Not sure I'll make it now. I'm sure you're going to call the police to report what happened. But honestly, I don't have time to wait around. Can I maybe give you my cell phone number and have you explain to the cops why I had to leave? I promise I'll head straight to the police station after my interview and answer any questions they have."

"Hold on, Mr. Atwell." Melissa put her hand on his forearm. "You don't have to run off to an interview. It would be an honor to offer you a position at EXIT Inc. I'm sure in a corporation as large as ours we have something that will fit your skills and offer you excellent opportunities."

AFTER SPENDING OVER two hours at the scene of the shooting with Cyprian and Melissa Cardenas and speaking to the police, Jace was finally back in his truck driving toward his house. He grabbed his phone and punched in a number.

"It's about damn time, Jace," the voice on the line said. "You should have called an hour ago. What's going on?"

"What's going on is that you were way too reckless with that van. You could have killed her. And your gun? Don't you know bullets can ricochet?"

"Yeah, yeah. Whatever. Did the plan work?"

Jace blew out a long breath. "It worked." He held up the EXIT business card that Cyprian Cardenas had given him. "Operation Trojan Horse has begun."

At Avon Books, we know your passion for romance—once you finish one of our novels, you find yourself wanting more.

May we tempt you with . . .

- **Excerpts** from our upcoming releases.

- Entertaining **extras**, including authors' personal photo albums and book lists.

- Behind-the-scenes **scoop** on your favorite characters and series.

- **Sweepstakes** for the chance to win free books, romantic getaways, and other fun prizes.

- Writing **tips** from our authors and editors.

- **Blog** with our authors and find out why they love to write romance.

- **Exclusive content** that's not contained within the pages of our novels.

Join us at
www.avonbooks.com

AVON

An Imprint of HarperCollins*Publishers*
www.avonromance.com

Available wherever books are sold or please call 1-800-331-3761 to order.

FTH 1013